Travell

BRANCH LOCATED AT:

~~CALHOUN BRANCH~~

~~FISH CREEK~~

~~HUMANITIES~~

~~RILEY BRANCH~~

~~SOUTHWOOD BRANCH~~

DARK TIDE

G·K
Hall
&Co.

DARK TIDE

A Novel of Suspense

William P. Kennedy

G.K. Hall & Co.
Thorndike, Maine

Published in 1995 by arrangement with St. Martin's Press.

G.K. Hall Large Print Core Collection.

The text of this Large Print edition is unabridged.
Other aspects of the book may vary from the original edition.

Set in 16 pt. News Plantin by Juanita Macdonald.

Printed in the United States on permanent paper.

Library of Congress Cataloging in Publication Data

Kennedy, William P.
  Dark tide : a novel of suspense / William P. Kennedy.
    p.   cm.
  ISBN 0-7838-1286-8 (lg. print : hc)
  1. Yachts and yachting — Caribbean Area — Fiction.
  2. Married people — Caribbean Area — Fiction.
  3. Hostages — Caribbean Area — Fiction.
  4. Large type books. I. Title.
  [PS3561.E429D3 1995b]
  813'.54—dc20   95-7160

With thanks to Barb and Mike,
Marilyn and Jack,
and the crew of *Wildcat*.

SATURDAY

TORTOLA

British Virgin Islands

The sun began to color the sky behind Beef Island, setting the water birds chattering, and silhouetting the distant islands that rose abruptly out of the sea. The night lifted like a theater curtain, and Road Harbor appeared as a dimly lit stage, with hundreds of tall masted yachts as its players. The boats stirred, and tugged at their lines. They began to groan as the air moved across their wire rigging, like a bow drawn across violin strings.

Peter Heinz heard the sound. He opened his eyes, blinked at the outlines of his hotel room, and saw the curtains stirring in the faint light of the window. He eased carefully out from under the bedsheet so as not to disturb the young black woman who was still sleeping next to him, and walked naked to the bathroom.

Her clothes were hanging from the towel rack, but he didn't recognize the colorful patterns of the blouse and slacks. There wasn't much from the night before that he could recognize. His head began to pound as soon as he switched on the light. He bent over the sink and splashed cold water into his face, then winced when he looked up into the light of the mirror. His fair skin was sickly and colorless, his eyes red and puffy and there was a small scratch across his cheek. He looked even worse than he felt.

What had happened? He vaguely remembered leaving the bar where he had spent most of the evening. And then the taxi driver had been waiting. He had started back to the hotel but then the cab driver had suggested another place. "Nice ladies, mon. They go crazy over a big guy like you."

He turned off the light before he opened the door, and then crossed carefully back to the bed. She was young, probably still in her teens. Heinz studied her face, and then remembered the girl that the taxi driver had brought up next to him at the bar. Small and wiry. Playfully shy. Delightfully surprised when she had run her fingers along the muscles in his arm. She had sipped her fruit-filled drink through a straw while he had been drinking dark rum over ice. He remembered telling her that it was the first rum he had ever tasted, and that he didn't usually put ice in his drinks. But he didn't remember leaving with her.

The taxi driver! That was how they had gotten back to the hotel. He had been waiting outside again, and had smiled into the rearview mirror while the girl unbuttoned her blouse so that Peter could enjoy her small figure. Then Peter remembered paying him, tipping him lavishly and telling him not to wait.

God, how much had he given him? Heinz searched through the dim light and found his clothes bunched up on one of the soft chairs. He tugged his wallet out of the pants pocket and carried it to the window where he could count the cash. He still had five thousand Swiss francs. And he still had most of the five hundred dollars he had bought in New York. The driver hadn't cost him much. He didn't remember paying the girl who was still sleeping in his bed. Hell, he didn't even remember going to bed with her.

She had gone into the bathroom, and he had begun undressing in the sitting area of his room. She had opened the bathroom door, and he had seen her naked body as she reached back to turn off the light. Had she come and sat next to him on the sofa? Or had he joined her in bed? He wasn't sure.

But she certainly hadn't helped herself to his wallet. And there was nothing else she could have taken. The cameras that were his only reason for being on Tortola were locked away in the hotel safe. His watch was still on his wrist.

He remembered the gun, an assault pistol with an extended magazine, and went to the closet to check it. It was a prized weapon with far more firepower than policemen generally carried, certainly worth a few hundred dollars to the local hoodlums. But he found it exactly where he had hidden it, under the graphite bottom of his suitcase. He sneered at his foolish caution. She never would have found it in a place that was designed to go undetected by airport security.

Still naked, he brought the gun back to the sofa and set it carefully on the coffee table. He released the magazine from the long hand grip that protruded from the square body just behind the trigger. With his thumb, he began snapping out the rounds, and let the dull casings with their heavy, blunt tips fall out onto the table.

11

The girl stirred at the sound, and Peter hesitated while she tossed restlessly in the bed. She threw off the sheet, too sleepy to care that she was wearing nothing. He could make out her slim legs, and the gentle curve at the small of her back. She looked more a child than a woman, yet very desirable and enticingly erotic. He vaguely remembered that she had nearly disappeared into his embrace as he had rolled on top of her, but he wasn't sure what had happened next. Had they made love? Or had he passed out from the dizzying effects of the rum?

When he heard her heavy breathing, he went back to emptying the ammunition. Carefully, he snapped the rounds back into position, and clicked the magazine back into the handle. He wrapped his palm around the grip and slipped his finger over the trigger, enjoying the feel of the weapon. Slowly, he raised it to the firing position and sighted across the top of the barrel.

He heard the girl gasp. He looked over at her and found her sitting up, staring wide-eyed at the gun. Peter smiled at her obvious fright, and then laughed when she realized that she was naked. She lifted the sheet over her breasts.

"What you doing, mister?"

Playfully, he swung the gun toward her. She pulled away, leaning back until she was pressed against the headboard.

"Hey, what you doing?"

He stood slowly and walked toward her, keeping the gun trained on her. As he approached, she slid carefully away from him, her fright turning into terror. He reached his free hand toward her.

"Come here. I'll show you."

She took his hand, but her eyes never left the gun. Then she followed him out of the bed, and over to the window that was now filled with a stream of sunlight.

Heinz eased her against the window sill and then moved around behind her. He reached the gun around her, until it was in front of her face and pointing out over the harbor. Then he pressed her face down against the side of the weapon.

"Aim out there," he told her. He found a target, a white yawl with graceful lines that was swinging at a mooring just inside the sea wall.

"You want to sink it? All we have to do is pull the trigger, and we can watch it blow up into little pieces."

She pulled her face away from the metal.

"You don't like guns?" he asked.

She shook her head. "I'm scared of 'em."

"You scared of me?"

She nodded quickly, and he enjoyed the thought that he had frightened her. "Why? Do you think I'm going to hurt you?"

"I'm scared of the people you were talking about. The people with all that money."

Heinz laughed into her ear. "That's why I have the gun. So nobody can hurt me. When I have it, I don't have to be scared of anybody."

"You just put it away. Okay?"

"Okay," he agreed. He lifted the weapon carefully over her shoulder, and then slid the cold metal barrel slowly down the ridge of her spine. The girl shivered, but never turned to face him. She stayed motionless at the window while he walked

13

back to the closet and put the gun back into his suitcase. As soon as he snapped the latch, he heard her run across the carpet and close the bathroom door behind her.

Peter stepped into his shorts. He was buckling the belt of his trousers when she came back out, wearing the slacks and the blouse but carrying the sandals in her hand.

"I be going now," she said, keeping a distance from him as she circled towards the door.

"Don't you want me to get you a taxi?"

She shook her head. "No. The taxi driver is my friend. He be waitin' for me." She was almost to the door.

"Come here," he ordered. "I have something for you."

She stopped, but she didn't move towards him.

"Come here," he repeated.

Slowly, she stepped back towards him.

Peter reached into the chair for his wallet, and took out a hundred dollars of the American money, folded it and then folded it again. Cautiously, the girl reached out for it.

He stepped past her hand, smiled at her, and then slowly slid the money down into the white bra that hung loosely over her small, dark breasts. She didn't even glance at the roll of bills. Her eyes were locked onto his.

He found the touch of her skin exciting, and thought for a second about picking up where his memory had shut down during the night. But he had partied enough. He knew that he had work to do.

"Thank you," he told her. He watched her back away a few steps and then hurry to the door.

1

Bill Chester leaned forward on the worn edge of the bench.

"Knock it down, Tommy! Knock it down!"

Twelve-year-old Tommy Newton shuffled at the foul line, bouncing the ball and then looking up at the iron rim with its torn netting. Bill could see his wide-eyed terror.

"Follow through, Tommy. Right over the rim!"

Martin Kominicki glanced at Bill out of the corner of his eye. "He can't even reach the rim," he smirked.

Bill ignored his fellow teacher. He had spent the previous afternoon working on foul shots, and one of Tommy's had rattled against the backboard and fallen in. He needed this one.

The boy flexed his knees and slowly raised the ball over his forehead.

"Nice and smooth," Bill whispered.

But Tommy's hands jerked forward. The ball flew on a line, just nicking the strings as it sailed out-of-bounds. His shoulders sagged and his head dropped in despair. He never saw the inbounds pass as the game rushed up court without him.

Bill glanced up at the scoreboard. They were down something-teen to six. He couldn't be sure how many points the other team had because three of the lights that formed the second digit on their side of the scoreboard had burned out.

"Shouldn't you be out of here?" Kominicki reminded him.

He turned to the wire-shielded clock on the far wall, and saw that it was after ten. "Oh, hell. I'm late. Take over, will you?"

Kominicki slid over to take Bill's place. "I don't know why in hell you even came in," he said. "You're supposed to be on vacation."

Bill was still watching the court as he stepped over the bench. "It's important," he explained.

Martin laughed. "What's important? Who cares about a grade school game?"

Bill tipped his head towards the kids who were rushing back down the court. "They do," he told Kominicki. "Take good care of them."

He backed away from the game until he bumped against the door. Then he turned, bolted down the corridor and out into the street. He jogged along the sidewalk, weaving around the occasional pedestrian, and dancing away from the castor-wheeled carts that were moving furniture from the parked trucks into the street-level showrooms. The furniture district was alive on Saturdays, when the vans that couldn't fit through the weekday traffic made their pickups and deliveries. Twice, he had to screech to a dead stop to keep from being impaled on the leg of an executive desk, or crushed under a Victorian sofa.

He raced across Third Avenue, holding up his hand toward an onrushing taxi, dodged around a bicycle messenger and then picked up his pace

16

as he ran toward Park Avenue. Bill was already rehearsing the excuse he would offer to Jeanne who, he guessed, was frozen into an angry silence. Not that she didn't have every right to be furious. He had left her alone to do all the packing for their trip. Kominicki was right. He never should have come in to school just to coach part of an unimportant basketball game.

His legs turned heavy, and he could feel the shortness of breath beginning to burn in his chest. He was surprised, even though he shouldn't have been. At thirty-seven, he wasn't exactly a kid anymore. And while he did spend a bit of time running the floor with his boys, most of his hours were confined to the classroom, and to the tiny office he shared with Martin. The fact was that he was a teacher, not an athlete. And teaching wasn't the best preparation for a mad dash across town, capped by his anxiety over being late for the start of their vacation.

Bill turned into a doorway, pushed open the inner door which was supposed to be locked, but never was, and kept his speed as he ran up the iron edged steps that led to his loft apartment. He had his sweatshirt peeled off by the time he turned at the landing, and was fumbling for his keys before he reached the heavy steel fire door.

"Sorry," he shouted as soon as he had mastered the two dead-bolt locks and stepped inside. "It won't take me a minute. I know just where everything is."

He tried to avoid Jeanne's ferocious gaze, but there was no place to hide. The apartment was essentially one big room, with a countertop defining the kitchen, and a small potted tree separating the sleeping area. Jeanne's decorating skills made it oddly fashionable, with each of the living areas clearly defined. But the only privacy was within the walls that enclosed the bathroom, and that was where Bill headed. He had the shower running full blast before Jeanne could get her anger into words, and he was already behind the curtain when she appeared in the doorway.

"We have exactly one hour and forty-two minutes to make the plane," she reminded him, her tone as matter-of-fact as a recorded telephone announcement.

His blond hair was already frothed with shampoo as he peeked over the curtain bar. "Plenty of time. Why don't you come on in here and join me?"

Jeanne's eyes flashed, and then she turned away abruptly. "Why can't you be serious?"

He raced across to the sleeping area wrapped in a towel, leaving a trail of wet footprints. "You all packed?" he called into the open space.

"Since eight o'clock this morning," her voice answered. Then, as an exclamation point, "And I'm not the one who wanted to take this trip."

"C'mon. You'll have a great time," he sang out as he fired his clothes into a duffel bag. "A whole week of sailing in the Caribbean. Rum punches every night. Swimming. Snorkeling."

Her answer came immediately. "A whole week jammed into a small cabin with people that I hardly know. That's not my idea of how we ought to be spending our first vacation in two years."

He was about to close the duffel when he realized that something was missing. "Hey, have you seen

18

my Yankee baseball cap?"

"I thought you knew where everything was," she answered unsympathetically. "You're just like the children you teach."

He tossed about in his dresser drawers and then dropped down to his knees and found the hat under the bed. It was only a minute later when he walked around the potted tree, fully dressed, dragging the canvas bag behind him.

"I'm ready," he announced.

"Is that what you're wearing?"

Bill looked down at the plaid cotton sport shirt, the faded khaki pants, and the scuffed loafers. "You don't like my outfit?"

He was tall and lean, with most of his strength in his arms and hands, an athlete beginning to go soft. Clothes didn't hang well on him, and he compounded the problem by his indifference to his tailoring.

"You'll look better when you comb your hair," she answered. His hair was thinning, but it was still long enough to hang down over his eyes. The wild hair and his angular, bony features occasionally made him look a bit deranged.

"Yeah," he agreed, rushing back into the bathroom where he remembered that he had forgotten to pack his toothbrush and shaving gear.

"Dammit!" Jeanne breathed.

"What's wrong?" he answered as he charged out of the bathroom.

"God, but I hate to leave the place like this."

His school papers were scattered across the kitchen counter, where he had been correcting them the night before. In their living room area, where soft designer chairs were positioned around the television and the stereo rack, there were two stacks of books on the floor, and more of his school papers piled unevenly on the bookshelves. Fabric samples that Jeanne had been studying for a decorating assignment were rolled against a wall.

"What's the matter with it?" he asked, following her eyes around the room.

"It's a mess. I should have taken yesterday off so that we would have had time to get ready."

Bill realized her frustration. "Just give me a minute. I'll straighten it up." He started gathering his papers from the counter.

"Don't!" It was a command rather than a request. "We don't have any place to put things, and we don't have any time. We have just one hour and twenty minutes to make our plane."

He left the papers and dragged the two bags toward the door which Jeanne held open.

"But when we get back," she threatened, "we have to have a serious talk. We can't go on living like this."

Bill left the duffel bags on the curb and jogged up to the Park Avenue corner to hail a taxi. Then he watched the meter tick as the cab crept through the dense traffic of delivery trucks. He could see Jeanne waiting impatiently, but the car seemed to take forever to reach her.

"We'll never make the flight," she predicted morosely. "We should have allowed for the traffic." She climbed into the taxi, joining the driver who was watching Bill struggle the bags into the front seat. "LaGuardia Airport," she said. "We're in kind of a hurry." The driver didn't seem at all impressed.

As soon as they were settled in the back seat, Jeanne began to review her check list. "Do we have the tickets?"

Bill tapped the pocket of his windbreaker. "Tickets," he reported.

"Cash for the porters?"

"Cash," he answered, tugging the wallet out of his back pocket.

"Travelers' checks?" She lifted the answer from her oversized straw handbag. "Travelers' checks," she announced. A second later, she produced an official looking brown envelope. "Passports."

She studied the list, which she had written on a small spiral-bound pad. "Hell, I didn't get half of these done. I didn't return the books to the library. And I never did the cost estimates on the Draper job."

Bill remembered the interiors she had designed for Draper and Oswald, Attorneys-at-Law; soft colors and rounded shapes that would give a pleasant personality to a corporate practice.

"When they see your designs, they won't care about the price," he flattered.

She started to smile, but then her expression turned to horror. "Oh my God!"

"What?" he asked her with an amused smile.

"I didn't pick up my birth-control pills."

He laughed. "Well, maybe we'll have more than pictures to remember our vacation by."

"Dammit! Be serious. That's the last thing we'd need." Children were a flash point between them. She was even more anxious than he was to start a family. But she was determined not to become pregnant until they had gotten their life in order. She had fixed ideas about a proper home for children, and they certainly didn't include a loft on a traffic filled street, or parents who weren't well launched in promising careers. Bill, on the other hand, was content with the life they were living, and thought now was as good a time as any.

He knew he had picked the wrong topic for humor. "There are drug stores in Tortola," he said indifferently.

Jeanne pushed the pad back into her purse and turned pointedly toward the window. She was relieved to see that the downtown Manhattan traffic was light on the avenue and that they were moving quickly. "Not that we'll have any use for them," she said. "There won't be much privacy with Marilyn and Howard in the next bunk."

"It's a big boat," he teased her. "There are separate state rooms."

"I'll bet we'll be able to hear Marilyn bragging right through the walls."

"Bulkheads," he said. "On a boat, they're called bulkheads. And I thought you and Marilyn had a great time when we were together."

"That was for an evening," Jeanne answered. "This is for a week. A whole week cooped up together on a sailboat, watching your Boston friends flaunt their success. This could be the voyage from hell."

He was hurt by the comment. "If you really didn't want to go, you could have said something."

She turned to him. "I did say something. I told

you it was a bad time. We're busy in the office. But you didn't hear me. Sometimes you don't hear anything."

They fell into a moody silence as they turned onto the ramp for the Triborough Bridge.

"What airline?" the driver asked, using the break in their conversation.

Bill looked bewildered. He reached for the tickets.

"Delta," Jeanne answered, as if Bill's not even knowing the airline made her point. The trip was his idea, something that Howard Hunter had suggested and Bill had agreed to when Howard was in New York on business. They weren't the closest of friends, often letting months pass between their telephone conversations. But they had kept in touch ever since they had been teammates at college. Howard had been the quarterback, and from what she gathered, the big man on campus. Even then, he had been the natural leader. Bill was a defensive back, a less exciting position which, she had decided, fit perfectly with his inclination to let life come to him. He was perfectly content to let Howard run the show, and had little desire to do anything that would bring a crowd to its feet.

Occasionally, when Howard's schedule allowed, they planned a day or a social evening with their wives. Howard had come up with the idea that they all share a cruising vacation on a charter boat out of Tortola. Bill had been more enthusiastic than she had seen him in years, but only for the short time while the idea was fresh and novel. He had quickly drifted back into his work at the school, and left all the details and decisions up to her.

That, she had admitted to herself, was the reason for the coolness she felt toward Howard and Marilyn. They always set the agenda, and then she and Bill followed along. They had everything together. Howard had built his architectural practice into a stunning business success, and Marilyn had used that success as a blueprint for position in her community. She was on the board of preservation societies, charitable committees, and the Junior League, and still managed to finish at the top of the B Flight at her country club. Face it, Jeanne had chastised herself on several occasions, you're jealous. In her more honest moments, she could admit that Marilyn wasn't bitchy. Marilyn was simply determined. She and Howard were going places, while she and Bill were wandering.

"New outfit?" Bill asked hoping to rekindle the conversation. She was wearing fitted jeans and an oversized sweater, a combination that she thought made her look younger.

"You gave me the sweater for Christmas," she answered.

"I've got good taste," he said, bringing the day's first smile to her face, "and you've got a great figure. Can't wait to see you in your bikini."

It wasn't true, but she enjoyed the flattery. She was slight and straight, more boyish than curvaceous. Her dark, short hair was cut more for its efficiency than for fashion. But she had large, blue eyes that sometimes smiled before her lips did, and it was the smile that made her attractive.

"I've got a one-piece speedo," she reminded him.

He shook his head furiously. "No way! No point in having a yacht if you don't have a naked nymph lounging on the bow. First thing we'll do is pick you up a string bikini. Something that you can really hang out of."

Jeanne noticed the cab driver examining her in the mirror. She leaned towards Bill and whispered, "I don't hang out of anything."

He pushed his hand between her thighs and she slapped at it playfully, her first light moment of the morning.

"This is going to be a great trip," he told her.

Jeanne nodded. "I guess I am looking forward to it. We both need a vacation."

She was genuinely happy for a moment. But then she realized that Marilyn would probably be wearing a string bikini. And if she remembered Marilyn's figure correctly, she would certainly be hanging out of it.

2

Traffic slowed along the Ft. Lauderdale beach drive as Cindy Camilli climbed out of the limousine. She was wearing black stretch bicycle shorts, and a yellow tank top that did little to hide the full shape of her breasts. A long blond ponytail hung from the back of her baseball cap. Her face could have been on the cover of a fashion magazine except for the bulge in her cheek, and the lollypop stick that poked out of the corner of her mouth. She pulled a knapsack out of the back seat, and then waited for the driver to lift the two aluminum travel cases out of the trunk.

"You need a hand?" she asked.

Manuel shook his head. "They're not heavy. Just bulky." The Spanish accent fit his dark complexion and wavy white hair. He set the cases on the sidewalk, and then stretched his back until he heard the bones crack. "A little heavy," he admitted.

"I don't know how in hell I'm gonna carry them," Cindy wondered aloud as she circled the cases.

"Just roll them," Manuel advised. He pulled a folding travel dolly from the trunk, extended the handle and then stacked the cases in position. Cindy helped him secure the freight with a bungee cord. Then she took the handle and tried a test run along the sidewalk next to the car.

"Not bad. I should be able to handle it."

"Want me to help?" the Cuban offered.

"Nah! No sweat. You better stay with the car."

She pulled her cargo through the ornate glass doors of The Commodore, a tower of condominiums that faced the ocean, and crossed the carpeted lobby toward the bank of elevators. A uniformed doorman rushed out of the small lobby office to intercept her.

"Mr. Linz's apartment," Cindy announced without stopping.

"Is he expecting you?"

She lifted the lollypop out of her mouth with one hand and pushed the button with the other. "I sure as hell hope so. I'd hate to be lugging these damn things around all afternoon."

"It's the penthouse," the doorman said.

She dragged the dolly into the elevator. "I know the way."

Walter Linz baffled her, she thought as the door closed behind her. At times, he seemed so careless. Having his chauffeur drive her around town in his limousine certainly wasn't the best way to avoid attention. And why would he meet her at his home where the doorman would certainly be able to identify her? Yet he had been meticulous in avoiding a paper trail that might link them. He had given her cash to purchase the camera equipment in her own name, and the cash she needed for the airline tickets. He had told her to use her own credit card in booking the hotel reservation. She guessed that he didn't particularly care what people thought they knew. His only concern was what they could prove.

The elevator opened into a private foyer where a circle of white Doric columns pretended to be holding up the ceiling. Cindy pulled the cases across the tile floor and pushed a doorbell that was next to the eight-foot double doors.

"Yes?" a friendly voice sounded through the speaker.

"It's me. Cindy."

"Ah, Cindy. And right on time."

She waited a few seconds until she heard the rattle of the dead bolt. Then Walter Linz swung the door open wide.

"Come in! Come in! Don't you look lovely." He stepped back, making no effort to help with the cases.

"You look pretty smooth yourself," Cindy answered, steering the dolly into the spacious living room. Linz was wearing pastel walking shorts with matching knee socks and a white cotton sport shirt. His round face and bald head were tanned to a deep, health-spa leather.

"Can I get you a drink? I'm having my morning Bloody Mary."

"Just a Coke. Diet, if you've got it."

He nodded, and walked off toward the kitchen. Cindy glanced around at the white leather sofas and the glass tables. The walls were a faint tint of coral framed with white woodwork. Large, colorful canvases hung on two of the walls. She eased open the sliders and stepped out onto the rooftop patio which had its own swimming pool and hot tub. From the railing at the edge she could look across the white beach and the lazy breakers, out to where the ocean blurred into a hazy sky.

Pretty nice, she thought. If Walter Linz wanted her for a mistress, at least the accommodations would be first rate. But in their several meetings, Linz had never offered even an inviting glance. He was the perfect gentleman, more a kindly uncle than a demanding boss. In her line of work, where attractive young women were a fringe benefit to management, Walter was unique. Despite his ruthless reputation and the fear he inspired in his associates, he had never demanded favors.

"Just ginger ale, I'm afraid." He was standing in the doorway, holding a glass toward her.

"That's okay." She took the drink as they walked back into the living room.

He nodded towards the cases. "Any problems?"

"Not a one. They had everything on the shelves. The guy didn't even seem impressed by the size of the order." Then she added, "It came to fourteen hundred bucks."

Linz settled into the sofa. "So. Let's see what fourteen hundred dollars buys."

Cindy got down on her hands and knees and opened the two cases. They were lined with black foam rubber, with shapes cut out that matched the dimensions of the equipment. One held two camera bodies, six identical camera backs, and four lenses of varying lengths and shapes. The other held square tinfoil packets of film, a power pack and an assortment of hardware clamps.

"Very impressive," Walter allowed. "Do you know how all this works?"

"Not really. I've never been behind the camera.

Only on the other side."

When she was younger, Cindy had tried modeling, hoping that it would be a glamorous escape from carrying cocktails in a topless costume. But "model" had proven to be as much of a fiction as the titles of the other jobs she had held since running away from her home in Minnesota. Waitress. Hostess. Entertainer. Escort. They had all involved pretending to be amused while sweaty hands groped under the edge of her panties. "Model" had meant bedding down with the photographer who was shooting pictures for her portfolio, and then sitting around in a bathrobe waiting for her scenes in an adult film.

"Well, you won't actually have to take any pictures. Just carry the cases, and then bring them back." Linz had gotten up and walked to the closet by the front door. He lifted a paper box from the shelf and then set it down next to the open camera cases.

"This is the film you'll be carrying."

She opened the box, and took out a dozen sealed film packets, identical to the ones that were already packed into the case. She juggled them in her hands, balancing their weight.

"Is this all?"

"That's it," Linz smiled. "What were you expecting?"

Cindy shrugged. "I don't know. Just that the last time . . ."

The last time she had made a trip for Walter, she had carried a suitcase of cash — stacks of large denomination bills wrapped as Christmas presents. The case had weighed over fifty pounds.

"It isn't cash," he explained. "Something much more valuable."

Her eyes narrowed. "Mr. Linz, I . . ."

"And it isn't drugs. I know you don't want anything to do with drugs, Cindy, and I respect that."

She looked back down at the film packs, her confusion obvious.

"They're financial instruments," he explained. "Pieces of legal paper that are of great value. I don't mind telling you that this is the most money you've ever carried for me. And that's because I trust you, Cindy. I have complete confidence in you."

She glanced up at him. "So, what am I bringing back?"

Linz crouched down and took the film out of the aluminum case. Cindy began replacing it with the film packets that Walter had taken from his closet shelf. He explained while they were working.

"Just check the cases with the security people at the hotel, and then wait in your room. You'll be contacted by a man named Heinz, and told where the photo session is going to take place. You bring the cases with you. Heinz will take these packets, and replace them with packs of exposed film. He'll also take the two camera bodies, and replace them with two identical camera bodies."

"That's it?" she asked.

"That's it," he assured her. "A few minutes work. Half an hour at tops, if Mr. Heinz decides to inspect all the film packs."

"And then I come back."

"No hurry. As long as you're down there, you

might as well take a few days in the sun. It's less suspicious if you don't seem anxious to leave."

He stood up and then studied the repacked case for a few seconds. "Just make sure that you leave these in the hotel safe. Fourteen hundred dollars worth of camera equipment would be mighty attractive to a petty hotel burglar."

He lifted the cases back onto the dolly and re-snapped the bungee cords. He hadn't answered her question. He hadn't told her what would be packed inside the camera bodies that she would be bringing back. But Cindy knew better than to ask. If it were important for her to know, he would have let her know. The only important thing was that it wouldn't be drugs. Walter knew that she had suffered through a short-lived cocaine habit. She believed him when he said that none of that shit would be involved.

He reached into the pocket of his shorts, took out a thick fold of currency and began counting through the one-hundred-dollar bills. "You said fourteen hundred for the equipment?"

Cindy reached for her knapsack. "Wait. I have a receipt."

"Don't bother. Fourteen hundred is fine. Just be sure you have the receipt with you when you check through customs. If you don't, they'll confiscate the cameras." He kept thumbing the bills. "Another eight hundred for your expenses."

"I'll keep track of everything," she promised.

He stopped counting, and shook his head in mock despair. "Cindy, dear, I want you to pad your expense account. I want you to have a good time."

32

She smiled. "Okay, Mr. Linz."

"And," he said, as he separated the money he was counting, "two thousand for your advance. I'll have the other two thousand waiting for you as soon as you get back."

She smiled giddily. "It sure beats hustling drinks." Cindy thought of the free time she would have on Tortola, and then remembered Steve Berlind, the charter boat captain she had met on her last trip for Walter Linz. They had hit it off well, and spent a great evening aboard one of the boats that he worked. If he wasn't out on a charter, she would enjoy getting to know him a little better.

But then Linz cast a dark shadow across her happy expectations. As he gave her the money, he added casually, "Oh, I'm providing you with the usual protection. You may notice Mr. Weston at the airport. He'll be on your flight, and will be staying at your hotel."

"Okay." For the first time, her voice sounded weak.

"You don't say anything to him, and he won't say anything to you. He'll just be there. In case you need him."

"Fine." She still didn't sound enthusiastic.

Cindy looked around the lobby as soon as she stepped out of the elevator, and then searched the street once she was outside. Now that she was carrying the "financial instruments," she knew that Al Weston would be nearby, scrupulous in safeguarding Walter Linz's investment. Walter had said that Al would be there to protect her, and she knew that was part of his mission. It was possible that the people she was meeting might get a little greedy. A young woman would certainly pose no obstacle if they tried to simply take the money without delivering the merchandise. Al Weston's strong presence could keep her from becoming an insignificant victim.

It was the other part of his assignment that frightened her. He was also traveling with her to make sure that she had no thoughts of straying. She had heard about one of Linz's earlier couriers, a young jock who had naively decided that his gym-sculptured physique made him invulnerable. He had entered the airport and then turned toward a different wing of the building, thinking that a flight he had secretly booked would carry him to financial security. The porters had found him in a men's room stall, his skull fractured and his jaw broken in two places. Weston had made sure that the word got around, so that other couriers who carried Walter Linz's merchandise would be very careful to catch the right planes.

The limousine swung around the corner and pulled up to the curb. Manuel popped the trunk, and then ran around the car to help Cindy load the cases.

"You seen Al?" she asked as soon as they were both in the car.

"Al? No. Is he coming with us?"

She shrugged, and then settled back into the soft leather seat. Maybe Al wouldn't be joining her yet. There was no need. She was locked inside the car with Walter Linz's driver, who had instructions to deliver her directly to the airport where she would catch the first leg of her flight to San Juan. Al would probably pick her up at the airport. She smiled as she realized that Walter was anything but careless. She was with his driver, about to be delivered to the supervision of his henchman. Ever since he had given her the new film packets, she had been completely under his control.

"Hey Manuel, keep your eyes on the road," Cindy said. "I've got to change my clothes."

He reached up and tipped the rearview mirror out of focus, a gesture he had learned when he was driving escorts and their johns. Mr. Linz had shown him the way to a more respectable life, just as he had done for Cindy.

3

Howard Hunter checked his Rolex, and then leaned forward over the chauffeur's shoulder so that he could confirm the time on the dashboard clock.

"Dammit!" he said in despair. The traffic feeding toward the tunnel that linked the Boston waterfront with Logan Airport had slowed to a crawl.

"Relax," Marilyn told him. "We have plenty of time. The flight's not for another two hours."

"We have baggage to check," he reminded her.

"Howard, this is supposed to be a vacation." She did an elaborate take on his white cotton slacks and blue racing jacket. "It's not a yacht race." Then she punctuated the statement by reaching up and pulling the peak of his captain's cap down over his eyes.

He pushed the cap up and squared it on his head, checking in the driver's mirror to be sure the soft cloth found the right rake. "Sorry," he admitted. "It's going to take me a couple of days to unwind."

"Relax," she repeated. "It will all still be here when we get back."

"I know." His eyes darted ahead through the windshield. He was plainly worried that the traffic

36

might come to a dead stop. "Maybe that's the problem. It *will* still be here. I should have gotten things settled."

Marilyn turned toward the side window and shook her head in despair. She had suggested that with the business problems he was facing, it might make sense to call the trip off. Or at least postpone it. New England was in the pit of a depression, with office plazas and shopping malls closing every day. The vacancy rate in the kinds of buildings that Howard designed was running over twenty-five percent. He hadn't been offered a new commission in the past ten months, and now the banks were foreclosing on some of the properties that he had put his own money into. It was a hell of a time to be sailing away to the Caribbean.

But he had put up a brave front, probably to reassure himself as much as for her benefit. "Nothing to worry about," he had insisted. And gradually, she had come around to think that the charter boat cruise probably wasn't the worst idea after all. Her husband had been talking about taking a boat for years. On a dozen occasions he had written away for yacht plans and charts of the cruising grounds. But in the past, with his business growing, there had never been time. Now, there was plenty of time.

"I suppose I should have taken your advice and postponed this thing," he said morosely.

Marilyn didn't answer, so Howard argued with himself.

"But we wanted to do this with Bill and Jeanne. If we put it off, it might have been years before all of us could get away at the same time. God knows how our schedules would work out. And nothing is going to happen immediately. The damn lawyers take months just to file a piece of paper."

She could have taken issue with the thought that she had ever been enthusiastic over a sailing trip with Bill and Jeanne. The fact was that she had been stunned when he had come home from a trip to New York and announced that the Chesters were going to be their shipmates. Marilyn had known Bill in college, a quiet, dedicated guy who was no match for Howard in the classroom, and was lost in the sea of uniforms on the football field. "Best defensive back in the conference," Howard had told her, in defense of his teammate. She had figured that defensive backs couldn't be very important, because Bill didn't get nearly as much attention as Howard did. Their wedding, right after graduation, had assembled the entire team as guests. Four years later, when they had gone to New York for Bill and Jeanne's wedding, there were only a handful of strangers in attendance. The reception had been in someone's tiny apartment, where a rooftop fire escape had been the most comfortable space.

Since then, she had spent no more than a dozen evenings with the Chesters. Pleasant enough, she remembered, but not people that she would call great fun. He taught in some kind of neighborhood school for poor kids, which didn't match the interests she and Howard had developed living in the Boston suburbs. And she was doing interior decorations for an office furniture company, a topic that didn't make for exciting conversation. No, they certainly wouldn't have been her first choice.

There were dozens of couples that Marilyn would rather have gone to sea with than the Chesters.

But she had spent her whole married life accommodating her husband's preferences. She had earned a reputation as a skilled hostess, catering to his business friends, and had learned to steer almost any conversation around to one of his interests. Given his love for sailing, it shouldn't be too difficult to find topics that Howard would enjoy. She guessed she could make it through.

Howard had a thirty-foot sloop docked near Plymouth less than an hour from their home, and at one time had headed out into Cape Cod Bay whenever he had a moment away from his work. He had enlisted their two children, Josh and Amanda, as his crew, and on several occasions coaxed Marilyn aboard for a day at sea. But the free weekends had become fewer and fewer, and Marilyn and the children had lost their enthusiasm. For Howard, sailing was every bit as competitive as football, and he tended to be much more concerned with the trim of the sails than with the enjoyment of his family. Once, when they had done a poor job of turning a mark in a yacht club event, he had become so enraged that Marilyn had thought he might have a stroke. Josh had said that he felt more like a galley slave than a guest at the captain's table and had found excuses to avoid spending his weekends before the mast. Over the past two years, the sloop had rarely left the dock, leaving Howard to do his sailing in the yacht club lounge.

He fidgeted when the traffic stopped in the middle of the tunnel. "Dammit," he cursed, and he checked his watch again. They were out of the tunnel and up on the skyway, with the airport in sight, when Howard admitted what was really bothering him.

"Probably no point in getting into our problems with Bill and Jeanne," he said, as if the thought had just occurred to him. "I wouldn't want to rain on their vacation."

Marilyn agreed immediately. "Let's not talk about business at all. I think that's what we're trying to get away from."

Over the years she had learned to read Howard like a first-grade primer. He could face up to the fact that his fortunes were failing. He was more than a match for the reality. But he could never confront the image of himself as anything but a winner. Given the choice between real achievements that were unknown to his friends, or an undeserved reputation for success, he would choose the latter without hesitating. He was less concerned with the specter of a major business setback than he was with the possibility that his friends might learn about his troubles. Image was everything.

That, she realized, was the cement of her husband's friendship with Bill Chester. Their images weren't in competition. If Bill had really been the best defensive back in the conference, then a defensive back was no rival for a quarterback. Bill could sincerely tell his friend how much in awe he was of a game Howard had just played without raising his own play for equal praise. She guessed that when the two men got together, Bill didn't spend time touting his work as a teacher.

He probably let Howard's obvious business success be the conversational center. And Howard would appreciate that. He needed the sincere admiration of the people around him. He needed friends like Bill.

4

Steve Berlind jumped out of the launch and pulled himself up onto the deck of *Cane Maiden*. He turned quickly and caught the duffel that the launch pilot threw up after him.

"Pick you up at sunset?" the pilot asked.

Steve gave his new command a quick glance. "Better not," he called down. "It's gonna take some time to get her shipshape."

The pilot gunned the launch engine. "Okay. Call on the radio if you change your mind." The launch pulled away and traced a white wake across clear blue water as it headed back toward the dock.

Steve didn't look like a yacht captain. With his bony build and slouched posture, he didn't seem to be up to the demands of the sea. The dark hair, pulled back into the stub of a ponytail, the cut-off jeans and the tie-dyed tee shirt were more fitting for a rock group follower than a commanding officer. But he caressed *Cane Maiden*'s lifeline like a lover, and he was as surefooted as a goat as he stepped across her wooden decks.

He had been assigned the cruise that morning, when he brought six vacationers back to the dock aboard a fifty-foot sloop.

"You're going out again tomorrow," the charter

manager had told him.

"Who've I got?"

"Some loudmouth from Boston. Two couples."

"Shit! I suppose the guy belongs to a yacht club."

"A commodore. And a member of the racing committee. The whole nine yards."

"Shit!" Steve had repeated.

The best charters fell into two groups. There were those who knew how to handle a yacht, and took a bare boat with no captain. And there were those who plainly admitted that they didn't know flotsam from jetsam, had no intention of doing anything more tiring than moving to keep in the shade of the mainsail, and wanted a full-time captain. The problem ones were the armchair admirals; people who had done just enough sailing to be dangerous. They wanted a captain for occasional services, but they were sure that they could skipper the boat by themselves. "Yacht clubbers," the charter people called them. They always showed up in nautical attire, and talked like characters out of *Billy Budd*. Then they got their foot caught in a bite of line, and had to be dragged back aboard after they disappeared over the side.

"What are we sailing?" Steve had asked. "A catamaran?" He was envisioning one of the fiberglass condominiums that charter fleets had fitted out with television sets and hot tubs to compete with the better resort hotels. They were topped with sails and could make decent headway, but most of them had the sea-keeping characteristics of a sand barge.

"*Cane Maiden*," he had been told.

"*Cane Maiden*?"

"That's what the guy asked for. He picked her out of the catalog."

Steve had been surprised. *Cane Maiden* had been designed for the open sea. The accommodations had taken second place in the builder's eye to her ability to point high into the wind. She wasn't usually the choice of the yacht clubbers.

He had sailed the boat before, and she was one of his favorites. Of his twenty-five years, ten had been spent aboard yachts, first racing in the Chesapeake, and then ferrying boats up and down the Atlantic coast for owners who wanted them moved with the seasons. He could tell the quality of a yacht simply by turning her bow across the wind. *Cane Maiden* was quality.

Steve walked forward and dropped his duffel down the forward hatch. Then he looked back down the length of his command. He needed to bring the sails topside from the lockers and get them rigged. Then he wanted to spin the compass and test the radio and the navigation equipment. Finally, he would check the charts and break out the navigator's instruments. In the morning, he would swab the decks, greet the tender when it brought the provisions alongside and help get them stowed. Then he would change into the company uniform, which consisted of white shorts, a monogrammed shirt and a baseball cap, and wait for his charter to arrive.

"*Cane Maiden*," he repeated to himself, shaking his head in disbelief. A guy who appreciated *Cane Maiden* couldn't be all bad, even if he was a loudmouth from Boston.

He had met them all. People like his father who

were obsessed with punctuality and who spent the week clocking their arrivals and departures with stopwatches. People like his mother, who mixed vodka in their morning orange juice and began asking about lunch while the day's wind was still too weak to rattle the rigging. People like his brother who simply enjoyed ordering their hirelings around. And like his sister, who got their kicks teasing the men by undoing the straps of their bathing suits. All the people he had tried to get away from when, at fifteen, he had run away from home and found a place as a winch grinder on an ocean racer.

Now, they were delivered aboard weekly to command his services. He resented their bullying, and he hated himself for letting himself be bullied. Someday, Steve kept telling himself, he would have his own boat. To his mind, it was the vision of freedom that a jailed convict might have as he counted the days remaining in his sentence. But the truth was that his bank account had never gotten beyond three figures. He was no closer to commanding his own vessel than he had been when he was fifteen. There was no salvation in sight. He would be ordered, bullied and seduced as far as he could look into the future. And he would hate every minute of it.

But maybe this trip would be a momentary reprieve. The guy had asked for *Cane Maiden.* Out of a thick catalog of gel-coated, aluminum-rigged, vinyl-padded cruising palaces, he had homed in on a true, down-to-the-basics sailing vessel. Maybe he was a seaman. Maybe this voyage would be different.

45

5

Cindy had noticed Al Weston lurking behind her at the Ft. Lauderdale airport. Now, here he was in San Juan, standing on the other side of the baggage conveyer as she waited for her camera cases to appear. He looked like a vacationer, in tan slacks, a subtle plaid sport jacket and a pastel golf shirt. The straw hat with its colorful band was certainly a playful touch.

But there was nothing playful about Al Weston. He was all business, and his business was discipline. His round face seldom smiled, and his thick neck and broad chest seemed threatening even now as he relaxed with one foot resting on the edge of the conveyer.

He had first met Cindy when he was the silent enforcer at a topless club where she had worked as a waitress. He had appeared out of the shadows when a six-man bachelor party loudly questioned its tab.

"Any problem, gentlemen?" he had asked politely.

"None at all," they had assured him as they began digging in their pockets. None of them wanted to step forward to state their case.

"Thanks," Cindy had told him.

He had acknowledged her gratitude with a wave of his thick fingertip as he sauntered back to his place at the end of the bar.

They had become better acquainted when there was a shortage at one of the cash registers. Al had gathered the waitresses together to review the procedures they used in completing and turning in their sales checks. Out of the babel of frightened voices, Cindy's had been the one that made sense.

"You!" The thick finger had pointed into her flaunted cleavage. "Come with me."

She had followed him into the office where hundreds of bar checks were stacked up on top of a desk next to coils of cash register tape. Weston had pulled back the chair and held it for her until she was seated. "Okay, you run the checks. I'll take the tapes. Let's see what we can find."

It was Cindy who had found the discrepancies. As she explained to Weston, the waitresses simply returned the amount of cash that was punched at the bottom of the check. Running frantically between tables, they never bothered to check the line items. But the bartenders could cancel the check, print a duplicate omitting some of the items and then pocket the difference. All they had to do was get rid of the original check.

She had studied the check stubs, then reviewed the tapes and found those with a high number of cancellations. While Al looked over her shoulder, she added the differences between the canceled amounts and the subsequent checks for one shift. "Four hundred and fifty bucks," she announced. Al did a mental calculation for a week's worth of shifts. The missing billing was in the ball park.

47

"Okay, thanks," he had managed as he pulled back her chair. As she walked toward the door, he had stopped her with a question.

"What the hell are you doin' workin' in a dive like this?"

"Lousy references," Cindy had answered.

He had nodded and turned back to his cash register tapes.

A week later, one of the bartenders was hospitalized after a street fight. Al had called Cindy in the next day, and handed her a stack of canceled bar checks. "Look what I found."

"Guess I was right," she had answered.

"Yeah. You were right."

Al had left the club a week later to take on greater responsibilities for the whole chain. Cindy had quit the next day after one of the patrons followed her out into the parking lot and tore off her blouse. She had been leaving her apartment to interview for a new job when Al's car pulled up to the curb beside her, and he had told her to get in.

"You workin'?" he had asked, as they circled the block.

"Not right now."

"None of the joints hiring?"

"I'm looking for something a little better."

"What's holdin' you back?"

"Lousy references," she had repeated.

They circled past the point where he had picked her up.

"I may have something for you. A friend of mine does a lot of business offshore. He needs couriers to carry the cash and bring back the merchandise.

Pay is pretty good. Four grand for a round trip. Usually takes only a couple of days."

"Four thousand," she had gasped. Cindy still owed a lot of money to drug people who enjoyed keeping her in their debt. She was desperate to pay them off and put together enough money for a new start. Four thousand for a week's work was the answer to a prayer. But then she hesitated.

"Drugs?"

He had shrugged. "I don't ask."

"Sorry, Mr. Weston. I don't want anything to do with drugs. I've done that scene already."

"It ain't always drugs. Sometimes it's other things."

"Then I'm interested," Cindy had said after a moment's thought. "Is it all legal?"

He had responded with the only smile she had ever seen on his face. "If it was legal, we'd use the mailman. But it's safe."

"You think I can handle it?"

He had glanced over at her. "Yeah. You look too dumb to be dangerous, but you're a lot smarter than you look."

She hadn't been certain that it was a compliment so she didn't answer.

"Listen, kid. You done me a favor. Now I'm doin' you one. My friend don't like his couriers getting caught, so he gives 'em a good cover and plenty of protection. It's as safe as anything else you been doin'. And the pay is a hell of a lot better."

She had nodded. "Sounds good. But no drugs, okay?"

"I'll tell him," Al had said as he pulled to the

curb, reached across her and pushed open the door. "You'll be hearing from me."

She had. In the past three months, she had run three errands for Walter Linz, always without a hitch. She had paid off her drug debts and then pulled down the legitimate loans she had from a bank. She had every reason to be grateful to Al Weston. And yet, she was afraid of him. In their past assignments together, he had never even spoken to her. But the lurking presence of his brutal reputation seemed a constant threat.

The camera cases poked through the small doorway, and began riding the conveyer toward her. She lifted them off, attached them to her dolly and pulled them toward the gate where Island Air's small commuter planes departed for Tortola. Even without glancing back, she knew that Al Weston was right at her heels.

6

Howard spotted Bill as soon as he came through the gate of the Boston flight, and charged across the San Juan terminal to greet him. As soon as Bill saw Howard, he moved toward him, and then crouched low in preparation for a tackle. Howard faked to one side and then cut to the other like a broken field runner. Bill ignored the fake, watched his friend's feet to pick up his move, then lunged suddenly and grabbed Howard around the waist. They spun around together, laughing loudly.

"Still the best damn safety I ever saw," Howard shouted. "Nobody ever faked you out."

"You still have all the moves," Bill answered. "You should have gone pro." They had completely forgotten the women who were following slowly behind them.

They backed away and studied one another. "You're keeping in shape," Howard complimented. "Not like me. Sitting behind a desk has taken its toll. I've gone to seed." It wasn't true. In the fifteen years since graduation, Howard had added no more than twenty pounds to his playing weight. He carried his six feet with military bearing. His dark hair was still full and there was no trace of aging in his soft, fair features.

Bill gestured towards Howard's nautical attire. "You look like you own the boat," he teased. "Where did you get the sailor suit?"

"It came with a cute little whistle," Marilyn teased as she caught up from behind. She and Bill embraced as if they knew each other better than they actually did.

Jeanne stopped just short of the gathering and eyed Marilyn cautiously. She took in the slacks and jacket of a safari suit and the colorful scarf of regimental colors. Suddenly, she felt as if she had been shopping at the Salvation Army.

"Marilyn, good to see you again. You look wonderful."

Marilyn stepped across the gulf to embrace her. "I'd look a lot better if I had your figure," she said. "How do you stay so young?"

It was a generous compliment. Where Jeanne was straight, Marilyn was curved. Where Jeanne's lines were certainly more fashionable, Marilyn's were more feminine. As she stood with her sunglasses dangling from her fingers, in her obviously expensive ensemble, she was the image of confident success that Jeanne aspired to. Marilyn was five years older, but the difference wasn't at all apparent. Her makeup was professional, and the hair coloring that made her a hazel blond had been done by an expert.

"Why don't you two go to the bar, while Bill and I check us in to the flight," Howard suggested. He was glancing up at the monitor where their final leg to Tortola was posted.

"The bar?" Marilyn asked. "Hell, Howard, it's still early."

"The sun's over the yardarm!" he laughed, as he started to pull Bill toward the ticket counter. The two women were left standing in uneasy silence.

Howard darted under the ropes, taking a short-cut to the reservation clerks. Bill followed at his heels until they reached the end of a short line.

"Want to see the boat?" Howard asked as they waited. He was already reaching into the pocket of his jacket. "She's a real classic." He pulled out a brochure and unfolded it dramatically as if he were unwrapping a present. Then he held the picture at arm's length, a color photo of a yawl with all sails flying as she heeled into the wind and churned up a white spray.

Bill smiled. "Wow!"

"She's called *Cane Maiden*. Fifty-four feet, flying fourteen hundred square feet of canvas. Look at those lines."

"Beautiful," Bill agreed. He tried to visualize fifty-four feet. He had no concept of fourteen hundred square feet of anything. "It looks . . . traditional."

"Damn right she's traditional. Built in the fifties when we still knew how to build a real ship. She's never been out of the water except for a scraping and a new coat of paint."

He turned the brochure over to show Bill the cabin layout. "Two staterooms aft. They should be the same, but if one's better than the other, we can flip a coin. Or we can switch halfway out."

Bill Chester shrugged. "Won't matter to us. Hell, Howard, you're the captain. You and Marilyn take whichever one you want."

"Full head," Howard went on, indicating a space on the port side. "Wash basin, head and a shower. Fresh water. It's cold water, but heck, the tanks are right up against the sea, and the sea water is probably eighty degrees."

Bill thought of the pleasure Jeanne took in long, scalding showers. "Should be terrific," he said, trying to build up to his friend's level of enthusiasm.

Howard went through the plan inch by inch, explaining every compartment and locker. When he reached the bow, he pointed to the crew's quarters. "That's where our skipper sleeps. He'll come in handy when we're window shopping up close to the coast. It's a good idea to have someone familiar with the area aboard when you're in shoal waters."

Bill nodded. It sounded like a damn good idea to him. But he wondered, "Won't he be sailing the boat?"

"No way," Howard answered. "You and I are going to do the sailing. Why should he have all the fun?"

"I'm not sure I know how to paddle a canoe," Bill laughed.

"Don't worry," Howard said as a clerk signalled them to the counter. "You'll know enough to sit for your mate's license by the time I get through with you."

Marilyn and Jeanne found a table in an open lounge and decided to launch their vacation by ordering tropical drinks. As they waited, they made their forays into safe subjects. Jeanne remembered that Howard and Marilyn had a couple of children — a boy and a girl, she thought. She asked about them without committing herself to the names that she couldn't remember.

"Josh and Amanda," Marilyn prompted politely as she took their photographs from her purse, and began describing two decent junior high school students who were just entering the most dangerous of their teen years. Her defense was to keep them busy with a round of activities that left them little time to get into trouble. At school, they were both on athletic teams and in science clubs. After school, their commitments ranged from singing in the church choir to packaging up old newspapers for the town's recycling program. And then there were the expensive activities which Jeanne already wanted for the children she had almost given up hope of ever having. They had each toured Europe with youth groups, gone south to spring training with their baseball and tennis teams, and bicycled across the country with a church group. "They're on a skiing trip right now," Marilyn explained. "The timing was perfect because we never would have left them alone."

Then Marilyn asked Jeanne about her decorating practice, and was surprised to find that she was interested in the reply. Jeanne was trying hard to bring character and differentiation to the sameness of the business offices that her company furnished. She described several of her battles, inevitably lost to budget cuts, and the frustration of settling for mediocrity. What she really wanted was a chance to open her own studio, with a much smaller clientele, so that she could concentrate on offices that would appreciate her skills.

55

"I certainly envy your work," Marilyn said.

Jeanne was stunned. "You . . . envy . . . my work?"

"The challenge," Marilyn explained. "Your determination to get somewhere."

Jeanne shook her head. "I think you're already where I'm trying to get. Your family . . . the children. I could have said that I envied you." She gestured toward Marilyn's outfit. "You just seem to have everything so . . . together."

"The children are my life," Marilyn agreed. "And, of course, Howard. But, still . . ." She hinted at a larger role than being Howard's alter ego and household manager. Jeanne's independent thinking appealed to her.

But Jeanne didn't see the compliment. Instead, she saw Marilyn and Howard in sharp contrast to Bill and herself. "We need to get better established before I can make the break and get out on my own," she confessed. "Bill really has to make some decisions about the school. It's not getting us anywhere. It's holding us back."

They were startled when Howard slid into the seat between them. "What about the school?" he demanded, forcing himself into the conversation.

"Ask Bill," Jeanne responded, nodding towards her husband.

Bill sat down across from Howard. "It's kind of shaky. The endowment is pretty well gone and the city isn't anxious to help out. We're starting to lose our staff."

"That's a damn shame," Howard said with an edge of anger. Then he addressed the table. "It shouldn't be allowed to go under. Not now, when

56

everyone is so concerned about education."

"Concerned," Bill agreed, "but indifferent. More and more kids, but less and less money. It's a community school that's getting pretty shabby. No one wants to get involved."

"Well, you're involved," Howard said. "You should be damn proud of the work you're doing."

Marilyn winced. Jeanne had just hinted her hopes that her husband would see the school for the dead end that it was. Jeanne wanted him to get out. Now Howard was encouraging his dedication.

"You know," Howard continued, "I just might be able to help. There are a lot of important people in my industry. Wealthy themselves, but also on the boards of some of the big charities. This might be just the kind of cause that would interest them."

Marilyn felt her temper heating. The important people Howard knew were posted in the lobbies of their country clubs for back dues. Like Howard, most of them were scrambling to keep up appearances. What the hell was the matter with her husband and his friends that they needed desperately to keep up their act?

"I'm glad you're still doing so well," she heard Bill say.

"Oh, it's a little slower than I like it," Howard answered with practiced nonchalance. "We're down a bit with the recession. But I can use the breathing room. No way I'd have been able to take a week for sailing if we were still racing at top speed."

Why, Marilyn wondered, was her husband lying to a friend who had just admitted his own difficulties? What did Howard think? That he would be less a man if he admitted that his cash cow had just fallen over dead? She had to stop him.

"Hey, you guys. I don't want to hear any business talk. This is a vacation," Marilyn said.

"Right," Jeanne agreed eagerly. She didn't want Howard blowing any more smoke about her husband's wonderful dedication. It was easy for Howard to be dedicated. He could afford it. What did he know about their problems?

"Show Jeanne the boat," Bill suggested to Howard.

He took the brochure out of his pocket and spread it across the table.

Jeanne smiled in genuine joy. "She's beautiful," she told Howard, as if he were personally responsible for the boat's lines.

"Best boat in the Caribbean," he answered, accepting the compliment.

Jeanne wasn't surprised that Howard had found the very best.

7

Howard noticed Cindy the second she strolled into the waiting lounge. She had changed into khaki slacks with a loose fitting, brightly colored blouse, and replaced the baseball cap with a simple ribbon that tied back her hair. The outfit was ordinary, but her figure was not.

"My, what big eyes you have," Marilyn said when she noticed that her husband was turning in his seat to follow Cindy's progress through the terminal.

"I was looking at her camera equipment," he protested with a sheepish grin.

Bill followed Howard's glance across the table. "Very nice equipment," Bill agreed.

Howard turned back to his friends. "She must be a professional."

"I wouldn't be at all surprised," Marilyn teased.

"A professional photographer." He glanced back toward Cindy. "I wonder what kind of cameras she's using?" He watched her as she stepped up to the departure gate that their flight would leave from. Then he turned to Bill Chester.

"Are you interested in photography?"

"No. Not really. Just snapshots."

"Have you seen this one?" he asked Bill, as he

opened his camera case and lifted out a thirty-five millimeter Nikon. While Bill watched, he attached a long, zoom lens. "I've got all the lenses for fine work, but for casual shooting, this little baby makes things a lot simpler. Here, take a look."

Bill took the camera, found a distant airplane on the runway, and turned the focus ring. "Hey," he said enthusiastically as he pulled the plane up close, "this is really something." He panned to several other targets, and adjusted the images to razor sharpness. "You won't miss much with this."

"Best you can buy," Howard allowed. "I thought about bringing the video gear. It's fun, with the motion and sound. But you can't beat film for color and fidelity."

Bill handed the camera back carefully, and Howard repacked it. "The lighting might be a problem. Down here, the sun is so damn bright that you have to know how to work with it." He nodded toward the gate where Cindy stood with her boarding pass. "She probably works with it every day."

Howard slipped the case over his shoulder as he stood. "Why don't you order us another round," he told Bill. Then he explained to Marilyn, "I'll be right back. I just want to talk with that girl and see if I can pick up some pointers."

"Make damn sure that's all you pick up," Marilyn called after him, bringing laughter from Jeanne and Bill. That was the reaction she was hoping for to make light of her husband's flirtation. Howard didn't mean to embarrass her. He just needed to demonstrate his prowess with attractive women, a card from the same hand as his need to be a financial wizard. But Marilyn was beginning to understand that Howard wasn't the only one who was playacting. She needed to pretend that she wasn't hurt, a demonstration of her own sense of security.

Cindy was leaning against the wall by the boarding gate, the aluminum cases stacked by her feet. She didn't notice Howard until he had stepped right in front of her.

"I think we're both heading to Tortola," he said with a wide smile.

"Looks that way," she answered.

He indicated the heavy cases. "You on an assignment?"

She looked puzzled.

"A photo assignment," he explained. "I assume you're a professional photographer. You wouldn't be taking all this just to send some pictures home."

"Oh, yeah. Right."

"Where are you going to be shooting? Inside or outdoors?"

She squirmed uneasily. "All over." She looked away from him, trying to discourage a conversation.

"I do some photography myself. Amateur stuff, but some of it is pretty good. Mostly thirty-five millimeter." He patted his case. "That's what I've brought with me. A Nikon body and a zoom."

Cindy responded with a hair trigger smile.

"You shooting thirty-five?" he persisted, nodding toward the cases on her dolly.

"Some," she allowed.

"Nikon?"

"Yeah. Nikon."

"Can't beat it," he said, pleased to find that they were in the same club. He began babbling about all the brands he had considered before he decided to go with Nikon. As he talked, Cindy glanced uneasily around the waiting area. She spotted Al Weston's straw hat above the top edge of a newspaper.

"Hey, can I ask you a question?" Howard said.

"Sure." Al's eyes appeared between the newspaper and the brim of his hat. They were riveted on her new-found companion.

"I'm worried about the light down here in the tropics. I hear it's a lot brighter than it reads."

"It's bright, all right," she agreed, although she had no idea what he was talking about. "You gotta watch it."

"What do you do?" Howard asked. "Take it up a stop?"

Al was folding his newspaper. He had pushed forward to the edge of his seat. Oh Christ, did he think she knew this guy? Did he think they had something going? The guy was carrying a camera case. Was Al watching to make sure they didn't exchange anything?

"Or do you just bracket everything?" Howard continued.

"That works," Cindy answered without taking her eyes off Al. Maybe Al knew him. Hell, maybe he was a cop. Or a narc. Maybe they were closing in on her.

"Which?" Howard persisted. "What do you recommend?"

Cindy's eyes darted around the groups of passengers. Did any of them look like cops? Some of the men were looking at her, and they hurried away as soon as she made eye contact. But that wasn't suspicious. She was used to men looking at her.

"Just bracket everything," she said, repeating the last words she had heard.

"Yeah," Howard allowed. "I guess that's the safest way."

She noticed that Al was looking around, apparently thinking the same thing that she was. Maybe this clown had back up.

"Look, you'll have to excuse me," Cindy said, taking the handle of the dolly. "I'm gonna stop in the ladies' room before we take off."

She managed a friendly smile as she walked around him. "Good luck with your pictures."

"Thanks. And thanks for the tip. Always a smart idea to ask a professional."

Howard didn't notice, but Al Weston's eyes followed him closely as he sauntered away.

"So, did you check out her equipment?" Bill Chester asked him as he sat down.

"Got everything I needed," he boasted.

"And all in under three minutes," Marilyn noticed for Jeanne's benefit.

"Very funny," Howard said, and then he joined in the laughter.

8

They dragged their own luggage through the gate
and out onto the tarmac, where the pilot hoisted
it into the cargo hatch in the back of the plane.
It was a twin-engine de Haviland turboprop, chosen for its ability to make the short airstrips that
were typically cut into the mountains. Inside, the
seats were almost miniature, and the passengers
had to duck their heads as they made their way
down the aisle.

Howard smiled at Cindy who was sitting in the
back, single seat. She acknowledged their recent
acquaintance with a tight nod of her chin. He took
a seat next to Marilyn on the double-seat side of
the aisle, behind Bill and Jeanne. Al Weston was
the last one to climb aboard, and he squeezed
down the aisle to the front single seat without
glancing at either Cindy or at Howard.

They took off to the east, using only a few hundred feet of the runway, and banked north out
over the water. The sea, up close to the shore
line, was nearly transparent. Rocky ledges were
visible far beneath the surface ripples, and the
small boats moving out of the harbor seemed to
be suspended in mid air. But as they moved further
off the coast, the ledge fell away and disappeared

into the steep cut of the Puerto Rico trench. The crystal water turned to a deep blue.

When they reached altitude, the howling engines settled into a pleasant rumble. A soft voice with an Appalachian twang came over the speaker and announced that St. Thomas was coming up on the right side.

Bill looked down on the brilliant color of the sea, suddenly dotted with the jet black tips of underwater volcanos. "You're going to love this," he whispered to Jeanne, "with your eye for color."

Howard leaned across Marilyn, and began focusing the zoom lens through the window. The shutter clicked, he made a quick setting adjustment and then the shutter clicked again. "Gotta bracket everything," he explained, still peering through the lens.

"Save some film for the boat," she reminded him.

The pilot's voice announced St. John, and the landscape below grew even more beautiful. Spires of wildly overgrown rock pierced the window-like surface, and beyond them a green mountain, edged with white sand, climbed out of the water. Howard pressed the camera closer to the window. The shutter fired in rapid sequence as the whine of the film advance tried to keep up.

At the front of the plane, Al Weston finally relaxed into the seat. The guy is a tourist, he reassured himself. No cop could be that good an actor.

As soon as they were past St. John, the engine drone turned into a whisper. The nose tipped down, and the plane began an easy descent over the Drake Channel. Looking across the aisle, Bill and Howard could see the peaks of Tortola's rugged spine. Through the right-hand window they saw the chain of long-dead volcanos and wildly green islands that formed the south side of the channel.

"Paradise," Howard whispered to Marilyn. The channel was only fifteen miles long, and less than five miles across. But it was rimmed with a hundred harbors, each framed with lushly grown rock. "You could sail here for the rest of your life and still never get to see it all."

"It's smaller than I expected," Marilyn answered. They were only up a few thousand feet, and yet all the boundaries of Drake Channel were clearly visible.

Howard smiled, remembering that her favorite time on their family voyages was when the boat was still tied to the pier. "You'll love it. You'll never be out of sight of land. And there won't be long dinghy rides to shore. In most of these places you can drop the anchor twenty feet from the beach."

The plane's wing nearly touched the southern slope of Beef Island, just off the eastern end of Tortola, and then began a gentle turn to line up with the runway. The landing strip cut completely through the north end of the island, with water at each end. The engines were silent as they touched down, and then gunned when the pilot raced toward the terminal. The passengers hurried out and waited near the tail as their luggage was unloaded.

Howard helped Cindy Camilli stack the aluminum cases onto her dolly. "Have a great shoot," he encouraged, "and thanks for the tip. I'm bracketing everything." He looked after her as she walked toward the gate. When he turned, he nearly tripped over the luggage that Marilyn was stacking by his feet.

Cindy's mouth was dry, and she began to feel a tightening across her chest. She was approaching the immigration counters, her first moment of real danger. Randomly, the officials selected passengers for a thorough interrogation and search of their luggage. There were a dozen questions they might ask for which she would have no answer.

"Do you have a contract for your photo assignment?"

She didn't.

"Where will the photographs be taken?"

She didn't know.

"Has this been cleared with our department of tourism?"

It hadn't.

And the inspection of her equipment could be as probing as they desired. They could make her empty the cases, disassemble the equipment and even tear open the film packs. She might argue that the equipment was delicate and that opening the packets would destroy the film. But that would be her problem, not theirs. They were empowered to prevent anything illegal — or even anything of commercial value — from entering their country. Walter Linz's plan was based on the fact that tourism was the economy of the island, and customs officials understood that they hadn't been hired to hassle the visitors.

Passport clearance was a single booth manned by a police officer in khaki shorts. "Vacation?" he asked as he thumbed through the pages and added his own entry stamp.

"No. I'm a photographer here on assignment. Publicity shots for one of the hotels."

He glanced at the cases and then handed back the passport.

She then turned toward the most dangerous test, a long wooden counter manned by customs officials who stared down the top of her blouse as she bent to lift the cases up for inspection.

"Anything to declare?" one of them said, as he snapped open the aluminum latches.

"Nothing that you haven't seen already," she answered with a suggestive smile.

"Open the cases," he ordered. He looked at the camera bodies, then lifted one of them out and examined it carefully.

"These are new?"

"Brand new. First time I've worked with this kind of equipment." She handed over the sales slips.

"Is it for sale, or for a gift?"

"No, it's for my work. I'm a photographer."

He examined each piece, and checked it against the sales slip. He didn't bother to count the film packs. Then he lifted the protective foam rubber and ran his hand around the edges of the case.

"Okay, you can lock them up." While she was closing the lids and setting the latches, he stamped the sales slip. "You'll have to check with us on the way out. You'll need the sales slip." Then he backed away from the table and lined himself up for the best view when she bent to reload the dolly.

Cindy turned her cases over to the first cab driver who approached her, and watched him load them into the back of a dust encrusted minivan. She climbed into the back seat and rolled down the window. "Road Town Harbor Club," she said. The car sprung to life and rattled out of the airport.

It was only six miles to her hotel, but the road followed the thousand curves of the shoreline, stretching it into a much longer trip. She had the taste of dust in her mouth and large sweat stains down the sides of her blouse when they swung into the hotel entrance. A porter in a sun helmet pulled the dolly and followed behind her as she crossed the small, open lobby to the registration desk. It took only a minute to register, and a few minutes more to deposit the cameras in the hotel safe. As she followed the porter through the lushly planted gardens toward her bungalow, she saw Al turn through the main entrance and pull up at the lobby. Once again, he seemed not to notice her.

Cindy locked the door behind her and left a trail of clothes to the shower. She dressed in a mini bikini, and settled into a lounge on the patio outside her room to await her phone call. "Take your time, Peter Heinz," she whispered to her unknown contact. She was lying in the sun with Road Harbor stretched out at her feet, a thousand boats floating on its glass surface. If she had to wait a few days for the call, this was as good a place as any.

9

Bill and Howard followed the two young men who staggered with their luggage toward the launch. Marilyn and Jeanne marched at their heels. They had been met by the charter company driver as soon as they had cleared customs, and driven in an air-conditioned van to an office at the head of the pier. Howard had signed the charter agreement and put down his gold card to pay for the provisioning.

"We're splitting everything," Bill had protested, digging for his own wallet.

Howard had waved away the offer. "We'll settle up later. This is easier."

Then two boys in short pants had scooped up their luggage and begun leading them down to the launch dock.

"*Cane Maiden?*" the launch pilot asked.

"*Cane Maiden,*" Howard answered. He took Marilyn's hand to help her aboard and then did the same for Jeanne. When he looked back onto the dock, the two porters were loading the last piece of their luggage into the bow. Bill peeled their tips out of his wallet and stepped over the gunwale. Howard brought the line with him as he jumped aboard. The engine gurgled and the launch slipped away from the dock.

They moved blindly down the channel between the floating docks, their view blocked by the dozens of yachts that were tied up side by side. The engine began to growl as they reached the end of the row and the small inner harbor appeared.

"Oooh!" Jeanne sighed when she got her first glimpse of the anchorage. The green hills dropped down to a narrow basin that was surrounded by rows of masts. The water ahead was filled with boats, moored close together in a flotilla that reached all the way out to the sea wall.

"I see her," Howard announced, pointing out over the starboard bow. "There, that one. With the bow sprit and the two masts."

"She's a beauty," the pilot said. "Prettiest yacht in the harbor."

"We were lucky to get her," Bill complimented Howard. Howard nodded enthusiastically.

The pilot added to the compliment. "You know your boats, sir. Most people want the newer ones. Takes a real yachtsman to appreciate *Cane Maiden.*"

"Ah, fuck," Steve Berlind cursed as soon as he could make out Howard standing in the approaching launch. When he took in the yachting jacket and captain's cap, his hopes that someone who appreciated *Cane Maiden* would be a true seafarer were dashed to pieces. "Dumb bastard is proud of being a clubby," he mumbled to himself. "Look at the asshole, decked out like Captain Bligh." The other man didn't look promising either. He seemed to be struggling just to keep his balance in the light seas of the inner harbor.

Steve sighted in on the two women, both with hands on their heads to hold their hair against the breeze. "Rich bitches," he decided, already certain that they would try to order him about like a cabin boy, and snap their fingers when they needed more ice for their drinks. He'd have to set them straight in a hurry.

"Ahoy!" Howard called as the launch turned to come alongside to starboard.

"Jeesus!" Steve whispered. "Ahoy, your ass." This was going to be a long week.

He caught the line that the pilot tossed up to him, and tied it to a cleat as the launch snuggled in. Then he watched as the two women climbed aboard, followed by the two men.

"Bring your gear up," he said to Howard and Bill without making any gesture to be helpful. They leaned over the side to catch the luggage that was passed up from the launch. When they had everything on deck, Steve uncleated the line and tossed it back into the launch.

"Smooth sailing," the pilot called as he gunned the engine. Steve followed him with a glare.

He stepped over the duffels, climbed out of the cockpit and swung his legs into the pilothouse hatch. "Bring it below," he told Howard. "I'll show you where to store it." Howard grabbed two of the bags and followed Steve down the ladder. He stopped abruptly when his feet hit the deck.

"Wow!" he sighed, as his face broke into a wide grin. She was even more beautiful than he had imagined. He stood in awe at the foot of the ladder, taking in the white lacquered interior, trimmed with polished teak, the stitched canvas cushions on the benches and quarter berths, the gleaming brass portholes. "God, this is shipshape."

They were tight quarters, much more restricting than the palatial layouts of modern cruisers. But they were workman-like. To his right was the galley, a propane stove with a latching oven that hung from gimbals. An ice chest with a butcher block cutting board as the countertop. Storage cupboards above the ice chest, and racks above the stove that would hold the china secure in even the heaviest seas. To his left was a navigation table, built over pigeon holes that held the rolled up charts. At the back of the table were broad, flat drawers for the navigator's instruments, and above the drawers was an electronic suite with the Loran equipment and the radio.

"Beautiful," Howard said. He stepped into the cabin and looked at Steve who was waiting impatiently. "I'd like to do some of the navigating."

The captain shrugged. "Not much to it," he allowed.

Aft of the navigation table was a louvered door that opened into the head. The space was primitive compared to the facilities that modern builders liked to install. There were no chrome fixtures or lighted vanity mirrors, but just a porcelain basin hung from the bulkhead under a small shaving mirror. The toilet had a wooden seat, and a heavy-duty pump handle protruding from its base. The shower was simply a spray nozzle hanging from the side of the basin. Drainage was through the lattice floor boards.

"Close the valve when you're done flushing," Steve said, pointing to the brass valve handle alongside the toilet pump. "And close that one when you're done showering." There was another valve handle that came up through the lattice boards. "You forget to close the valves and you'll be ankle deep in sea water."

Bill looked over Howard's shoulder as he listened to the instructions.

"Those are your quarters," Steve intoned, pointing his chin toward two other doors that were at the rear of the space. Bill opened one, and found a minimum double bunk built into the gentle curve of the hull, ventilated by a single porthole. There was a neat row of drawers underneath, and a hanging locker at the far end of the space. He measured the length of the bunk against his own height and realized that it would be a tight squeeze.

Steve led them forward and down a step into the narrowing space that was shaped by *Cane Maiden*'s prow. There were benches to either side, with pilot berths above them, and a folding table mounted on gimbals amidships. The table length was cut short by the trunk of the mainmast that dropped down through the deck overhead, and disappeared into the deck below. Light streamed through a glazed greenhouse, just aft of the mast, that opened onto the deck above. There was a ladder that climbed the mast into the greenhouse.

"You get a lot more air in here through the hatch than you get in the staterooms," Berlind told them. "The ladies might want to sleep in the pilot berths if we get a still night."

They probably will, Bill thought glumly, his fantasies of a wildly passionate tropical vacation beginning to drift out of focus.

Steve pointed out the hanging lockers forward of the benches, and the additional drawers beneath the seat cushions. "Store your gear anywhere. As soon as you're finished, come up topside and I'll take you through the rigging."

Howard started toward another door that was forward of the hanging lockers. "What's up here?"

"My quarters," Steve answered, bringing Howard up short. "There's a head and a deck hatch, so I won't have to go through your spaces. Only time I'll be in your way is when I'm at the chart table."

He squeezed between Howard and Bill and dashed up the ladder to the cockpit.

"Not the friendliest guy I've ever met," Bill told his friend.

Howard shrugged. "Sailing is serious business," he said.

Bill frowned. "I thought it was supposed to be fun."

Jeanne and Marilyn tried to put on their best faces when they came below and saw their cabins, but they were both disappointed.

"Last time we slept in a bed that size," Marilyn told Howard for the benefit of the group, "it was the back seat of a Chevrolet."

"You're lucky," Jeanne joined in. "Bill and I had a Volkswagen."

"Hey, this is a cruise," Howard reminded them. "You want to spend your time on deck, not down below in the sack."

"Excuses, excuses," Marilyn teased.

The women began folding the clothes into the tight drawers and lockers. Bill and Howard climbed back up topside for their tour of the deck and the rigging, which their young captain conducted with all the pleasantry of a drill sergeant. He marched them around the pilot house, forward to the bowsprit and began reciting dimensions and operating procedures as if he planned to give an examination at the end of his course.

Cane Maiden was a fifty-four-foot yawl, with a fifty-five-foot high mainmast that carried eighty-five percent of her sail area, and a twenty-five-foot mizzenmast set aft of the cockpit. Her mainsail and forward triangle delivered most of her power, the mizzen serving to balance the boat and give her a gentle helm. The foretriangle carried two sails, a mast top roller-reefing genoa connected to the point of the bowsprit, and a forestaysail that was controlled by a club boom pivoting on the prow. The main could be reefed by rolling it into the boom.

"She was re-rigged a few years back for one-man handling," Steve explained. "The original rigging needed a couple of experienced hands." He looked directly at Howard when he added, "You don't get experienced hands in the charter business."

Howard didn't notice the dart. "Beautiful setup," he said, testing the tension on the starboard shroud, one of the wires that supported the mast. "She should be a joy to sail."

As they walked aft, Steve lectured on the hull design. *Cane Maiden* was a deep *V* with a fin keel and a skeg forward of the rudder. That gave her a bit more drag than cruisers with a shallow draft and a straight keel, and made her turn more leisurely. She was no close course racer. But she had

76

great stability in rolling seas, and held her course close to the wind.

"How's the helm?" Howard asked when they stepped down into the cockpit. He laid a gentle hand on the chest-high wooden wheel.

"Light to windward without the genoa," Steve answered. "Maybe a little to leeward when the genoa's full."

Howard nodded knowingly.

Bill smiled in bewilderment. "Glad you guys know what you're doing."

"Won't take you long to get the hang of it," Howard assured him. "Nothing to it."

Jeesus, Steve Berlind thought to himself. This guy is the biggest idiot yet.

10

Cindy Camilli twisted uncomfortably on the chaise, suddenly aware of the film of perspiration that coated her skin. She blinked her eyes open and followed a sticky rivulet that was oozing down her belly. Then she sat up and looked longingly at the clear surface of the hotel pool, partially hidden behind hibiscus plantings only a few hundred feet away. A swim would feel great. She could run down across the manicured lawns, dive into the pool and be back at her room in less than five minutes. No one would know that she had left. Even if the call came in, the chances were that the phone would still be ringing when she returned.

But she had her instructions. Check in, and then wait in her room until she was contacted. Have her meals and her drinks sent up so that she would always be by the phone. When the call came, simply answer with "yes," or "no." Get her instructions. Write the time and the place on a note pad. Then go outside the hotel, find a pay phone, and call Al Weston. Al would be leaving the lobby when she returned to the hotel. He would take the note as they passed. It was a simple procedure that isolated Al from her and kept him completely unconnected with the transaction that was to take place. If something went wrong, there would be nothing to prove that Al was even there. Nor would there be any record that could link the deal back to Walter Linz.

"You just follow instructions," Al had told her when she was preparing for her first assignment, "and everything will be okay. Get creative and you can get yourself into trouble." She had always followed instructions to the letter and, as Weston had promised, there had never been any trouble.

She pushed up out of the lounge, went back into the room and called in an order for a Diet Coke and a tuna salad sandwich. Then she untied her bikini as she stepped into the shower and turned the faucet to cold. She shuddered as the icy blast hit her hot skin, and then settled comfortably into the stream.

Cindy had never planned to be here. The thought of bagging money through hotel rooms and placing secret calls to someone like Al Weston had been nowhere in the dreams that had drawn her out of middle-class drabness in Minnesota. She had been realistic, with no expectations of being discovered for stardom, nor hopes of finding a fortune. All she had wanted was a chance at the adventure and excitement that she saw nowhere around her.

Her hopes had ground to a halt in the middle of her high school years, at a time when her popularity was peaking. She had grown from a pretty child to a stunning young woman, and found herself the center of attention of the jocks who ran the school. Her grades had dropped as she threw herself wholeheartedly into the social swing, but not far enough to be alarming to the abandoned mother who was trying to control her.

"Cindy has everything," she overheard a friend say. And that was her downfall, because she was smart enough to understand that "everything" wasn't very much at all. "Everything" was a numbing routine of rote class assignments, menial after-school jobs, and evenings of rock music piped through a television set. It was catty gossip, overdoses of cosmetics and cigarettes sneaked in the girls' washroom. Romance had consisted of pulled zippers and frantic groping sessions in the seats of parked cars. Her first intimacy had been an embarrassing disaster with a basketball player who had turned up at a house where she was baby-sitting, and it had been interrupted by the shocked parents who returned home earlier than expected. Her mother had been mortified, then enraged, and had begun lamenting that her daughter would never amount to anything.

Gradually, Cindy had realized that her mother was right, but for very different reasons. The woman was afraid that her daughter would never find a respectable place in the local community. Cindy was afraid that she probably would, and the prospect deepened her despair.

College was the only socially approved avenue of escape, but four years of living on a distant campus wasn't a realistic hope. The cash that Walter Linz had unfolded so casually was more than had ever been in the family bank account. What had been realistic was graduation, a service or clerical job, and then marriage to a local boy whose prospects were as limited as her own.

She had wanted something better, although exactly what that might be was by no means certain. Maybe nothing more than a chance. If she could just get to someplace exciting, maybe something more would happen to her. Gradually, she had been able to harness the courage to make her break.

Her mother had threatened with frightening images of Cindy's inevitable abuse at the hands of uncaring cities, and then pleaded with sad predictions of her own loneliness and disgrace. In the end, she added her spare cash to her daughter's savings, and helped finance her flight to Florida.

At first, the excitement had been elusive. The jobs she found as a waitress in tourist hotels and a clerk in supermarkets had been every bit as dreary as the ones she had fled in Minnesota, and a good deal lonelier. She saw two choices. One was an embarrassing return to her hometown. The other was to market her only real assets, which were a good face and a great body. She had steeled her courage and opted for the latter. And then, the excitement had come too quickly for her to handle.

A job as a leggy cocktail waitress had led her to the bedroom of the manager. He had touted the fortune to be made as a topless dancer, which had won her a chance at a career in modeling and then a screen test for amazingly explicit adult movies. Her acting performances had made her a favored passenger in a small-time drug dealer's stretch limousine. Traveling the narcotics circuit had introduced her to cocaine, and the cost of even her minor habit had made evening work with an escort service a financial necessity. Cindy was smart enough to realize that she was moving in circles that went nowhere, but still too naive to jump off the carousel. This has to stop, she told herself every day, but instead the ride kept turning faster and faster.

Then, on her twenty-second birthday, a john had done her a favor. He had beaten her senseless, breaking her jaw with his fist and two of her ribs with his foot. Her enforced stay in the ward of a county hospital had ended her experiment with drugs and changed her views on excitement. The small scar under her right eye had been a very small price for her education.

She was going home, Cindy had decided, just as soon as she could put together a bit of money. And that was exactly what she had been trying to do when she met Al Weston and was introduced to the opportunity for a fast fortune in the service of Walter Linz. But as she stood in a cold shower, unable to leave her room for even the few minutes it would take to dive into the swimming pool, she knew that she was still on the merry-go-round. Walter Linz valued her precisely because she was of no value at all. He could abandon her the instant that one of his commercial transactions went sour. He had taken great pains to make sure that, should she be caught, she would have no links to anyone. But this would be her last job as a courier. She had paid off nearly all of her debts. Most of the money she earned would be hers to keep; more than enough to go home and make a fresh start. She was enjoying the thought when she heard the impatient pounding on the hotel door. She stepped out of the shower, and tied a bath towel around herself as she dripped across the room.

The bellboy's eyes widened when she opened the door. First they darted over her shoulder in search for the man he assumed was sharing her room. Then they focused over the top of her towel as she leaned over the service cart to sign the tab. Cindy took her sandwich and soft drink, and kicked the door closed with her heel as she turned back into the room, giving the boy a final glimpse of a long, naked leg.

She ate and then paced for a few minutes while deciding whether to get back into the bikini for another hour of sunning or to dress for the evening. She was in the process of tucking a white peasant blouse into a gauzy cotton skirt when the telephone rang.

"Yes."

"You the photographer?"

"That's right."

"This is Heinz. The shooting is tomorrow afternoon at two o'clock. Parson's Boatyard. The storage shed. You know where that is?"

"No, I don't."

"Take a taxi. Any of the cabbies can get you there."

"All right."

"Bring all your equipment. And plenty of film."

"Okay." Then, as she wrote the information, she repeated: "Tomorrow at two. Parson's Boatyard. The storage shed."

"Looking forward to meeting you," the voice said suggestively. Then the line went dead.

Cindy spent a minute standing over the phone, trying to visualize the person she had just talked with. He had an accent. German, she guessed, thinking of the close-cropped, blond-haired stereotype. She slipped into her sandals, took her note and room key and left the hotel.

It took her fifteen minutes to find a pay phone, and she could already feel the dampness under her blouse. She juggled the change into the telephone and dialed the hotel.

"Mr. Weston's room, please."

Al picked up on the first ring.

"Yes," he said.

"I'm all set," Cindy answered. "I'm about fifteen minutes away."

"Fine. I'll be seein' ya."

He hung up.

She folded the instructions in her hand and started back to the hotel. As she was strolling up the path to the lobby she saw Al, in his colorfully banded straw hat, coming toward her. He never made eye contact as he took the note.

Couldn't have been easier, Cindy thought when she stepped back into her room. And she still had time for a swim. But if it was all so easy, why was she beginning to taste the fear that was pushing up into her throat?

11

They sat in the dark cockpit, talking softly as if they were in a church. There was enough light lingering in the sky to hold the shapes of the mountains, but the harbor was dark, except for the reflections of anchor lights that sparkled on the wave tops. Their voices were the only sound.

"One more swim," Howard suggested. He was still wearing his bathing trunks which had nearly dried in the warm air. He looked toward Bill who had pulled a pair of jeans over his swimsuit and was wearing a battered sweatshirt.

"I'm game," Bill nodded, but he made no move toward the swim ladder that was hanging over the side. Instead, he raised the rum punch that he had been sipping. "As soon as I finish this."

Howard nudged Marilyn. "You coming with us?"

"No way," she answered. "This is too perfect. I'm not going to spoil it by getting back into a cold, wet bathing suit."

Jeanne shivered at the thought. "The shower was cold enough," she said, siding with Marilyn.

"Then don't wear bathing suits," Howard teased the women. "Bill and I will keep our eyes closed until you're in the water."

Marilyn looked at Jeanne. "Don't trust him. Howard has a big telescope in his office window."

They were getting along better than either of the women had expected. As soon as they had stowed their gear they had changed into their swim outfits. Jeanne had been quietly pleased when Marilyn appeared on deck in a one-piece suit cut very much like her own. Maybe she wouldn't have to endure a week-long fashion show. Howard had led them over the side with a near-perfect jackknife off the bowsprit, and they had spent an hour swimming around the boat and floating in its shadow. The only interruption had been when the charter company launch came alongside to pick up Steve. "Be back before midnight," Steve had mumbled while he looked over the women. "Hope the damn thing capsizes," Howard had said as the launch pulled away.

Jeanne and Marilyn had left the men in the water and climbed back aboard to get the dinner started. Their conversation came easily, and they had shared a laugh as they tried to decipher the directions for the propane stove. Howard came aboard and mixed his own version of a rum punch, and then they had all settled down to a round of cocktails and a light dinner. The women had taken turns in the shower while the men took care of the dishes. There had been plenty of topics for small talk.

When he couldn't drum up any enthusiasm for another swim, Howard settled for a fresh drink. "It doesn't get any better than this," he announced as he stretched out on the port-side bench. "I'm really looking forward to the challenge."

"This is all the challenge I want," Marilyn whispered, looking up at the stars that filled the blackening sky. "I'd be happy just to sit here at the mooring."

"Boats don't belong on a mooring," Howard contradicted, "and sailors don't belong in a safe harbor. The whole point is to take her out to sea and challenge the elements. See what she's made out of and see what you're made out of. Otherwise, you might as well stay home."

Bill smiled. "I don't know, Howard. This sure beats home." He turned to Jeanne. "Much better view."

"But it's supposed to be much more than a view," Jeanne answered. "More than just watching life go by. That's what you're saying, isn't it Howard?"

"You're damn right." He swung his feet down to the deck. "Boats that sit in the harbor begin to rot in the keel. Before long they're good for nothing. It's the same way with us. We need to sail out and face the wind. You can't get anywhere if you stay tied to the mooring."

Jeanne was nodding enthusiastically. "It sounds exciting. God knows, there's not much of a challenge in what I've been doing."

"You'll see," Howard continued. "You put some sail up, and *Cane Maiden* will suddenly have a mind of its own. It'll take you flying out of the harbor and you won't know what's out there. The wind picks its own direction and the sea can get damn unfriendly. If you're not ready for it, you can get into a hell of a lot of trouble. So you have to take charge. That's the first challenge. Proving

87

that you're in command. You can't just hang on for the ride. You have to take charge of the elements and make them work for you."

Marilyn smiled to the others. "This is Howard's idea of a vacation. To me it sounds like boot camp!"

"Then," Howard went on, riding right over Marilyn, "you have to decide where you want to get to. And you make the boat take you there. That's the challenge. Getting where you want to go no matter what you're up against. That's the fun." He turned to Bill. "You understand what I'm talking about?"

"Yeah," Bill agreed. "And it does sound exciting."

"It's like when we were playing football," Howard said. "You come up against someone who wants to run right over you. And you dig in and stop him in his tracks. That's when you find out what you're really made of. That's when you find out if you've got what it takes."

Bill shrugged. "I never took football that seriously. It was just a game. Exciting. And a lot of fun. But, still, a game. I guess I hope this trip will be exciting, and a lot of fun. I didn't think of it as testing myself, or finding out what I'm made of."

"But you get my meaning," Howard insisted. "The challenge of getting where you want to go no matter what the sea throws up against you. The feeling of being in charge."

"Sure. And I'm looking forward to it. Although I can understand Marilyn. When I look around, this is a pretty nice harbor. Maybe I don't need to go somewhere. Maybe I'm already there."

Marilyn stood up and stretched. "Where I need to go is to bed. This has been a long day."

Howard agreed, and he followed his wife up to the hatch. "Don't stay up too long," he called back to Bill. "I've got a big day planned for you tomorrow."

Bill smiled as Howard disappeared below deck. "He hasn't changed a bit. The night before a football game, he used to pace the dorm room like a caged lion. Every Saturday was total warfare."

"His energy is contagious," Jeanne said. "He really needs to make things happen."

Bill agreed. "That's what made him a great football player. I suppose it's what makes him so successful in business."

He stood, took a last look around the sparkling harbor, and then suggested to Jeanne that they turn in. She promised to follow him down, but lingered to spend a few moments by herself.

Howard was right, she thought. You couldn't get anywhere if you stayed tied to the mooring. You had to throw off the line and head for the open water. That was the problem with Bill and her. They were living their lives tied to a mooring. That's what her job was. Something that barely floated on top of the water and wasn't ever going to go anywhere. And that's what Bill's school was. A safe haven. A place where he could keep out of the weather. What had Howard said about boats that don't put out to sea? They rot! Wasn't that exactly what was happening to the school?

Bill knew that. He had said himself that the place was failing. And yet he couldn't break free from it. Was it because he had the courage to fight for something he believed in? Or was he afraid to measure himself against the open water? Jeanne had never doubted his courage. That's what she had found so attractive about him. He didn't need to be part of the crowd. He didn't need anyone else's approval. He had the courage to be himself.

Had she been wrong? Was the school something he truly believed in? Or was it a safe harbor where he could be sure of calm seas?

Was that what made her attractive to him? That she was safe? Predictable? Was that what she had become? A mooring that was content to bob up and down without trying to get anywhere? A calm sea that would never rise up into a storm? What would happen when she cut free and ventured out on her own? Would Bill support her? Or would he resent her for rocking the boat?

Something had to change. Of that, she was certain. But did she have the courage to risk winds that picked their own direction, and seas that could get very unfriendly? Did her husband?

SUNDAY

12

Howard was up before sunrise and out on deck when the first pale trace of light was beginning to outline the steep slope of the shore. He stood alone in *Cane Maiden*'s cockpit, listening to the distant chatter of sea birds, and the rattling of the rigging in the gentle morning air. The sea, the sky, and himself. If only his life were really that simple.

In the hustle of traveling, the thrill of boarding the boat, and his first relaxing evening aboard, he had forgotten about the crumbling empire he had left at home. But he had found plenty of time to think about it during the night. Marilyn had lounged over more than her half of the tight bunk that they shared and, rather than wake her, he had spent most of the night balancing precariously on the edge. Even the rum-laced nightcaps that they had all enjoyed in the cockpit hadn't been sufficient to relax him into a real sleep.

Everything was falling out of control. He couldn't bring in more commissions for his work because construction was dead in the water. And he couldn't cut the outflow of expenses because most of them were in long-term contracts and leases. Each new bank statement was inevitably lower than the last with the balance plunging towards zero. Nor could he manage his liability for the buildings that held his personal investment. One was foreclosed, the other half-empty. The investments which had seemed so promising were suddenly worthless at best.

Worse than the drop in his assets was his rapidly deteriorating self-image. Howard was used to being a winner. And he won because he was a stand-up, take charge person who could gain control of a situation and then outwork and outthink his competitors. What was crippling him was that he couldn't take charge. His fate had slipped through his own fingers and passed into the hands of faceless bankers and lawyers. He had become just another victim of the economic malaise that was sweeping the northeast, his affairs lost in a pile of paperwork that would be processed in due time. He was waiting helplessly for the mills to grind, a grain completely undifferentiated from the thousands of others. He couldn't win because he wasn't even an important player in the game. The thought of his lost identity was more difficult for him to admit than the reality of his lost fortunes.

He set his hands on the idle wheel and looked up at the bare rigging. Hoist some canvas, he thought, and cast off the mooring. Then he would be back in charge. Reduce the numbing complexity of his business affairs to just a ship and the wind and he would quickly be back in command, turning his world to fit his will. That was why, he realized, this cruise was so important to him. He needed to feel his own importance. He needed to stand tall among his shipmates and be the one they looked toward to set their course.

Bill Chester ambled up through the hatch, setting down two mugs of steaming coffee as he swung his legs out onto the deck. "Fresh brew," he announced as he handed a mug to his friend.

Howard looked around the brightening horizon as he sipped. "What do you think? Ever seen anything like it?"

Instead of the scenery, Bill focused his attention on the towering mast, with its web of shrouds and stays and the countless blocks and lines. "What I think is that it's a damn good thing you know what you're doing. This is all bewildering to me. I'm afraid I'm not going to be very much help."

Howard leaped at the opportunity. "Nothing to it. Here, let me show you."

They walked the deck as they drank their coffee, with Howard pausing to lecture and demonstrate at each line and every fitting. He showed Bill how the sails were hoisted and how they were trimmed against the wind, close-hauled when they were beating into the weather, and let out when they were running before the wind. Then he demonstrated the operation of winches that would deliver the force needed to pull the giant sails against the power of the air. "Maybe today you should concentrate on trimming sails," he decided. "Just listen to my commands. Nothing more complicated than 'haul her in,' or 'let her out.' You'll get the picture just by watching. And for God's sake, don't worry about making a mistake. No harm in sailing a little sloppy on our first day."

He stopped the lecture as the red cherry shape of the sun popped above the horizon, whitening the sky and sparkling off the sea. Suddenly, they were both casting long shadows.

"Jesus, but this is beautiful," Bill gasped.

Howard nodded. "It's simple. Uncomplicated," he allowed, his eyes still fixed on the sunrise. Without looking at Bill he added, "I wish I'd been able to keep things simple, the way you have. The school. The kids. It must be nice to be focused on something so important."

"Crazy," Bill answered, with a slow shake of his head. "I've often thought about all you've been able to accomplish. You've built so much. A battered old building and a bunch of noisy kids seems sort of trivial by comparison."

Howard caught himself. "Oh, don't get me wrong. There's a lot of satisfaction in seeing your ideas rise up in concrete and steel. It's just that at a moment like this simple things take on great importance."

Steve Berlind's head poked up from the forward hatch. He spared the sunrise a glance, and then lifted himself up onto the deck. "What's your pleasure, gentlemen? A leisurely breakfast? Or are you ready to get under way?"

Howard looked to Bill who responded by shrugging his shoulders. He turned to Steve. "I'm ready to take her out."

Berlind smirked. "She's a lot of boat. Maybe I ought to get her off the mooring."

"I can handle her," Howard said. He laid a reassuring hand on the wheel. "You just give me a heading from the last channel marker to Norman Island. We'll have breakfast over the reef."

Steve tried to look unconcerned. "Okay," he sing-songed. "She's your charter." He walked aft to the pilothouse hatch and dropped down below to the chart table.

"Let's put up some sail," Howard ordered Bill, walking forward to the mainmast. He pulled the main halyard tight around the winch. "Haul her all the way up," he told Bill, "and then tie her off here." He connected the forestay halyard, and began hauling side by side with his friend. As the two sails rose up the mast, Howard began laughing. "What a way to start a day."

Bill was suddenly aware of the huge size of the canvas he was lifting. The main began fluttering, then snapping as it took more air. Even in the light morning breeze the force was enough to push the boat into a slight heel and drive it across the water until it was pointing straight into the wind.

Howard cranked on the winch until the working jib was tight against the forestay. Then he pulled the line through the clamp to tie it off. Bill followed his example, hauling down on the halyard until the last wrinkle disappeared from the mainsail.

Howard was already in the cockpit freeing the mainsheet, and then the jib sheet that controlled the swing of the club boom. Now the boat steadied as the sails swayed gently back and forth over the deck. He turned aft to the mizzenmast, hoisted the small spanker sail and freed her sheet. "Looking good," he called to Bill.

Bill was leaning back, in awe of the enormous spread of sail that they had raised into the sky. The mast towered over his head to the height of a five-story building. The sails, impotent while they were aimed dead into the wind, were snapping angrily. He could hear the wire stays singing.

"You sure you can handle this?" he asked. There was an edge of fear in his voice. Suddenly both he and Howard had become insignificantly small.

Howard came forward and guided Bill up to the foredeck. "Give me a hand," he said, bending over the mooring line. He began to haul in, expecting the yacht to slide towards the mooring buoy. He was startled when the line stayed taut and *Cane Maiden* didn't budge.

"Heavy son of a bitch," he gasped.

Bill bent down beside him, wrapping his big hands around the line. The muscles in his arms rippled as he pulled against the weight. Slowly, the line began to creep across the deck and the boat inched forward. Howard used the slack behind Bill's grip to unfasten the line from the cleat. Then he tied it off with a single turn.

"Hold it here until I tell you to cast off."

Bill nodded that he understood.

"Soon as the line is over, I want you to back the jib to port."

He could see that Bill wasn't following him.

"Get to this side and pull the boom into the wind. That will push the bow that way." He pointed over the starboard bow. "And stay clear of the track and sheet. When you let it go, the boom will ride over to the other side. You don't want to get caught in the lines."

"Okay," Bill answered as he deciphered his instructions.

Howard dashed back to the cockpit just as Steve appeared through the hatch with a rolled-up chart. "We're ready to cast off," he said.

Berlind studied the sails. He pointed to the small

spanker that was flying from the mizzenmast. "You sure you want that one up? It'll turn you back into the wind."

"No problem," Howard assured.

Steve answered with a despairing shake of his head. "She takes time to turn," he warned. He looked aft at the other boats moored astern. "You don't have much room to fall back."

"I can handle it," Howard said.

Berlind stowed the chart under a shelf on the forward bulkhead. "It's your show," he announced.

Marilyn appeared in the hatch, her hair hidden under an oversized straw hat. "What's going on up here?"

"We're getting under way," Howard answered. "Come on up."

"I'd keep the cockpit clear," Steve contradicted.

Howard was visibly annoyed. "They won't be in the way."

Marilyn came up and slipped into the cockpit beside Howard. Jeanne followed at her heels.

"Cast off," he called up to the bow. Bill slipped the mooring line off the cleat and let it run off the deck and into the water. Instantly, *Cane Maiden* began slipping slowly astern. He danced around the club boom, took its end in his hands and pulled it into the freshening breeze. Ever so slowly, the bowsprit began drifting to starboard. When he released the boom, it snapped across the deck until the sail was fluttering uselessly.

Howard watched patiently as the air caught the side of *Cane Maiden* and turned her slowly across the wind. But when he glanced astern, his patience vanished. The boat was gathering speed as it drifted back toward the next row of moored yachts. His head snapped back and forth as he measured the rate of turn against the rapidly closing distance that separated him from a collision.

"Haul in the main," he snapped at Steve. At the same instant he bounded across Marilyn's feet as he rushed to haul in the jib and then the spanker. Steve jumped to the order, smiling as he did. The yacht clubber was getting himself into serious trouble.

The sails stiffened, checking *Cane Maiden*'s drift. She heeled gently and slowly began making headway. Howard rushed back to the wheel, pushing passed Marilyn and Jeanne who began scurrying around the cockpit, trying to get out of the way. With the boat beginning to move, he eased the wheel slightly to windward, trying to steer away from the collision without pointing so far up into the wind that he would luff the sails and lose power.

"We've got it," he called to Steve.

Steve glanced up at the spanker sail that he had told Howard not to fly. "I don't think so," he nearly laughed.

Cane Maiden was still moving too slowly for the rudder to take effect. But the wind on the spanker had exactly the effect that Steve had predicted. It pushed the stern downwind, turning the boat into the breeze. The sails luffed, and *Cane Maiden*'s speed died. Once again, she was drifting helplessly back into the moored fleet. A grinding collision was only seconds away.

"Christ," Howard cursed. He spun the wheel,

trying to turn her out of the wind. But with *Cane Maiden* nearly dead in the water, the rudder was useless.

Steve watched his panic with growing amusement. "How's it going, Captain?" he asked.

"She's not responding," Howard shot back. He hit the engine starter so that he could power his way out of the impending disaster. But the engine had been long idle. It growled and sputtered, but wouldn't catch. He looked at the moored yachts, now only two boat-lengths away. "Shit, we're going to hit them." He spun the wheel violently, hoping that reversing the rudder into the boat's backward drift would produce the turn he needed.

"Won't work," Steve taunted him. "Not enough speed."

Howard thought about leaving the wheel and preparing to fend off as they reached the idly floating yachts. But *Cane Maiden* was no day sailer. She was a big boat, moving with the wind. There was no chance that he would be able to hold her off the first yacht she reached. He could envision the crunching collision with its hopeless tangle of sails and riggings.

"What are we going to do?" he pleaded.

Steve Berlind sprung into action.

"First thing we're going to do is get you off the wheel." He pushed Howard aside, letting him settle uselessly onto one of the benches. "Then we're going to douse the goddam spanker." He slipped the mizzen sheet. "And kill the main." In a second, he had changed the setup so that the jib was his only working sail.

"Back the jib," he ordered Bill Chester, who

was still on the foredeck. Bill repeated the operation he had already performed. He pulled the club boom to port. Instantly, the bow began to swing.

Howard's eyes were riveted on the moored boats they were closing against. But Steve never spared them a glance. There was nothing he could do about them, so he kept his attention focused on their only route of escape, watching the bow turn away from the breeze. As soon as Bill let go of the boom, the jib snapped across the bow and caught the air.

"Now let's get some power," Steve chanted as he hauled the main in close. He slid back behind the wheel. "And get our asses out of here." He turned toward the impending collision in order to bring his speed up rapidly. Howard looked on in disbelief. Steve was aiming them toward disaster. But he was too confused to protest.

Cane Maiden slid across the bow of the closest moored yacht, the mooring buoy bumping against her side, and they could feel the mooring line slipping under the keel. It would move easily across the bottom until it reached the sharply protruding underwater skeg, just forward of the rudder. Then it would catch, and swing the two boats together.

"Now or never," Steve said, swinging the wheel violently to starboard. With the spanker fluttering idly, the rudder took immediate effect. The stern swung out away from the mooring line. *Cane Maiden* broke free and turned into the narrow space between two of the moored boats. Steve brought the rudder back amidships.

The sails began to flutter as *Cane Maiden*'s stern

moved to windward. Berlind would have eased out the sheets to set the sails for running before the wind, but the boat he had nearly hit was too close aboard. "Stand clear," he ordered. "Ready to jibe." He reached out, put his hand on Marilyn's straw hat, and pushed her down to her knees. As he did, the main boom swung across the deck like a scythe and the sail furled. The speed that had been lost in the turn began to rebuild.

Cane Maiden was now running down the side of the moored yacht, starboard rail to starboard rail. Howard looked in breathless silence at the narrowing gap between the two boats. They couldn't make it, he feared. She was a fifty-foot yacht, leisurely to the helm, and Steve was trying to handle her as if she were a small day sailer. It couldn't be done.

They slid silently by the close aboard yacht, their railings only inches apart. Every eye was focused on the inevitable collision. But while the others were waiting for the awful scraping sound of the two hulls hitting, Steve was carefully gauging the swing of his stern. He eased the wheel to starboard, pushing the stern further away, steering *Cane Maiden* in a precisely-drawn arc that matched the curve of the other yacht's hull. The space narrowed, but the two boats never touched.

She slid away from danger, breaking out into the open channel between the rows of moored boats. "Stand clear," Steve sang. "Ready to jibe." He threw the rudder to port. The sails crossed the deck, catching the wind that was now coming over the port beam. She gained speed as she moved between the moorings toward the sea wall that enclosed the harbor.

"Tend the sheets," Steve ordered Howard, establishing his role as captain. Howard came to life, lifted himself off the bench and moved to the winches.

"We're turning up," the captain said. When he reached the last boat in the line, he started around her and into the wind. Howard ground the sails in close. *Cane Maiden* heeled and raced toward the harbor entrance.

"Turning down," Steve intoned. He swung back to starboard and Howard let out the sails. The boat settled into a powerful broad reach and charged between the sea wall lights.

"What was that course to Norman Island?" The island was clearly visible, dead ahead. He didn't need a course.

Howard jumped up and found the chart that Steve had prepared. "One nine five from the last marker," he read.

"Think you can steer one nine five?"

"Sure. Sure." Howard slid in behind the wheel, reddening in embarrassment. He had nearly lost the boat within the first three minutes of cutting free from the mooring. In front of his wife and friends he had been shown up as a deckhand.

Bill ambled back from the position he had maintained on the foredeck. "Is sailing always that exciting?" he asked innocently.

"It's not supposed to be," Steve answered as he passed Bill. He was stepping out of the cockpit and moving toward the forward hatch that led to his quarters. "I'm going to wash up. But yell if you need me."

The women settled onto the cockpit benches. Bill climbed in and stood behind the wheel, next to Howard.

"Son-of-a-bitch could have told me about the spanker," Howard whispered. "He set me up for a collision."

"He sure can handle this thing," Bill answered. "I was scared shitless. He was as cool as an ice cube."

"I wouldn't have had any trouble if he'd taken down the fucking spanker."

Bill looked up at the solid curve of the sails and the steady heel of the deck. "Well, you're not having any trouble now. You look like you were born behind that wheel."

"I know what I'm doing," Howard insisted.

Bill nodded. "You sure do. When do my lessons begin?"

Howard smiled. Apparently his friend had been unaware of his humiliation. "You start right now. Take the wheel. Get the feel of it."

Bill hesitated. "I'm not going to sink us or anything?"

"She's all yours," Howard answered. He took his hands away and slipped them into his pockets. The wheel began to crank to port. Bill grabbed it and held it steady.

13

"You can feel the power in the sails," Howard began. "Head too far into the wind, and you'll sense the canvas dying. Head too far down, and they'll begin to flutter. It's a balancing act — the course you want to steer and the angle of the sails."

"Where am I heading?"

Howard tapped the compass binnacle. "One nine five. When you're dead on it, sing out. I'll trim the sails." He stepped around the helm to the winches.

"One nine five," Bill Chester called. Howard slipped the sheets until the sails were perfectly shaped. When he looked back, he saw the awed expression that had replaced Bill's nervous smile.

The canvas was silent, formed like steel against the breeze. The boat was heeled, holding at a steady angle, presenting its long shape to the sea. White foam whistled past the railing which was almost touching the surface. The bow rose and fell gently.

Without sensing his own transformation, Bill was becoming the link between the wind and the waves. The resistance of the water was flowing upward, through the wheel and into his hands. The power of the air was reflecting downward, from the sails into the rigging, and then into the deck beneath his feet. His knees were flexing, settling his body into equilibrium despite the awkward cant of the boat.

"Jesus," he whispered. "This is unbelievable." A broad smile broke across his face.

His presence spread through the cockpit, touching them all like the heat from a fire. With the wheel in his hands he had become a holy man, radiating a divinity that they could feel. Marilyn smiled, delighted to see a man rejoicing in simply being a man. Howard looked from Bill back to the straight wake of a perfectly steered course. "Looks like we've found a sailor," he said to the women.

Jeanne frowned as she watched him, suddenly reminded of the first time they had met. It was at a loft party, a noisy, laughing affair of young couples and a scattering of singles, with conversations centering around achievements and professional prospects. The host — she couldn't remember who he was — had steered her over to a tall guy, too casually dressed, who seemed to be on the outside of activities, looking in.

"What do you do?" she had asked after they had gotten past their names and their connection to the other guests.

"I teach."

She had nodded that she was impressed. "What field are you in?" She had expected a long-winded explanation of an academic discipline that was in vogue.

"No field. Just kids."

"Children? Little children?"

"I'm at the Twentieth Street settlement school.

I teach grade school and coach some of the sports."

She had known that her disappointment had registered, but he had been polite enough not to notice. At least that was what Jeanne had thought. But as they chatted, she realized that he was used to people being disappointed that he had no field. It simply didn't matter to him. He didn't need anyone's approval but his own.

That was what she saw now. A man whose life rose from within himself. That was what she had fallen in love with. And it was that same self-sufficiency that she was now beginning to despise.

Steve felt the confident hand at the helm all the way forward in his cabin at the forepeak. There was an eerie silence, even though the sea was crackling against the bow. There was a dead calm, even though the deck beneath his feet was rising and falling with the waves. He popped his head through the hatch, glanced at the rigid fix of the sails and then looked back toward the cockpit. He could hardly see Bill Chester, so precise was his fit into *Cane Maiden*'s lines.

He pulled himself up on deck and walked aft without ever touching the lifeline for support. Silently, he slipped into the cockpit and took a position alongside Bill. For a full minute, he watched the hands work the wheel, and studied the results in the canvas high above his head and in the sound of the sea whistling past.

"What do you think?" he finally asked.

"She's alive," Bill answered. "I can talk to her."

Steve nodded. Then he asked, "Want to hear her talk back?"

Bill smiled.

Steve leaned toward Howard and whispered as if they were sharing a pew in church. "Let's put up the gennie."

Howard began hauling on the genoa sheet, unfurling the huge genoa that was rolled around the head stay. As he pulled, the corner of the sail appeared and began flapping in the air. As more and more of its area unrolled, it flew away from the bow, snapping like a whip as it toyed with the wind. Then, when it was fully deployed, Howard hauled it back, along the starboard lifeline, stretching from the point of the bowsprit past the mainmast, and reaching from the surface of the speeding sea all the way to the masthead. As he pulled her tight, she filled with air. The mast creaked under the strain and the shrouds hummed as they tightened.

The power of the sail hit *Cane Maiden* like a foot on an accelerator. She leaped forward, heeling even further. The wake over her rail began to steam into a fine spray that flashed colors as it refracted the sunlight.

Bill nodded as if listening to a heavenly voice. His hands anticipated the force that would drive the bow off the wind, and moved the wheel a fraction of a turn. He looked forward. The bow, which had been rising and falling, took command of the rolling waves. It steadied like the aim on an arrow, and fired into the sea.

"You guys want something to drink? Some coffee?" Marilyn offered, breaking their trance.

"Okay," Howard said, still trimming the genoa.

"Sure," Bill echoed.

Marilyn started down into the hatch.

"A mug of tea," Steve called after her. "Hot tea." He looked at Bill. "I don't know why, but it has to be tea when I'm underway."

"Marilyn," Bill called into the empty hatch. "Change mine to tea, too." He smiled at Steve.

"With a piece of lime," Steve yelled after Marilyn.

He and Bill made eye contact.

"Put some lime in mine," Bill asked.

The sails were groaning and the seawater hissing. *Cane Maiden* broke away from the land and into the luminous blue of the Francis Drake Channel. Marilyn pushed the tea and coffee out onto the pilothouse overhead, and Jeanne passed the mugs around. Then the women went below to change into their bathing suits.

"You want to take her?" Bill offered Howard.

"No rush," Howard answered from his seat on the starboard bench. "I'm getting a big kick out of watching you enjoy it."

"You're the captain," Bill said.

Steve grimaced. "I'm going forward. Give me a call when we get close to Norman Island. You'll need me to anchor her." He moved forward along the windward lifeline, and disappeared into the bow hatch.

Howard slid over to Bill. "That prick is going to ruin this trip. Son-of-a-bitch is treating us as if we worked for him."

"Maybe he's coming off a bad charter. He'll probably loosen up."

"He sabotaged me this morning just so he could come to the rescue. He should have briefed me on the way she handles."

Bill sided with his friend. "Yeah! I guess he did enjoy pulling us out of the fire. But you said we'd need someone who knew the harbors and the anchorages."

"We do. But not some punk with a chip on his shoulder. When we get in tonight, I'm going back to the charter company and ask them to put somebody else on board."

"Maybe we should take him ashore with us. Buy him a drink. Give him a chance to get to know us."

"I'd rather just get rid of him," Howard said.

Bill nodded. "Whatever you say. It's your cruise." Then he stepped away from the wheel. "Here, you take her. I'm having all the fun."

Howard took the helm, and his anger vanished almost instantly. He sighted the green height of Norman Island over the bowsprit, and turned up a bit to aim right at it. "Can you haul in a bit?" he asked.

"Aye, aye, sir," Bill laughed, and he jumped to the winches.

Marilyn came topside, wearing a two-piece suit over the very attractive figure that Jeanne had feared. She held her straw hat on with her hand.

Howard whistled appreciatively. "You can see why I want you to get the hang of this," he announced to Bill. "I plan on spending most of my time below."

"Not in that bunk," Marilyn teased. "You'd throw your back out." She glanced around, found the port deck next to the pilothouse to her liking, and stretched out to take the sun.

Jeanne poked out of the hatch, and turned her

head slowly. "God this is beautiful. It's like a photo in a travel magazine."

"Only it's real," Howard corrected.

She came up slowly, wearing a loose blouse over the top of her one-piece suit, and carrying a plastic bottle of suntan oil. Then she took a seat on the bench, pulling her knees up in front of her. They fell into a pleasant silence, each of them breathing in the setting.

Howard gave the helm back to Bill and lifted his camera out of its case. He turned the lens toward his friend and fired a couple of pictures of Bill's tour at the wheel. Then he slipped up next to the women, instructed them to ignore him, and tried for some candid portraits.

"Howard, maybe you want to take this," Bill called as he realized how quickly they were coming up to land. Norman Island was only six miles across the sound from Road Harbor, and they were already more than halfway there. Peter Island was close at hand off the port bow. And *Cane Maiden* was gaining speed as the sun rose higher and the wind freshened. Bill was apprehensive about racing so close to land.

"You're doing fine," Howard answered. He used the moment to try the auxiliary again, and kept cranking until the engine fired. He left it in neutral to charge the batteries and then went forward to get some photos of the steep cliff at the end of Peter Island as it passed just thirty yards off the beam. Then he dashed back to the cockpit and spread out the chart of Norman Island. He began plotting an anchorage in the bight that formed the island's natural harbor.

112

"You're going to take her in?" Bill asked in surprise.

Howard set the chart beside the helm. "You and I are going to take her in. We don't need that smartass."

Marilyn sat up and looked over the pilothouse into the cockpit. Jeanne made wary eye contact with Bill.

"What do you want me to do?" Bill asked Howard.

"Go forward and check the anchor chain. Make sure you can slip the shackle quickly, so that when we get in close, you're ready to let go."

Bill thought he understood. He squeezed past Marilyn as he went forward.

The western point of Peter Island slipped past the port beam. The tiny top of Pelican Island was close off the starboard bow. *Cane Maiden* was heading evenly between them with the entrance to the bight dead ahead.

Steve came up as Bill passed the forward hatch. He watched as Bill studied the anchor shackle, and then looked aft at Howard.

"He planning on making the anchorage?" he asked.

"Yeah. He knows what he's doing."

"The wind off the hills can be pretty tricky."

Bill turned to Steve. "Why don't you go back and tell him? He'd appreciate the advice."

Steve boosted himself onto the deck. "I thought he knew it all."

"Nobody knows it all," Bill answered.

Steve ambled aft, filling his eyes with Marilyn's body as he stepped over her. Not bad, he thought.

Maybe she'll decide to stay aboard while her old man goes ashore. He had bunked down with several of his passengers during his stint in the charter business. One of them was still writing him letters.

As he swung into the cockpit he asked Howard, "Where are you going to put her?"

"Eastern end, close into Treasure Point."

He nodded his approval. "Less crowded. And closer to the caves."

Pelican Island passed abeam, and Howard eased to leeward to round Water Point at the north end of the bight. Steve moved automatically to let out some sail. Marilyn shifted up to her knees so that she could see the landfall. Jeanne moved close to her and stood beside her.

"I hope this isn't going to be another fiasco," Marilyn whispered.

Cane Maiden charged past the point, still under full sail.

"You might want to furl the genoa," Steve suggested.

Howard nodded. "Good idea."

Steve hauled in on the furling line that rolled the genoa sail out of sight. Immediately, the bow tended to windward.

"Maybe the mizzen too," Howard said.

Steve took down the spanker, letting the boat run on its main and the working jib.

They were still carrying good speed when they crossed the entrance to the bight and headed toward the southern shore. Howard picked his anchorage and steered toward it. Within seconds, they were up against the beach.

"Close enough?" Howard asked.

"Maybe fifteen feet," said Steve, referring to the depth.

"Let's do it."

Howard swung the wheel to windward. *Cane Maiden* came about smartly, her sails luffing as she aimed into the wind. Her speed began to die. He leaned over the rail to watch the flow of the sea along her side. The boiling foam had become a lazy ripple. She was losing all the momentum she had carried through the turn. He waited until she was dead in the water, and even beginning to move aft under the push of the wind.

"Let go!"

Bill opened the shackle. The chain rattled across the deck and disappeared over the bow.

The boat drifted further back.

"Watch it! The wind can be gusty," Steve advised.

"Thanks!"

She moved back slowly, and then picked up speed in a sudden puff. Howard kept calculating the amount of chain that the anchor was pulling across the foredeck. When he thought he had enough scope, he called to Bill, "Check it!"

Bill raced the anchor line around the cleat and tied it tight.

Howard hit the auxiliary engine starter and shifted the prop into slow astern. The boat backed until the anchor chain was pulled taut. When he shut down the engine, *Cane Maiden* leaped forward and then settled securely.

"Nicely done," Steve said.

Howard didn't answer. To his critical ear, it

sounded like another surly remark. "Any idiot can drop an anchor," is what he thought he heard.

Steve lowered the inflatable dinghy over the transom and then pulled it alongside to starboard. Bill and Howard went below, changed into bathing suits and then reappeared on deck. Together, they helped Marilyn and Jeanne into the dinghy, climbed aboard themselves and then fired up the tiny outboard engine.

"You coming?" Bill called up to Steve.

"I've been here," Steve answered, showing no particular interest.

Howard shook his head as they pulled away from *Cane Maiden*. "Real head case," he said, nodding back toward Steve.

14

Cindy Camilli closed her room door behind her, and walked along the path that curved among the bungalows to the lobby. She glanced around, expecting to find Al Weston peering between the palm trees. He was nowhere in sight, but she knew that he wouldn't be far away, probably parked out at the end of the driveway, waiting to fall into line behind her taxi.

She went to the desk and presented her vault key. It didn't take the desk clerk more than a minute to return with her two camera cases, and summon a bellboy to act as Cindy's bearer.

There was a taxi waiting, another battered van with dusty windows. The driver was swaying to the rhythm of a reggae band blasting from the portable radio on the seat beside him.

"Do you know how to get to Parson's Boatyard?" Cindy asked.

He nodded, his head bobbing with the beat of the music. Cindy slid in and then the bellboy loaded the cases in beside her. The driver shifted gears and vaulted over a speed bump, setting the car rocking on its worn out shocks.

"Parson's is out of business," he commented idly, as if the information were of no consequence.

"You sure?"

He shrugged. "Ain't nobody worked there for over a year."

"Can I get in?"

"Ain't nobody there to stop you."

The yard was on the eastern side of the town, close to where the harbor met the Francis Drake Channel. They would take the main road through the small, meandering town, climb into the slope of the mountains, and then come down on the eastern shoreline.

"How long?" Cindy asked as they turned onto the street.

He shrugged, still keeping the beat. "Maybe ten minutes. Maybe twenty. Not long."

She peeked back over her shoulder. A clean, blue sedan was turning onto the road behind them with a large, masculine figure silhouetted behind the wheel. She breathed a bit more easily. During the morning, she had tried to relax by the edge of the pool, but the apprehension over her approaching meeting had kept her coiled like a spring. She wasn't looking forward to her rendezvous, but at the same time, she was anxious to get it over with. The thought of Al Weston, only a few car lengths behind, eased her tension.

She rehearsed her plan. Go into the storage shed. Stand out in the open where she could be easily seen. And wait. Her contact would be under cover, somewhere close by where he could watch her arrival and be certain that she was alone. He would let her stand there, probably for ten to fifteen minutes, just to make sure that no one was joining her. Then he would approach.

When she saw him, she would take a few steps

back, away from the cases. He would approach, open the cases, and examine the payment. When he was satisfied, he would make the transaction, close the cases and leave. Perhaps there would be an "okay," or an "everything's here." But more than likely he would signal the end of their meeting with a simple nod. There was no reason for conversation because, if all went well, there was little chance that they would ever meet one another again.

Al knew the routine, so he would be careful not to be seen. Somewhere short of the meeting place he would pull his car to the side, get out, and follow on foot. More than likely he would find a hiding place outside the boat yard, a point where he could observe without being noticed. He had probably visited the area, either yesterday, after her phone call, or early in the morning. Most likely, he had already picked out his observation point.

The van entered a town, a small cluster of cinder-block houses with stores and bars along the road's edge. It had to slow because the shoppers had spread out from the narrow sidewalks and were using the road as a thoroughfare. She checked again. The blue sedan was still following.

Weston didn't like to be driving so close. He should be further back, perhaps allowing a car or two to get between them so that the taxi driver wouldn't keep seeing the same car in his rearview mirror. Not that there was anything suspicious about his car. But on an island of derelict vans and pickups that had been rusted out by the salt air, his new model rental car was easy to spot.

He wanted to back off, only there was every chance that a flow of shoppers, and the goats that wandered among them, could cut him off. He knew where Cindy was headed, and felt certain he could overtake her on the single road that wound around the water's edge. But he was uncomfortable at the thought of letting her and her baggage out of his sight.

He saw the gaudily painted delivery truck moving down the side street, and watched it slow as it approached the intersection. His attention snapped back to Cindy's taxi, but at the same instant he realized that the truck wasn't stopping. When he looked back, it was still rolling, and then suddenly it accelerated onto the main road. Al was on his brakes instantly, and for a split second it seemed that the truck would clear past his left front fender. But then he felt his car lurch to the right and heard the rumble of metal and the tinkling of shattered glass. Both cars stopped together, with Al's fender folded against the side of the truck.

He was out in an instant and around the front of his car before the truck door opened. The driver, a skeletal black man wearing a sport shirt and a baseball cap, eased out, studied the damage for an instant and then flashed a wide smile at Al. "You hit me, mon!"

Weston's fists tightened, but he checked his rage. "No damage," he answered. The side of the truck was slightly dented, and a patch on the metal had been scraped bare. But the damage fit unobtrusively into the pattern of scrapes and dents that decorated the rest of the truck's body.

"No damage? Look, mon. Your whole fender's bent. You got no headlight."

"That's okay. It's covered. Just pull back so I can get around you."

The shoppers had circled the accident. "Hey, mon!" one of them said to Al. "He cut you off. I see it. It's his fault."

The driver turned on the shopper. "You crazy? He drove right into me. I was just turnin'." He pointed toward the street he had just left, and then began reenacting the collision with his hands. "I'm just turnin'. I got plenty of room, but I got to stop because of the crowd. And he drive right into me."

Al pushed his face in front of the driver's. "There's no problem. You're not damaged, and I'm insured. So let's just get outta here."

The driver pointed at his accuser. "This guy say it was my fault."

"I don't give a fuck what he says. It's no problem. Just pull back so I can get around you."

"But he say . . ." the man kept arguing.

Al took his arm and lifted him back into his truck. "Get this shit heap outta my way. You hear me?"

"Hey, mon. You can't . . ."

"Move it!"

The driver recognized that Al wasn't going to tell him again.

"Yeah. Sure. No damage. Everything's okay." He settled behind the wheel and pulled his door shut.

Al ran around his car and slid back in.

He heard the truck engine grind weakly, and

then saw its hood shake as the engine coughed, seemed to catch, and then died.

The driver twisted over the ignition key, and once again the motor turned over. There was a series of blasts that tried to meld into the roar of a running engine, but once again the motor died.

Al bounded back out from behind the wheel.

The driver turned to him and shook his head apologetically. "Needs to cool a minute. Then it'll start. No problem, mon!"

Al glanced passed the battered hood. Cindy's cab was nowhere in sight.

15

They motored around the point to the water-filled caves that were the island's treasure, and steered into the black-walled vaults. Shafts of light aimed through the broken holes in the ceiling, turning patches of dark water into shimmering emerald. Voices seemed to sing as the wind squeezed through the crevices.

With their flashlights, they could see down into the water and follow the strange, gaudily colored fish, who were eating furiously at the plants on the rock walls. They found hundreds of tiny orange-colored crabs scampering along the walls at the water's edge. Jeanne pointed to a sea turtle who wandered by, and Bill laughed out loud at her obvious pleasure.

"Another world," he told her, and she answered, "A beautiful world."

They paddled out to the reef that guarded the caves. Jeanne fixed her mask and fell over the side. She sucked in air and then dove beneath the surface, becoming part of the world where minutes before she had only been a spectator. Dozens of fish rushed up to meet her. She turned back to the boat. "Get in here," she yelled. "It's incredible."

Bill dove in beside her and followed her along the bottom and then, with a kick of his flippers, up the side of a stony wall. They broke the surface together. She pushed the mask back off her face and then laughed at Bill, whose mask was half filled with water. He lifted his own mask, smiled at her and then pulled her close to kiss her.

"Uh oh!" It was Howard's voice in the water next to them. "Breeding ground," he yelled. He took Marilyn by the hand and kicked out toward another cluster of coral. "I think they want to be alone," he announced loudly, as he and Marilyn swam away.

"This is wonderful," Jeanne told Bill.

"It's going to get better," he said, and he slipped his hand down the top of her bathing suit.

Jeanne pulled away. "It could always be like this. There are so many things we could do. If we just make up our minds."

He could fill in the rest of her thought because she had said it before. They could be living a more exciting, more adventurous life. Like Howard and Marilyn. If only he would change. Give up the shabby school building in a dying section of a troubled city. Put his efforts into something more promising. She wanted to break out. She wanted him to help her.

"We'll work it out," he said. "But we're here now. Let's just enjoy it." He tried to caress her, but Jeanne turned away abruptly and kicked off after Howard and Marilyn. Bill was always promising to work it out. But nothing ever happened.

They swam for an hour that passed in minutes, diving down along the walls of the cliffs, blowing bubbles at the fish, and then drifting back to the surface. They were pleasantly exhausted when they climbed back aboard the inflatable, and motored back to *Cane Maiden*.

Marilyn and Jeanne went below to assemble a fruit salad lunch. Howard tried to raise the rum punch to an art form while Bill and Steve set the Bimini tent top over the cockpit to protect them from the sun.

"Join us," Marilyn offered to Steve, but he preferred a quick dive over the side and then returned to the loneliness of his cabin.

"That boy is disturbed," Marilyn decided.

They devoured the fruit salad, and then lounged lazily around the cockpit, sipping the rum punches as they planned the rest of their day.

"There's too much to do," Howard complained cheerfully. "Too much to see. Damn it, Bill, we've got to make this an annual affair. Only next time, we'll take two weeks. Hell, we ought to take a month and really do it right."

It was easy for Bill to nod in agreement at the pleasant thought. "It certainly wouldn't make me mad."

Then Howard blundered into the topic that Marilyn had cut short in the airport. "Hell, you teachers have the whole summer off. We could plan a summer trip. We could take a whole month."

"Bill doesn't have the whole summer off," Jeanne corrected icily. "His school stays open."

Howard looked surprised. "You keep the kids locked up for the whole summer?"

Bill began explaining that the school was as much

a community center as an educational facility. They kept the sports programs running, and supplemented them with local field trips. "The kids wouldn't have much going for them if we shut down," he said.

As he spoke, Jeanne's eyes narrowed in anger. Why couldn't he see what was happening all around him? There was a bigger world of opportunity that Howard and Marilyn were enjoying. They could talk realistically about devoting weeks and months to shared pleasures. She and Bill were locked into a tiny corner that was defined by the needs of his damn school.

Bill caught her glance, and remembered how she had turned away from him in the water. "But right now, everything is up in the air," he offered hopefully. "The school may not make it through the summer, and Jeanne and I have been talking about making a change." He smiled and poked Howard in the shoulder with his fist. "Maybe I'll get a cushy job like yours, and be able to join you for a month."

"Well, if you're serious, we ought to talk," Howard said, about to expand on all the things he could do to help his friend.

"That's the last thing we ought to do," Marilyn interrupted. "Didn't you say there was more snorkeling right around here? Why don't we get to it?" She was already up, picking up the dishes.

Howard caught her meaning. "Great idea! Let's get under way. It's over at the Indians, just beyond Pelican Island. We can be there in a minute. We won't even bother to hoist the sails. We can motor over. Be there before you know it."

They sprang into action, babbling with new-found energy. Only Jeanne remained quiet, still nursing her anger. She had heard what her husband had said. But she just couldn't believe him.

16

Weston's jaw tightened as he watched the driver twist the ignition key, and jump up and down on the gas pedal. It was worse than before. The cranking noise began to drop in pitch, and the engine wasn't even trying to catch. The black man looked up and tried a smile. "No good, mon. I think she's dead."

Al ran back into his car, started the engine, and tried to back away. He was hoping that he could swing into the side street that the truck had left, and find his way around the shopping district. But as his car began to move, the truck lurched toward him. They were hooked together. His bumper was locked under the battered chassis. Neither of them was going anywhere.

Cindy felt a cool breeze coming in through the open window as soon as they were free of the town. The driver forked to the left and began climbing along the edge of the hill. Suddenly the water came into view above the tops of the houses, and the smell of salt air rushed in.

"Won't be no time, now," the driver called back to her over the din of his radio. Then he asked, "You want me to wait for you?"

"No, I'll be a while. Can you come back for

me in an hour?" She didn't think it would take that long. Probably half an hour at most. But she was afraid a waiting taxi might spook her contact.

"I can wait. No extra charge."

"No, I might be longer."

He shrugged. "Okay. Be back in an hour."

She turned in her seat. The road behind her was empty. But she wasn't concerned. Al would be there in plenty of time.

She got a clear view of Parson's Boatyard as her taxi turned and started down a road toward the waterfront. It looked like a nautical junkyard, a fenced-in compound with rusted hulls and bare wooden boat ribs scattered about in no particular order. There were a few finger piers sticking out into the harbor, one of them tipped on an angle and half awash. A half a dozen small boats were tied to the piers, two of them nearly sunk. The only structure that resembled the shed specified for her meeting was a corrugated metal building with waving sides and a gaping hole in its roof.

"You sure this is where you're goin'?" the driver asked.

"Parson's Boatyard?"

"Yeah. It's Parson's Boatyard."

Sections of the chain-link fence were missing. The large, swinging gate was off its hinges.

"Maybe I should wait."

She shook her head. This was probably the place. Her contact wouldn't want to make the exchange in her hotel lobby. The abandoned shed would suit him just fine.

"Pick me up in an hour. Right here, by the gate."

He sat and watched as she pulled the cases out of the back seat and loaded them onto the dolly. Then he spun into a U-turn that kicked up a cloud of dust, and labored back up the hill.

As soon as she was alone, Cindy felt the broiling heat of the midday sun. She glanced up the road looking for Al's car and then scanned the flat, scarce underbrush that surrounded the compound. The tension began tightening around her as she started through the open gate, the dolly bouncing at her heels.

Everything she saw was long dead. The boats, raised off the ground on wooden racks, hadn't been near the water for years. The paint that was flaking on their hulls was older than she was. Random lengths of chain were rusted permanently into their snake-like shapes, and the occasional loops of line were rotted into seamless heaps. The only sound was one of the shed's metal roof panels banging easily in the breeze, well on its way to tearing off.

She glanced through the wide door of the shed into a dark interior. A neatly defined square in the center of the dirt floor was brightly lit by the sunlight pouring in through the hole in the roof. In the gloomy corners, she could make out the shapes of old hulls, and the hoist that had once been used to move them out to the water.

Cindy moved further down to the water's edge, squinting at the light that reflected off the surface of the harbor. Far to her right, she could see the sea wall with the hundreds of masts standing over its top. Her hotel, which she couldn't locate, was among the cluster of white buildings on the hillside beyond.

She looked down at the small flotilla of decrepit boats that she had noticed from the taxi. It was then that she spotted the new outboard motor hanging from the stern of a small, tidy runabout. Suddenly, she could taste the dryness in her mouth. Her contact had apparently already arrived. She went back to the shed, took one last look around hoping to see some sign of Al Weston. Then she dragged the dolly through the opening and went inside.

The heat hit her like a hammer. The metal walls not only radiated the sun's heat, but also blocked out the cooling relief of the wind. The place was a giant oven. She rolled the cases into the center of the glowing patch of daylight and then backed away to the edges of the shadows. It was just two o'clock.

The minutes passed slowly, counted by the rattling of the roof overhead that banged in steady tempo like the beat of a clock's second hand. Cindy kept her eyes trained on the door and the small section of the boatyard that she could see through it. Nothing was moving. The shadows seemed to be fixed permanently. She could feel the perspiration trickling down the small of her back, and realized that the light cotton skirt was clinging to her legs. She glanced at her watch, and found that only five minutes had passed. If the son-of-a-bitch decided to keep her waiting in this heat, she'd probably be dead when he got there.

"You the photographer?" The voice was the same one she had heard on the telephone, this time a stage whisper from the shadows at the other end of the shed. She could feel her heart beginning to pound.

131

"Yes," she said, matching the conspiratorial tone.

There was movement in the darkness. Then he stepped into the light, exactly the person she had imagined when she heard him on the telephone. He was young, broad-shouldered, and athletic, with close-cut blond hair. He wore a dark windbreaker over white slacks and carried a canvas shoulder bag. She took a hesitant step forward to meet him.

"Sorry to keep you waiting. This should only take a second." But he didn't move toward the camera cases. He was more interested in Cindy, and he took his time as he examined every curve of her body. With the light clothes clinging to her skin, he had plenty to look at.

"Whenever you're ready," she advised.

He smiled easily, keeping his eyes on her as he moved to the cases. He knelt down on the dirt floor and snapped open the case that held the camera bodies and the lenses. He moved it aside, and then opened the film case.

"When did you get in?" he asked, without looking up from his work.

"Yesterday," she answered. "Yesterday afternoon."

He had lifted the film packs out of their slots in the protective foam rubber and was in the process of counting them.

"Nice island," he commented idly. "Lots of places to have fun." The accent, Cindy decided, was German. Or Swiss. Someplace over there. He selected one of the packets at random and tore the seal. She could see printed documents of some

132

kind as he slipped them out and counted their edges. He pushed them back, and then tore the edge of another packet.

"All these the same?"

"I don't know," Cindy answered.

He closed the second packet, then reached into his bag and took out two camera bodies. He worked quickly, exchanging the bodies with those Cindy had carried.

"I'm going to stay around for a day or two," he said without stopping his work. "Maybe we could get together."

Cindy thought of Al Weston. "I don't think that would be a good idea."

He nodded as he put Cindy's cameras into his shoulder bag. "Probably not," he agreed, "but it might be fun. There are lots of things I could show you." A smile spread across his face.

It turned to open-mouthed amazement the instant that a gunshot blast snapped through the building and echoed off the metal walls. The walls were still singing, rattling like a snare drum, when there was a second blast and then a third. Heinz's body snapped with each new sound, dancing as if his puppeteer were jerking violently on his strings. With the first shot, he bounced to his right, catching his fall by slamming one hand into the ground. He started to rise up, turning his face toward the open door when the second shot knocked him back on his haunches. He was twisting with palsied motions, trying to get back up on his knees when the third shot knocked him flat on his back.

Cindy watched his death dance in horror, her

piercing scream locked silently in her throat. She wanted to rush to help him, but instead, she backed slowly away, further into the darkness. She watched the body, brightly illuminated in the square of sunlight, twitch for a few seconds and then go motionless. She was still staring at it when she noticed a shape move into the space of the open door.

He was backlighted, as she must have been when she had first entered the shed. She wasn't sure of anything, except that the silhouette was holding a long-barreled pistol extended in both hands and was moving carefully into the shed. She backed further away from the bright arena of slaughter, moving deeper into the shadows.

The figure faded into the darkness, then suddenly reappeared as he stepped into the sunlight. It was her taxi driver, still in the colorful sport shirt, but no longer bouncing to an island rhythm. He was as taut as a stalking cat, moving toward the splayed form in the dust with his pistol pointing steadily at his victim. He stopped when his toes were nearly touching the feet of the courier and lowered the muzzle toward the staring face.

"No!" Cindy gasped involuntarily, her hands leaping up to her mouth.

The driver wheeled toward her, the gun swinging quickly in her direction. He squinted into the darkness. The gun flashed, and its deafening crack rattled through the structure. Cindy froze, her pounding heartbeat jerked to dead stop. She stared back at the man who seemed to be looking directly at her. The rattling stopped and the building went silent.

"You in there, miss?"

She wasn't thinking at all, just frozen still in silence.

He waited. "You come out of there, miss. You come out before I have to come in and get you."

She stood absolutely still.

"You come out," the nasal voice demanded. Then, softer, "I'm not going to hurt you."

She was riveted on his motionless form. He seemed to lean toward her, and then he took a careful step in her direction. The aim of the pistol never wavered.

"You hear me? You come out here."

Another careful step. He was squinting down the gun barrel, directly at her face. How could he not see her?

Behind him, the fallen form began to rise out of the dust. Peter Heinz had silently lifted his head, and was struggling to raise his back off the ground.

The driver fired another blinding flash that crackled around the metal wall. He stopped. Listened. His head tipped to an angle as he tried to see into the darkness, to separate his victim out of the tangle of shadowy shapes. He steadied the pistol and then eased another step toward the edge of the lighted square.

Behind him, Heinz was sitting, balancing on one hand. The other hand was moving down inside his windbreaker.

"You come out, miss. You can't get away." The driver was almost to the edge of the shadow. "You come out now!" His face turned slowly, scanning the darkness.

He was leaning into another step when his head suddenly snapped around. His body spun quickly, the gun whirling away from her and toward the ghost that had risen behind him.

There was a roar of gunfire, the shots sounding too closely together to be counted. The driver's smooth swing was cut short of his target. His arms flew out and he fell straight back over his heels. The shed went silent.

Cindy gaped at the flattened body that only an instant before had been closing on her. Over its pointed toes, she could see Peter, his eyes looking right through her as if she weren't there. Slowly she became aware of the metal roof, knocking like a heartbeat high over her head. For a second, she stood motionless, looking curiously at the still players who were laid out in the lighted center stage. Her fists squeezed and then her body began to shudder.

She forced herself to take a step forward, and then another. Her eyes focused on the closest form, the driver, who was spread-eagled in the sunlight, his head cut off by the edge of the shadow. She moved in a wide arc, circling around the body to keep it at a distance. She stopped when she reached the dividing line between the daylight and the darkness. Only when she was certain that he was dead did she step toward him.

He was flat on his back, his arms and legs outstretched, the pistol still tight in the grip of his hand. She was puzzled that there wasn't a single mark on the body. The tropical shirt wasn't even in disarray. But she gasped when she was able to make out the face. One of the cheeks was missing, and there was a red hole where the nose should have been. Both eyes were popped out of their sockets.

She staggered back, feeling the bile flooding up from her stomach as she jerked her head away. She gagged, and bent over from the waist, expecting to be sick. But nothing came up.

She turned toward Heinz. He was still sitting, his torso rocking gently, his chin slumped down on his chest. She lowered herself to one knee, leaned closer, and saw his two hands, spread over a large, boxy gun that rested in his lap.

"Are you . . . alive?" Cautiously, she reached out a soothing hand and touched the colorless cheek. The weight of her finger upset the delicate balance of the body. The torso slowly began to tip backward, and then gathered speed until it crashed onto the dirt. Cindy breathed in relief when she saw the face was unmarked and the eyes were peacefully shut. There was a hopeful instant when she expected some sort of miracle. But then she saw that the white shirt under the opened windbreaker was clotted with blood.

"Oh shit," she breathed. And then she repeated it in half voice. "Oh shit." She stood slowly, her eyes pinned on the bloody shirt. Then she broke her stare, turned, and took in the entire lighted arena. One man was dead at the edge, his face cut into a horror. Another was balled up at her feet. Between them were her open camera cases, the neat stacks of film packets, and the toppled shoulder bag.

"Oh shit," she said, on the verge of hysteria. Without thinking, she turned and raced toward the open door.

137

"Al!" she screamed suddenly, aiming her voice in no particular direction. "Al!" Her wail echoed hollowly throughout the shed.

She stopped as soon as she was slapped by the sunlight, and then staggered weakly so that she had to catch the door edge, to steady herself. "Al, you son-of-a-bitch. Where the fuck are you?"

She glanced around. The bones of the yachts were silent and still. Nothing was moving in the scraggly fields that stretched outside the fence. Cindy looked toward the gate. The empty taxi was half off the road to one side of the entrance. Then she searched up the hill. The road was empty, heat waves rising from its dry, dusty surface.

She started to scream Al's name once more, but then she caught herself. If he hadn't heard the gunshots, then he was too far away to hear her scream. She turned cautiously and looked back into the shed. The stage drawn by the square of sunlight was exactly the way she remembered it.

Cindy swallowed hard. Get ahold of yourself, she thought. Think! What happened? What went wrong?

Her cabby had come back. Back long before his hour was up, and parked his car and then crept up to the building. Why? What did he know?

A thief, she told herself. A fucking petty thief. Probably came back to see who she was meeting. Probably had nothing more in mind than taking the cameras and a little cash. Most likely walked in on something that he didn't understand.

No, that couldn't be it. He didn't come back just to steal. He came back to kill. He had fired at her courier before he had even entered the building. Fired first, as if he expected the man to be armed. He must have known what was in the cases. Known it was so valuable that he would have to kill in order to get it.

No! Because if he knew what was in the cases, why didn't he just take them from her? He must have had the gun with him in the taxi, when they were driving down a deserted road to an empty boatyard. He could have pushed her over the edge of the road, or followed her into the boatyard and left her dead in the corner of the shed. So he didn't want just the cases. He must have wanted what the courier was bringing as well.

Jesus, he must have known about the whole deal. But then why would he have driven away and then come back? And if he knew about the whole deal, why was he waiting on line with all the other taxis at the hotel? He would have been waiting here, at the boatyard, for the deal to come together.

Wait! He wasn't on line with other taxis. He was parked right in front of the hotel door. Could he have been expecting her? Waiting for her to come out? Maybe he knew about the trade, but just didn't know where it was supposed to take place. Then he would have needed her to show him the way.

But how could he have known? The only ones who knew were her and the courier. And Al. Jesus, could Al be in on this?

She looked around again. Al, for Christ's sake. Where the hell are you? You're supposed to be here. Where the hell are you?

She wanted to run. But where? Out the gate and back up the hill? Where? To what? She spun

139

completely around in her confusion, turning away from the door and back toward the inside of the shed. "Get hold of yourself, Cindy," she whispered. "Start thinking, or you're going to be dead."

She should take the film packages. And the camera bodies. That was what this was all about. She should take them because they were her only protection. She remembered thinking that she was dispensable. If something went wrong, Walter Linz and Al Weston could just turn away and leave her to the authorities. Or to the killers. No one could trace her back to them. But there was a fortune scattered across the dirt floor inside the shed. If she took it with her, then she wouldn't be dispensable. Someone would have to sort all this out and come to her.

The money would keep her safe. Walter Linz would take care of her if she saved his money.

She took a deep breath, straightened herself, and then walked carefully back into the square of sunlight. She kept her eyes away from the two shattered bodies, focusing her energy on the scattered merchandise that lay between them. Carefully, she repacked the film packets into the protective slots in her case. She threw the lighting hardware aside, and fitted the camera bodies that the courier had brought into their place so that she had everything of value in one case. She closed it, put it on the dolly and then fastened the cord. She stood up to leave when she saw the oversized automatic pistol protruding out from under the courier's body. Carefully, she reached out and slid it into her hand.

She was surprised at its weight. Cindy had never held a gun in her life, and she fitted her fingers carefully around the grip. She noticed the square clip that protruded from the bottom of the weapon, and remembered that it held the ammunition. There were others just like it connected to the leather holster that she could see under the dead man's windbreaker. Carefully, she reached toward the body and took the spare magazines. She put them, together with the gun, into the straw bag that hung from her shoulder.

Just walk, she told herself, through the gate and up the hill. Just get moving. You'll think of something. She stuck her head out through the door, and once again panned the deserted yard. Her eyes were searching over the empty boats tied to the sinking piers when she saw her answer.

The boat. The new one with the outboard motor. That was how Peter Heinz had gotten there, and how he was planning to leave. Of course! A smart move. One way to make certain that he wasn't followed was to leave by boat. He could speed out into the harbor and then disappear into the fleet that was moored behind the sea wall. Cindy broke into a run as she dragged the dolly out of the shed and down toward the docks.

She loaded the case into the boat, and then climbed aboard. She tried not to rush as she studied the instructions that were written all over the equipment.

"Forward," "neutral," and "reverse," were printed on the gearshift lever. The throttle was marked "fast" and "slow." A red button was labeled "start." She pushed the button. There was no response.

"Oh, shit." She stabbed at it again and again, and then screamed at it. "Do something, you son-of-a-bitch. Do something!"

She tried to stem her growing panic. Carefully, she moved the lever to neutral, and pushed the throttle up to fast. As soon as she touched the red button, the engine roared to life.

"Slow it down," she told herself, easing back on the throttle until the roar had become a hum. Then she pushed the transmission lever to forward. The boat jumped ahead until it was snapped back by the mooring line. The bow swung in and crashed against the dock, nearly throwing her out of the seat. "Dammit," she cursed. She pulled the transmission back to neutral, and the boat eased back against its lines.

Cindy untied the lines and pushed the bow away from the dock. She set one lever on slow, and then bit down on her lip as she put the transmission back into gear. The engine kicked up a gentle wake, and the boat eased out into the harbor. Carefully, she pushed the throttle forward until the engine's gurgle turned into a steely whine. The boat lifted its bow and kicked up a wash of white water as it raced toward the distant sea wall.

17

The boat had already disappeared behind the sea wall when Al Weston crested the hill. The layout of the boatyard was familiar to him. He had driven the road the evening before, and spent a full hour studying the surroundings and selecting his vantage point. In his line of work, it was best not to leave anything to chance. But the smooth routine he was anticipating had been shattered by the accident in Road Town. And now there was another surprise. Cindy's taxi was parked near the gate.

He slowed, letting the car coast down the hill in low gear. Had the cab returned already? If it had, then Cindy should be near it, loading her cases into the trunk. But she was nowhere in sight, which probably meant that her contact had not yet showed. She would still be inside the shed, waiting to make the exchange. He smiled at the thought that he had made it on time.

But the smile vanished as he came nearer to the gate. The dusty minivan looked empty. Where in hell was the driver? Cindy wouldn't have brought him inside with her. He should be slumped behind the wheel, dozing as he waited.

Al turned toward the gate and moved slowly

past the parked car, rising up in his seat to get a better look inside. It was empty, and suddenly his apprehension turned to fear. Something was wrong. Something was terribly wrong. Either the driver had gone in after Cindy, or someone else had gotten rid of the driver. Someone who was following her and didn't want any interference from her cabbie. He kept his speed slow until he had reached the end of the battered fence. Then he pulled abruptly to the side, checked the clip in his automatic, and eased himself out onto the road. He moved down toward the water until he found a flattened section of fencing, and then crept behind the cover of the grounded boats as he worked his way to the shed.

He hesitated when he reached the last boat that could provide him with cover. There was fifty feet of open space that he would have to cross to get to the building, and he searched carefully, looking for any sign of life. The yard seemed to be as dead as a cemetery, with no hint that anyone had been there for months. Crouching low, he raced to the corner of the shed and flattened himself against its steel wall. He waited again, now listening for a shot that, if well aimed, he would probably never hear. Then he began moving along the wall, turned the corner and started inching toward the open doorway. When he reached it, he sprang through the space, his automatic clutched in both hands and already aimed at the target he was anticipating. He blinked into the patch of sunlight, and then saw the two figures sprawled in the dirt.

Carefully, he edged around the door and moved

into the shadows, circling the center stage where the two bodies lay. Someone might still be lurking inside, waiting for him to step into the bright light, and Al took the time to make sure that he had the building to himself. Only when he had searched the dark corners did he approach the grim scene in the middle.

He identified the driver, recognizing his colorful sport shirt. He bent down, looked at the pistol still clutched in his hand, and saw that it had been fired. It was an old revolver, not the sort of weapon that a professional would carry. Maybe the guy was freelancing, he thought. Next, he crossed to the second body, turned the face up with the toe of his shoe, and decided that this must be the courier that Cindy was supposed to meet. He took in the shoulder holster, designed for a large, automatic pistol, and then glanced around the area until he was certain that the pistol was missing.

One of the camera cases lay open before him, with two camera bodies placed beside it. He opened the bodies, and wasn't surprised to find that they were empty. Then he noticed the tiny scraps of paper on the ground near the case. Weston picked them up and read the promotional lettering that had been hastily torn. They were pieces from the film pack wrappers, which indicated that the packets had been opened and that the transaction had probably taken place. He stood slowly, trying to put together the chain of events that led up to the carnage.

There had been a gunfight. Either the two men had shot each other, or there had been a third party who had shot them both. It wasn't likely that the two men had killed each other, so he concentrated on the idea of another person being present. Someone other than Cindy. She simply didn't fit the bill. He figured he knew Cindy like the back of his hand. There was no way she could ever fire a bullet into anyone.

The third person had left the scene, taking with him the case that held the film packs, the replacement camera bodies and probably the missing pistol. Obviously, he had also taken Cindy. But why would he take the messenger with him? Once he had the money and the merchandise, she was no good to him. Unless Cindy knew the other person and they had planned right from the beginning to leave together.

Who knew about the exchange? He did. Cindy did. And the courier who had called her the previous evening. But the courier was crumpled dead at his feet. If the rip-off had been his idea, chances were that he would have escaped with money.

So that left Cindy. Cindy? Weston couldn't believe it. There was no way she would have the guts to pull this kind of double cross. But what other explanation was there? She knew the time and place of the meeting, which meant that she could have arranged the interruption. And that would explain why she would have vanished along with the cases.

The whole thing had probably been well planned. The traffic accident which had seemed only an annoyance, now seemed to have been a deliberate ploy to separate him from Cindy. And who else could have arranged it? It had to be someone who knew that he would be following close behind, and no one but Cindy knew that. They had taken great pains to cover up his role in the operation.

But he still didn't believe it. She wouldn't have the nerve. She wasn't smart enough to set something like this up. Or was she? Hadn't she figured out how the bartender was handicapping the cash register? Besides, she didn't have to work out all the details herself. All she had to do was cooperate with someone.

He was still trying to fit the random pieces of evidence together when he glanced at the spread form of the taxi driver. What was the fucking taxi driver doing inside the shed? Cindy wouldn't have brought him inside. Unless he was in on the plot. That made sense. The truck that had cut him off could have been watching for the cab, waiting on the corner of a street that the taxi driver had been told to take. So the driver was a minor player. Probably someone paid to pick Cindy up and drive her along a predetermined route. Someone who became expendable once he had done his job.

Unless he was a major player. Al couldn't be sure that Cindy had ever reached the shed. All he knew was that the cases with the film packs had been there. The driver could have delivered them by himself. Jesus, if he knew what was in the cases, he could have dumped Cindy anywhere along the route. So maybe Cindy wasn't part of the plan. Maybe she had been its first victim.

Easy enough to find out, Al figured. He'd search back up the road. And if he didn't find Cindy discarded by the roadside, then the only conclusion was that she had left with the money. A fucking cocktail waitress had made a fool of him.

But first, he had to get rid of the bodies. He didn't want to leave any evidence for someone to stumble across and for the police to investigate. He had to find Cindy, and find her fast, either out on the road or someplace in the islands where she had gone into hiding. He didn't want any competition from the police.

He searched the cab driver's pockets and found his keys. Then he stripped the shirt off the body and wrapped it around the shattered head. He dragged the body out into the yard and down to the water where he slid it under one of the piers. Next, he pulled the young man's body to the water's edge. He searched around the yard, found a rusted anchor with its fall of chain, and tied it around the two corpses. He towed them out to the end of the finger pier and then watched them sink under the weight of the anchor.

Al went back to the gate, started the taxi, and drove it across the yard and into the shed. With the headlights on, he was able to steer into a dark corner, and then cover the car with a boat canvas. He gave the area a final search, kicking dust over the bloodstains that the two bodies had left behind. Then he walked back to his car to begin a slow, careful search along the road that climbed up the hill.

He was almost hoping that he would find Cindy dead. He didn't want to think that she had betrayed him. He couldn't bring himself to admit that a cocktail waitress had outsmarted him.

18

They were exhausted when they dragged them-selves back aboard *Cane Maiden*.

The afternoon of snorkeling over the Indians had passed by quickly, lost in chasing schools of sunnies and angelfish through the branches of coral. Jeanne had begged to stay for just one more hour, and Bill had felt more energetic than he could remember.

"What's the rush?" he had asked Howard when Howard and Marilyn suggested that it was time to call it a day.

"We've got a long night ahead of us," Howard had answered with a wink. "Dancing 'til dawn." Reluctantly, Jeanne and Bill had followed their friends to the dinghy. It was only when they were motoring back to the yacht that they realized how tired they were.

"You don't feel it while you're in the water," Bill had explained, flexing his aching shoulders. When they pulled alongside, Howard could hardly lift himself up to the deck.

"You'll never make it through dinner," Marilyn teased him. "We'll have to carry you down to your cabin."

"Bull! I'm up for a big night ashore," Howard

boasted. He snapped a lens onto his camera. "Let's get everyone together. We're going to want to remember this day."

He moved them about the deck to line them up with the most spectacular backgrounds. They shuffled about, following his directions, and then forced lively, excited poses while he twisted them into focus.

"We're really going to do the town tonight," he promised as he set the camera back into the case. He swiveled his hips in an exaggerated reggae beat.

There was a moment of silence while they tested the strength left in their limbs. It was Jeanne who announced, "I'm up for it!" Her glance to Bill was almost a challenge. "I don't get many opportunities for fun. I want to make the most of it."

"I'd die if I stepped on a dance floor," Marilyn protested.

Bill was still reading Jeanne. Then he told Marilyn, "I guess we ought to keep these two party animals company."

"Get some drinks started," Howard ordered the women. "Bill and I have to put the sails up."

Steve came up on deck as soon as he heard the halyards squeaking through the blocks. He watched the sails flutter and felt the boat swinging into the wind.

"You taking her in?" he asked Howard.

"Yeah! I'll need you to snag the mooring."

"Maybe your friend should snag the mooring. You might need me in the cockpit."

Howard was about to tell the young captain that

150

he wouldn't be needing any help. Then he remembered the morning's near disaster. "Okay," he nodded.

Bill went forward to crank in the anchor. Howard started the engine and eased forward, slacking the anchor chain. He used the engine to keep the boat into the wind until Bill had the anchor secured on deck. Then he pointed the boat across the wind to fill the sails, and killed the power. She heeled to port as she caught a starboard reach, and began driving northward toward the shape of Tortola which filled the horizon.

There was a scream from below, followed by hysterical laughter. Marilyn raised up through the hatch holding a tray of rum painkillers. "That was Jeanne in the shower. Apparently she prefers her water hot." She brought the drinks up on deck and then settled on the bench next to Howard. Bill sprawled on the bench across the cockpit, and watched the bow wave racing past along the rail.

"Best day I've had in a long time," he told his friend. He raised his glass in toast. "I've got to hand it to you, Howard. You certainly do know how to play."

"Day's just begun," Howard answered with a mischievous wink. "And this is only the first day of the week."

Steve tossed down his drink, set the glass down and started forward toward his quarters. "Call me when we get close to the sea wall." Howard and Bill watched him until he disappeared down the hatch.

"Son-of-a-bitch doesn't know how to be pleasant," Howard told Bill.

151

Bill nodded. "Yeah, something is bothering him. But let's not let it bother us."

"I'll drink to that," Marilyn said.

Howard frowned at them, and then his face broke into a smile. "Fuck him!" he agreed. "I'm having too much fun to care."

It took Howard just one tack to bring *Cane Maiden* into the harbor, and another to line her up with the mooring. Steve returned to the cockpit just as they were beginning their approach.

"You want me to kill some sail?"

Howard agreed, and he watched while Steve rolled in the genoa and dropped the spanker. Then he turned into the channel between the moored boats, reached up until they were at the float they had left in the morning. Howard swung into the wind, and when the boat stopped, Bill was able to reach over the bow and pick up the mooring line.

Howard strutted away from the wheel. "What do you think?" he asked the captain.

"Okay," Steve said, refusing to compliment the perfect approach. "Long as nobody got killed."

They took turns in and out of the head as they dressed for a casual dinner. Then Steve raised the dock on his radio, and summoned the launch that would take them ashore. As the sun was turning to red across the harbor, they settled down to dinner on the veranda of a waterfront cafe.

"To the good life," Howard proclaimed, raising his cocktail. He leaned toward Bill. "To hell with the big city. Maybe we ought to pack it in, move down here."

Bill smiled at the thought. A pleasant dream,

but nothing that he could take seriously. "Do they need teachers on Tortola?"

"There are other things you could do besides teach school," Jeanne cut in.

"Damn right there are," Howard chimed. "You can do anything you want."

Bill still wasn't taking him seriously. But Jeanne was pushing her husband toward a decision and wouldn't let the opportunity pass. "Maybe Howard can help you. Make some suggestions. Get you some introductions."

"Be happy to," Howard offered.

Marilyn was suddenly apprehensive. She couldn't let Howard dangle empty promises in front of his friend, or let Bill and Jeanne pin their hopes on his empty boasting. "Hey, I thought this was going to be a big night on the town. It's starting to sound serious."

"I am serious," Howard persisted.

"It's important to us," Jeanne told Marilyn.

Marilyn threw her husband a warning glance. "I don't know, Howard. Are you sure this is the right time for straight talk?"

He understood her meaning. He was the one who didn't want to air his problems in front of his friend. She was warning him that if they talked, the conversation would have to be honest.

"No. You're right. We're all on vacation. Plenty of time for this later, when we get back."

Jeanne's displeasure was as obvious as Bill's relief.

Howard raised his glass again. "Tonight, the only subject is reggae dancing!"

19

After dinner, they followed the rhythmic music to the open porch of a loud cafe, and then followed the laughter up a flight of wooden stairs to a room that was jammed with boaters. Howard flashed a tip at the waiter, and followed him to a table at the edge of the dance floor. A bank of amplifiers, aimed directly at them, made conversation nearly impossible, so they lost themselves in the island rhythm. Howard jumped up to dance, and when Marilyn didn't follow, he turned to Jeanne. She was up eagerly, and in an instant was in his arms, rocking across the floor in the shuffling dance step. Howard broke from her, and challenged her with an exaggerated spin. Jeanne answered with a sashay of her own, bringing a wide grin to his face.

"Let's show these amateurs how it's done," he shouted above the music when they came back together. "Let's kick ass!" He pushed her away, into the center of the crowd, and then gyrated toward her to the tempo of the music. Jeanne fashioned her own step, and moved toward him provocatively. They met in a wild spin that cleared the other dancers back and gave them the middle of the floor.

Finding himself the center of attention, Howard

rose to the occasion, passing Jeanne under his arm, and then shuffling slowly under hers. Jeanne took the cue and writhed around him, her eyes closed and her head bobbing with the beat. "Hey," Howard called, as he led her on a pass around the audience they had created, "I didn't know white women could dance like that."

"I'm full of surprises," she answered, and she improvised another spin to prove her point.

He nodded toward their table. "C'mon. Let's get those dead asses up on their feet." They did a jerky stroll over to the table, where Howard scooped up Marilyn, and Jeanne dragged Bill out of his chair.

Marilyn fell into step with her husband. "Howard, you idiot," she whispered through her laughter, "you'll kill yourself. I'm going to have to bury you at sea."

"With full military honors," he answered as he threw her into a spin.

Bill managed the first few turns with Jeanne, but then laughed helplessly as she marched away from him with one hand on a thrust-out hip. "I can't keep up with you."

"Damn right you can't." Her tone was more serious than humorous. "But you better try."

The song ended, and they fell back into their chairs. Howard gulped for air, and then tossed down his rum punch to quench his thirst. Bill complimented Jeanne on her dancing. "You're going to have to give me lessons," he said.

Marilyn fanned herself with the menu. "Where the hell are those 'cool tropical breezes?' " Howard signaled the waiter for another round of drinks.

They were being set on the table when the band leader shouted, "Limbo."

"That's my cue," Howard cried. He reached his hand out for Marilyn.

She shook her head. "Not on your life. Where am I going to find a chiropractor on this damn island?"

Jeanne was already out of her chair. "Let's go for it," she challenged Howard, taking his hand and leading him toward the line of couples that was forming in front of the bamboo bar. "Let's kick ass." She never glanced back at Bill.

"You're sure you don't want to try this?" Bill offered Marilyn. "It looks like fun."

"Are you planning on winning?" she asked.

"Hell no."

She smiled and nodded. "Okay. Just for laughs."

They shuffled forward with the line, and then leaned back on their heels as they danced under the bar. At the starting height, it was a simple maneuver that left everyone in high spirits. The line danced easily under the bar at its second height, with only two of the couples knocking it off its pins. They all groaned when it was set still lower, and this time a dozen couples failed the test.

"Now it's getting interesting," Howard called to Marilyn and Bill when the bar was dropped down to within three feet of the floor.

"Now it's getting impossible," Marilyn told Bill.

Half the couples dropped out, some upsetting the bar and others collapsing onto the floor as they tried to balance down low. Howard and Jeanne passed easily, keeping up their dance rhythm as they slithered under. Bill was able to glide through, but he slowed as Marilyn struggled to wiggle beneath.

"Why do I think that half of these people are looking up my dress?" she asked Bill as they circled for their next pass.

"Probably because they are," he told her.

The bar went down another notch, and one after another the couples failed the test. Howard and Jeanne struggled a bit, but still got by with plenty of clearance. Bill's knees seemed too high as he started through, but once he slipped them under, he had an inch of space to work with. Marilyn's knees made it under, bringing a howl of approval from the merrymakers as her skirt slipped up around her waist. But there was a collective groan when it became obvious that her chest wasn't going to clear. The bar lifted as it rolled up the underside of her breasts and then slipped off its pins. She toppled onto her back as the bamboo rod clattered down on top of her.

She acknowledged the applause as Bill led her to the edge of the crowd. "A noble effort," he teased. "If there's a lechery prize, you've got it won."

There were four couples left when they set the bar down to within two feet of the floor. The fallen dancers moved in close to cheer the surviving couples. The band leader held up the prize, a cheap trophy with its comical figure leaning backwards at a ridiculous angle.

"We're going to win that sucker," Howard promised Jeanne, the laughter gone from his expression.

She rubbed her hands down the sides of her

skirt, which was already pasted to her legs. Then she kicked off her shoes. "We can make it," she said confidently.

The first pair started under to wild shouting and rhythmic clapping, and were halfway through when they fell in unison onto their backs. A sigh of disappointment squeezed from the crowd, followed by a round of applause.

"I don't think anyone can get under that," Bill laughed toward Marilyn.

"Howard will," she said, with no hesitation. "For his sake, I just hope to God no one else does."

"He's having fun," Bill reminded her.

"He always does," she answered joylessly, "as long as he's the one who's making it under the bar."

Another couple started under, wide legged, their backs nearly resting on their heels. They struggled for balance, inching forward until their chins were at the bar. Then they ducked their heads under and stood on the other side. There was a wild explosion of applause.

"That's our competition," Howard whispered to Jeanne. She nodded in recognition of the enemy.

The third pairing started under, but hit the bar almost immediately. They stood for an instant, shaking their heads, and then looked up smiling into the roar of applause from their friends. Then the bar was reset for Howard and Jeanne. The band raised its volume and the circle of onlookers drew a tighter noose.

They moved forward, dancing to the tempo, leaning back carefully as they approached. Their faces were set as seriously as a doctor's reaching for the scalpel. Side by side they inched to the bar, their legs spreading to balance their bodies, which were cantilevered backward over their heels. Their knees slipped under, the bar wobbling as it was touched. Howard sucked in his stomach, his midsection undulating around the curve of the bamboo. Jeanne froze as her breast tipped against the barrier. The bar rose, and then settled back into position. Their heads ducked and they danced through to the other side.

There was a roar of approval as Jeanne and Howard embraced. "Way to go," Bill shouted. He turned to Marilyn. "This is exciting."

"This is combat," she answered, nodding her head toward Howard. "Total war."

Bill noticed that his friend's expression was taut. There was a cold glint in his eyes. Jeanne was leaning in close to him, inhaling his determination, unaware that her skirt was bunched up to her waist. Her blouse was soaked against her skin, showing more of her body than she liked to reveal. They rocked to the tempo as the bar was set down another two inches and their competitors lined up for their approach.

The other couple dropped close to the floor, their motions more lithe than Howard and Jeanne's had been. They danced forward, their knees trembling under the strain as they slipped under. They danced easily, passing their thighs and then their torsos safely under. The bar was up to their chin when the man's feet suddenly lost traction. He struggled to keep them together as he balanced with his hair touching the floor, but they slid slowly out of control. He tried for a final thrust past the bar, but his footing gave out, and he settled spread-eagled on the floor, pounding with his fists in mock frustration. The crowd cheered, and the couple's friends rushed forward to rescue them.

The man turned towards Howard. "It's all yours," he smiled.

"You bet your ass it is," Howard answered through clenched lips. He glanced at Jeanne. "Ready?"

Her expression was as tense as his. She stared at the bar almost in rage.

There was no music in their movement as they moved toward the challenge. Howard's face flushed as he leaned back, his weight leveraging an enormous force against his knees. Beads of perspiration glistened on his forehead and across his chest as his shirt rode up. When Bill stole a glance at Marilyn, her fist was pressed to her lips in genuine fear. Jeanne's blouse had slipped up to her chin, revealing her bra which was nearly transparent against her wet skin. Her body was still as she kept herself from breathing. The howling room went dead in a steamy silence, the staccato of the steel drums the only sound.

They twisted their knees outward, flattening them under the barrier. Then they edged forward in short, nearly palsied movements. A single pair of hands began clapping the tempo and then others joined in. Howard sucked in his gut, which seemed to be sliding along the underside of the bar as he moved ahead. Jeanne inched forward, until her breasts were the obvious barrier.

She rolled her shoulders, contorting and then flattening her figure. There was a collective gasp

160

as her breasts passed underneath. Howard and Jeanne were both struggling for balance with the bar across their throats. Jeanne turned her head, her cheek touching the floor as she slipped her face free. Howard kept staring upward at the barrier, tipping his face back as his weight rose onto his toes. His forehead cleared and he fell forward, catching himself an instant before his knees reached the floor. He sprung up, took Jeanne's hand and lifted her slowly to her feet.

The room exploded with screams of approval. Bill rushed forward, lifted Jeanne in his arms and swung her in a circle. Howard stood aside, trying to restart his breathing. Lost back in the crowd which had surged forward, Marilyn struggled to keep from crying.

Jeanne rushed to Howard and threw her arms around him. "We did it," she yelled into his face. "We're one hell of a team."

He nodded in agreement. But he was already looking over her shoulder at the trophy that the band leader was carrying toward them. Holding it high above his head, he led Jeanne through the crowd, cheerfully accepting the handshakes and back slaps that were lavished on him.

"I guess I still have it," he announced to Marilyn when he reached the table.

"You've still got it," she answered, circling her finger by the side of her head. "Only a genuine nut would damn near kill himself for a bowling trophy." She smiled, grateful that he had won. Winning was the only thing that would keep him laughing.

"I must have been quite a sight out there,"

Jeanne said, realizing that her clothes had been in disarray when she had gone under the bar.

Bill laughed. "You left a trail of horny men. Me included. I hope your back doesn't act up before we get back to the boat."

"Damn, but I got a kick out of winning."

She leaned forward to examine the trophy. "That's yours," Howard said, sliding it in front of her. "I couldn't have won it without you."

20

Jeanne and Howard walked arm and arm toward the launch dock, carrying the trophy between them. They explained their triumph to the launch captain as they climbed aboard and shared a seat in the stern. Bill and Marilyn sat forward, facing their triumphant partners.

"I think a round of drinks is in order as soon as we're back aboard," Howard announced to general sounds of approval. "Then I think we ought to mount this thing right on top of the compass binnacle, so our smartass captain can see just who he's dealing with."

The launch pilot smiled at the suggestion. "Steve giving you a hard time?" he asked.

"No, not at all," Bill answered in defense of the young captain. "He just takes his job seriously."

"Too damn seriously," Howard contradicted. "I keep waiting for him to pull out a cat-o'-nine-tails." He laughed uproariously at his own joke.

"He's a fine sailor," the pilot said. "The best we've got."

"Not when I'm in town," Howard told him.

They were approaching *Cane Maiden*, which was completely darkened except for the single anchor light.

"Looks like he's already turned in," the pilot noticed. Then he asked, "You folks going out early tomorrow?"

"First thing," Howard answered, "for a five day swing around the islands. But tonight, we're going to celebrate."

The engine was doused as they pulled alongside, and Marilyn noticed the complete silence of the harbor. She could hear the small waves lapping against the wooden strakes. Howard's voice would carry like a pistol shot. "Maybe we ought to turn in, too," she tried. "We've only got a few hours until morning."

"Nonsense," Howard protested as he scampered aboard. "We've got some celebrating to do." He reached down and took Jeanne's hand as she jumped aboard. Bill held the launch in close for Marilyn and then stepped up onto the deck. The engine droned and the launch pulled away, headed back toward the pier.

Howard pulled open the pilothouse hatch. "I'll fix the drinks." Jeanne followed at his heels. Marilyn and Bill fell into line, headed below to gather around the saloon table.

Howard blinked in the darkness below deck and fumbled for the light switch. "Where the hell is that damn lamp?" he mumbled.

"There's one over here," Jeanne answered. She began to feel her way across the cabin toward the navigation table.

They were startled when a beam of light fired from the forward end of the saloon, and glared blindingly into their faces.

"Stay right there," Steve Berlind's voice ordered

out of the darkness.

"What in hell . . ." Howard protested, trying to block the light with his hand.

The beam pointed up the ladder and illuminated Marilyn and Bill.

"You two get down here." Then it slipped back to Howard and Jeanne. "Just do what you're told, and no one gets hurt."

"Goddammit," Howard snapped. He took one step forward and then pulled to an abrupt halt. He could make out two figures in the back glow of the flashlight. One of them was his captain, and he was pointing an automatic pistol straight into Howard's face.

Bill stepped carefully down to the lower deck and slid close to Jeanne. "What's this all about?" he asked calmly.

"This is what it's all about," Berlind whispered, brandishing the gun. "I'm giving the orders, and you're doing exactly what I tell you."

"Why, you little prick . . ." Howard cursed. He started forward, reaching toward the gun. He saw the light beam dart across the overhead. By the time he saw the flashlight swinging toward him, it was too late to block it. The heavy case blasted against his forehead. His knees buckled, and he staggered backward, falling into Marilyn's arms.

"Jesus," she screamed.

Bill jumped forward and caught his friend before he could fall. "For God's sake." He glared at Steve, but found the gun now pointing directly into his own eyes.

"Any one of you tries a stupid stunt like that,

and you're gonna get a lot of people killed," Steve warned. He focused on Howard who was touching the bloody gash on his forehead with his fingertips. "You, I'd enjoy wasting. I don't like loudmouths." Then he scanned the others. "It doesn't mean shit to me whether you're dead or alive. Just as long as no one gets in my way. You understand?"

Their eyes were locked on him, but no one answered.

He looked at Bill. "Keep everyone calm. Everyone follows orders and you'll all get out of this alive. Make sure your dumb friend . . ." he nodded toward Howard, "stays in line. I ain't gonna say this again."

"What's going on?" Bill demanded.

Steve shook his head. "That's none of your fucking business. I'm not answering questions. I'm giving orders."

He scanned their frightened faces to be sure that his message had gotten through. "Okay, now. I want all of you to go back into your cabins. Nice and slow, so that I don't get spooked."

They remained frozen in confusion.

"Move," he snapped, raising the pistol toward Howard's face. "Now!"

Bill took Howard's shoulder and nudged him toward his cabin. Marilyn opened the door and slid in behind her husband. Then Bill turned to Jeanne and steered her toward their cabin.

Steve turned to the figure beside him. "Lock them in," he ordered.

Cindy Camilli stepped out of the shadows and moved toward the open stateroom doors. She stopped when she saw her prisoners waiting in the doorways.

"All the way back," Steve ordered, waving the gun.

They retreated from the doorways, piling up at the after bulkheads of the cabins. Cindy moved toward them and closed the doors in their faces. They heard her slide the dead bolts, locking them inside.

Steve's voice called through the louvered doors. "Anyone sticks a head out before I tell you, and I'll blow it off. You want to see the sun rise just stay inside and keep your mouths shut."

They heard footsteps on the ladder as their two captors climbed up into the cockpit, leaving them below.

Jeanne clutched Bill's arm. "What are we going to do?"

"Exactly what he says," he answered. "As long as he's got that gun."

She was trembling. "What are they going to do to us?"

"Nothing," he told her. He put his arm around her and pulled her close. "They're not going to do anything as long as we don't threaten them."

"Bill, I'm scared."

"I am too. But we're going to be all right. If we keep our heads, we'll be all right."

"I'm going to kill that motherfucker," Howard was mumbling as Marilyn pressed a handkerchief to his forehead.

"For God's sake, Howard, he has a gun." She lifted the handkerchief. "This isn't too bad. You're bruised, but it's a small cut."

He knocked her hand away. "Little bastard

167

doesn't know who he's messing with."

"Jesus, Howard. Please don't do anything stupid. He could kill us all."

"You recognized the girl, didn't you? That fucking photographer I was talking to at the airport. Probably setting me up. Probably laughing at me the whole time."

"It doesn't matter, Howard. We have to follow their orders. They have a gun."

"Screw the gun. After I empty it into his head, I'm gonna shove it down her throat."

"Please, Howard . . ."

Marilyn was interrupted by a noise from above, the squeak of the halyards running through their blocks.

"What's that?"

Howard listened for an instant. "The son-of-a-bitch is putting up the sails."

On cue, he felt the deck moving under his feet as the boat began to swing on its mooring.

In the next cabin, Jeanne clutched at Bill. "What's happening?"

He listened carefully, and then felt the swing of the boat. "I think they're raising the sails."

"Now? At night?" Her voice was faint with terror. "Where are they taking us?"

He gestured for her to be quiet so that he could listen. There were footsteps overhead. Someone was walking forward.

"We're being kidnapped," Jeanne gasped, the words struggling against her near hysteria.

There was a metallic banging sound at the bow. Then he heard the mooring line snapping across the deck.

He and Jeanne lost their balance and fell into the bunk as the boat suddenly heeled to starboard. They heard Howard and Marilyn topple against the bulkhead that separated their two cabins. Then there was silence, broken only by the sound of the sea rushing past the hull next to their bunk.

Bill pulled himself up, and struggled up the sloping deck until he was leaning on the inside bulkhead. He tapped gently, and then called in a stage whisper. "Howard. What's going on?"

The cockiness was gone from Howard's voice when he answered hoarsely. "I think they're taking us out to sea."

MONDAY

21

Al Weston stepped up on the pontoon and lifted his big frame into the seat of the helicopter. He reached out to Johnnie Igoe, took the compact Uzi assault rifle that Johnnie had been carrying, and then the cloth bag of ammunition clips.

"Remember. If you find her, don't do nothing," Al said for the third time in the past half hour. "Just hang on to her until I get back."

Johnnie Igoe nodded impatiently. "Yeah, yeah. I got it. Don't worry." He was painfully thin, constantly in motion with nervous energy. His eyes darted from side to side as he talked, never quite focusing on the person he was talking to.

"I ain't worrying, Johnnie. But if she gets off this island then we all better start worrying. She's got a couple of million bucks with her."

"If she's on the island, she won't be gettin' off. Trust me."

"I trust you, Johnnie. That's why I brought you down here. It's just that if you find her, I don't want you bustin' her up. Okay?" Al had always trusted Johnnie Igoe. The man was as loyal as a hunting dog. But he also had a nasty streak.

"Okay," Johnnie promised, "but it would help if I knew what she looked like. That photo ain't worth a damn if she's wearing clothes."

"The picture ain't that important. She's a young, good-looking girl carrying an aluminum suitcase. That shouldn't be too hard to spot."

Paul Canavan, the helicopter pilot they had hired, helped Al stow the gun and ammunition under the seat belt in the tiny back seat. Then he showed his passenger how to lock his shoulder harness.

"We'll start to the west, looking for anything headed toward St. Thomas or Puerto Rico," Al told his pilot while he was being buckled in. "Then we'll swing south around St. Croix."

"There's a lot of boats out there," Paul said.

"Then we should stop talking and get going," Al snapped angrily.

Johnnie Igoe backed away as the starter whined and the rotors began to swing slowly. He was back in the car by the edge of the field when the helicopter kicked up a swirl of dirt and struggled into the air.

It had been a long night for Al. He had been on the telephone constantly with Walter Linz, out to the airport to meet the plane that carried Igoe and two other men that Linz had sent as reinforcements, and then back to his hotel for an angry strategy meeting. They had all been tense, realizing that their chances of finding Cindy weren't good, and that the odds grew longer with every passing hour.

"She could be anywhere," Igoe had protested when he heard the assignment and saw the list of nearly a hundred hotels and rooming houses that Weston wanted checked. "Hell, with an operation like this, chances are she was off the island an hour after she took the goods."

The low point had been when Johnnie had tossed the photo of Cindy on the coffee table. It was the only picture they had been able to find, a publicity glossy from Cindy's brief career as a topless dancer, that focused on her figure rather than her face.

"For chrissake," Al had screamed. "Is that the best you could find? There's a thousand girls in the dance halls that look like that."

"That's what I told Walter," Igoe had agreed. "The only way you'd recognize her is if she shows up at the airport with her tits hanging out. And that ain't likely."

Of the four men, Al was the only one who would recognize Cindy at a glance. So it made sense for him to stay on Tortola to cover the airport. But he had already figured out that there were two likely scenarios. In the first, she was taken away by people she didn't even know, who had pulled off the robbery without her help. In that case, she was already dead. In the second, she was working with the people who had made off with Walter Linz's money. In that case, she probably wouldn't be walking up to an airline ticket counter to buy a seat on a commercial flight. They would have planned a safer escape, probably aboard one of the many boats that left the island every day. Given the odds, Al had decided that he should be the one to check out the boats, leaving the others to watch the airports and marinas, and canvass the hotels.

"Our chances of finding her are slim to nil," Igoe had concluded.

Al had lost his patience. He picked up the telephone and handed it to Johnnie. "Why don't you call Walter and tell him that his two million bucks ain't worth looking for."

"Hey, I was just saying . . ."

"Don't say anything. Just start looking. I know it's a long shot, but finding Cindy is the only chance we got."

Johnnie had gone out to make arrangements for chartering the helicopter. The other two men that Linz had sent had split the list of hotels and started visiting them. Al had gone out to a pay phone to brief Walter on the steps they were taking.

"I think you've made the right decisions," Walter Linz had answered calmly. "I agree with you that Cindy probably wouldn't have betrayed us. She's probably at the bottom of the channel. But she is our only lead. I think you're doing the right thing by looking for her."

Linz had indicated that he would do everything possible at his end of the call. He already had people out talking to Cindy's friends to see if she had made any new acquaintances. One of his people had given the super in her building a hundred dollars, and was in the process of searching her apartment. "If anything turns up," he had promised Al, "I'll leave a message at your hotel saying 'call for news.' You can get back to me."

Through it all, Al had been amazed at how composed Walter Linz had remained. Hell, it was a lot of money. He had expected his employer to fly off into a rage. But Linz had never raised his voice. He had listened, analyzed and then acted. Their discussions had been logical and unemotional. Slowly, it had dawned on Al that while a

176

couple of million dollars was a vast fortune to him, it was by no means an extraordinary amount to Walter. Obviously, he did lots of big deals and had already discounted his risks. He wanted every conceivable step taken to recover his money. He wanted to find out where his procedures had broken down, and who had betrayed him. When he found out, he would certainly take corrective action to make sure that it never happened again. But what Weston had realized was that Linz was running a very sizable operation that did lots of business at many locations. He would be careful not to jeopardize his entire empire by overreacting to disastrous results from any one of his deals.

The helicopter climbed out of the darkness into morning light that was beginning to fill the sky. It cleared the western tip of Tortola and raced out over the narrow channel that separated the island from St. John. There were two boats, already underway, leaving white trails in the sea below. Al signaled the pilot to dive down for a closer look.

What was he looking for? Cindy, of course. If he could catch her out on deck or in the process of scampering into hiding, the link to the money would be instantly reconnected. But that was a long shot. The helicopter's engines gave warning of its arrival. If Cindy were alive, she wouldn't stay out on deck waiting to be identified.

Maybe a careless mistake. Maybe a boat would tip its guilt by taking sudden, evasive turns. Maybe someone would bring a gun up topside to warn him away.

Or, maybe a familiar face. Al knew many of

the Florida operators who dabbled in contraband, and who were close enough to Walter Linz's operations to learn about the payment that Cindy was carrying, and perhaps the merchandise that she had been sent to acquire. If one of them were racing away from Tortola, hours after the transaction had been attacked, the coincidence would warrant further investigation.

At a minimum, he was looking for the names of the boats that were generally lettered across their sterns. He could check the names with the marina operators back on Tortola, and identify any yachts that had been in harbor the day before. Then he could follow up, finding out who owned or chartered the boat, where it had come from and where it was heading.

As they pulled close to the first boat, Al shook his head and waved the pilot away. It was an open day sailor, probably no more than twenty feet long, with two couples in the cockpit. Certainly not the kind of boat that would attempt a long, deep-water voyage, nor be used to transport a team of professional thieves.

The second boat was more interesting, a forty-foot, flying bridge cruiser, rigged for deep-sea fishing. She had plenty of cabin space below, good speed, and the sea-keeping capabilities that would easily carry her to Puerto Rico, or even the southern Florida coast. The pilot eased up to her stern, and Al wrote down her name, *Miss T.* Her port of registry was San Juan.

They window-shopped along the port side, the loud popping of the rotors causing four men to scamper up from the pilothouse and into the cockpit for a gawking look at the helicopter. They were all in shorts and loud tropical sport shirts, appropriate attire for an overnight fishing party out of San Juan. There was nothing to cause Al even a moment of suspicion.

He took the battery powered bull horn that was clipped against his seat. "Hello." His greeting was returned with frantic waving. Then one of the men ducked down into the pilothouse and returned with a hailer of his own. "Hi," he called back. "How can we help you?"

"You boys coming out of Road Town?"

"No. San Juan. We been out all night."

"Catch anything?" Al asked.

"Not yet. But we have all day."

It all seemed completely natural. They were having a good time, and getting a big kick out of talking to a helicopter.

"You see anyone coming out of Road Town?"

The three figures in the loud shirts conferenced for a moment. "When?" their spokesman asked over his loud speaker.

"This morning. Maybe last night."

Another conference, and then the voice came back. "No, but we were north of here last night. We just came into the channel this morning."

"Thanks," Al answered, lifting his hand in front of Paul to indicate that he was finished with his conversation, and they could go back up to continue their search.

"You're welcome. Any time," came the fading voice from the cruiser, *Miss T.*

Al pointed ahead, signaling the pilot that he should close on St. John and then continue past, all the way up to St. Thomas.

Christ, he thought as he resumed scanning the horizon, he had no idea what was suspicious. The fishing party certainly seemed legitimate. The poles were in place, and rigged, and there were tackle boxes all over the deck. But if he were using a boat to take a hit squad and a couple of million dollars off an island, he'd probably make damn sure that it looked innocent. He'd probably outfit everyone in vacation garb, and maybe even put a fresh caught tuna on board to hold up as evidence. What was he expecting? Guys dressed in black suits with big bulges under their coats?

His fists clenched in frustration. Finding Cindy aboard one of the yachts cruising around the Drake Channel was probably going to be every bit as impossible as finding her at the bottom of the sea.

22

They were all alert to the sound of the footsteps on the ladder that came from the cockpit down to the pilothouse deck. Jeanne had been lying in the bunk, her eyes closed but her mind wide awake. Bill, who had spent the night sitting on the bunk's hard wooded edge, had been listening for any sound of activity from above. Marilyn hadn't even tried for sleep. She had sat up in her bunk throughout the night, her back propped against a pillow. Howard had paced back and forth endlessly for the two and a half strides it took to reach from the after bulkhead of the cabin to the locked door at its forward end.

They all heard the footsteps pause just outside their doors. Then they heard the dead bolts slide free, one after the other. The steps retreated quickly up the ladder, and then came Steve Berlind's clipped words.

"You can come out now. Get breakfast started. But stay below. Anyone sticks a head up through one of the hatches, and I'll blow it off. Understand? Stay below deck!"

Bill eased forward, opened the door and stepped out into an empty cabin. He staggered momentarily in the open space, having difficulty adjusting

181

to the slope of the deck. He was able to steady himself by grabbing the edge of the ice chest.

He heard the latch click on Howard's door, and watched the door ease open slowly and his friend's wide-eyed face peek around its edge. "What in hell . . ." Howard started, but Bill silenced him by raising a finger to his lips.

"Let's get the girls started on breakfast," he whispered to Howard. "Let them make a lot of noise. Meanwhile you and I will take inventory of everything down here. Everything that might be useful."

Howard nodded as he listened. Good idea, he thought. Inventory your assets before you decide on the best course of action. He leaned back into his cabin, and waved for Marilyn to join him.

"Cook something," Bill whispered to the two women. "They have to be hungry. Let them smell the coffee. And the bacon, if we have any. Talk! And bang some pots."

Marilyn nodded that she understood. Jeanne seemed too frightened to understand what her husband was saying, but she followed Marilyn's lead and began pulling things out of the ice chest. Bill gestured for Howard to start searching the saloon at the forward end of the pilothouse. Then he started at the rear, carefully opening each drawer of the navigation table.

He noticed that the back had been taken off the radio; he examined it carefully and saw that the power cord had been disconnected from the internal power supply. It was obvious that Steve had been busy while he was waiting for them to return from shore. He had disconnected the cord and probably stuffed it into his pocket. The radio would be useless until their captor replaced the cord.

The dividers were gone from the instrument drawer. There had been three pair, each with a sharp metal point for swinging an arc and measuring precise distances on the charts. Steve must have realized that they could be used like a stiletto, and had taken them away. Left behind were the parallel rulers and soft, plastic protractors that couldn't threaten anyone. There were manuals, bound volumes of star tables, and lists of radio and Loran frequencies. Nothing that could serve his purposes.

He crossed to the galley side. The pots and pans were still in place, but the two long kitchen knives were gone. The ice pick had been removed from inside the cover of the ancient ice chest. Even the heavy soup ladle was gone.

Bill looked forward to where Howard was searching. Howard threw up his hands in frustration. The entire pilothouse had been picked clean of everything heavy, hard or sharp. If they were tempted to confront the automatic pistol that Steve had waved in their faces the night before, it would have to be with their bare hands.

The coffee began to perk, and Marilyn tossed the sliced bacon on the skillet. Appetizing aromas filled the space.

Howard came aft. "We've got to do something," he whispered to Bill.

"We are doing something," Bill answered.

Howard looked in confusion at the domestic activities that surrounded him. Then he snapped,

"We have to get that gun away from them."

"First thing we have to do is get up on deck. Then we can start thinking about the gun."

Bill went to the ladder and climbed the first two steps. Then he called up, "You guys want something to eat?"

"Yeah." It was Steve's voice, hard and demanding. "Some coffee."

"Tell him to go fuck himself," Marilyn said. "I'm not his maid."

Bill put a quieting hand on her shoulder. "Okay," he called topside. "I'll be bringing it up. My head and shoulders will be coming up through the hatch."

There was a pause. Then Steve's voice answered. "No. One of the women can bring it up."

"Bastard," Marilyn hissed softly.

"I can't do that," Bill yelled. "They're afraid of the gun. It will have to be me, unless one of you wants to come down."

Another pause. Then Steve's voice. "Come up real slow."

He took two of the mugs and filled them with coffee. "Cream? Sugar?" he asked out loud while he was pouring.

"Jesus," Howard whispered, "what is this? A diner?"

But Marilyn was catching on to what Bill was doing. She put packets of sugar and a pitcher of milk on a tray next to the coffee mugs.

"One with cream," came Steve's voice.

"I'm coming up," Bill answered. He started carefully up the steps. "Turn that gun away, will you? We don't want any accidents."

"Just bring the coffee," Steve's voice snapped.

He pushed the tray through the hatch ahead of him, and then raised his head slowly. He was blinded by the bright blast of daylight and had to blink his eyes back into focus. The captain and the girl were sitting on the bench at the back end of the cockpit. Steve had one hand on the wheel. In the other, he held the pistol which was resting against his leg.

"Get it," Steve told Cindy. She jumped up, but then slowed cautiously as she moved toward Bill.

"Hold it out," Steve ordered. "Arm's length."

Bill stretched the tray toward the girl. She reached for it carefully, as if she expected it to snap on her like an animal trap. As soon as she had her fingers on the tray, she backed away quickly.

"Thanks," she mumbled.

"Don't mention it," Bill answered.

He looked around at the flat sea that was flying past them. *Cane Maiden* was on a reach, and probably making close to her best speed.

"Get back down below," Steve ordered.

Bill nodded and started down. Then he stopped, and suggested almost as an afterthought, "You want some breakfast?"

The girl looked up, eagerly accepting the offer.

"Yeah," Steve answered. Then he added suspiciously, "Same procedure. You tell me before you come topside."

"Right," Bill answered as he disappeared below.

He went straight to Howard. "They've got all the sails up. And there's some land off to the left.

In the distance. Looks like a big island."

Howard looked through the porthole and found the sun on their port side. "We're headed southwest," he figured. He dashed to the navigation table and found one of the charts. "St. Croix," he announced. "We're probably right about here."

Jeanne was looking over his shoulder. "Where are they taking us?" She was frightened at the expanse of wide open sea that lay ahead of them.

"Could be anywhere," Howard answered, waving his hand over the chart. "Maybe the Dominican Republic," he guessed as he pointed to the eastern end of Hispaniola. "Hell, they could be going all the way down to here." His finger dropped down to the islands off the coast of Venezuela.

"That's five hundred miles," Bill said.

Jeanne's hand flew to her mouth. "Why? Why are they taking us?"

Bill put an arm around her. "We don't know yet. But we're going to find out."

Marilyn began putting strips of bacon and scrambled eggs onto the plates. "Some vacation," she smirked. She looked at Bill. "You better tell them that I don't do windows." He smiled, realizing that Marilyn was doing better than any of them in keeping her composure. She put a fork on each plate. "I don't suppose there's any rat poison on board."

Bill took the two breakfasts. "I'm coming up."

Steve's voice answered, "Nice and slow. I want to see your hands before I see your face."

He lifted the plates through the hatch and then followed behind them into the sunlight. As Cindy came forward, he held them out to her. She snatched them away and retreated quickly to the after end of the cockpit.

"Can we come up on the foredeck?" Bill asked innocently. "After breakfast."

Steve's eyes narrowed with suspicion.

"We can come up through the greenhouse," Bill continued quickly. "And then go forward to the bow. We'll be right out in the open where you can see us. We can't cause you any trouble from all the way up on the bow."

"No way," Steve decided. Then he ordered, "Get below."

Bill saw that the gun was resting on Steve's lap while he held the coffee cup in his free hand.

"Look, it's pretty sick down there. We're all feeling queasy with the whole cabin tipped on an angle. It would help if we could come up for just a few minutes. Just for a breath of air."

Steve set his mug on the bench, and let his hand fall across the automatic weapon.

"You've got the gun," Bill pressed. "And we'll be out in the open in front of you. There's no way we can cause you a problem."

The girl looked from Bill to Steve. "It'd be okay, I guess. Wouldn't it?"

Steve didn't acknowledge her at all. He stared at Bill while his fingers fitted around the grip of the pistol. "I'll think about it," he decided. "Now get below."

Bill nodded, and then dropped back down into the cabin.

Marilyn had already spread the drop leaves on the gimballed table, and set out their breakfast.

Bill motioned them all forward and then slid onto one of the benches. They joined him around the table.

"What the hell is going on?" Howard demanded, leaning across towards Bill.

"I'm not sure," he said. "It doesn't make a lot of sense. I think the girl is more frightened than we are. I think she's more afraid of Steve than she is of us. She really jumped at the opportunity of having us up on deck."

"Bullshit," Howard snapped. "She's working with him. She's the one who locked us in our cabins."

"They're kids, Howard. I don't think they know what they're doing."

Jeanne's eyes widened. "Then they're not going to hurt us?"

"I don't think they want to hurt anyone," Bill told her.

Howard pointed to the red welt on his forehead. "Bastard tried to brain me last night. What do you mean, they don't want to hurt us?"

"You were attacking him," Marilyn reminded her husband.

Howard snarled. "Dammit! He was pointing a gun at me."

"Right!" Bill said. "He could have shot you. But he didn't. I think he's hoping that he won't have to shoot anyone. Look at what he did with the cabin. Took out anything that we might use as a weapon. If he was planning on shooting us, he wouldn't be worried about weapons. Or about us using the radio."

"Then why are they kidnapping us?" Jeanne begged.

There was a long silence. Then Bill admitted, "I don't know. That's what we have to find out."

They toyed with their breakfasts, too distracted to eat. Bill picked up the plates and carried them to the sink. Then he went to the bottom of the ladder.

"You want more coffee?" he called. "I'm coming up to get your plates."

"Why in hell are we waiting on them?" Howard demanded of Marilyn.

She held up a hand to silence him, and listened for the response that would come from the cockpit.

"Come up slowly," Steve's voice cautioned.

Bill lifted the coffee pot from the stove and started up. When his face broke out of the darkness, he saw Steve and the girl still seated on the rear bench. Steve's hand was still on the pistol.

"Why don't I refill the coffee, and then take the plates?"

Steve nodded to Cindy who lifted the cups as if they were live hand grenades and brought them to Bill.

He showed her the coffee pot. "Just hold them close. I'll pour."

"Be damn careful," Steve warned.

Bill filled the two mugs and Cindy retreated. "Okay, I can take the plates now."

He waited while Cindy stacked them and brought them forward.

"How about letting us up now? All the way forward. Just for a couple of minutes."

Steve nodded. "Yeah. Okay. Just come up slowly. One at a time. And I want to see everyone's hands first."

189

Bill clattered back down the steps. "We're going up on deck," he told his friends. He went forward to the saloon, jumped up on the ladder, and then pushed open the window of the greenhouse.

He turned to Jeanne. "You ready?"

She shook her head furiously. She was afraid to even look at their captors.

"Marilyn?"

She got up on the ladder next to Bill, and found that her face was already above deck level.

"Put your hands through." He took her by the waist and lifted her up through the open hatch. Howard then climbed up next to him and pulled himself out through the opening.

"Come on, Jeanne. You'll be all right. You don't want to stay down here alone." She reacted instantly to 'alone' and stood up next to Bill. He boosted her through, onto the deck and then he followed behind her. They sat in a tight circle on the high side of the deck, the women leaning against the greenhouse structure, while the men's backs were pressed against the lifeline.

"That has to be St. Croix," Howard said the instant Bill sat next to him. He looked at the island that had fallen back to their port quarter, and then up at the sun. "We're still heading southwest."

Marilyn wasn't paying attention to her husband. She was looking forward, gulping in great draughts of the onrushing breeze. But Jeanne was hanging on Howard's words. "What does that mean?"

"If he holds this heading, it means we're headed toward Venezuela." Her terror was immediate. "But he could turn at any point to another tack. Maybe westward, into Puerto Rico. Or eastward, toward the Leeward Islands."

"That's closer, isn't it?" Jeanne asked hopefully. A short trip seemed safer than a long one.

Howard nodded. Then he stole a glance aft, into the cockpit, and saw Steve and the photographer from the San Juan airport huddled together behind the wheel. "We've got to get that gun," he mumbled to Bill out of the corner of his mouth.

Bill nodded. "We will. Give it time."

"Dammit," Howard snapped, "we don't have time. We're getting further away with each minute."

"First, let's see if we can't win their confidence. Then, maybe, we can figure out what this is about."

Howard looked up at the sails, feigning disinterest in his captors. He leaned closer to Bill. "I already have it figured out."

Marilyn and Jeanne both snapped their attention to him.

"This has to be some kind of a drug deal. Those weren't cameras that little bitch was carrying. It was probably cash. She bought the drugs, and now we're sailing them out of the islands. Maybe south of Cuba and up into the Gulf. Or maybe we're rendezvousing with another boat. Or a sea plane."

The women thought, and then turned to Bill for his reaction.

"Could be," he agreed. "But why would they be taking us?"

"As cover," Howard answered instantly. "Figure it out. We're signed out of Road Town for five days of cruising. That means no one is going to be looking for us for five days. If they just took

191

the boat and left us on the beach, we'd have reported it. The authorities would be hunting for them right now."

Bill nodded. It made sense. But then he offered, "Except they could have dumped us during the night. Why do they need us alive?"

Jeanne joined the conversation. "In case someone comes near. Then they'd want us out on deck so everything would look normal."

"Right," Howard said, jumping on Jeanne's comment. "If there was a drug buy, it could be that the police are looking for them. Maybe the coast guard. We'd be out on the deck with our hired captain at the wheel. Just the way we're supposed to be. Everything would look normal."

"So he needs us as window dressing."

"Until he delivers the stuff," Howard agreed. But then he added morosely, "After that, he doesn't need us at all."

"Then he'll kill us," Jeanne suddenly realized. "He won't want any witnesses."

"That's why we can't wait around," Howard insisted. "We've got to take over this boat now, and get it headed back into Tortola."

Bill nodded toward the cockpit. "Except he's got the gun. And if we frighten him, he might make a mistake and use it."

"The longer we wait, the more dangerous it gets," Howard said.

Jeanne reached out to Howard and grabbed his arm. "What are we going to do?"

"We've got to rush the son-of-a-bitch and take the gun away from him."

Marilyn turned away abruptly. "Jesus, Howard.

Stop talking nonsense. When was the last time you disarmed a drug dealer?"

"We have to do something." Howard's voice was rising.

"We have to wait for an opportunity," Bill cautioned.

"We can't wait, dammit! We're sailing into our graves."

"Howard is right," Jeanne chastised her husband. "We have to do something." She looked hopefully to Howard, waiting to find out what the something might be.

23

Al Weston looked down on the approaches to San Juan harbor, and then turned to his pilot. "This is far enough," he yelled over the engine noise. "Let's swing south and do a turn around St. Croix." Paul Canavan nodded that he understood. The copter banked into a left turn and flew over the eastern edge of Puerto Rico before it moved back out over the sea.

There was no point in searching inside the harbor at San Juan, any more than there had been any reason to fly over Charlotte Amalie in St. Thomas. There were so many yachts in the big harbors that it was impossible to tell them apart. Besides, if they had already made port in St. Thomas or Puerto Rico, there would be no way to head them off. Once ashore, they could take commercial flights to any number of cities along the eastern seaboard of the United States. Or they could take an executive jet to just about anywhere.

That's what Al would have done if he had been on the other side. Get off Tortola immediately, and head for either St. Thomas or San Juan. Then take the first plane out, before Walter Linz had time to react and cover the airports.

It was as close to being the perfect theft as he could imagine. The only identifiable people were Cindy, her taxi driver, and the courier. Two of them were dead and the other was missing. The merchandise was untraceable. The bearer bonds could be cashed in by anyone, at any time, no questions asked. And the uncut diamonds that the bonds were intended to purchase were a commodity. Finding them in the New York or Amsterdam diamond markets would be like trying to find a particular grain of wheat in a silo. Even the location was genius. Walter liked to use the Caribbean islands for his transactions because there were hundreds of points of entry and exit, and lax customs geared more to accommodating tourists than stopping contraband. You could bring anything in from anywhere and out to anywhere without raising any suspicions. Now, the thieves enjoyed all the advantages that Linz had so carefully arranged.

His only hope was finding Cindy on Tortola, grabbing her at the airport or one of the marinas, or finding her aboard a fleeing boat. He had the island covered, and he was checking on the boats that were still at sea. There was nothing more he could do.

For the past three hours he had been darting about the western approaches, swooping down on any boats that might be used for an escape. There had been several of them surrounding St. John and traveling the southern shore of St. Thomas around Charlotte Amalie. And several more, running between St. Thomas and Puerto Rico. He had focused on the power cruisers because that was the kind of boat he would have chosen himself.

Something big enough so that it could put to sea in any kind of weather, and fast enough so that it could make one of the major ports in a few hours. Why would you choose a sailing yacht that would have to tack back and forth, and might slow to a crawl if the wind died?

Only two of the boats had reported that they were coming out of Road Town. They were the least likely targets, because someone escaping with Walter Linz's money probably wouldn't admit that they had just left the scene. He would check the names of the others when he got back to port to see if any of them had been in the harbor the previous day. If he found anyone who had lied about being in Road Harbor, it would certainly be worth a follow-up.

As he flew south, there were far fewer boats than he had flown over during the morning. He was leaving the cruising grounds behind him and heading out into the vast openness of the Caribbean. Anyone out this far was probably keeping a commercial schedule.

The pilot pointed a bit to the west of dead ahead. In the haze, Al could make out a small tanker riding low in the water, coming toward him. He shook his head. No point in heading toward her. The fortune he was looking for would fit in a suitcase. It didn't need a deep draft vessel. Besides, this one was heading toward the Virgins, not trying to run away.

To the east of his heading, he could make out the outline of an island, and see the first hint of its green hills. "St. Croix?" he yelled at the pilot. Paul nodded. Then he tapped his finger on the glass of the fuel gauge, which was registering half full. Al nodded that he understood. They would continue to the west of St. Croix, swing south of the island, and then come back up over the eastern passage. That should bring them back to Road Town with a safety margin left in the tanks.

24

They had gone in silent procession, back down through the greenhouse and into the cabin below. Howard and the two women were at the table, hunched close together over cold glasses of fruit punch. Bill was carefully examining the back of the radio, hoping that he might be able to use the cord from one of the lamps to reconnect it to a power source.

"You're wasting your time," Howard mumbled. "We have to get that pistol before we can call anyone." Then he explained to the wives, "Someone tries to board us while he still has the pistol, and we'll find ourselves in the middle of a gunfight."

Bill walked back to the table and squeezed in beside Jeanne.

"I think I can jury-rig it when we need it."

"Howard says it won't do us any good," Jeanne snapped. "What are we waiting for?"

He answered calmly, knowing that she was becoming more frightened with each passing minute. "I guess we're waiting for him to get careless. If we can convince him that we're not a threat, he may let himself get distracted."

Howard slammed his fist on the table. "Dammit,

Bill, these people are professionals. They're not going to let themselves get distracted. What we've got to do is find some way to lure him down below. And then jump the little bastard."

Bill had thought of the same thing. The only problem was that they would have only one chance. One desperate lunge at a man who was holding an automatic pistol. All he needed was the fraction of a second it would take to pull the trigger. And then one of them might be dead.

"You get him talking," Howard continued, "and I'll grab for his wrist. If I can get the gun pointed away, then there's four of us to take him down."

Easily said, Bill thought. But Howard had moved toward Steve the night before, and Steve had been much too quick for him. There was no reason to believe that anything would change.

Marilyn had come to the same conclusion. "What are you talking about, Howard? Something you saw on television? The last thing we need is you trying karate on a guy with a machine gun."

"No, he's right," Jeanne said angrily. "We have to try something." She looked at Bill. "Are you just going to wait for him to decide it's time to kill us?"

In the cockpit, Steve had left Cindy at the wheel while he let out the sails. The wind was shifting around to the east and blowing a bit stronger because of a storm he was keeping well clear of. But as soon as he had filled the sails they had begun to flutter. Cindy hadn't been able to hold the heading, and now *Cane Maiden* was heading up and losing power. Steve snatched the wheel away from her and let the bow fall off.

"I'm sorry," she said, as soon as he had everything settled. "I don't know what I'm doing."

"It's all right. We're okay."

She sat back on the bench and pulled her knees up to her chest. "You decided where we're heading?"

He nodded. "Yeah. There's a storm coming up from the southeast. As soon as we're around it, I'm going to turn her and head for St. Kitts. I got friends down there. From the charter fleets. We should be able to get some help, no questions asked."

"I still think we should go back," Cindy said.

"We went through that last night."

"They're not going to stop looking for me. They'll keep looking until they know I'm dead."

"It's a big ocean," Steve said. "Anyone who saw us sailing out will say we were headed southwest. Where we're really going is southeast. So it's going to take them a lot of looking. All we have to do is lay low for a couple of months. Then we're set for the rest of our lives."

"They'll never let us spend it," she warned. "I'm telling you, I know these people."

"They can't stop us from spending it. It's all untraceable. Hell, we could spend it in one of their joints and they'd never even know."

"I'm scared," she said for the hundredth time since Steve had come up with their plan.

"Cindy, listen to me. A couple of million dollars just fell into our laps. When you came aboard last night, we were just a couple of losers. I was taking orders from that loudmouth, and all you had was enough to get yourself back to where you ran from in the first place. Now we're rich. All we have to do is gut it out for another couple of days. And then we're home free. Nobody knows you're alive. Nobody knows we're together. Nobody knows we have the money. It's like they lost it, and we found it."

"I didn't know what to do. I wanted to bring it back. But I was scared. I didn't know anyone to go to. Except you."

"Why would you bring it back? If you brought it back, what would they have done? Tell you you're a sweet kid, and given you an extra couple of hundred? We've been losers too long, Cindy. Now we're going to be winners."

It all made sense. It all sounded easy. Except Steve had never seen Al Weston when he was mad. Steve didn't know what happened to people who crossed the thugs she had worked for. They ended up in the trunks of cars with holes through their heads. And those were the lucky ones. She had heard about a girl who was sold to one of the Colombians for the six hundred dollars she had stolen, and taken down to a whorehouse in the jungle. For six hundred dollars! What would they do with someone who walked off with a couple of million?

"You hear something?" Steve was suddenly alert, turning slowly to search the horizon.

"What?" Cindy asked. "I don't hear anything."

"A boat. Maybe a plane. It sounds like an engine."

She listened carefully, and then heard a noise coming over the stern. She turned, using her hands as a sun visor. "There!" she said. "It's a plane."

He followed her pointing finger and saw the

small shape coming from the north.

"It's a chopper," he whispered. "Jesus, I think it's a chopper. Take the wheel!"

Steve raced forward to the hatch and screamed down. "Get the girls out on the foredeck. Now! Then I want both you guys up here in the cockpit. You hear me?"

There was no response from below.

"You hear me?" he screamed. "Or do I have to come down there and start shooting?"

Bill and Howard stared at each other.

"What's going on?" Howard asked.

"I don't know. We better do what he says."

"Move! Now!" It was Steve's screaming voice.

Bill jumped up on the ladder. Marilyn followed instantly and boosted herself out through the greenhouse hatch.

"C'mon. C'mon," he ordered Jeanne. She climbed the ladder and then Bill boosted her through the opening. The two men then raced aft.

"Come slowly," Steve's voice cautioned them. "I want to see your hands first."

They heard the helicopter engine as soon as they stepped up onto the deck. Bill followed the sound and could make out the distinctive, bug-like shape in the distance.

"Now listen, and listen good," Steve began to lecture. "We're all going to be topside, just like a bunch of happy cruisers. But Cindy is going to be below. Right under the greenhouse. And if anything goes wrong — if she even thinks anything is going wrong — she's going to start firing at your wives. You understand me?"

Bill looked at Cindy as she took the pistol that

202

Steve was handing her. Her hands were trembling under the burden she was accepting. For an instant, he thought of firing one tight punch right onto the point of her chin. Even if she survived it, he couldn't believe that she would come up firing. She seemed too frightened, too uncertain of the cautious step she was taking toward the cabin.

But Steve's words cut him short. "The guys in that helicopter might be hired killers. If they even think that we're the ones they're looking for, they'll cut us all to pieces. But I'm warning you. Your women will be dead before you guys hit the deck. So play it smart. Wave at them. Nice and friendly. Like you're having a great vacation. You understand?"

Howard nodded.

Bill watched Cindy climb down into the cabin. He looked forward. Marilyn and Jeanne were sitting with their backs against the framing of the greenhouse, looking back toward him as if expecting instructions. "Just wave," he shouted to them. "Everything is going to be all right."

Bill and Howard moved to the bench on the starboard side. Steve settled behind the wheel, clearly more concerned with the approaching helicopter than he was with Howard and Bill.

"What's going on?" Bill asked the captain in a calm, conversational tone.

"Shut up. It's none of your business."

"If these guys are going to start shooting, it's our business," Howard snapped.

"Just shut up. If nobody panics, we'll be okay. They don't know who we are."

"Who are they looking for?" Bill persisted. It was easy to defy Steve's orders now that he didn't have the gun. He remembered the name that Steve had called the girl. "Are they looking for Cindy?"

"Just shut up. Okay!" Now it was a plea more than an order.

Bill pushed harder. "Who are they? Cops?"

Steve smiled cynically. "Maybe. But maybe they're killers. So just play it smart. Act like you're all tourists and they won't know any better."

"What are they after?" Bill demanded.

He felt Howard's hand lock around his arm. "For God's sake," Howard begged. "Are you trying to get us all killed?"

Bill looked toward his friend, bewildered. A moment ago, Howard had been planning to attack an armed gunman. Now he was begging Bill to submit quietly.

The droning of the engine was growing louder. They could hear the popping of the rotor blades against the wind. The helicopter was beginning its sloping descent directly toward them.

"Just keep calm," Steve said. "As soon as they get close enough to see our faces, I want both of you to start waving. Tell your wives! Wave! And smile!"

The helicopter settled a few feet off the water, its downdraft kicking up a misty spray and carving swirls into the surface. Then it eased up close to the windward quarter.

"Hello," Al Weston's voice boomed over the megaphone.

Steve waved, and then the women on the foredeck followed his lead.

"Are you out of Road Harbor?"

Steve exaggerated his nod as he indicated that they were.

"Where are you headed?"

The young captain released the wheel and held up his hands, indicating no place in particular.

Weston was impatient with pantomime responses. "Can you talk to me over a hailer?" He held out the power megaphone that he was using. Steve knew there was a hailer on board. He had carefully removed it from the pilothouse the night before, and stowed it forward, in his cabin at the bow. He wasn't about to go forward to get it, so he held his hands in a gesture of helplessness and shook his head.

Weston turned inside the helicopter to consult with his pilot and then aimed his megaphone back toward Steve. "Can you come up on channel four?"

Steve thought for a moment and then nodded that he could. He turned to Howard. "Take the wheel. Just hold our heading." He jumped up on the pilothouse and then started down the hatch. Before his head disappeared, he yelled back to his prisoners. "Just remember. The gun is down there with me. Anything goes wrong, and I start shooting."

"We should tell him," Howard said, nodding toward the figure in the helicopter. "This is our chance."

Bill eased closer to the helm. "Those guys aren't police," he told Howard.

"We have to take that chance," Howard repeated, his voice cracking. "What are we waiting for?"

Bill looked at the menacing figure leaning out of the helicopter. "We're not going to start a gunfight," he answered. "I like our chances better with Steve and the girl."

"We've got to tell him," Howard insisted. But he made no motion toward the helicopter. He kept his attention on the wheel. "Dammit! Do something!"

Steve's head came up through the hatch. He had the radio microphone in his hand.

"This is *Cane Maiden,* up on four," he said.

Weston's voice boomed from the radio in the cabin below. "You leave Tortola this morning?"

"Yeah! Real early. My charter wanted to do some sailing."

"Where you headed?"

"No place in particular. Probably just window-shop St. Croix and land someplace for dinner." It was the right answer. Exactly what a charter boat would be doing. Then Steve asked the right question. "Why? What's up? Somebody lost?"

"Just looking for someone who's needed back on Tortola. Who you got aboard?"

Steve gestured to the two couples on deck. "People on vacation. Just cruising."

"Anybody else?" Al's voice asked. They could see him talking into a microphone only fifty feet away. But his voice was echoing out of the hollow of the pilothouse.

"Just me. I'm the charter captain."

Al studied the boat. An old rig. Not what anyone would use as an escape boat. He looked at the two women up forward, one with tanning lotion dabbed on her face, and the other wearing a big hat. If this were an act, they were the most convincing tourists he had seen all day. He studied the captain. Typical of the young sailors that the charter companies employed. And then at the two men in the cockpit. His eyes focused on Howard.

"One of those guys looks familiar," he mumbled to the pilot.

Canavan responded by tapping the fuel gauge. If Al wanted to do a swing around the south of St. Croix, they had to get moving.

"I swear I seen him someplace before. Just can't place him."

"What do you want to do?" the pilot asked.

Al pressed the key on his microphone. But his eyes stayed fixed on Howard as he talked with the captain. "You seen any other boats headed out this way? Any cruisers?"

Steve answered instantly. "Not since this morning. There were a bunch of them heading west." Then he repeated, "What's up?"

"Where are your passengers from?"

"New York, and Boston." Steve answered. "That's where they flew in from."

It all rang true. There was nothing to make Al suspicious, except a vague recollection that he had met Howard Hunter before. But where the hell was it? Certainly not in New York or Boston.

"I seen that guy," he told the pilot.

"Probably around Road Town," Paul offered. "Look." He hit the gas gauge again. "We have to get moving or we'll be burning up our reserve."

Al nodded. "Okay, let's go." Then, into the microphone, "Sorry to bother you. Thanks for your help."

"Don't mention it," Steve said. He threw a friendly wave as the helicopter lifted off the water and then banked away to the east.

"Wave, dammit," he yelled at the women on the bow. They waved furiously at the chopper as it flew away.

25

"Okay. You guys get forward," Steve ordered. "Get up there with your wives." He climbed out on the leeward side of the pilothouse, leaving the high deck free for Bill and Howard to move up. Howard released the wheel and scampered forward. But Bill held his ground next to the helm.

"Get forward, I said."

Bill shook his head. "Not until you tell me what's going on. Those guys were after Cindy. Why?"

"Never mind. All you have to know is that she has your wives covered. You want her to start shooting? I told you to get forward."

"I don't think she's going to start shooting anyone," Bill answered.

Steve suddenly looked frightened. He was out in the open, without the pistol, and his prisoner was calling him down.

The unattended wheel began to spin slowly as the boat eased into the wind. The genoa started to flap, and the boom swung across the boat toward Bill. Steve used the moment to spring back into the hatch and race down the ladder. When he reappeared seconds later, he had the gun in his fist. He climbed out, and then Cindy came up behind him.

"What are you going to do?" Cindy was begging Steve. "They did what you told them."

Steve stepped down on deck, keeping the pilothouse between Bill and himself. "I told you to get forward. I won't tell you again."

"Do what he says," Howard screamed from the bow.

"Bill, please!" It was Marilyn's voice, pleading with him.

"You're making a mistake," Bill said calmly, holding his ground. "This isn't you against us. It's all of us against the guys in the helicopter. We're all in this together."

The barrel of the pistol raised up toward his eyes.

"Why don't you tell us what you're up against? Maybe we can help you. We don't want anyone to get hurt."

Cindy looked from Bill, back to Steve. "Maybe they *can* help us," she said.

"Keep quiet," he ordered.

"Steve, they'll be coming back. They're not going to give up on us. Maybe these people can help us."

His head snapped towards her. "I said shut up."

"She's right, Steve," Bill said, siding with Cindy. "And when they do come back, we better be here to wave at them or they're going to know. You need us."

"Tell them," Cindy pleaded. "We need them."

"We don't need anyone," Steve screamed.

"Let us help you," Bill said. "If we work together we can get through this. Tell me what's happening."

210

Cindy grabbed Steve's arm. "Please. Let's tell them."

He shook free of her grip, and then started slowly toward Bill, his finger tightening around the trigger. "I don't need any help from you. I'm in charge, and I know what I'm doing. And you're going to follow my orders, or I'm going to blow you over the side. You hear me, big man? I've taken all the crap I'm going to from assholes like you. I'm in charge. I'm giving the orders."

Bill saw that he was about to snap. He raised his hands in surrender. "Okay. Okay. You're in charge. I'm going forward. Just like you said. I'm going forward." He started easing toward the bow, keeping his hands in the air even though he wanted to grab the lifeline to steady himself. If Steve was going to kill him, he was going to do it right now.

But the gun didn't fire. It relaxed in Steve's hands and the barrel began to lower. Bill turned and scampered up to join his friends.

Steve turned on Cindy. "Don't you ever turn against me, you hear?"

She nodded submissively.

"We've got everything we need. We don't need any partners, you understand?"

She nodded again. But then she asked, "What are we going to do when they come back?"

He looked up at the helicopter that was now a buzzing dot, fading into the distance. "Maybe they won't be coming back."

Bill slumped down next to Howard.

"Jesus," Marilyn said. "I thought he was going to kill you."

Howard looked straight into his face. "You're crazy."

Jeanne's face was slumped down between her knees. "I thought you were going to do something," she reminded Howard.

"I was," he said, addressing the two women. "I wanted to signal to that helicopter. When he was below, setting the radio, I wanted to signal that we were in trouble." He turned to Bill. "But you wouldn't go along with it."

Bill fired back. "Think, for God's sake, will you, Howard? That guy wasn't a cop. He was someone looking for Cindy."

"So what?" Jeanne demanded. "He could have helped us."

Howard nodded vigorously. "All we had to do was tell him that Cindy was aboard."

"And then what?" Bill demanded.

Howard stuttered for a second, but he had no answer.

"They were a lot more frightened of the guy in the helicopter than they were of us. Why Howard? Why?"

Howard slammed his fists against the deck. "What the fuck difference does it make?"

Marilyn was trying to follow Bill's thinking. "Because if he found Cindy, he was going to kill her. Maybe both of them."

Bill nodded slowly. "Yeah. Cindy knew that guy. She said earlier that they should bring something back. The way I figure it, Cindy took something that belongs to him. Something damn valuable. Valuable enough, so that he's out in a helicopter looking for it."

"Drugs," Howard interjected, recalling his earlier explanation.

"Maybe," Bill agreed. "But the guy doesn't know that there's any connection between Cindy and Steve. When they saw the helicopter, Steve hid Cindy below, out of sight. But he had no problem staying up on deck himself."

"So?" It was Jeanne, demanding an answer.

He threw up his hands. "I'm not sure, yet. The only thing I know for sure is that our captain and his girlfriend are on the run. They have something that belongs to some dangerous people, and they're running for their lives. They're using us for cover, just to make this look like an innocent charter boat."

Howard snarled angrily. "That doesn't change anything. We've still got to get the gun away from that punk."

"Howard, they need us. They don't want to kill us. The only thing that would put us in danger would be if we tried to attack them. If we threatened them. Either that, or if we did anything to bring the guy in the helicopter back. So we have to wait. Just go along with them, and try to win their confidence."

"We have to get the gun," Howard repeated. "We're never going to win their confidence. Dammit, Bill. The guy was just about to kill you."

"Yeah," Bill admitted. "I went too far. But the girl is already on our side. She was begging him to work with us. Now all we have to do is help Steve see it that way."

Marilyn nodded, but Jeanne shook her head. "Howard's right. You should have grabbed him

213

while he was up on deck without the gun. You should have done something. Don't you see, every minute we wait just makes it that much more dangerous." She looked at Howard. "What are we going to do?"

"I don't know," he said brusquely. "But I'll tell you one thing. I'm not going to wait around for something to happen to us."

Bill begged, "Howard, for God's sake, don't give them any reason to start shooting."

"You're wasting time," Howard snapped at his friend. "What we need is action."

They were sitting in a morose silence when a gust of wind snapped back the brim of Marilyn's straw hat, and then lifted it off her head. She was too late in grabbing for it, and turned in time to see it fly into the jib, and then fire aft with the draft of air reflecting off the sail.

"Damn," she said, as if the hat were important, but none of the others commented. They were each lost in their individual scenarios of how the dangers that surrounded them would play out.

Steve's bellowed order broke into their thoughts. "You two guys! Get back here! Send the girls below. Now!"

Bill pushed up off his haunches. Howard rolled onto his knees and stood carefully. "What's he want?" he whispered to Bill.

"What's he going to do?" Jeanne's voice was a frightened whisper. But Bill's attention was locked on the captain, who was waiting behind the wheel. The gun was still in his hand.

"I'm coming about," Steve told them as they edged toward him. "We're turning to the southeast and heading away from where those guys would expect to find us, if they decide to come back for another look. I need you to tend the sheets."

He motioned them down into the cockpit with the barrel of his gun. Howard seemed the most submissive, so he ordered Bill to handle the main sheet, which was secured on the forward bulkhead of the cockpit, farthest from where he was standing. He assigned Howard to tend the genoa, which would require him to free the sheet on one side, and then cross the cockpit directly in front of the helm. The gun was aimed at Howard. "Don't get any smart ideas," he warned. "Anything happens, I'll sure as hell get one of you." He signaled Cindy to move along the after bench, further away from the helm.

"Ready about!" he announced, and then he turned the wheel across the wind.

Cane Maiden responded instantly, her bow crashing head on into the mounting seas and sending a spray up over her decks. Her sails fluttered idly for an instant, and then swung across her decks as they caught the wind over the other bow.

Howard set the gennie instantly, but Bill let the main go slack. "Bring her in more," Steve ordered, and Bill cranked in the main until she began to pull.

"Where are you taking us?" Howard asked. He was talking over his shoulder, hesitant to turn toward the gun that he knew was aimed at his back.

"None of your business," Steve told him.

Howard looked forward at the dark gray that was settling on the horizon. "Looks like you're taking us straight into a storm. We should be

215

heading toward land."

Steve sneered. "You think you'd feel safer waiting for that guy in the helicopter to come back?"

Bill turned back toward the helm. "It doesn't have to be this way, Steve. We're in this together. We should be working together."

"Get below!" he responded, gesturing with the pistol.

Bill started to turn away toward the hatch, but he saw Cindy looking pleadingly toward her partner. "We can help you," he told her sympathetically, almost as if he were in charge instead of Steve.

"I said get below!"

For an instant, all of Steve's attention was focused on Bill. He wasn't looking at Howard, who stood only a few feet away from him, on the other side of the wheel. It was the chance that Howard had been talking about. He would never get any closer to the man who held him prisoner. The automatic had swung away from him and was focused on his friend. He could grab for the gun. He could launch a punch at Steve with a simple spin of his shoulders.

Instead, he looked anxiously at Bill. "Do what he says." Bill looked at Howard and then at Steve. Then he climbed up to the hatch with Howard following right behind him.

As soon as they disappeared, Cindy jumped up and rushed to Steve's side. "Where are we going?"

"St. Kitts," he told her, "just like we planned."

"What are we going to do with them? As soon as we get ashore, they'll go straight to the police."

He shook his head. "I don't know yet."

"We could pay them," she said. "If we work with them, they could cover for us for a couple of days. You said that was all we'd need. Just a couple of days to get away."

"We don't need anyone," Steve told her again.

"But what are we going to do with them?"

26

Johnnie Igoe was waiting by the car as Al walked away from the helicopter. "Anything?" he asked.

"Names of a lot of boats we gotta check up on. No sign of Cindy. How about you?"

"Nothing on Cindy. Her things are still at the hotel. Nobody's asked about them." As he climbed into the car beside Al he added, "We did find your truck driver."

Al was surprised.

"It wasn't all that hard. That piece of shit he's driving stands out in a crowd."

Al had told them about the truck that cut him off and separated him from Cindy. "Maybe it was just an accident," he had admitted. "But it's one hell of a coincidence."

Igoe's sidekick had suggested that they check the body shops where the driver would probably take it to have the dent fixed. "The whole truck is one big fucking dent," Al had answered. "He ain't going to take it to a body shop." Then he had described the truck and the patches of colors in which it was painted. He had told them that if it were still on the road, it wouldn't be too difficult to recognize.

"So? What did he say?"

"Nothing, yet. Figured we ought to wait for you."

Al checked his watch. "We're going back up again in a couple of hours. We still have to search to the east."

"Couple of hours is all we need," Igoe assured. "The guy is scared out of his mind."

They drove from the airport along the shoreline, turning through the endless switchbacks that climbed up and down the edge of the hills. The sun was filtered through a cloud cover that was beginning to move in from the south, and the wind was kicking up dust that quickly coated the windshield. Igoe led Al into the boarded-up shed of an abandoned produce market on the eastern edge of Road Town. The driver was sitting deathly still in an old wooden chair, afraid to look up at Johnnie's partner who was leaning against the wreckage of a long produce table. His eyes widened into bright white circles as soon as he recognized Al Weston.

"Hey, mon. We don't need this. I got money. I'll pay." He started out of the chair, hoping to do business with Al. His guard grabbed him by the collar of his shirt and pulled him back down into his seat.

"I'll pay you, mon," he offered again as Al walked toward him. But Weston seemed not to hear. When he reached the chair he swung a roundhouse right that sent the driver hurtling backward and the chair toppling over on its side. Igoe reset the chair, and then Al picked up the terrified man and threw him back into it.

"Who told you to cut me off?"

The driver shook his head and tried to clear his eyes. "Told me what, mon? Nobody told me."

This time it was Weston's left fist. The man rolled sideways and would have fallen again, but Johnnie Igoe caught him and pushed him back into the chair. "Tell him, fella," Johnnie advised. "Tell him before he gets mean."

The driver dabbed at a split lip that was already flowing blood. He blinked at the hazy form of Al Weston taking off his jacket, and saw the shoulder holster with the black handle of an automatic.

"You cut me off yesterday. Somebody told you when I'd be coming by and what street I'd be on. Somebody told you to cut me off and block the street."

The man shook his head. "It was an accident, mon. It was my fault and I'll pay. I got the money."

Al grabbed the man's hand, pulled it toward him and bent the fingers back in a wrist lock. "It was no accident. Somebody told you to do it. And I'm going to start breaking your bones, one at a time, until you tell me who it was." To make his point, Weston bent the man's pinky back until he heard the bone snap. The driver screamed, his whole body twisting with the pain.

"You're making him angry," Johnnie advised. "You still got a lot of bones for him to break."

Weston began bending back the ring finger.

"It was Terry! It was Terry," the man screamed.

Al held the finger on the point of breaking. "Who's Terry?"

"The taxi driver. The one who picked up the girl."

220

He let the ring finger relax. But he still had the man's arm stretched out in front of him.

"What did he tell you?"

"He hear about this girl from some drunk fella in a bar. The guy say she have a lot of money to buy something. Terry figure maybe a couple of thousand dollars. But he figure that she have a bodyguard. So he tell me to cut off any car that follows his taxi. He say he pay me a couple of hundred dollars. Maybe more if there's more money there."

"How'd you know Terry?"

"He rip off lots of tourists. Sometime cash. Sometime cameras and stuff. When I help him he pays me."

"So, what happened?"

"I see his car, and see you following, mon. So I cut you off. Only Terry don't pay me. I can't even find him."

Weston put pressure back on the finger, and heard the driver yelp with pain. "I think you're lying to me."

"That's bad," Johnnie whispered to the truck driver. "That means he's going to tear out your tongue."

"Jesus, mon. I don't know nothing. Terry just going to rip off the lady. I swear, mon. That's all I know."

The bone in the ring finger snapped, and the driver let out a piercing scream. He stood up out of the chair, but Johnnie stuffed him back down. He was still whimpering when Al took his middle finger. "Please, mon," he screamed. "That's all I know. Terry was just going to see what she got for the money and then rip her off."

"How did Terry know she was buying something?" Weston demanded.

"He meet this guy in a bar. A German guy. Terry trying to sell him a lady. But the guy is pretty drunk. He keep bragging about how much money he's going to collect. Then he tell the lady all about this buy he's making. He tell her about the girl who's bringing the money and how he's going to have her next."

Al began bending the middle finger. "You're lying," he decided.

Johnnie told him, "After he breaks all your bones and pulls out your tongue, he's going to gut you like a fish."

"It's true! It's true," the man begged.

"How'd he know that I'd be following the lady?" Weston asked suspiciously.

"The guy was drunk, mon. He shooting off his mouth."

"What did the guy look like?"

"Please! I don't know. I never see him. Terry say he a young kid. Sound like a German or something. Mon, all he tell me is to wait until he pass and then block the street. I swear. That's all he tell me."

Al released the hand, which was already discolored and puffy. He looked at Johnnie. "What do you think? Some stupid free lancer?"

Igoe shrugged his shoulders. "It happens," he answered.

Al looked down at the trembling driver. "Your friend Terry own a gun?"

"Yeah, mon. Old English pistol. He keep it under the seat."

"He ever shoot anyone?"

The black man was crying. "I don't know. Maybe. Terry get mean sometimes."

Al thought of the carnage he had found in the shed at Parson's Boatyard. The cab driver was still clutching an old English pistol, and the blond-haired man who had died beside him certainly fit the description of a young German.

The driver sat slumped in the chair, petting his wounded hand and whimpering. There was no way the guy was a professional. Just a small-time punk, probably like his friend Terry. He was certain that the man had no idea what he had become involved in. If he were part of a two-million-dollar heist, he wouldn't still be driving his battered truck around town where he'd be easy to spot. The truck would have been cut up and buried. He'd either be on his way to South America in a business suit, or he'd be lying someplace up in the hills with a hole through his head.

Al reached into his pocket and brought out his wallet. He peeled off a hundred dollars and stuffed it into the pocket of the man's shirt. "You tell anybody about me, and I'm coming back to finish the other fingers." He nodded to Johnnie and his friend and then led the two of them out the door.

"You gonna leave him?" Johnnie asked.

"Yeah." He looked at Igoe's partner. "You follow him. My guess is that he'll go straight to a gin mill and drink half of that money. I think the guy is a loser."

He and Johnnie got back in their car and headed out to the airport.

Johnnie asked, "So, what do you figure?"

"I figure the whole thing was an amateur fuck-up. Nobody serious would hire that jerk. A loud-mouthed courier. A greedy purse snatcher who figures he's stumbled on a big score. Like you say, it could happen."

"So where does that leave us?"

"Maybe in pretty good shape. I think it means that Cindy is still alive, and probably has all the money."

Johnnie was startled.

"Look, she goes to the exchange. The money and the goods are all there. And then this punk shows up figuring it's gonna be like taking candy from a baby. Only this time the courier isn't drunk. So they shoot it out, which explains why I found both of them in the shed."

"Cindy ain't in on it?" Johnnie asked.

Al shook his head. "I don't think so." He smiled at the thought. If he were right, then he hadn't been outsmarted by a damn cocktail waitress.

"So, then where is she?"

"Maybe hiding under a bed. Everybody is dead. I don't show up. She's scared out of her pants. So she takes everything and runs."

"Runs where?"

"That's what we have to find out. But probably not very far. What we have to do is keep shaking this tree until she falls out."

"Then we don't need to keep looking for boats," Igoe suggested.

"Bullshit!" Al answered. "We keep checking everything until we find her."

They drove around to the general aviation hanger and pulled up near the helicopter. Al

224

started out of the car when he saw the pilot walking toward him.

"No more flying today," the pilot announced. "We're grounded."

"Says who?" Al demanded.

"Says the weatherman. There's a hell of a storm blowing up out of the southeast. We'd be flying right into it."

"I gotta check the eastern approaches. The boat I'm looking for could be out there."

The pilot shook his head. "Any boats out there will be running for the beach. This is one hell of a storm."

27

They sat tensely in the saloon, bracing themselves against the sharp heel of the boat. They could feel the rise and plunge of bow, and hear the blast of the sea as *Cane Maiden* plowed ahead.

Howard had identified the sound of the roller-reefing mechanism as the big genoa was taken down and wrapped around the masthead stay. "He's taking down some sail," he had informed the others. And then he had added, "About time. He's been carrying too much sail for this kind of weather."

Now he could hear the rush of the wind and the furious banging of the rigging. "We ought to be in port," he announced. "He can't single-hand a boat this size in heavy seas."

Both of the women were frightened. The sunlight that had been pouring in through the greenhouse had gone dark, turning the cabin into a dreary prison cell. They felt all the despair of prisoners, their lives out of their control, totally at the whim of hostile strangers who were controlling them at the point of a gun. But more than the moment, they were terrified of the hours ahead. Each of them had run all the possibilities, and neither had found an outcome that left them safe.

"They're going to kill us," Jeanne said, without looking up at the others. There was no question in her voice. It was a statement of fact.

"They're not going to kill anyone," Bill countered, with more assurance than he really felt. He reran his explanation that the four of them were the cover for Steve and Cindy's escape. "They're in over their heads, and they're frightened. She's already begging for our help. It's not going to take him long to understand that he needs us."

Howard lifted his eyes from his own thoughts. "I should have jumped him," he whispered through clenched teeth. "I had my chance." He explained to his wife, "He wasn't looking at me. Bill had him distracted. All I had to do was throw one punch." Then he looked at Jeanne. "But he had the gun pointing right at Bill. I just couldn't take the chance."

"You made the right call," Bill responded. "We don't want to push this guy over the edge. Just keep him calm. And keep talking to him."

Jeanne's eyes narrowed. "You're going to keep talking to him? For God's sake, that's all you ever do is talk. This time you've got to do something."

"They're kids," he answered his wife. "They're in some sort of trouble and —"

"He's got a gun, you fool!" Jeanne screamed into his face. "And you almost talked him into using it on you. Don't you understand? We need to get the gun away from them, and then we need to get rid of them. We need a plan."

Marilyn defended Bill. "He was right about the girl. She wants our help. She's frightened."

Jeanne turned away from Marilyn in disgust.

"Jesus! She was standing under the hatch pointing a gun up at us. Does that look like she wants our help?" Then she clutched Howard's arm. "Tell us what to do."

Howard slid out from the table and tried to balance against the angle of the boat. "First thing we're going to do is make sure that they're both together, in the cockpit."

He had managed just one step when *Cane Maiden* shuddered, and snapped hard to port. The deck pitched and fell toward its edge, throwing Howard backward into the bench that he had just left. Marilyn, with Jeanne in her arms, hurtled forward, halfway across the table. She screamed in fright.

The boat rolled further onto its side, driven by a force that seemed determined to turn her upside down and shake her to death. Cups and dishes broke loose from their racks over the galley, and crashed down on the deck. The coffee mugs that had been left on top of the ice chest, fired across the cabin and smashed on the navigation table.

"It's going over," Howard yelled, his arms folded across his face to protect himself from Marilyn and Jeanne who were about to plunge down on top of him. Bill, who had been thrown against the back of the bench, managed to get his hands up to keep the two women from falling.

Then, just as suddenly as it had snapped over, *Cane Maiden* began to right herself. The gimballed table, which had tipped high over Bill's head, began to level. Jeanne and Marilyn rolled backward into the far bench.

They were tossed forward as the yacht's bow

blasted into a wave. But then they settled back into their seats when the boat steadied into a moderate heel.

Howard clutched the edge of the table in both hands. "Christ," he managed, more as a prayer than a curse. Jeanne clung to Marilyn.

Bill looked up and saw sea water running down the glass panes of the greenhouse. "We're all right," he told the others. "Everything is all right." He looked uncertainly at Howard.

"It's a hell of a storm," Howard said. "He can't handle it. He should have run to port."

Fear came into Jeanne's eyes. Marilyn clutched her and glared at Howard. "It's all right," she said threateningly. "Don't say things like that. It's all right."

They sat perfectly still, as if afraid that even their slightest motion might tip the boat over again. They listened to what had become a steady howl of wind, and felt the rumble as the boat battered its way through the sea. Jeanne eased carefully out of Marilyn's arms, retreating to the forward end of the bench, as far away from the others as she could get. She wrapped herself in her own arms and shrunk into an empty isolation.

The wind's groan turned into a scream as Steve slid open the after hatch. "You guys. Get up here. Leave the women below."

Marilyn's expression tensed. Jeanne seemed not even to hear the command.

"Come up slowly," Steve shouted over the clattering of the rigging. "Put on the slickers. And life jackets."

Bill and Howard moved aft, clutching to handholds as they balanced against the motion of the pilothouse. They took the foul weather jackets out of the lockers, and then helped one another fasten the straps of the life preservers. Bill was first up the ladder, and felt the slap of the driving rain as soon as his face was raised through the hatch.

He saw a lightless sky smeared with rolling black clouds. The sea was churning into peaks that rose high above the deck, and then seemed to explode into geysers of salty spray. The sails were pulled taut, like sheets of curved, dull metal.

"Tie this around your waist." Steve tossed him a canvas belt that trailed a length of wire cable. "Snap the fitting into the track."

For the first time, Bill noticed the metal tracks that were screwed into the top of the pilothouse and along the decks near the life rails. The fitting at the end of the cable locked into the track so that it could slide fore and aft, but couldn't be pulled free. He understood that it was a safety line to keep him from falling overboard. He cleared the hatch and crawled out on the pilothouse overhead. Howard recognized the safety line as soon as Steve tossed it to him. He followed Bill up and went out on the windward deck. The two of them looked back at Steve and Cindy, both in life jackets, and awaited their orders.

Steve gave the girl the pistol. She moved forward timidly, sliding her safety line along the leeward deck track. Then she climbed up on the pilothouse, close to Bill, undid her belt and dropped down through the hatch.

"We're going to reef in some sail," Steve explained. "Go where I tell you and do what I tell

230

you. Don't do anything dumb. You get Cindy upset and your wives are going to pay for it."

They heard Steve's threat, but they weren't really paying attention. They were both focused on the pyramids of angry water that surrounded them, making *Cane Maiden* seem ridiculously small, and the blasts of wind that threatened to tear the sails to pieces.

Steve explained the crank that stuck through the main boom. He would head the boat up a bit to take some strain off the sail. Then, by turning the crank, they would be able to roll the mainsail halfway down into the boom. The operation would require two hands; one to turn the crank, the other to slack the main halyard so that the sail would be free to slide down. The two men eased forward along the pitching deck, fighting for each step against the force of the wind. They were aware that the safety lines protected them, but still afraid to move without a secure handhold.

When they were at the mast, Steve eased the boat's heading closer to the wind. *Cane Maiden* began to plunge as she took the seas head on, and sheets of water blasted up from her bow, showering down on Howard and Bill. But the steel-like surface of the sail began to soften into angry ripples. The fabric started cracking like a whip.

"Okay, reef her down!"

They read the order more from the captain's expression than from the sound of his voice. Even though he was only thirty feet away, it was difficult to hear him over the whine of the wind and the clatter of the rigging. They reached out for the mast, fighting against the wind and the constant

231

battering of the spray. Bill took the crank while Howard freed the halyard so that it could slide around the drum of the winch. As Bill turned, the sail shrank, filling an ever smaller part of the angle formed by the mast and the boom.

"Hold it there!" Steve screamed. The sail reached only halfway up the mast and halfway back along the boom. "Tie it off."

Bill could feel the difference as soon as Steve eased the bow back off the wind. The heel of the boat was less severe than it had been. The bow stopped its furious plunging into the waves. The howl through the sails seemed to quiet.

"Come aft!"

They looked at one another, and then eased cautiously back toward the cockpit, dragging their safety lines along with them.

"That's far enough," Steve said as soon as they were down into the forward end of the cockpit. "I want you both up here on deck." He watched his two prisoners make eye contact and knew what they were thinking. "You wouldn't be dumb enough to try anything. You guys wouldn't last ten minutes out here without me."

"Where are we heading?" Bill asked.

"East, into the Leeward Islands. But for now, we're going wherever this weather takes us."

Bill didn't understand, but Howard knew exactly what the captain was saying. In the heavy squall, Steve had to keep *Cane Maiden* into the wind and sea. Otherwise, she could turn over.

She was carrying the working jib forward, and the small spanker aft on the mizzenmast. He had just reefed the main in to half its size. The total was less than half of the boat's full sail capacity, but in the heavy wind, more than enough to keep her moving into the sea.

"This is pretty bad," Howard said, gesturing to the waves which were breaking into whitecaps at their peaks.

"It'll get worse," Steve answered, showing no particular concern. "That's why I want you up here. I may need you."

They had choices, Bill knew. They were alone in the cockpit, two of them against one, and he had little doubt that he could handle the young captain by himself. Steve's protection was that his accomplice held their wives at gunpoint. But he had studied Cindy and seen her fear. He was almost certain that nothing could bring her to execute the two women she was guarding. The threat was empty.

He could simply climb up to the hatch, ignoring Steve's orders that he stay put. Then he could go down the ladder, stepping down next to Cindy. "It's over," he could say, "we're going to help you," and then hold out his hand. For an instant, she would be confused. She might glance at the people surrounding her just to be certain that they posed no threat. Just to reassure herself that they weren't as dangerous as the man in the helicopter. He knew what she would decide. He was certain that she would hand him the pistol. Then he could go back up to the windswept cockpit, with the gun in his belt, and tell Steve, "It's okay. Now we're all in this together."

But he was uncertain of Steve. There was a brooding anger in the young man that made it easy for him to order and bully. No matter how much sense it might make, he didn't think that Steve would give up without a fight. Maybe he would abandon the wheel and rush forward to try to keep Bill from going below. There would be a struggle, and in the battle he might have to batter the young man senseless. Which would leave Howard to take the wheel and battle the storm.

As if to remind him of the danger, a gust tore at the sails and heeled *Cane Maiden* over to port, plunging her leeward deck into the sea. His hands clutched under the edge of the cockpit to keep him from falling out across the deck and over the side. He held on for his life while the yacht groaned under the strain, deciding whether to fight its way back against the sea, or to simply surrender to its death roll.

To his right, now high above him, Howard had both arms wrapped around one of the winch heads. His legs were churning as he struggled to get a foothold on the wet duck boards that formed the cockpit deck. His eyes were wide with fright. Behind him, Bill could see Steve, still planted behind the compass binnacle. He was powering the wheel into the force of the wind, excited by the danger. By driving the rudder over, he was using the speed of the boat and the power of the waves to turn the bow back into the sea. And as she turned, *Cane Maiden* began to right herself, slowly at first, and then with a crisp snap.

"Jesus," Bill prayed as he dragged himself back to his feet. Howard found his footing, but his arms kept their stranglehold around the winch head. Steve calmly brought the rudder back to amidships, and studied the compass as he found his heading.

Bill eased over to Howard. "Can you get us through this?"

Howard didn't understand.

"If we take over from this guy, can you handle the boat?"

Howard didn't answer. He bit down nervously on his lip and turned cautiously to look at a new wave that was swelling up off the starboard bow. Then he mumbled. "We shouldn't be out here. He should have run for port when I told him to."

Bill made his decision. They would never make it through the storm without Steve. He took a new handhold and waited for Steve's next order.

In the cabin below, Cindy pulled her way back up to the ladder. She had been braced against it, half-sitting on one of the rungs, when *Cane Maiden* rolled. The motion had thrown her off her feet, and sent her sliding under the navigation table. The automatic pistol that had been cradled in her lap had bounced across the deck ahead of her.

She had scrambled for the gun, and after she had it back in her hand, had tried to stand so that she could see the two women she was supposed to be guarding. But the deck now rose steeply away from her. Her own weight held her pinned against the shelves and drawers under the table.

She had waited for what seemed an eternity, expecting them to pounce on her while she was helpless. Then, like a room in an amusement park fun house, the cabin had begun moving back toward level. The deck, which had been a blank wall in front of her, gradually settled beneath her.

She looked forward as she clutched at the ladder. Her prisoners, who had been thrown across the saloon table, were now falling back into the bench in a tangle of bare arms and legs. One of them was screaming in fright.

"It's okay," Cindy yelled. "Don't be afraid. Steve's been through a lot of storms. He knows what he's doing."

She wanted to ease their fear. They were nice people, and she hated to see them so frightened. Then she looked down at the terribly lethal rapid-fire automatic she had been waving in their faces. And then nothing made sense.

28

They were moving deeper and deeper into the center of the storm, feeling the steady battering of the wind, and watching helplessly as the sea grew more angry. As they crested the top of a wave, Bill and Howard could look down into the valley into which *Cane Maiden* was falling. And then, behind the trough, there was another mountain of water rising higher than their mast top.

All around them, there were mountains, swelling, rising, settling and then disappearing. Like snowcaps, each was topped with a churning foam of white water that exploded into spray, and then rolled down the slope of the wave like an avalanche. *Cane Maiden*, which had seemed towering to Bill when he first looked up at her masts, now seemed pathetically small. She was insignificant in comparison to her surroundings, and was about to be swallowed up without a trace.

The wind was building. Where it had jabbed at them in sudden, quick gusts, it now pounded in steady hammer blows. Even the small cover of sail that *Cane Maiden* was carrying seemed dangerous. The wind was determined to tear it off the masts, or rip the masts away from the shrouds that supported them.

The rain had become a torrent, a constant sheet of water driving sideways, directly into their faces. It filled their eyes, the salt spray stinging as they wiped the water away.

They heard Steve shouting behind them, and turned toward him to try to read his command. "We've got to reef her in all the way!"

Bill stepped back toward him, but this time Steve didn't seem concerned that his prisoner was coming near. He needed his crew, and he knew that they desperately needed him.

"The main!" Steve yelled. "You two go forward and reef it all the way in."

Bill nodded vigorously, and then moved up to Howard. "He wants the main reefed all the way in."

"It won't do any good," Howard answered, his eyes fixed on the peak of the steep hill that *Cane Maiden* was climbing. "We can't make it."

"We have to make it." Bill checked his safety line and climbed up on the pilothouse. Howard watched him for an instant and then crawled out of the cockpit and onto the windward deck. Carefully, they began moving forward from handhold to handhold.

The wave ahead broke, and a roaring wall of white water charged down at them. The bow buried, and the white churning fury rolled over the deck. Bill's legs were knocked out from under him. He crashed down on his chest, and as his grip was torn from its hold, felt himself sliding in the wash. He slipped over the edge of the pilothouse, rolled down onto the leeward deck, and then began sliding toward the life rail, caught helplessly in the torrent of water. Then he felt the jerk of the lifeline, and came to a stop with one leg dangling over the side.

Slowly, he dragged himself back to his knees, and clutched at the handhold that ran along the edge of the pilothouse. Directly across from him, he saw Howard, who had escaped the force of the wave by pressing himself low against the side of the pilothouse.

"We can't make it," Howard screamed. He was turning back toward the cockpit.

Bill looked forward. They were at the crest of a wave, riding high above the floor of the sea. He darted forward, scampered up onto the cabin overhead, and clutched the mast.

Steve turned the boat up, taking some of the pressure off the half-sized main. With one hand, Bill freed the halyard. With the other, he began turning the crank.

Howard saw him struggling, and realized that they had several seconds before *Cane Maiden* would dive into the next trough. He climbed up next to him and took the halyard. Bill wound the sail down until it disappeared into the boom. Then they moved carefully back and tumbled into the small safety of the cockpit.

Steve nodded at them, but kept his concentration focused on the wheel. The boat was now flying just two small sails, the working jib forward, and the spanker off the stern. With the main down, the spanker had less force to overcome, and it pushed the stern downwind. That pointed the bow up, and made it easier for Steve to hold the boat closer to the wind. She stood up straighter, and seemed to find a better balance.

But they were sliding downward, along the back side of the wave, picking up speed as they rushed toward the next looming wall of water. Howard nearly strangled the winch head with his choke hold as he waited for the bow to plunge under. She dropped into the trough, surrounded by towering, watery mountains that seemed about to fall over on top of her and drive her to the bottom. But the bow began to ride up the next slope, and once again they were climbing up toward the breakers that were charging down at them.

They crashed again, sending another wave rolling over the deck toward them. The men ducked low under the cockpit bulkhead so that the torrent would rush over their heads.

Marilyn heard the rumble of the wave an instant before it hit the bow, and took hold of the half bulkhead that divided the saloon from the galley. She felt the boat shudder, and battled to hold her footing. Jeanne, at the other end of the bench, had both arms wrapped around the mast trunk. Her face was buried into her shoulder, and her eyes were squeezed shut. Cindy was pressed against the ladder, with her arms locked around the steps. The gun, still clutched in her hand, was pointing toward the deck.

The glass crashed over their heads. They looked up to see one of the greenhouse hatches break open. In the next second, a flood of sea water poured down on top of them, blasted off the table and then rushed aft. Jeanne watched it in silent terror, certain that the saloon would fill. Cindy screamed, and then looked up the ladder, debating whether she should rush up to the deck to save herself. Marilyn cowered while the flood was pouring down on top of her. But the instant it stopped, she jumped up on the bench and tried to pull the hatch closed.

The wooden framing had been smashed at its center. The glass panes were shattered, and two of them had fallen through. Even with the hatch bolted down tight, the saloon was open to the sea. She had to find a way to close the opening.

"We've got to block this," she yelled to the other women. She looked down at Jeanne. "Quick! Pull off one of those seat cushions. Roll it up." Then she ordered Cindy, "Get some rope. We need something to hold it."

Jeanne stood cautiously and began rolling the cushion she had been sitting on. She stared fearfully up at the open hatch, clinging to the trunk of the mast while she worked. Cindy took a new grip on the ladder slats and didn't move.

"Cindy, Goddammit, get up here. We have to block this off."

She hesitated. She was supposed to be guarding them. But what was the point in guarding them if the boat was sinking?

And then Marilyn was struggling for balance as the bow pitched up. She held on to the hatch locks over her head, and tried to plant her feet solidly on the bench. There was another blast against the bow, and then a new wave flooded down into the pilothouse. She held her ground while the stream poured over her, soaking her to the skin. When the rush stopped, she was still up on the bench, clinging to the hatch.

The water rolled aft, splashing over Cindy's legs, and making her decision for her. She let go of the ladder, looked about frantically, and then stuffed the pistol in between the manuals on top of the navigation table. She eased forward toward the gear locker.

"Jeanne! Get me the seat cushion."

Jeanne passed it up to Marilyn, still keeping her grip on the mast trunk. Marilyn began jamming it into the greenhouse opening.

"Here!" Cindy pulled a coil of line out of the locker and held it up to Marilyn. The bow was beginning to dive, and once again Marilyn was struggling for balance. The bow blasted through another wave. Her feet slipped off the wet bench, and for a second she was hanging by one hand from the hatch. Then she fell down on top of Cindy. The two of them sprawled across the deck just as a new flood washed over the shattered hatch and poured down on top of them.

"The greenhouse is open!" Looking forward, Bill could see the flickering light coming up from the saloon. He could make out the crushed framing and was able to watch the water as it disappeared into the opening. He stepped back toward the helm. "The greenhouse is broken through," he screamed into Steve's face.

Steve put one foot on the bench and raised himself up so that he could see over the pilothouse roof. He nodded when he understood the emergency.

"Pull the cover off the dinghy," he told Bill. He indicated the canvas tarpaulin that was tied over the rubber dinghy. It was a huge square of cloth, with lines attached to its corners. "Untie the after end first. If the wind gets under it, you won't be able to hold it."

Bill looked aft. He understood that Steve wanted him to take the tarpaulin forward and tie it over the top of the open greenhouse hatch. But to get the tarpaulin, he would have to crawl out onto the open deck behind the cockpit, and over the top of the dinghy. If he lost his grip, he would go straight over the stern and into the sea.

Steve pointed to a track that ran along the windward deck next to the cockpit. "Hook your safety line in here."

As he turned forward, Bill saw the next wave rushing down toward them. He ducked low just as it blasted over the bow and surged over the deck. He didn't waste a thought on the water that he knew was pouring through the hatch. Quickly, he unfastened his safety line and carried it to the track that Steve had indicated. Then he climbed out of the cockpit, and out on top of the dinghy. Laying flat on top of the canvas that was stretched over the rubber boat, he reached out timidly for the tie lines.

As soon as he freed the first line, the corner of the canvas began flapping wildly. He tried to ignore it as he worked the second line free and then the third. Now only one corner of the tarpaulin was secured. It was his own weight that was keeping it from blowing away.

Steve turned away from the helm long enough to get a grip on the closest edge of the canvas. Then he screamed over the wind. "Get back in. Bring it in with you."

Bill slid slowly off the dinghy, trying to drag the cloth with him, keeping it pinned under the weight of his body. Steve tugged on the near end with one hand while he tried to manage the wheel with the other. But the drag of the loose, flapping end was too much for them. It was starting to get away.

"Lend a hand," Steve yelled forward to Howard, who was still clinging to the jib winch.

Howard looked at him dumbly.

"You son-of-a-bitch! Get back here and lend a hand."

Howard eased aft to the full length of his safety line. He was able to grab the edge of the canvas under Bill, so that Bill could drop back into the cockpit. Working together, the three men were able to roll the tarpaulin into the cockpit.

"Fold it up tight," Steve instructed. "Leave two of the lines from one edge free. When you get up there, you have to tie the two forward lines before you try to spread the canvas. Then the wind will blow it back over the greenhouse."

Bill nodded and began folding the canvas, keeping it low and out of the wind. Howard suddenly understood what they were going to try to do. They would have to carry the canvas forward, all the way to the mast. Then they would secure its forward end, spread it back over the greenhouse and then secure the after end. They would be out on the open deck for a long time, taking the full impact of the waves that crashed over the bow.

"You're crazy," Howard screamed at Steve. "We'll never be able to get up there."

Steve didn't answer. The storm was trying to

force the bow up, and he was having trouble holding *Cane Maiden*'s angle on the wind so that he could keep up speed. He would have to reef in the spanker sail a bit just to take the pressure off the helm.

Marilyn had climbed painfully back up onto the bench. With one hand, she held the rolled up seat cushion. With the other, she clung to the locking latch on the broken hatch. She tried to maneuver the cushion up into the hollow of the greenhouse, but with only one hand to work with, she couldn't keep it from unrolling. Cindy saw the problem and climbed up beside her, bringing the coil of rope. "I'll hold this end," she told Marilyn.

"Just keep it from unraveling," Marilyn answered. With Cindy's help, she was able to concentrate on packing one end of the rolled cushion into the opening without having the other end fall away. "I think this is going to work," she told her young helper.

Cindy nodded eagerly. "I think so!"

The boat rolled and tossed, but the two women were able to hold on. They had most of the cushion packed into the space when the bow slammed into another wave.

As *Cane Maiden* shuddered they staggered, spinning against one another but still managing to keep their footing. Then the sea washed overhead and poured down through the open glass. The weight of the water pushed the rolled cushion out of the opening. Marilyn felt it slipping through her fingers, but Cindy was able to hold on despite the rush of water that soaked her. She pushed it up against the glass, blocking a good part of the flow.

When the bow jerked upward and the tide fell away from over their heads, the cushion was still halfway into the hollow.

They worked quickly, both understanding what they were trying to do so that no conversation was necessary. When their makeshift packing was in position, they gave up their grips on the latches. Marilyn held the cushion and Cindy began tying the rope in a web across the latches. If she could get it tied off tightly enough, then the line would hold the packing pressed against the broken hatch. It would still leak, but the torrents that had been pouring down on top of them, plastering their clothing against the contours of their bodies, would be blocked.

Jeanne came out of her frightened trance and let go of the mast she had been clinging to. She wrapped her arms around Marilyn's legs, holding her steady so that she would have two hands to work with. "Thanks," Marilyn called. "Hold on tight." Cindy fastened the line around another latch. And then they were struggling once again to hold the cushion in place as another wave roared over the broken hatch. This time, there was only a trickle that came down on top of them.

As soon as the wave had rolled by Bill and Howard, the men secured their lifelines to the tracks that led forward. They climbed up onto the deck and eased forward on either side of the pilothouse. Bill held the tarpaulin tightly folded against his chest. The bow was still rising, riding over the sea, and they knew they had to get as far forward as they could before it dove into the next wave. But still, they moved slowly. There were threatening spires of water all around them, reaching well up over the height of the mainmast. It seemed that any one of them might simply slide over *Cane Maiden*, covering it forever.

Steve risked turning a bit further off the wind. *Cane Maiden* heeled a bit more, but with her sails full, she would ride steadier. It was more frightening to the two men going forward, but probably less dangerous. He was fighting against the force of the small sail that caught the wind behind him. He knew that he would have to reef it down a good way if he were to be able to keep his heading and hold his speed.

Bill and Howard were forward of the mast when the next wave attacked them. They squeezed the railing on the edge of the pilothouse and crouched low, but still the force of the sea drove them back. Bill, on the downwind side, clung desperately as his legs were carried out from under him. Howard was battered painfully against the side of the pilothouse. But the instant that the rush of water was by them, they drove themselves forward toward the bow.

Bill tied one of the free lines around the port life rail, knotting it amateurishly. Then he crawled across the deck and held the other free line out to Howard. Their hands came close, but then *Cane Maiden* pitched, forcing Bill back across the deck. He took another hand hold and started across again. This time he made it all the way to the windward rail and began tying the line.

Another wave washed over the starboard bow. Bill grabbed the lifeline with both hands and the tarpaulin slipped away from him, carried aft by the flow. But the two lines held. The canvas spread out over the top of the greenhouse with its after end snapping wildly. Howard was able to catch the securing line on his side and begin tying it off.

Below deck, Marilyn and Cindy saw the tarpaulin close over the broken glass. The trickle of water stopped instantly. They were bewildered for a second, but then broke into laughter when they understood what had happened. "We did it," Marilyn nearly sang. She threw her arms around Cindy, forgetting for the moment that they were balancing on top of the benches. "We did it!" she yelled down to Jeanne.

29

Bill worked his way aft during the tense lull between waves, caught the last free line from the tarp, and tied it off to the life rail. The cloth was now stretched over the entire foredeck, bulging up at the point where it covered the greenhouse. He was laughing with success when he made it back into the cockpit, and aimed a thumbs-up at Howard.

"Nice going," Steve complimented. "Now get behind me and reef the mizzen down about half-way."

Bill looked up at the sail. There was no crank on the boom.

"You have to tie this one down," Steve said. "Fold it onto the boom and tie it off."

Bill didn't understand.

"Show him," Steve ordered Howard.

Howard looked cautiously at the open deck and the tangle of lines that secured the dinghy. The small rubber boat was bouncing in the wind, trying to tear itself free. It was a risky working platform at best.

"Reef it in!" Steve repeated.

Howard unhooked from the forward track and brought his safety line to the after end of the cockpit. He had just connected it when the bow took another wave, and a new cascade of water rolled across them. He clutched the windward mizzen shroud, afraid to climb up.

"Then take the wheel," Steve said. "Just hold it off the wind. I'll get the sail."

Howard waited until *Cane Maiden* rose up above the waves. Then he released the shroud and dashed over to the helm.

"Right here," Steve said. He hesitated an instant until Howard seemed to have the course. Then he sprung out of the cockpit and took hold of the mizzenmast. Quickly, he released the sheet to slack the sail. He was just beginning to gather it in when *Cane Maiden* plunged her bow into the next churning roller.

The wave roared over the cockpit, hit Steve and spun him around the mast. The halyard slipped out of his grip and, as he tried to catch it out of the wind, his other hand came free. The blast of the water drove him backward, his feet tangling in the moorings to the dinghy. Then, without a sound, he vanished over the transom.

"Steeeve!" Bill screeched like the wind. He raced aft but was suddenly pulled up short by his safety line. "Steeve!" He darted forward, losing traction on the slippery deck, and unclipped the cable from the track. Then he carried it aft, and reconnected it as he jumped up on top of the dinghy. "Steeeve!"

At first, all he saw was the wild wash that trailed behind the boat. He blinked the rain out of his eyes, but there was no sign of the captain.

"Howard! What do we do?"

Howard hunched closer to the wheel. He should turn up into the wind to kill his speed so that he wouldn't run away from the man lost overboard. But, with the spanker sail blowing freely, the bow was being pushed down wind by the pressure on the jib. He was having trouble holding it.

"Howard," Bill screamed from the transom. But Howard didn't answer. Instead, he squeezed his grip on the wheel even tighter.

Then Bill saw Steve snap out of the water only a few feet astern, jerked up by his safety line that was slicing through the wash. He realized that Steve was being dragged through the sea, and he snatched at the cable to pull the captain forward, along the leeward side.

"I'm losing her!" It was Howard's cry of panic as he battled the wheel. *Cane Maiden* was turning completely across the wind, exposing her windward flank to the sea. She was beginning to slip sideways, down the slope of the wave that she had been climbing only seconds before, and threatening to ride over the man struggling in the water. Bill eased the cable, letting Steve fall aft. He lifted the safety line over the transom, and then leaned out over the dinghy to recover the captain over the stern.

"I can't turn her," Howard screamed. The force of the sea now controlled the boat. With the jib hauled in close, the wind was heeling her precariously. Then the next wave rumbled down the mountain of water, crashed against the upturned hull, and drove *Cane Maiden* further over. She broached across the wild white water and rolled on her side. Her towering mast stabbed into the sea.

TUESDAY

30

As *Cane Maiden* rolled, Howard was flung off the helm, into the half-sunk corner of the cockpit. His safety line held him in the boat, but he was struggling to keep his head out of the water. Bill hung vertically from the dinghy, his body on deck, his legs dragging in the sea. Steve, who had drifted under the stern, was being dragged under the boat by the safety line that was caught over the transom. They were all helpless, pinned into their suddenly upside-down world by the inertial forces the boat was generating as it slid sideways before the wave.

The pilothouse had gone mad. The leeward bulkhead was now the deck, and the deck had become a towering wall. The three women had fallen across the cabin, and then locker and cabinet doors had broken open, sending kitchenware, books and deck gear crashing down on top of them. Sea water spilled through the makeshift patch in the greenhouse. They couldn't move. Their only defense was to cover their faces against the shower of debris, and to pray that they could stay above the rising water level in the cabin.

Cane Maiden was in free-fall, helpless before the wave. The entire port deck was under water. On the starboard side, her bottom was turned up all the way to the curve of her keel. At the stern, her rudder and propeller were out of the water, both useless. Her fate was in the powerful wave that drove her. It would either bury her mast and turn her completely over, or it would slide beneath her and go on its way, leaving her to try and right herself.

Bill hauled himself up the dinghy, which rose like a sheer rock face above his head. Howard struggled in waist-deep water, reaching out for a handhold on the compass binnacle. In the water, Steve was being battered against the underside of the stern, trying to push himself clear so that he wouldn't be dragged under.

Then, as suddenly as it had started, the death fall ended. *Cane Maiden* bobbed up on top of the wash, and slid gently down its other side. With a loud groan, she lifted her rigging out of the water, and began to roll back upright. Howard was able to stand in the now knee-deep water that was draining out of the scuppers at the rear of the cockpit. He was able to get hold of the wheel. Bill was no longer climbing, but was stretched out across the top of the dinghy. In the water, Steve was close aboard on the starboard side, caught by his safety line that was tangled under the stern.

The jib was still close-hauled. It filled as soon as it rose out of the water, and began pushing the bow further down wind. *Cane Maiden* was turning completely about, pointing her stern into the trough it was now entering, and toward the roll of white water that was already forming atop the next crest.

Howard tried to stop her swing and turn her

back into the seas. But the wheel was locked. It wouldn't move and he couldn't work it free. He looked around in panic, and saw the cause. Steve's lifeline, which Bill was once again holding, was fastened to a port side track. Steve was in the water to starboard. The cable was wrapped under the stern and was probably laying across the rudder. Until Bill could drag Steve against the rush of the sea and around the stern, *Cane Maiden* would have no steering.

"Cut him free," Howard yelled to Bill. He jabbed his finger furiously at the clasp that was fitted into the track. "Pull the release. Let him go."

Bill understood. If he freed the line, then they might be able to bring Steve back on board over the starboard side. But the sea was churning wildly. More than likely, he would be pushed away from them. And even if he weren't, there was little chance that Bill could reach down to him from the rising and falling deck. The safety line was Steve's best hope. He shook his head, refusing Howard's order, and tugged at the cable.

"Cut him free, dammit!" Howard left the frozen wheel and lunged at the cable fitting. He snapped it out of the track. "Let go! He's going to kill us."

The image of Steve pointing the rapid-fire pistol into his face flashed through Bill's mind. Howard was right. The man had threatened to kill them, and now his lifeline was a new danger to all of them. But he couldn't simply open his hands and let Steve drift away. As the cable slipped through his fingers, he tightened his grip, finally catching the clasp that Howard had released. He began edging around the dinghy toward the starboard side, where Steve's head would reappear momentarily, only to disappear in the next swell. He pulled the line taut, lifting Steve's shoulders out of the water. The young captain was able to reach up and get a grip on the gunwale.

Howard felt the wheel spin free and realized that the rudder was no longer fouled. He turned aft to determine his best direction back into the wind. But he froze when he saw the next tumbling wave racing downhill toward the stern.

For an instant, the new wall of water pushed down on the transom, lifting the bow. But then its force rushed under the stern, lifting the back of the yacht, and driving its bowsprit downward. *Cane Maiden* began surfboarding, racing forward ahead of the wave that was rolling behind her.

Howard twisted the wheel back and forth, trying to keep behind the bow and prevent the stern from sliding around to one side. If he lost the stern, then the boat would broach again, certain to be knocked over just as it had been before. Bill was spread across the dinghy, with the spray pounding down on top of him. He held himself aboard with one hand that clutched the mizzenmast. The other hand was dug into the soft collar of Steve's life jacket. Steve clung to the edge of the deck, his legs flailing in the air as he tried to hold them above the power of the thrashing water.

From the helm, Howard looked down over the bow and saw that it was beginning to bury. The bowsprit was already skimming over the surface. He felt his stern tipping to port and rising even higher. If the bow plunged, then the sea would throw the stern past it, sending *Cane Maiden* into a lethal cartwheel. There was enough power in the wave to snap her in half. He spun the wheel, trying to steer the boat back into line. It turned freely. The rudder, with as much pressure from behind as the boat's movement was generating from ahead, was useless. He dropped down on his knees and hugged the wheel stanchion, waiting for the worst.

But the race ended. The boat slowed and the bow bobbed up. The white water that had been roaring behind them was now passing beneath the keel. Once again, *Cane Maiden* had dodged her destruction.

Steve was able to lift his face over the gunwale, and then swing one knee onto the deck. Bill shifted his grip from the collar of the jacket to Steve's belt, and dragged him over the deck and into the cockpit.

"Slack the jib," he ordered Howard. He hit the starter on the engine, and set the speed for full ahead. Then he bounded up onto the dinghy next to Bill, and began gathering in the spanker. He reefed her halfway down and then told Bill to haul in the halyard and tie her off. He left it flapping as he rushed down into the cockpit to set the jib drawing.

Then he was back at the helm. With the jib drawing and the engine racing, *Cane Maiden* was moving. Steve turned her to starboard, hoping to get the bow back into the wind before the next wave struck. As soon as he felt the wind shifting to the starboard side, he hauled in the mizzen sheet. The spanker caught the wind and drove the stern around. *Cane Maiden* began climbing the next mountain, rising toward another confrontation with the tumbling white water. Her bow was pointing up when the sea hit. She sliced through, tossing the wave's power aside, and shrugging off the water that rolled down her deck.

Steve flicked the bilge pump switch to start pumping out the water that she had taken on while she was pinned on her side. "Trim the jib," he told Howard. He reached back himself to set the spanker. The boat heeled gently and gathered speed.

It was only then that Steve's shoulders sagged. He took a deep breath and settled back against the bench. Bill reached over, took the end of his safety line, and snapped it back into the deck track.

Steve nodded. "Thanks." Then he remembered the hands that had clung to his lifeline and had lifted him out of the sea. "Thanks," he repeated.

"Yeah," was all the acknowledgment that Bill could manage. Then he added, "I ought to check below." He unbuckled and transferred his lifeline to the pilothouse. Then he slid the hatch open and dropped down the ladder.

He stepped into shoetop water that washed back and forth, carrying the debris that had fallen from the lockers. The three women were sitting together, braced into the saloon benches. Marilyn and Cindy were staring across at one another. Jeanne was hunched down, her arms again wrapped around the mast trunk. Bill saw that Cindy was no longer holding the gun.

"You all right?" he asked.

"I think so," Marilyn answered.

"Jeanne?"

She nodded, but she didn't even look up at him.

"Cindy?"

When she turned to him, he jaw a welt on her forehead, and a smear of blood wiped into her hair. "I'm okay."

"How are we doing?" Marilyn asked.

"We're going to make it. Steve has everything under control."

He sloshed forward and laid a reassuring hand on Jeanne's shoulder. "I think the worst is over."

The cabin shook as the bow cut through another wave. "It's still flowing up there, but Steve and Howard can handle it."

She clutched the mast even harder.

Bill worked his way aft and climbed the ladder. By now, he understood the boat's tempo through the wild seas. The bow dove as soon as they crested a wave. There wouldn't be another one until they had climbed halfway up the next mountainous swell. It was safe to open the hatch and go back out.

In the cockpit, Steve was once again standing behind the helm. Howard was crouched in the front corner of the cockpit where he could take a secure handhold and duck under the wash that would soon be coming over the deck.

"It's easing up a bit," Steve announced. Howard straightened up and looked across the bow. He wasn't convinced. But as he scampered down from the pilothouse, Bill could feel that some of the sting had gone out of the rain. The wind wasn't driving it as furiously. The contours of the mountains that surrounded them seemed to be softer.

"It still scares the hell out of me," he admitted.

"Me too," Steve said.

The bow rose and then crashed through another row of surf. Steve slipped the prop into idle and turned the engine down to low. Even with the minimum canvas she was flying, *Cane Maiden* was sailing faster than the auxiliary could drive her. She didn't need the propeller. The engine was running just fast enough to keep the batteries charged, so that the pumps would keep working.

Crest after crest slipped beneath them. Bill could see the waves flattening, and feel the rolling that had replaced the boat's violent pitching. They seemed to have regained control from the sea. They were setting their own direction, no longer at the mercy of the waves.

They stood together in the cockpit for over an hour, ducking low under the spray, but no longer threatened by its force. There were no words shared among them. Each of the men had disappeared into his own private thoughts.

The rain stopped, something that Bill became aware of when he saw Steve brush back the hood of his foul-weather slicker. He did the same, and then combed out his matted hair with his fingers. He looked up, and saw a faint point of light blinking over head. He laughed out loud, and pointed out the star to Howard.

"I never expected to see one of those again."

Howard glanced up, but didn't answer.

31

"Steve Berlind."

Al Weston had repeated the name as he wrote it down, balancing the paper on the small counter in the phone booth while he cradled the phone against his shoulder.

Then Walter Linz had told him, "The address is 'Drake . . . something . . . charts.' It's hard to read. It's written in pencil on the corner of the envelope. But it's in Tortola. Tortola BVI."

Linz had bribed the manager of the small, off-the-beach apartment house where Cindy rented a room over a back alley. His men had then tossed the place looking for any evidence of where she might have gone and the names of anyone she knew. All they found were two postcards, signed "Steve," and one short letter with a return address on the envelope.

"She must have met this guy on her last trip down there for us," Walter had speculated. "I gather from the letter that they spent a couple of nights together aboard a boat."

"I'll find him," Al had promised, although Steve Berlind didn't sound like much of a lead. A guy who could handle a multi-million-dollar theft wouldn't keep in touch with his co-conspirators by writing postcards in pencil. Still, he was a friend that Cindy might have run to. And if he owned a boat . . .

Then he reported on his lack of progress. He had interrogated the truck driver who had cut him off, and he pretty much believed that the guy was telling the truth. Cindy's cab driver was a small-time thief who stumbled onto something far bigger than he could imagine. It didn't look like a careful plan involving professionals. Cindy was probably a victim rather than a conspirator.

They hadn't been able to find her. She had never returned to her hotel and she wasn't in any of the other hotels. She hadn't left the island by plane, at least not by a commercial flight. Al had explained how he had checked boats leaving Tortola and then had checked with the marinas and with harbor control. The boats that had claimed not to have been in Road Harbor had been telling him the truth. None of them had logged in to Road Harbor before Cindy had disappeared, nor moored with any of the marinas. And the boats that had been coming out of the harbor all seemed to be legitimate. There was nothing suspicious.

"What's your best guess?" Walter had asked him.

"I think that if Cindy was still alive, she'd have brought me the money. I figure that maybe the cabbie had a partner. Another cheap crook who took Cindy and the money. That's what I got Johnnie Igoe doing. He's asking around to find out who the cabbie was friendly with."

"Be careful," Walter Linz had cautioned. "I know you have to ask questions. But we don't want the authorities to begin asking questions about us."

Al had understood Walter's concerns. It was okay to spend a little bribe money to get information. But if he hurt anyone badly, he might draw in the police. Linz could afford to have an occasional deal go sour. Even one as big as this. But he couldn't afford to have the police start picking up his people, and then plea-bargain their way back to him.

He had walked back to the hotel, getting himself drenched in the rain that was pounding the island. Then he had started through the telephone book looking for "Drake . . . something . . . charts." The closest listing was Drake Channel Charters. He dialed the number, and asked for Steve Berlind.

"He's out on a charter," he was told. Al had decided it was worth checking out. There wasn't much else he could do. He couldn't get back up in the helicopter until the weather cleared.

Now he was standing in a small office at the head of one of the piers in Road Harbor, waiting patiently while a vague young man in shorts and a tee shirt thumbed through a stack of charter contracts.

"Yeah, here it is. Steve Berlind." The clerk scanned the form. "He's got two couples out on *Cane Maiden*. They boarded on Saturday."

"*Cane Maiden*?" The name rang a bell. "Let me see that." Al took the contract and read it carefully. The boat had been reserved several months ago, long before the deal that had gone bust had even been thought of. The contract was with a

Howard Hunter, who described himself as an architect from Newton, Massachusetts. The other passenger was a schoolteacher from Manhattan. Both were traveling with their wives. There was nothing to suggest people who would be involved with untraceable bearer bonds or uncut diamonds. But still, the name of the boat seemed familiar.

"You got a picture of *Cane Maiden*?"

"Sure! Here somewhere," the young man answered, gesturing toward the three file cabinets that were behind him. "What's this all about?"

"It's about you making a hundred bucks," Al answered. He took the roll out of his pocket, found a hundred, and dropped it on the counter. "You got a name?"

The clerk went wide-eyed at the money. "Tyler. Tyler Sherwood." He turned to the files. "People call me Ty."

"Nice to know you, Ty." Weston waited while his new friend checked the files.

"Here she is." He took a color photo print out of a manila folder, studied it for a second and then passed it to Al. "She's a beauty!"

Al recognized the old wooden yawl that was shown heeling under full sail. It was one of the boats that he had buzzed. "Was she in harbor on Sunday? In the afternoon, or maybe Sunday night?"

"I don't know. I'd have to check."

Al nodded toward the hundred dollar bill. "Why don't you do that," he said.

The young man lifted a log book up onto the counter and began thumbing its pages. Al took the photo over to the window and studied it in the gray light that was filtering through the rain-drops. He had talked with dozens of boats the day before. Where had he seen this one? He checked the notes he had written in the helicopter, and found *Cane Maiden* at the end of his list. Sure! It was the end of the trip when they were running low on fuel. The guy who didn't have a hailer and had to come up on the radio. That must have been Steve Berlind.

"Out past St. Croix," he read from his notes. "Charter boat from Road Harbor. Might put in on St. Croix."

He remembered. There were the two women out on the deck, and their husbands in the cock-pit. One of the guys had taken the wheel while the captain went below to tune the radio. But there was something else. Something that had bothered him but that he hadn't written down.

Yeah! The guy who took the wheel. Al remem-bered thinking that he knew him from someplace. He had mentioned it to the pilot. They figured he had probably seen the guy around Road Town. But where the hell was it?

"She was in Saturday," Tyler called over the counter. "Went out Sunday morning and came back in Sunday night. Then she went out again early Monday."

Right, Al thought. That was what the captain had told him over the radio. He had said that they left Road Town early Monday morning. Didn't seem that he had anything to hide.

And yet, the timing was right. Cindy's meeting had gone bad late Sunday afternoon. The boat came in Sunday night and went back out early

Monday morning. If she had been working with Steve, that's about the kind of schedule they would follow. But, Al reconsidered, if she had been working with Steve, then she and he would be alone. They wouldn't be taking a couple of vacationers for a boat ride.

His mind spun with possibilities. Maybe Steve was the cabbie's accomplice. He could have deep-sixed Cindy and taken the money aboard *Cane Maiden*. Then it would make sense that he would be carrying on with his charter cruise, making everything seem normal.

But that didn't work. *Cane Maiden* was out to sea in the afternoon, so Berlind couldn't have been at Parson's Boatyard. Unless . . .

Al tried another scenario. Cindy could have run to Steve looking for help. And once he heard about the money, he might have decided that he didn't need Cindy. He could have taken the money and tied her to the weight at the end of a mooring.

Except his passengers would have seen her. He couldn't get rid of the girl and then just say, "Okay folks, let's go cruising." Of course, he might have met her on the beach and left her there. Or maybe the vacationers were ashore when Cindy came out to the boat. It could have worked out that the couples in Steve's charter never saw the girl.

He walked back to the counter, picked up the bill and stuffed it into the young man's pocket. "Any way you can find out whether Berlind was ashore Sunday night? Or whether his passengers came ashore?"

"No, we wouldn't know that," he answered.

"That's up to the captain and the passengers. Once they take the boat, they can do pretty much what they please." He thought of the money that had just been placed in his shirt. "If there was any way, I'd sure find out for you."

Al nodded. "That's okay." Then he asked, "When's *Cane Maiden* due back in?"

The kid checked the contract. "Friday night. The people have a flight back to New York on Saturday."

"She putting in anyplace before then?"

"Anywhere she wants. Like I said, it's pretty much up to people who chartered the boat."

It all sounded innocent, too normal to be suspicious. If Berlind had to bring the boat back to Road Town, then he certainly wasn't on the run. But, still, there was something that bothered him about *Cane Maiden*. The guy who had taken the wheel. Al couldn't place him, but he was certain that he knew him. And if he was right, then someone he knew was on the same boat with the one person on Tortola that Cindy knew. A hell of a coincidence.

Weston reached into his pocket and dropped another hundred dollar bill on the counter. "There's a couple of things you might be able to do for me." Tyler seemed more than anxious to oblige. "I want you to find out where *Cane Maiden* is now, and get me the names of any ports where she put in. Or where she's thinking of putting in. Can you do that?"

"Yeah. I can raise Steve on the radio and ask him."

Al thought for a moment. "I don't want to spook

this guy," he said. "Last thing I want to do is worry him. This isn't all that important. Fact is, one of the ladies on board may be the wife of a guy I'm working for. If she's there, it could help save some alimony."

"Oh, yeah," the kid said knowingly. "But Steve won't get spooked. There was a storm last night. Nothing unusual about our dock master checking up on the boats."

Weston took the second hundred dollar bill from the counter and pushed it into Tyler's pocket on top of the first one. "You can see why I wouldn't want anyone knowing that I was asking."

The young man shook his head. "No one will ever hear anything from me."

Al started to put the picture back on the counter. Then he asked, "Can I keep this?"

"Sure."

"I'll be back in a couple of hours."

He walked out of the office and onto the dock. The rows of tied up yachts seemed to go on forever. Then he looked at the photograph. It was no wonder that he remembered *Cane Maiden*. She had different lines; a very distinctive stance. But, he admitted to himself, that wasn't the real reason. It was the guy who had taken over the wheel. The more Al thought about it, the more positive he was that he knew him from somewhere. It seemed he had some sort of problem with the man, sometime in the past. He wasn't just someone he had happened to notice in Road Town. But where was it? Who was he?

32

The seas were still heavy when a dull sun pushed through the gray horizon. The swells were higher than the deck, and *Cane Maiden*'s bow sent up a white spray each time it plunged. But they were no longer in any danger. The wind had dropped to the point where Steve was able to run the spanker up all the way, and raise the main to better than half its full height. They took off their safety belts so that they could move about the deck freely. Bill and Howard went forward, removed the tarpaulin from over the greenhouse, and opened the hatches to let drying air into the cabin below.

Marilyn found the stove steady enough to light a fire and put on a pot of coffee. Jeanne and Cindy worked side by side lifting the debris from the deck, and repacking those items that could be dried.

As the sun rose, the gray surface flattened and began to show its blue color. The men took off the oilskin slickers and tugged at the clothes that were stuck to their skin. Bill and Howard hoisted the mainsail all the way to the masthead, and then Howard took over the steering while Steve went below and tried to plot a Loran fix. But the radio and navigation equipment had been submerged when the boat rolled. The controls of the radio panel had been smashed by falling debris. Nothing was working.

When Steve came back up on deck, he spent a few minutes evaluating the soft waves that were swelling up from the south and decided that there would be no problem sailing across them. He ordered a course change to a more westerly direction.

"Where are we?" Bill asked.

"I'm not sure. But a lot further south than I wanted to be."

"Where are we heading?"

"Toward St. Kitts."

Howard asked, "How far away?"

Steve couldn't be precise. "We should be able to make it late tonight. Maybe sometime early morning. Depends on the wind."

The sun began to heat the air. Marilyn and Jeanne came topside through the open greenhouse, and sat out on the bow. Cindy came up into the cockpit and stood close to Steve for a few minutes. Then she worked her way forward and joined the women.

They were sailing normally, making good speed across rolling seas. There was no longer anything to fear from the weather. But now yesterday's tension was returning. Even though he wasn't holding the pistol, Steve was still in charge. He was still following a plan that determined their fate. And he wasn't sharing it with anyone.

The sun climbed higher. Bill peeled off his shirt, and Howard went below to find dry clothes. He came back up dragging a soaked duffle. It had been under his bunk when the boat rolled onto its side, filling half his cabin with sea water. Carefully, he began laying wet clothes out onto the bench to dry.

"Maybe it's time to put up the genoa," Steve said.

Reflexively, Howard started up to the deck. But Bill stopped next to the helm.

"First, it's time for you to level with us. Like I said, we're all in this together. I think we have a right to know just what it is that we're in on."

Steve glanced from Bill to Howard. Then he looked back up at the sails. "Cindy and me have a problem with some pretty nasty people. We can work it out. It's nothing you want to get involved with."

Bill turned so that he was face to face with the captain. "That's no good, Steve. You pointed a gun at me. You pistol-whipped my friend. That sure as hell makes us involved. I want an answer. What are we involved in?"

Steve smiled sheepishly. "You weren't in any danger. We couldn't have shot anyone."

Bill's muscles tightened as he remembered the moment when Steve had the gun aimed at him and had been about to pull the trigger. It took all his strength to keep from smashing a fist into the smug face. Then he felt Howard flashing past him.

"You little son-of-a-bitch," Howard blurted as he moved around the helm. His jaw was set and his eyes were suddenly alive with rage. His right fist fired over the top of the wheel. Steve began to duck away, but the blow glanced off his cheek and sent him sprawling across the after bench.

273

Howard leaped on top of him. His hands locked around the young man's throat. "I'll kill you, you fucking bastard."

Bill grabbed Howard and tried to drag him off Steve. Howard lost his grip on the young man's throat, but managed one more punch that crashed into Steve's ribs.

"It's over, Howard! We're past that!" Bill said as he struggled with his friend.

Howard tried to tear free so that he could get back to the murder that he had started. "It's not over. Nothing is over until that little prick is either dead or in jail."

Bill fell back into the port side bench, hauling Howard down on top of him. Steve sat up slowly and weakly. His eyes were glazed and there was an open cut on the left side of his face. Howard flailed at him, but couldn't break Bill's bear hug. Slowly, his struggling stopped. As Bill eased his grip, Howard knocked his hands away. But he made no move toward Steve. He stood slowly, and stared down at his former captor. Then he pointed a warning finger. "It's not over. You hear me?"

From the bow, the women looked on in amazement. The explosion had come so suddenly out of the dreary silence that Cindy had scarcely started to her feet when Bill had pulled the other two apart. She settled back slowly.

Steve got back to the wheel and eased *Cane Maiden* back to her course. He touched his cheek and found blood, then indicated the bruise on Howard's head and said, "Look, we're even. Okay?" Howard started toward him, but Bill stepped in the way.

"I'm sorry," Steve offered.

Bill turned on him. "That's not good enough! What you did rates a hell of a lot more than 'I'm sorry.' I want an answer. We want to know what's going on, and we want to know now."

Steve was nodding before Bill finished. "Okay, you're right." He glanced at Howard. "I was going to tell you." He looked back at Bill. "When you dragged me back on board last night, I knew there'd be no more guns. I knew I was going to cut you in. But I just haven't figured everything out. It isn't simple. It's complicated. And it's dangerous."

"What the fuck haven't you figured out yet?" Howard demanded. "Where you're going to dump our bodies?"

Bill made sure to keep himself between the two men. Howard's rage peaked every time he looked at Steve. He looked across the wheel. "Maybe we better figure it out together."

"Yeah," Steve agreed. "We're all in it together."

"In what?" Howard demanded over Bill's shoulder.

Bill got Howard settled on the windward bench and then sat beside him. They both stared at Steve, who kept his place behind the helm.

"Cindy was down here as a mule," Steve began. He saw their instant confusion. "A courier. She was carrying a lot of money for some people in Florida. Not cash. Bonds."

Howard sneered with grim satisfaction. He had been right. "In the camera cases," he added for Steve.

"Yeah. In the camera cases. She was supposed

to meet another courier in Tortola. She was going to exchange the bonds for something he was bringing."

"Drugs?" Howard demanded.

"No, not drugs. Diamonds. But the whole exchange went crazy. The taxi driver who drove her to the meeting came back. He shot the other courier. He was about to kill Cindy when the courier shot him. They both died right in front of her."

"Jesus," Bill muttered, visualizing the young woman surrounded by the carnage.

"She panicked. She didn't know what the hell to do. The guy who was supposed to be backing her up never showed. She didn't know whether he was dead, or whether he was working with the cab driver. She figured someone else was going to show up and maybe kill her. So she grabbed everything and ran."

"Ran to you?" Bill asked.

"We know each other. Cindy's been down here before. We spent some time together. Nothing serious. But I'm the only name she knows on the island. So she went to the dock and asked if I was around. One of the guys knew I was, and brought her out to the boat."

"While we were ashore," Howard surmised.

Steve nodded. "She had all this money, and she was frightened out of her wits. She didn't want to take it back to shore because she was certain someone would be looking for her. All she wanted to do was get away. To sort of disappear until she could figure how to get the money back to the guys she works for. So I said I'd help her.

The only thing I could do was take her aboard with you guys."

Howard and Bill thought about what they had just heard. Bill asked, "Why did you wait for us? Why didn't you just leave?"

"That's what we were going to do. That's what Cindy begged me to do. Just pull off the mooring and leave. But I didn't know how long you guys were going to be. You might have been coming out in the launch while I was still inside the sea wall. You would have gone screaming to the charter company, and they'd have been out looking for me before I cleared the channel. There would have been a big commotion, and the people Cindy was running from would have been waiting for us on the dock. I had to wait for you and then take you with us so that no one would know we were running away."

"Running to where?" Bill asked.

"I've got friends on St. Kitts. I used to skipper for a charter company down there. I figured they'd get us to St. Martin, and then on a plane going to Europe. Or maybe South America. Hell, if we could lay low for a while, we could probably get back to the States. I could scuttle the boat. People would just figure that Cane Maiden had gone down. No one would know that Cindy was aboard. And no one would come looking for me if they figured I was lost at sea."

Howard understood. "You were going to take the money with you. The bonds and the diamonds."

"What were we supposed to do?" Steve snapped. "Bring it back? You saw the guy in the helicopter.

What was I supposed to say? 'Hey, friend, I was just holding your money for safekeeping.' You figure a guy like that would just say, 'Great! Very kind of you. Thanks a bunch'? Cindy witnessed two killings that maybe this guy arranged. I know all about the money. We're witnesses! The two of us would end up at the bottom of the bay."

"You were taking the money," Howard repeated. "That's what this is all about. The money."

"No!" Steve insisted. But then he backed down. "Not at first, anyway. Cindy was just trying to stay alive. But then I figured, hell. No one knows where the money is. So we might as well take it with us." He saw Howard's eyes narrowing. "Well what would you have done? It didn't belong to an orphanage, for chrissake! We took it from a bunch of crooks. It wasn't like we were hurting anyone."

Howard turned away abruptly. Listening to Steve justify his actions was stoking his fires. He wanted to throttle the obnoxious kid.

"It's easy for you," Steve taunted. "You're rich. You could just throw it over the side and it wouldn't matter. But it's different for Cindy and me. All we ever got from anyone was a lot of shit. People like you, who think you know it all just because you got a lot of money. Getting into her pants. And fucking me over. Well, this was our chance. We were done taking other people's shit."

Howard wheeled and started off the bench. Bill jumped up to restrain him. Howard jabbed a finger over Bill's shoulder and into Steve's face. "I wasn't into anyone's pants. And I wasn't fucking you over."

"No? The hell you weren't! You come aboard in your fucking sailor suit and start ordering me around like I was a goddamm deckhand. I'm a captain, goddammit. A better one than you'll ever be!"

Howard was twisting and pushing, trying to get past Bill. And now Steve was coming around the wheel, ready to fight Howard. Bill had to wrestle his friend back onto the bench. "Take it easy, Howard. Take it easy. We still have things to work out. Bashing this kid's face in isn't going to do us any good."

Steve backed up to the helm and tried to find his course while his anger settled. Howard nodded to Bill that he was back under control. "I don't like some punk risking my life for a couple of thousand bucks," he explained to Bill.

Steve laughed. "It's more than a couple of thousand bucks, my friend. A lot more."

"I don't give a rat's ass how much it is," Howard fired back. But he made no move toward Steve. He relaxed into the bench and let Bill settle beside him.

"It wasn't a bad plan," Bill agreed with Steve. "Except . . ."

Steve nodded. He knew where Bill was heading. "Except what were we going to do with you," he said, finishing Bill's thought. Then he looked up helplessly at the sails, and searched the sky as if he might find an answer there.

33

Bill waited for several seconds. Then, in a calm tone, he asked, "What were you going to do with us?"

He waited, but Steve wouldn't even look in his direction. So he brought the question to its only conclusion. "The only way you could get away with it would be if all four of us went down with *Cane Maiden* when you scuttled her."

Steve managed to look at the two men. "Yeah. You're right. But I couldn't have done that. I admit I thought about it, but I knew I couldn't do it. That's what I've been trying to think through. How do I get you people out of this without putting Cindy and me in danger. I was going to pay you. Pay you a lot. I figured maybe you could give us a couple of days' head start before you got in touch with Tortola. Maybe you could say that the boat went down, but that you got off in the dinghy. You could say I went down with the boat. Or that we got separated. Or something. That's what I was trying to figure out."

"You were going to pay us?" Howard asked, spitting out the words in anger. "For what you've done to us . . . and our wives . . . you were going to pay us?"

"I didn't mean for it to sound that way."

Howard was struggling to stay in his seat. "How the hell else could it sound?"

Steve stumbled through his explanation. "Look. Suppose — just for a minute — suppose that I could put you ashore on an empty beach. Say in Nevis, or St. Kitts. I know a lot of places where you could land without anyone seeing you. I put you ashore with the dinghy. Right in close so there's no danger. And then Cindy and me disappear with the boat. You hide out for a couple of days. And then you find a road and let yourselves get rescued. All you have to say is that the boat was going down and that I put you off in the dinghy. For your own safety. You don't know what happened to the boat."

He looked from one to the other for a response. Howard said nothing. Bill nodded that he was following the plan. But his eyes were narrow with suspicion.

"Meanwhile," Steve continued, "Cindy and me can reach my friends. They'll take the boat out and scuttle it. And then they'll help us get away. When you guys tell your story, they'll start searching for the boat. When they don't find it, they'll figure it went down sometime after you got off. They'll figure I went down with it. There won't be anything to connect Cindy with me, and there won't be any reason to keep looking for me."

Bill stood up slowly and turned his back on the captain. He looked out over the gentle swells, rerunning what he had just heard. "I like it a hell of a lot better than us going down with the boat," he concluded. "At least you weren't going to kill us."

"Yeah," Howard agreed sarcastically. "I guess you figure that makes you some sort of humanitarian." He jumped up from the bench and turned on Bill. "Why the hell are we even listening to this son-of-a-bitch? We ought to be kicking the shit out of him."

Bill ignored his friend and turned back to Steve. "We can't do it. That would make us part of the cover-up. We could get into a lot of trouble. With the police. With the guys you're running away from."

"That's what we'd be paying you for," Steve answered.

Howard wheeled. His anger was still at the edge of exploding. "You think we'd risk jail for a couple of thousand dollars? You think we're as stupid as you are?"

"A couple of hundred thousand dollars," Steve said.

Howard's furious expression went blank immediately. Bill's eyes widened.

"It's a lot of money," Steve said. "I know you'd be taking a risk, but it wouldn't be for nothing."

"A couple of *hundred* thousand dollars?" Howard repeated softly. It wasn't really a question. He was certain of what he had heard. He was just trying to believe it.

"It doesn't matter," Bill concluded. "We can't do it. We need a better plan."

Howard settled slowly back down on the windward bench.

"What we're going to do," Bill continued, "is

282

turn this boat around and head back to Tortola. We get off with our wives, and you and Cindy take the bonds and the diamonds back to where they came from."

"We can't," Steve said. His tone was suddenly frightened. He was pleading when he repeated, "We can't do that."

"Why not?"

"Because they'll kill us."

"Why? Why would they kill you for bringing back their money?"

"They'd kill us because we know about the money."

Bill shook his head. "Cindy already knows about the money. She was working for them."

"They'd kill her for trying to run away with it. They'd know they couldn't trust her. And they'd kill me for helping her."

"I don't believe it," Bill argued.

Steve's voice was beginning to crack with the fear he felt. "You don't know these people. Cindy says killing isn't a big deal to them. It's the way they do business. That's why she was so scared. They won't stop to figure out who was playing square with them and who was trying to cheat them. They won't give a damn if Cindy was frightened and that she panicked. They'll just take their money and kill all the witnesses. They won't think twice about it."

Bill studied Steve suspiciously. Then he looked at Howard.

"He may be right," Howard admitted. But his answer didn't ring with certainty. He sounded more confused than positive.

"And don't think you guys can just walk away. You think they won't figure out that you know about the money, too? You're witnesses. You could cause them trouble. Believe me, they'll come looking for you."

The words punched like a fist into Bill's gut. He hadn't figured that there would be any danger to them. Now he pictured the man in the helicopter coming after Jeanne. He suddenly understood the fear that had been in Steve's face. Slowly, he settled back on the bench next to Howard. For a long moment, the only sound was the run of the sea.

"I'm sorry," Steve said. He seemed to mean it. "But there's no easy way out of this."

The sails rattled in a gust. Then they went quiet again.

Bill finally spoke. "She should have taken the money back to them right away. If she'd gone straight to them, they wouldn't have had any reason to hurt her. They'd have been grateful, for God's sake."

"I know," Steve answered. "She never should have come to me."

Then Bill felt anger. "Why didn't you tell her that? Dammit, you could have told her that waiting — and running — put her in danger. That there was no escape. You could have called for the launch, sent her back to the dock, and told her to go straight back to her friends."

"The guy she was working with never showed up. She thought maybe he was dead."

"That's bullshit," Bill snapped. "Even if she was frightened, you knew that was her only chance. She could have taken the money straight back to her hotel. Whoever she was working for would have known where to find her. All she had to do was hand the money over to her boss. Then she'd be in no danger. Christ, she probably would have been paid extra for saving his deal."

"I suppose so," Steve admitted. "But at the time —"

Bill cut him off. "So why didn't you tell her that?" He began pounding away like a prosecutor cornering a lying witness. "Why did you come up with a stupid plan that put everyone in danger? Her. You. And now us. Why?"

Steve sagged. "Because I wanted the money."

Bill watched his shoulders slump, and his fingers begin fidgeting on the curve of the wheel.

Howard's voice was almost too soft to hear. "You rotten bastard. This is all your fault."

"Jesus," Steve explained, as much to himself as to the others. "It just seemed so right. All this money falling into our laps. All I had to do was sail out of there, and they'd never find us. Hell, they wouldn't even know enough to look for us."

There was another silence, with just the sound of the wind tapping at the edges of the sails. Then Bill reached his decision.

"I think we better get this thing turned around."

But he didn't move. Howard stayed on the bench, his face now resting in his hands. Steve still hung from the wheel.

Finally Steve said, "You're taking me back to my execution."

And then Howard added, "It could be dangerous for all of us." He saw the surprise in Bill's eyes. "I mean for *us*. You and Jeanne. Marilyn and me.

285

I don't give a damn about this punk! But I don't want to put us in danger."

Bill glanced forward and saw the women on the bow, keeping their painful silence as the boat sliced through the sea. Jeanne was sitting against the front of the greenhouse with her knees tucked under her chin, looking straight ahead. Marilyn had gone below, and brought up her soaked clothes. She was stretching them out on the leeward deck. Cindy was sitting on the windward deck. She appeared to be sunbathing, but it was easy for Bill to imagine the thoughts that were torturing her.

"I think the women have to be in on this," he said. "It involves them just as much as us."

Howard nodded, but with no great enthusiasm. His mind seemed to be lost in the dilemma that Steve had just posed.

Bill went forward, stepping around Marilyn's clothes so that he could reach Jeanne. He spoke to her softly, then took her hand and helped her up. The others followed as he led her aft along the windward deck.

When they were all assembled, he turned to Cindy. "Steve just told us what we're all involved in. I think you ought to tell Jeanne and Marilyn. Then we have some decisions to make."

Cindy began talking instantly. It was a confession that she had been dying to make, and she jumped at the opportunity in a torrent of words that came almost too quickly to comprehend.

She began with her assignment and her trip to Tortola, admitting that she had acted as a courier several times in the past. She told them about Al

286

Weston, how he watched her, and what had happened to other couriers who hadn't followed his instructions. Then she told them about the meeting at the boatyard, the sudden, deafening crack of gunfire, the taxi driver who tried to kill her, and then the new explosion of shots that had left her standing between two dead, bleeding corpses.

Jeanne listened with dumb fascination, her eyes unblinking and her face without expression. Marilyn reacted silently to the words. Her hand reached out and touched Cindy's arm in a gesture of support.

Then Cindy told about her escape across the harbor in a boat which she had abandoned at an empty berth, and her careful, frightened movements around the harbor as she tried to find the pier where Steve's boat was tied during their earlier rendezvous. She had been on the dock when the two couples had come ashore, although at the time she had no idea that they had come from the boat that Steve was captaining.

"I wasn't thinking when I came aboard," she told them. "I was too scared to think. When we decided to run, I had no idea where I'd be running to. I just wanted to get away."

She looked directly at Marilyn and then at Jeanne. "I never thought how I'd be hurting you. I didn't want to hurt you. But Steve said that we couldn't leave you. And I saw he was right. I understood that we'd have to take you with us. But I didn't mean for you to be . . . like . . . prisoners, or anything. I didn't mean for you to be afraid."

She turned to Bill and Howard. "I wasn't thinking. And then, when we . . ." — she found the

287

memory difficult — ". . . were holding a gun on you, and ordering you around . . . it was too late. I didn't want to do what we were doing, but I didn't know what else to do. Do you know what I mean?"

It was easy for Bill to nod his acceptance of what he knew was intended as an apology. He had recognized the fright in her eyes as soon as he saw her in the daylight. He had understood that she was caught up in something that she couldn't handle.

But Howard gave no hint of understanding. He stared coldly at Cindy as she went on with the story.

"Once we were out at sea, I began thinking. I knew there was no way I could . . . hurt you . . . or put you in danger. I wanted to turn around and go back. To let you go and try to find someone who would take back the money. It seemed like the only answer. But then I got confused. I thought if we went back, maybe they would kill me. Maybe they'd kill us all. I just didn't know what to do."

She looked around, first at the men and then to the women for some expression of understanding and forgiveness. All their eyes were turned away.

She looked at Steve, who had kept busy with his steering all through her story. "Steve? What are we gonna do?"

"Steve isn't deciding," Howard hissed through a set jaw. He took Bill and their two wives in his glance. "We're the ones who are going to do the deciding."

Bill began explaining what their alternatives were. He outlined Steve's plan of putting them ashore, and using them to establish the story that would cover Steve and Cindy's escape. Then he explained his own view that they should turn *Cane Maiden* around and head back to Tortola.

Both Jeanne and Marilyn sided immediately with Bill. Until he raised the possibility that their connection to the money could put them in danger.

"I don't think it's a real problem," he speculated. "My guess is that these people will be damn glad to get their money back." He spoke to the two wives as he continued, "But Steve is right about one thing. I don't know them. I don't know how they think or how they might act. So, I guess we have to at least consider that they might think of us as witnesses."

He turned toward Cindy. "What about it?"

She shook her head. "I don't know. I don't know what they'd do. Al scares the hell out of me."

"It's not fair," Jeanne nearly screamed. "Why should we be in danger for something we didn't do?" But she knew the question had no meaning the moment she asked it. They weren't talking about what was fair. They were talking about their best chance for survival.

Marilyn wasn't sure about the danger to her and her friends. But she believed Cindy, and she didn't think they could simply leave the girl to whatever fate might await her on Tortola.

"She was pointing a gun at you," Howard nearly screamed.

"She doesn't know how to use a gun," Marilyn fired back.

Jeanne sided with Howard. "Why are you worrying about them?" she demanded of Marilyn and Bill. "They were planning to kill us. They could still get us killed. We should be worrying about ourselves."

Howard leaped out of his seat and started for the hatch. "This is crazy. Jeanne is right. Why are we even talking about helping them? I don't want to hear any more of this."

"We need your help to think this through," Bill yelled after him. But Howard disappeared down the hatch.

They continued without him. Marilyn asked Cindy what would happen if she and Steve went straight to the police.

"I'd have to hope that they kept me in jail forever, because Weston and his friends would be waiting for me the day I got out."

Steve interrupted. "Our best chance is if you help us to just disappear. They don't know that Cindy is aboard *Cane Maiden*. All you'd have to do is say that I was lost. Put us ashore. Go back in the boat and don't say anything about Cindy. Just say I went over in the storm."

Bill thought, "It might work. Howard ought to be able to sail us back to Tortola."

Steve pressed the opening. "And we'd share the money with you. We'd make it worth your while."

Marilyn shook her head. The money wasn't the issue. She was trying to decide whether they could really help the two young people without putting themselves in danger. But Jeanne looked straight at Steve. "You already owe us something for what you've put us through. You wouldn't be doing us any favors. You'd just be giving us what we deserve."

Cindy was anxious to agree. She was genuinely sorry for the terror she and Steve had caused the two couples. She was anxious to make amends.

"This bullshit is stopping right now!"

They spun toward Howard's voice as he stood up out of the hatch. "I'm taking charge."

He had the automatic pistol in his hand, and he stabbed the barrel toward Steve and Cindy. "I don't give a damn about these two bastards. The only thing that counts is what's best for us." He stepped down from the pilothouse onto the windward deck and started into the cockpit.

"Howard, for God's sake. . ." Bill started.

"I don't need anything from you," Howard hissed at his friend. "I told you to cut that motherfucker loose. If you hadn't dragged him back we wouldn't have this problem."

Bill was stunned. His friend was clearly out of control, and he was waving a pistol. He moved cautiously, putting himself between Howard and the women.

"Howard!" Marilyn started to get up. "What are you doing?"

"I'll show you what I'm doing." He swung the gun toward the open side of the cockpit and squeezed the trigger. The blast was sudden and deafening. The women ducked away, their hands clamped to their ears. Steve dropped down behind the helm.

"Jesus," Bill screamed as he started toward Howard, but his prayer was drowned out by the gunshots that tossed the sea off the port side into an angry spray. Then, just before he could grab for the gun, the shooting stopped. The echo died quickly.

"That's what they were going to do to us," Howard yelled into Bill's face. "This thug . . ." The gun jabbed toward Steve, then it snapped toward Cindy, ". . . and his slut were going to line us up on the rail and blow us over the side."

"No! No we weren't," Cindy begged.

Howard didn't even hear her. He turned the gun back on Steve. "That's what you were planning for us, wasn't it? A couple of quick shots and then on your way with the money."

Steve shook his head. "No." He backed away. He could see the cold hatred in Howard's face as Howard followed him around the wheel.

"Well I'm in charge now." Howard raised the gun until it was pointing right between the young man's eyes. "You have any problem with that?"

"No," Steve said. "No problem. We'll work together. There's plenty of money for all of us." He had retreated as far as he could, up against the leeward bench.

"Put down the gun, Howard!" Bill ordered. It would take him only two steps around the wheel to be within reach of Howard and to be able to grab for the pistol. But his friend was at the edge of his temper, and his finger was already squeezing the trigger. Steve could be dead before Bill took his first step. Bill held himself as still as a statue. "Put down the gun!"

Howard didn't seem to hear him. He kept moving after Steve. "Where is it? Where's the money?"

"It's here! Aboard!"

"Where is it?"

Steve understood that the money was the only thing that was keeping him alive. "It's hidden. You'll never find it."

"Tell me where it is!" Howard was screaming. The hand that held the pistol began trembling with rage.

"Tell him," Cindy yelled.

"It's hidden." Steve said. "I'll get it for you. But first put away the gun."

"Tell me!" He grabbed Steve's shirt, pulled him close and pressed the barrel of the pistol under his chin.

"I'll get it," Cindy begged.

"No," Steve warned her. "He'll kill us."

Howard pushed Steve ahead of him to the edge of the cockpit. He twisted the shirt and dug the point of the gun into Steve's neck.

"Where's the money?" His voice was now a breathless whisper. "I won't ask again. Where's the money?"

Steve knew he would be dead the instant that Howard had the money. It was his only bargaining chip. But the gun was pressing into his throat. With the back of his hand, he knocked the pistol aside and then made a grab for Howard's arm. He held it tight as they wrestled onto the deck. Howard flung him away. Steve grabbed wildly as he fell over the lifeline. Then he dropped backward into the sea.

34

The sky had cleared over Road Town, and the winds had settled to occasional gusts. Al Weston was having a cup of coffee with Johnnie Igoe in the hotel restaurant before leaving for the airport where his helicopter was waiting.

"If you ask me, we're wasting our time," Igoe said, tearing open his third packet of sugar. "Your lady is at the bottom of the channel wearing a couple of hundred pounds of anchor chain. Somebody else has got the stuff. We don't even know who we're looking for."

"Maybe," Al allowed. "If she was working with someone, then you're probably right. If someone got his hands on the money, then why in hell would he need Cindy?" He broke a piece off his danish and dunked it in his coffee. "The problem is that I just don't believe that she was working with anyone. I think she just got scared and ran."

"Then why ain't she showed up? She knows where to find you. If she wanted to bring the money back, she'd have called you by now."

Igoe had given Weston a full report of his activities. They had revisited all the hotels and combed the marinas without finding a trace of Cindy. They had paid visits to some of the other cab drivers who were friendly with Cindy's driver. All of them had laughed at the notion that their friend might be working with a big-time syndicate. "Mon, every time he get a little money, he go straight to the bar," one man had told them.

"He be back soon," another had promised. "He just gone off for a couple a days with a couple of bottles and a lady. He be back, soon as the rum run out."

And they had inquired cautiously with some of the established underworld types who dealt in drugs for the tourists and managed the inter-island smuggling. They had offered attention-getting rewards for anyone who could turn up Cindy. "A hundred grand is serious money for these sleeze-bags," Igoe had told Weston. "They really took this island apart lookin' for her. And they didn't turn up nothin'."

Then Weston had reported on his efforts. He told Igoe how he had run down Cindy's boyfriend on the island. "The guy brought a charter boat into Road Town Sunday night, and he sailed out of here on Monday morning."

Johnnie had been impressed. He liked the timing. But then Al had added that he had overflown the boat and remembered seeing vacationers on deck. Johnnie thought *Cane Maiden* was a dead trail, arguing that people running away with a couple of million in stolen bonds and diamonds wouldn't have tourists along for the ride.

"Drink up," Al said, as he tossed a ten on top of the check that the waitress had brought.

"You're really going up again?" Johnnie asked, wagging his head in disbelief. "I don't know what

295

the hell you expect to find."

"I gotta' do something," Al explained. Then he mentioned that they would be stopping off at Drake Channel Charters. "The kid is going to find out where *Cane Maiden* is cruising. While I'm up, I'm going to give her one more look."

Johnnie waited in the car while Al went down the gangway to the charter company shed. Tyler Sherwood was waiting behind the counter. As soon as he saw Weston, he threw up his hands in a gesture of frustration.

"Sorry, Mister. I have nothing for you. We can't raise *Cane Maiden*."

Al's expression showed that he didn't understand, so the clerk explained.

"We've been trying to call her on the radio. On the company channel. She hasn't answered yet. But we'll keep trying, and I'll let you know as soon as we get ahold of her. Where can I find you?"

"Why wouldn't she answer?" Al asked.

"She's probably in port somewhere. Maybe the tourists wanted to do a little shopping. Berlind could have gone ashore with them."

"Is that usual?"

"No. The captain is supposed to check in with us whenever he's leaving the boat. But sometimes they forget. Our dock master is a little concerned because of the storm last night. I guess it was pretty bad out there. But it's too soon to get worried. If she was having a problem she would have called on the emergency channel."

Weston didn't like what he was hearing. If she had made port then she was a lost cause. If the money had been on *Cane Maiden*, then it could be anywhere in the world once the yacht reached land. And if she were still at sea, then why wouldn't she be answering? Unless *Cane Maiden* was running and didn't want to talk to anyone.

"Can I see that contract form again? The one with the information on the vacationers."

"Sure." Tyler tossed through the papers and handed Al the charter agreement.

He re-read the same innocent information that had disappointed him earlier in the morning. An architect from Boston and a teacher from New York. Not the kind of people who would be leaving bodies in the storage shed of a deserted boatyard. And the charter date. They had booked the boat months ago. There was no way they could have guessed that it would be the week when Walter Linz decided to make a big diamond buy. He read their travel arrangements. They were due back in on Friday to catch a plane on Saturday. Why would thieves hang around for a week after they made their score? These guys just didn't work out. Maybe Johnnie was right. Why in hell was he going back up in a helicopter? What did he expect to find?

He noticed their incoming travel arrangements, flights into San Juan, and then a puddle jumper over to Tortola. It was then that he remembered where he had seen the man who took over *Cane Maiden*'s helm. At the airport in San Juan.

The guy with the camera case over his shoulder. He had walked up to Cindy and spoken with her for a couple of minutes. And Cindy had seemed nervous. He remembered her eyes darting around the waiting area as if she were afraid of something. As if she were trying to make sure that no one saw them together.

Al remembered his own reaction. He had been suspicious. Even alarmed. They had been close together. The guy had been doing most of the talking, and Cindy had been listening. He remembered noticing the guy's camera case, and watching closely to be damn certain that nothing was exchanged.

Cindy apparently knew him. And she knew Steve Berlind. Then both men show up on the same boat. A boat that had left Road Harbor a few hours after the money had disappeared.

"Can you find out if *Cane Maiden* put in on St. Croix?" He had seen the boat out past the island, apparently sailing out into open sea. Berlind had told him they might turn back into St. Croix, which would be the logical thing to do with a storm coming up. If he hadn't put in on the island, then maybe he was still heading out into the Caribbean, trying for South America or planning a turn west for Hispaniola.

"Yeah, we should be able to do that," the young man told him. "He would have logged in with the authorities. I can check it out."

Weston reached for the roll of bills in his pocket. "You think you could check it out *now?*"

"Sure. No sweat. Just give me a minute to run down to the dock master's office." He was already around the counter and on his way through the door.

Al paced the small office like a caged animal. He didn't know what had happened in Parson's

Boatyard. He didn't know where Cindy had gone, whether she had gone willingly, or whether she had gone alone. All he had to work with were two leads: the man who had met Cindy at the airport, and the young charter captain who had written her postcards and a letter. They both were on *Cane Maiden*. And, unless she had put in on St. Croix, *Cane Maiden* was sailing away. He had to find the old wooden yawl. If she were still at sea, then his money was probably aboard. If she were in port at St. Croix, then that was where he should pick up his search.

He saw the kid running back up the ramp, and went to the door to meet him.

"She's not in St. Croix," the clerk told him. "And she still hasn't come up on the radio. But we're going to keep trying to raise her."

Al stuffed another hundred into the young man's pocket. Then he gave him the hotel and room number where he was staying. "There will be someone there all afternoon. Soon as you hear anything, give a call."

He repeated everything he had learned to Johnnie Igoe as they drove to the airport. "I'll be heading straight out in the direction that the boat was heading yesterday. I'll go as far as the fuel will take us. You stay by the phone. You hear anything, call the helicopter company. They'll get the word to me."

"Maybe you ought to take a plane," Igoe thought out loud. "What's it been, nearly twenty hours since you saw her? She could be out another hundred and fifty miles. I don't think your helicopter can go that far."

"There was a bad storm out there," Al reminded Johnnie. "She wouldn't have gotten very far. But I'll talk to the pilot. Maybe we'll gas up on St. Croix."

Al took the automatic rifle with him when he boarded the chopper. This time, when he settled down next to *Cane Maiden*, he was going to take a much closer look.

35

Bill saw Steve bob to the surface in the middle
of the wake that *Cane Maiden* was trailing. He
ripped the red life ring out of its rack on the after
bulkhead of the cockpit and threw it over the side.
"Turn it around, Howard. Dammit, turn it
around!" He grabbed the wheel, but realized it
was a useless gesture. He could turn the bow, but
he knew he wouldn't be able to handle the sails.

Cindy rushed to the rail where Steve had gone
over the side, but Howard caught her and pushed
her away. "If you want him, then go get that
money." His voice was suddenly soft, more cun-
ning and threatening than when he had been shouting wildly. Moments before, he had been out of
control. Now he seemed to know exactly what he
was doing. "When I see the money, then I'll go
back and get him."

Marilyn was screaming. "Go back for him. Howard, for the love of God, go back for him."

"The money's up in Steve's cabin," Cindy
pleaded. "I know where it is. Don't leave him
there."

"You want to save him," Howard said, biting
off his words, "go get the money." He didn't need
the gun anymore. He was in control because he

was the only one who could bring the boat about. He pushed the pistol under his belt. "Get the money," he repeated. "Then we'll decide whether to go back for him."

"Howard, please," Bill was begging him. And Marilyn, who had run aft and seen the struggling figure in the water, was pulling at her husband's arm, pleading with him. Jeanne was the only one who wasn't in a panic. Howard had taken command, and she was following his lead.

Cindy jumped up on deck and raced forward along the windward rail.

"She's gone for the money," Marilyn pleaded. "Turn back now, before it's too late."

Howard smiled, pleased with his new role. He shrugged off his wife's grip. "I'll decide when we come about."

Bill saw Steve swimming toward the life ring. He waited until he was sure that he had hold of it. Then he rushed forward to help Cindy. When he looked down the hatch, she was struggling to lift a heavy aluminum case out of the rope locker that was just forward of Steve's berth. He jumped down, wrestled the case up through the hatch, and then followed it onto the deck.

"It's here, Howard," he shouted from the bow. "We've got the money. Now turn us around."

Howard was enjoying his total authority. He held the wheel casually in one hand. He made no movement to swing the rudder over. "Open it," he ordered, pointing to the case.

"Jesus," Bill mumbled as he began fumbling with the clamps. Cindy, who came up behind him, helped him undo the latches. When he lifted the

302

lid, he was confused to find nothing but stacks of film packages. "Where is it?" he snapped at the girl.

She grabbed one of the packages that had been torn open, pulled back the wrapper and held it in the air. "Here! It's right here!"

Howard leaned back against the edge of the cockpit. "Bring it here. I want to be sure."

"For God's sake, Howard," Marilyn begged. She looked over the stern. Steve had become nothing more than a small black form in the distance. She couldn't see whether he was still holding on to the life line.

Cindy ran aft waving the open film pack in the air. Bill snapped the case closed and began lugging it back toward the cockpit. Howard took the packet, peeled the wrapper back further and studied the face of the certificate. Then he handed the package to Jeanne. "Count them," he told her.

"There are more of them in here," Bill said, as he struggled the case into the cockpit. He grabbed the jib sheet, which would be the first thing he would have to tend during the turn. "Now turn us around, Howard. And tell me what to do."

"Slack it off," Howard ordered. "Then get ready to slack the main." He swung the wheel to starboard, starting the bow swinging across the wind.

"Watch your heads. Get down!" Marilyn slumped onto one of the benches so that the main boom could clear over her head. Cindy crouched, but fixed her eyes on the small, distant form of Steve. He was several hundred yards astern, and disappeared from sight each time he fell into the hollow behind a swell.

Cane Maiden bobbed almost to a standstill as she crossed the wind and her sails died. The boom swung lazily over their heads.

"Haul her in!" Howard ordered Bill. The jib caught the wind which was now coming over the port bow, and began to fill as the boat continued through her turn. Howard dropped the wheel long enough to haul in the main sheet and tie her off.

The yacht rocked in the swells as she began to ease ahead on her new course. She heeled a bit to starboard as the main caught the full force of the air. Then she began picking up speed.

"I see him. There he is!" Cindy had moved to the front end of the cockpit, and she was pointing out over the windward bow. She climbed up on the deck and ran forward where she would be the first to reach Steve.

"How do we do this?" Bill asked.

Howard indicated the locker under the starboard bench. "Break out a line. I'll bring him alongside and then you can throw him a line."

Bill went to the locker. Marilyn ran forward to join Cindy on the bow. Jeanne stood carefully and took a position next to Howard. She shielded her eyes against the sun and squinted out over the sparkling surface.

"I don't see him. Where is he?"

Howard pointed out over Cindy. "Right there."

Steve rose up as he crested one of the gentle swells that were being formed by the wind. He was just a dot, scarcely visible, with only his head showing. Then he disappeared behind the foredeck as *Cane Maiden*'s bow rose up over a swell.

She was on a broad reach, her fastest sailing

angle, with the jib, the main and the spanker curved out over the side. Her heel was becoming more pronounced and she was building up speed rapidly. Steve was a good half mile ahead, but at the rate *Cane Maiden* was moving, she would close the distance in a few minutes. If Steve had caught the life ring, he was in no danger.

"Thank God you took over," Jeanne said to Howard.

"Someone had to," he answered, checking over the falling bow to pick up Steve in the water. Then he nodded toward Bill and Marilyn who were leaning over the side, anxious to make the rescue. "Look at them! You think Steve and that bitch would be leaning out to rescue one of us?"

She shook her head. "I'm afraid to be on the same boat with them."

"Don't worry about them." He patted the gun that was stuck through his belt. "This is what made them dangerous. And now we have it. We won't be taking any more crap from those two."

"Thank God," Jeanne repeated.

Then Howard told her, "I had that rotten bastard over the side. Last night, while we were handling the storm. The only thing holding him was his lifeline, and I pulled the damn thing free. We were rid of him. Then Bill pulls him back on board."

She seemed shocked. "Why?"

"Damned if I know. And, then, this morning, he's trying to decide how we can save their asses. Putting us all in danger. For what? Dammit, the bastards kidnapped us. They were planning on killing us. Why should we be worried about what

305

happens to them?"

"Bill . . ." Jeanne threw up her hands in despair.

"The little fucker says he's going to pay us. Can you beat it? Pay us for putting our lives on the line. Dammit, but I wanted to wring his neck. Christ, I would have punched his head off, but Bill stepped in again and saved him." He pounded the wheel with his fist. "Pay us! For what we've been through we have more right to the money than they have."

Jeanne looked down at the film packet in her hand. "There's a hundred thousand dollars here. And there's a couple of dozen packets in the camera case."

Howard blinked toward her. Then he looked down at the packet. "A hundred thousand? In that one pack?" He shook his head. "They can't all be like that."

Marilyn's voice screamed from the foredeck. "He's over there. You're turning away from him." She was pointing out from the port bow. Howard could now make out the figure clearly. He could see the shape of the head, and one arm waving in the air.

He eased the wheel up toward Steve, and began taking in on the mainsail sheet. "Haul in the jib a bit," he called to Bill. Bill came back in from the rail and trimmed the jib sheet. Howard reached behind him and tightened the spanker sail.

Cane Maiden heeled even more, but seemed not to give up any of her speed. She was no longer rising and falling over the swells, but was pinned into the sea by the pressure on her sails. The bow was carving cleanly through the water, throwing up a curved wake of white water. The space between the bowsprit and the man in the water was closing rapidly.

"Where should I be?" Bill asked.

Howard didn't understand.

"For the rescue. When I throw him the line. Where should I be?"

Howard pointed toward the leeward rail. "Right there's okay. I'll bring her into the wind at the last second. He'll be close aboard, right off the side."

Bill nodded. He coiled the line in his fingers, and took a stance up on the leeward deck, next to the pilothouse.

On the bow, Cindy shifted from the port side up toward the bowsprit. The charging yacht was heading straight toward Steve. Marilyn looked back at Howard. "What should we do? Should we try to reach for him?"

"You don't have to do anything," he screamed back, into the breeze that the boat's movement was generating. "Bill is going to throw him a line."

"What are you going to do with him?" Jeanne asked. Just the thought of having Steve back on board was frightening to her.

"I'm going to take him below and lock him into one of the cabins. The girl goes into the other cabin. Believe me. You're not going to have to look at either of them."

He leaned out over the side so that he could see the water dead ahead. Steve had one arm wrapped over the life ring, and was waving with the other. He was still too far away to recognize. But the dot in the water now had a face and shoulders. The ring was clearly visible.

In the water, Steve could see the two women leaning out over the bow. They were waving back at him, assuring him that they had him in sight and that his rescue was only moments away. He could see the bow spray that *Cane Maiden* was throwing aside. Her heel, and the set of her sails told him that Howard was coming toward him at his best possible speed. In another few seconds, the boat would be on top of him. Then she would veer sharply into the wind, luff her sails and drift to an easy stop right next to him. He remembered how skillfully Howard had brought *Cane Maiden* to a stop at the mooring buoy. The guy wasn't all that bad a sailor. He guessed that when the boat stopped he would be able to reach up and grab her gunwale.

Howard was hanging out over the windward deck, with one hand stretched into the cockpit to keep the wheel steady. He could make out Steve's features, less than two hundred yards ahead. Bill was leaning out over the starboard rail, the heaving line coiled in his hand. He raised the line so that Steve could see it. His only doubt was whether Steve had enough strength left to grab the line and hang on. If he seemed to be faltering, Bill was ready to go over the side and swim the line out to him.

Steve watched the bow carving toward him. When he looked up, he could make out Cindy's face and see that she was shouting at him. He stopped waving, put both arms over the life ring and pushed himself up out of the water. He saw Howard's face, peering out over the boat's port side. On the other side he could see Bill, waving the rope in the air. There was no problem. *Cane Maiden* was going to turn her starboard side to him. She was going to turn up into the wind, creating a calm lee under her starboard freeboard.

For the first time since he had surfaced in the water, he began to wonder what would await him back on board. Howard must have gotten control of himself. Otherwise, *Cane Maiden* never would have turned back. He hoped they would see things his way, and understand that their only safety was in helping him and Cindy to escape. They could split the money. Even half of what was aboard would be more than he and Cindy would ever need. And the other half would pay them handsomely for the problems they had been caused. Everything was going to work out.

He had just convinced himself that he was safe when he realized that the boat should be turning. *Cane Maiden* was less than fifty yards away and was still racing directly toward him. Howard knew what he was doing. He should be easing the bow up into the wind and taking off speed before he got too close.

And then he understood. *Cane Maiden* wasn't going to turn. She was going to sail right over him. He raised one arm and began waving furiously. "Head off!" he screamed. "Turn up!"

The women on the bow were waving back at him. They didn't understand.

"Turn up!" He was yelling with all the strength that was left in him. But the women didn't hear. They were smiling, as if the boat's galloping speed was his salvation.

"Turn up!" The racing bow was bearing down on top of him, about to cut him in half, just as easily as it was cutting through the sea.

He let go of the life ring, and kicked off to leeward, trying to swim out of the way. But there wasn't time. The blade-like bow was less than twenty yards away, rushing at him with tremendous speed.

"Where is he?" Howard yelled from the cockpit. "I've lost him. I can't see him."

Cindy pointed dead ahead, over the bowsprit. Marilyn suddenly realized what was about to happen. She screamed back toward her husband. "Turn! Turn! You're going to run him over."

Bill had to lean out further to keep Steve in sight. It wasn't until the young man let go of the ring and began swimming furiously, that he understood the danger.

"Turn!" he screamed at Howard. "You're going to hit him."

"Which way? Where is he?" Howard yelled.

Steve saw that he had no hope of swimming away. He could hear the hiss of the bow cutting through the sea. The bowsprit flashed by over his head. He could read the suddenly horrified expressions of the two women who were reaching over the bow. He sucked in air, and dove down.

He saw the boat's keel in the nearly transparent water. He tried to kick down even deeper. Then the underwater blade of the bow hit the back of his head like the edge of an ax. The water went black.

36

Bill heard the thud under the boat. He turned away from the lifeline and raced back into the cockpit. On the bow, the two women shrieked. Cindy stared down into the water as the bow wake tossed the life ring to one side. Marilyn turned and ran aft along the windward rail, looking down into the white wash that tossed up from under the boat.

"You went over him!" Bill yelled at Howard as he jumped up on top of the dinghy.

Howard threw the wheel into the wind. "Where? I couldn't have. I lost sight of him." He looked over the stern into the wake. There was no sign of Steve.

The bow had driven him down, and then the curve of the keel had rolled across his body, crushing the bones and driving the air out of his lungs. The propeller and the rudder had each struck their blows, one into his head, and then the other into his chest.

"Do you see him?" Marilyn called as she rushed into the cockpit. "We sailed right over him."

"I can't find him! I can't see him!" Bill answered.

Cane Maiden's sails luffed when she settled into

the wind. Her momentum kept her moving forward even though she no longer had any power. She rolled upright, and was suddenly balancing uneasily on the dancing swells.

"I couldn't see him," Howard screamed to anyone who might listen.

Bill was studying the curved wake of the boat. There was no sign of Steve. All he could see was the life ring that was floating innocently behind them. "Turn us around," Bill snapped. "He has to be back there." Then he saw that the white wash behind *Cane Maiden* was spotted with crimson. "Jesus, we hit him. Howard, for God's sake, turn us around."

Howard went pale. "I didn't see him," he told Bill as he began maneuvering the wheel. "I thought I had room to turn up."

Cindy and Marilyn rushed to the rail on the port side. Jeanne went to the starboard side of the cockpit. Bill went to the sheet winches so that he could follow Howard's orders for trimming the sails. Howard let the boat fall off the wind so that the air was coming over the starboard side.

"Let them out," he yelled at Bill. But he couldn't check the swing of the bow, and Bill couldn't manage the sails quickly enough. The boat turned past its mark, and the sails jibed, swinging furiously across the deck. *Cane Maiden* heeled and began moving in the wrong direction.

"He's behind us," Marilyn said, running aft to try and keep the point where Steve disappeared in sight. Then she saw the bloodstain. "Jesus, we've killed him."

"I didn't mean it," Howard told her. "I thought

he was off to starboard. I thought I was turning clear."

The boat came all the way around again, and the sails luffed uselessly.

"Take them down," Howard ordered Bill. "Reef in the main and just drop the jib." He fired up the auxiliary engine.

"You went right over him," Cindy screamed at Howard.

He shook his head. "I thought I had room. I was trying to turn up."

The luffed sails came down easily, and the auxiliary started the boat moving slowly. Howard was able to steer her around back over the ugly mark in the water. They all leaned out over the lifelines, searching straight below them. The water was clear, and in the bright sunlight, they were able to see several feet below the surface. But there was nothing to see. No sign of Steve except for the colored marker of his blood which was fading away.

Howard turned the boat in a series of S turns, back and forth across his original wake. By the second pass, the bloodstain had vanished. They used the floating life ring as their mark and continued the search pattern.

"I never meant to hit him," Howard kept saying to his shipmates. They were all leaning out, studying the waves, even though they were beginning to realize that there was nothing to find. "I didn't mean for him to go over the side. He tried to get the gun back from me. You saw that. I just wanted to scare him. Let him know that we were in charge. Even when he was in the water, I knew we'd be able to get back to him. It should have been easy to pick him up. I don't know what went wrong."

He brought the boat through another gradual turn. "I only lost sight of him for a second. There was plenty of room for me to turn. I don't know what happened."

"It was an accident, Howard," Jeanne agreed.

Marilyn gave up the search. She stepped down into the cockpit and put her arms around her husband.

Howard broke away from her. "We have to keep looking. He may be okay."

Bill climbed down from the rail. "It's been too long, Howard. He's been under too long."

Cindy buried her face in her hands and began crying. Marilyn turned to comfort her.

"Just one more pass," Howard said.

Bill nodded. "Okay. One more pass."

Howard turned again, but he was no longer sure of his mark. The bloodstain was gone. The life ring had drifted away. "Where should we look?"

"Over by the ring," Bill answered. "He probably would have drifted in the same direction as the ring."

They slowed to a crawl as they came close to the ring. Bill stared down into the water, and Jeanne moved up close to him.

"He's gone," Bill told his wife. He dropped down on the deck, reached over the side, and lifted the ring aboard.

37

Al Weston was looking down at empty sea. It had been half an hour since they had refueled on St. Croix, and there had been no boats to check out for the past twenty minutes.

"How far out are we?" he asked the pilot.

"Maybe fifty miles," Paul Canavan said. "The charter boats don't come out this far."

They were flying on the same bearing from St. Croix that *Cane Maiden* had been on when they had seen her the day before. And they were flying the course that the yacht had been sailing.

"How far do you figure she could have gone?"

A boat like *Cane Maiden* could cover 150 miles in a day, more or less depending on the wind and the tide. But in a storm, she would have all she could do to hold her bow into the wind, and keep from being driven back by the sea. "No more than a hundred miles," the pilot answered. "She couldn't be more than fifty miles further out ahead of us."

"How long will that take?"

"Maybe another half hour. And that's about as far out as I want to go. This thing floats. But it's not a boat. If we had to set down in any kind of waves, it might turn over."

"Okay," Al agreed. "Another half hour. Then we'll head back."

He glanced down at the radio, which had been quiet since their takeoff. That meant that the charter company still had no contact with *Cane Maiden*. She had either made a port and been abandoned, or she was still on the run. There was nothing he could do if she were in a harbor. Except wait, until she was found, and then pick up his search wherever she had put in. He had to play it as if she were still at sea. And if she were, then this was the only direction he had on her.

"Suppose she turned west," he speculated with his pilot. "Suppose she ran away from the storm, and turned for Puerto Rico. Or the Dominican Republic?"

The pilot checked the chart. "Well, she'd be pretty close to Puerto Rico by now. Maybe even in port. She'd still have a way to go to reach the Dominican Republic."

"Can we come back that way?" Weston asked.

The pilot nodded. "We can certainly take a look by Puerto Rico. But we can't run very far toward Hispaniola. Not enough gas."

Al squinted out through the glass bubble. His visibility was unlimited all the way to the hazy line where the sky and the sea seemed to come together. There didn't seem to be much point in flying further out. Maybe it was best to hold the heading for only another fifteen minutes, and then swing west toward the southern coast of Puerto Rico.

The radio crackled with the helicopter's call letters. Al didn't recognize the voice, but the pilot seemed to know whom he was talking to.

"I've got a message for your passenger," the voice said.

"Ready to copy," the pilot answered.

"*Cane Maiden* not in any of the usual ports. She hasn't put in at St. Croix. Apparently still cruising at sea, but not answering radio calls. Charter company thinks she may have lost her antenna in the storm. They expect her to call in when she reaches port."

The pilot looked at Al who nodded that he understood the message. "We've copied," he said into the microphone.

"Call in, my ass," Al cursed. "The son-of-a-bitch is running."

He looked out at the blank sea ahead, and then decided.

"Let's turn west, and see if she's trying for Puerto Rico."

38

Far to the east, more than a hundred miles from where Weston was searching, *Cane Maiden* was underway again. She was on a starboard tack, heading north, moving slowly in the light breeze that had come up behind the dying storm.

Howard knew that they had been heading southwest the day before, and then had turned to the southeast. He couldn't calculate what the storm had done to their position, but he knew that they had spent the morning back on an eastward course. That had to put them southeast of St. Croix, over near the Windward chain. No matter what their exact position, the course back toward the Drake Channel had to be to the north.

He kept pleading his innocence as Bill raised the sails, and turned for one last look over the stern when the sails were trimmed and the boat began moving. "I never meant to kill him," he told Bill, and then Marilyn. "All I wanted to do was let him know that we were in charge. That we were taking command and that we were the ones who were going to decide what to do with the money."

Bill nodded that he understood what Howard was saying. But his expression was uncertain. He had witnessed his friend's confusion when they had first cut free from the mooring and Steve had had to come to his rescue. Howard could certainly make a mistake in handling the big boat. But he had also seen him anchor perfectly, and then, later, bring *Cane Maiden* to a dead stop only inches from the mooring they were returning to. He wanted to believe that Steve's death was one of Howard's mistakes.

"I mean, I was furious with him. Christ, he had been threatening to kill us. I guess I wanted to take him down a peg or two. But I never thought of killing him. I figured that we'd lock him below and then turn him over to the police."

"That's what you said," Jeanne reminded him. "You said you were going to lock him in one of the cabins."

"That's right," Howard announced for all to hear. "I never figured we'd have any trouble bringing him back on board."

Marilyn embraced him. "It's all right, Howard. It . . . just happened." But as much as she wanted to believe her husband, she wasn't completely sure. She remembered the crazed rage that she had seen in his face, and the sight of him jamming the gun into the young man's neck. At that moment, there had been no doubt in her mind that he was capable of killing Steve. And she remembered what he had said to Cindy. "Get the money. If you want me to go back for him, get the money." Was it the bluster that she had heard so often from her husband? Or had he really been bargaining Steve's life for the stolen fortune?

Bill took the wheel while Howard went below

319

and tried to get a fix on their position. He was gone a while, and then brought his charts back up on deck. It would take him time to reconstruct the courses they had sailed and the time that they had held each heading. All he could do in the meantime was hold their northerly course, and keep moving in the light air and gentle seas. It would be hard for them to miss one of the many islands that were ahead.

Howard relieved Bill at the wheel. Jeanne and Marilyn roused themselves from their stunned shock. No one had eaten since the day before. They went below to fix sandwiches even though no one seemed interested in food. Cindy stayed behind on the leeward deck, looking vacantly out to sea.

"I feel as if everyone is sneaking glances at me," Howard admitted to Bill. "As if they think I'm some sort of mad-dog killer."

"We've all been through a lot. It's been a terrible ordeal."

"You believe me, don't you?"

Bill answered with what he wanted to believe. "It's a big boat. It had picked up a lot of speed. You haven't had a lot of practice handling it."

"I was just trying to protect us. You and Jeanne and Marilyn. I thought I had to take over. I thought I was the best one to make the hard decisions."

Bill didn't answer.

"Jeanne said she was terrified until I took over," Howard continued. "I think she understands what I did."

"We were all frightened," Bill admitted. "But if we had only picked the kid up out of the water, everything would have been okay."

"When you think about it," Howard said, "it isn't any different than if we had lost him during the storm. I mean, he was over the side with his safety line fouled around the rudder. It would have been right to cut him loose then, to save the boat. To save the rest of us."

Bill couldn't make himself believe that it would have been right. Maybe there was some sailor's rule about letting go of everything to save the ship. But he knew he couldn't have let go of the line and let Steve drown no matter how much danger they were in. He hoped that Howard wouldn't have been able to steer the bow over Steve just to guarantee the safety of his friends.

"I think I'll try to rig up a power cord to the radio," Bill announced, turning away from the uncomfortable conversation. "Maybe I can get it working. They may be trying to reach us from shore. And maybe I can alert someone about our problems. We're going to have to explain to the authorities what happened to our captain."

"It's no good," Howard told him. "It was under water with the Loran. And something must have fallen against it. The tuning controls are bashed in."

Bill went up on deck and walked forward. He hadn't really held out much hope for being able to get the radio working. He just needed to be alone with his thoughts.

Marilyn brought up a tray of sandwiches, and Jeanne followed with pitchers of cold drinks. But there were no takers.

"C'mon," Marilyn said, trying to be a cheerleader. "We can't change what happened. We've still got a long way to go. We have to eat." She went up to Cindy and used the food as a pretext for starting a conversation. "I'm sorry about Steve. Did he mean a great deal to you?"

Cindy shook her head. "He was just a guy."

"But you liked him."

"He was like me. A loser. But we got along." She swallowed hard and then added, "He was trying to help me. When I ran to him, he tried to help. I was thinking that if I hadn't gone to him, then none of this would have happened. He'd still be alive."

"What happened isn't your fault," Marilyn consoled. "We all made a lot of mistakes. I think maybe we should have all trusted each other a little more."

"I didn't think Steve was like that," Cindy interrupted. "I mean, with the gun. And threatening everyone. I think he was just scared."

"We were all scared. Maybe too scared to think clearly. Howard isn't like that, either. But he was very frightened. Not just for himself, but for all of us."

Then Cindy admitted what she had been thinking. "It was the money. It was the money that changed Steve. He never would have run like he did if he wasn't thinking that maybe he could keep the money. And I guess I thought it was a good idea. We really didn't think it through. Either of us. It all happened too quickly."

Marilyn offered the food again, and this time Cindy bit at the corner of a sandwich. She turned suddenly to Marilyn. "Steve wouldn't have killed

322

you. When we were alone in the cockpit . . . when you people were down below . . . he kept trying to figure out what he was going to do with you. He talked about bringing you in real close to shore and then letting you go in the rubber boat. Or maybe putting you ashore someplace and then sending his friends back to find you. But he never talked about killing you."

Jeanne brought a cold drink up to the bow, where Bill was holding the lifeline rising and falling gently with the motion of the boat. She stood beside him while he sipped.

"Thanks," he said. "It tastes good."

She offered a sandwich but he shook his head. "Maybe later. I don't think I could swallow right now." He looked toward the west where the sun was beginning to redden the horizon. "I'm sorry for what you've been through," he said.

Jeanne admitted that she had been terrified and was embarrassed that she had been of so little help. She apologized for having retreated into herself and for having been focused only on her own safety. But she added, "I'm glad Howard finally took over."

Bill looked at her curiously. He wasn't sure that he still knew her. She didn't seem to care about what had happened to Steve. Howard had made her feel more secure. It didn't seem important to her that the young captain had been killed in the process of Howard taking over.

"I'm sorry about Steve," Jeanne said, as if reading his thoughts. "It must have been terrible. Being crushed like that, under the boat. But I just can't bring myself to cry over him. Not when I saw him almost kill you. Not when I think about what he might have done to us."

He weighed her words, and then asked, "Do you think it was an accident?"

She seemed shocked by his question. "Of course it was an accident," she snapped back angrily. "Howard was trying to rescue him. He even told me what he was going to do with him when he had him back on board."

"Yeah," Bill agreed. "I guess that's what I think too. Howard and I aren't very close. But I think I know him well enough. I guess I'm not surprised that he decided to take over. Howard always thought of himself as a take-charge type. But when the chips are down, I don't think he would really want to hurt anyone. Not unless something has changed him."

When they walked back to the cockpit, Marilyn had coaxed some food into Howard. Bill offered to take the wheel.

"Just hold her at three four zero," Howard instructed, indicating the floating compass rose. "That's just a bit to the west of dead north. I think that should be taking us pretty much toward home."

Bill brought the marker to three four zero.

Howard looked up at the sails and added, "It's going to be a while. We're not making much time. There isn't a lot of wind."

He stood beside the helm and glanced down at the heading on the compass, out at the swell of the waves and then up at the curve of the sails. Everything seemed to be in order.

"You know that none of our problems are

solved," he finally said to Bill. "Steve being gone doesn't mean that the girl isn't still in trouble. The money is still here, and that means that all of us are still potential witnesses."

"I know."

"We still have to talk about it. We still have to think it through."

"In the morning, Howard. Let's talk in the morning. I'm not ready for it now."

"Sure," Howard said. "We have plenty of time. There isn't a lot of wind." Then he asked Bill, "You want to get some sleep? I'll take the first watch."

Bill backed away from the wheel. "Yeah, I guess I'm beat. I could use a couple of hours." He stopped on his way to the pilothouse hatch and looked at the western sky, now glowing a deep red. There were clouds on the horizon, painted crimson by the sun. A golden shaft reached across the surface of the water and touched the side of the boat.

"Beautiful," Bill said.

"Beautiful," Marilyn agreed. "Truly beautiful. Maybe it's a good omen for tomorrow."

Bill held his hand out to Jeanne. "Not yet," she answered. "I'll be down later. After the sunset."

He went through the hatch. Marilyn climbed back up on deck to be near Cindy. The young girl had talked freely to her, and Marilyn thought that she might need to talk some more.

Jeanne went to the helm and stood next to Howard. "I don't blame you for anything that happened today."

"Thanks," Howard acknowledged. "I've been

feeling like I did something awful. But all I did was what had to be done. I'm sorry I . . . he got killed. But it was his own fault. None of this would have happened if he hadn't taken us prisoners."

She stood beside him until the color began to fade out of the sunset. Then she said, "I counted the packets in the camera case."

His face jerked toward her.

"There are twenty of them. All about the same size and weight. I think there's a hundred thousand in bonds in each of them."

He whistled softly, pulling the air in over his teeth. "Two million dollars?"

"I think so," Jeanne said.

WEDNESDAY

39

He was drowning, thrashing about madly, trying to keep his face above the surface. The white side of the boat was only a few feet away. But he couldn't reach it. He was swimming with all his strength, but he wasn't moving. He couldn't seem to get any closer.

Jeanne was standing on the deck, in a gossamer white cotton dress. She was looking down at him, watching with great interest, but not reaching out to help him. If she would just lean down and stretch out her arm, he could catch her hand. And then she could pull him closer so he could hold on to the boat.

He tried to scream her name. "Jeeeeanne!" But his voice wasn't making any sound. She didn't seem to understand that he was drowning. Or maybe she just wasn't concerned.

He stroked out furiously, and suddenly he was up against the side. His kicking was splashing water against the smoothly painted, pure white strakes. But it wasn't water. Each splash threw a red stain up against the boat, and then the tiny red droplets rolled down, leaving a crimson trail.

It was blood. He was drowning in blood. But Jeanne wasn't trying to save him. It was the dress.

She didn't want him to splash the blood on her white dress.

"Jeeeeeanne!"

Bill bolted upright and blinked at the heavy darkness. He was in his cabin, jammed into the tight, undersized bunk. The air was damp and stale, and he was gasping for breath. Rivulets of perspiration were running down his chest.

"Jesus." He braced his hand against the wooden side of the bunk and fought to calm himself. "Jesus."

Slowly, the cabin began to appear out of the darkness. He could see the lantern that jutted out of the bulkhead over his head, and the handles on the doors of the locker. He looked around. There was faint light coming through the porthole behind him, the nighttime glow of the sea that was passing by outside. He held his arm up and read the time from his wristwatch. One-thirty. He had been asleep for nearly four hours. He swung his legs over the side and searched for his deck shoes. Then he eased the door open and stepped carefully into the darkened pilothouse.

He saw Jeanne stretched out on the bench in the saloon, walked quietly toward her and bent to kiss her cheek. She stirred for an instant and, in her sleep, turned her face away. Marilyn was in the pilot bunk, above the bench on the starboard side. He moved noiselessly to the ladder, and climbed up onto the deck.

Howard was sitting behind the helm, making slow, minute adjustments to the wheel. "Good morning," he said facetiously as Bill slipped down into the cockpit. "Have a good nap?"

"I'm sorry. I didn't mean to leave you up here alone."

"The girls were up for a while. I've only been by myself for about an hour," Howard explained. He looked up at the clear sky that was flashing thousands of stars. "And it's not a bad night to be alone. Look at that sky."

Bill glanced around. "Where's Cindy?"

"She took a blanket up on the bow. I think she wants to keep her distance from us."

They stood together for a few minutes, entranced by the stars. "Perfect night," Howard said. "Flat, calm sea. Unlimited visibility. Easy sailing." He demonstrated as he added, "You can steer with just one finger on the wheel."

Bill looked into the faintly lighted compass. "Still steering three four zero."

"Yeah. We're moving in a straight line. But we're not moving very far. We could use a bit more wind."

Bill laughed. "I think that storm was all the wind I'll ever need."

He slipped in behind the wheel to relieve his friend. "You'll have to use my bunk," he said. "Everything on the port side is still wet."

Howard watched for a moment to be sure Bill had the proper heading. He took one last look at the sails, and gave each of the sheets a perfunctory tug. Before he climbed up to the hatch he said, "Give some thought to how we should handle things. When we get back to port."

"I probably won't be able to think of anything else," Bill answered. Then he asked, "Did you come up with anything?"

"Not really. We still have a lot of problems. But I'm hoping that we can all agree to say that Steve went over during the storm. It will be a lot easier for me than explaining how he happened to be in the water." He waited, but Bill didn't answer, so he continued, "It doesn't really matter how he was lost. No matter how you look at it, it was a terrible accident. It's just that after all we've been through, I don't think any of us needs a formal inquiry."

He slipped slowly down the hatch.

Did it matter? Howard's words set Bill's mind swirling. Did it make any difference whether Steve had been driven overboard by his battle with the sea, or by his struggle with Howard for command of *Cane Maiden*? And once he was in the water, did it matter whether he died by an accident of nature, or by the accident of Howard's miscalculation? He was dead. He was dead because . . .

Why was he dead? What was it that truly destroyed him? Howard's rage? Or his own stupid arrogance? Had Howard killed him? Or, had he killed himself when he locked four innocent people in the hold and played games with their lives? Why did he do it? Why would a young man point a pistol into the face of a stranger and threaten to kill him? Why would he give the gun to a naive young girl and order her to shoot two innocent women if his authority should be challenged?

The money. He had said so himself. "I wanted the money." It was the sight of the money that had changed him. That made an insane plan seem perfectly logical. He had gone overboard to protect his stolen fortune. And then he had died.

Howard hadn't brought him the money. Howard never had any reason to kill him. So, maybe it didn't matter whether he was lost in a storm or crushed under *Cane Maiden*'s keel. Either way, it was his greed that had destroyed him. So, why should Howard be dragged through an inquest? Why should he pay a price because he had been caught up in someone else's madness?

He saw Cindy on the starboard deck. She had been hidden behind the pilothouse, but she stood slowly and began walking back to the cockpit, dragging her blanket like a child.

"Hi," she said as she sat on the starboard bench. She pulled her knees up to her chin and then wrapped the blanket over her shoulders.

"You all right?" Bill asked.

"Yeah. I guess so." She looked over the side at the starlight dancing on the tips of the waves. "I guess I really screwed up."

He wanted to say something consoling, but he didn't think that was what Cindy was looking for. He guessed that she hadn't been asleep when she was lying alone on the deck. She had been thinking of everything that happened, and realizing that there was no way she could undo any of it. She was just hoping to talk.

"This was going to be my last trip. I was going to clear a couple of thousand bucks. Enough to get home. And then I was going back to see if I could sort of start all over again."

Her chin slumped, and she fell into a silence that he suspected she didn't want. So he asked, "Where's home?"

She talked softly, almost to herself, but wanting

him to overhear her. She began with life in her hometown, and sounded jealous of the simple routine she had once hated. Then she recounted the shouted battles with her mother.

"So I left. I just got on a plane headed for Florida. I didn't know where I was going, or what I was going to do. It was just that something had to be better than what I was doing."

She shook her head slowly as an admission of her stupidity. She had really screwed up, she seemed to be repeating. Only now, she didn't mean just the last three days on the boat. She was indicting her entire young life.

Then Cindy talked about the work she had done in Florida. Hostess, dancer, cocktail waitress, escort. And the kinds of people it had connected her with. There was no particular order to her reminiscences. She skipped from one degrading ordeal to another, offering each as a further example of her own futility. She was blaming no one but herself.

She omitted the grim details. She didn't go into the ugliness of being groped and abused by the dance hall managers in their back offices, or into the hotel rooms where her escort assignments generally led. Of her ordeal with drugs, she only mentioned that she had "used the junk," and that it kept her from saving any money.

But it wasn't hard for Bill to fill in the details. Every day, he worked with young people whose self images were fragile, and who put too cheap a price on their personal worth. He knew how eager they were to sell their futures for a chance at adventure, and how easily they were exploited.

Cindy was an attractive young woman anxious to get ahead. There were dozens of ways of taking advantage of her.

She reached the terrifying moment when guns had been firing all around her, and when she backed into a dark corner of the shed while bullets whizzed past her face. She told him about standing between two dead bodies, one with only half a face and the other staring at her through dead eyes. She had been alone, her protector nowhere in sight. It was easy to understand why she would have fled in panic, and gone along with any plan that promised to take her away from the island.

"I didn't care about the money," she said. "I mean, not about how much there was. Steve kept saying that we'd be set for life. That we could go anywhere we wanted and do anything we liked. All I wanted to do was get back home and try to start over. That didn't take much money. What I was supposed to get paid would have been plenty.

"I know it was dumb, but I never wanted you people to . . . get hurt. And I never wanted anything to happen to Steve. If I hadn't run to him with the money . . ."

"You didn't kill Steve," Bill interrupted. He was remembering his thoughts about why Steve had really died. "He made his own choices. He went for the money, and he did whatever he had to do to keep the money. That's what got him killed. And you never hurt any of us. That first morning, when I brought the coffee up on deck, I knew you weren't going to shoot anybody. You were more frightened than I was."

Cindy nodded thoughtfully, admitting that it was

true. "It was dumb for me to be guarding your wives. Steve told me to just hold the gun. He said I'd never have to fire it. So I kind of posed, figuring they wouldn't do anything if I looked dangerous. I guess it was wrong, but I never would have hurt them."

Then, as if nothing she had just relived mattered in the least, she dipped her chin back to her knees and sighed, "It's all my fault."

They were quiet for a while. Bill watched the gentle rhythm of the bow as it rose and settled. He listened to the soft rattle of the sails, and the wash of the sea along *Cane Maiden*'s sides. Nothing suggested the storms that he knew were raging in the young woman's mind.

"We can still get you back home," he finally told her. "There has to be a way."

40

It had been a long and discouraging night for Al Weston. He had landed back on Tortola with nothing to show for the afternoon spent in the air. His only hopeful moment had been when they sighted a yawl, under full sail, racing along the southern coast of Puerto Rico. They had swooped down, but found a more modern design, larger than *Cane Maiden,* and with nothing of its distinctive character.

He had gone directly to Drake Channel Charters and learned that they still had no contact with the boat. None of the usual ports of call had logged in her arrival. Nor had she responded to any of the company's radio messages.

"So, where is she?" Al had asked.

Tyler had thrown up his hands. "Anywhere. Like I said, the captain takes the boat wherever his charter wants to go. Usually they hit a couple of ports. But sometimes the people just want to sail around, anchor off the beaches, swim over the side. Stuff like that. It's their vacation."

"Then nobody's out looking for them," Al concluded.

"I guess not. There are hundreds of boats cruising around the Drake Channel. You can't start

337

a search and rescue every time one of them doesn't call in."

Al wanted to throttle the kid. "Maybe she's not just cruising around," he wanted to scream. "Maybe she's running away with a couple of million in bonds and another couple of million in diamonds." But that was only a guess. *Cane Maiden* might be his best hope but she was still a long shot. More than likely, the architect from Boston and the school teacher from New York were as legitimate as they sounded. More than likely, there was nothing of great value aboard.

"Keep me posted," he had told the clerk, and then headed back to his hotel room.

Over a sandwich and a bottle of beer, he had listened to Johnnie Igoe's men tick off the list of dead ends they had chased down. Two more friends of the cab driver had been found and questioned. They had laughed at the thought that he might be in on a big theft, and had described a small-time crook who could be brutal, but was very rarely effective. "He talks a lot," one of them reported, "but he never has more than a hundred dollars in his wallet."

Customs officers had folded the offered money into their pockets and checked through three days' departure records. No one had left the island with a commercial camera setup. And the private jets that had taken off from Beef Island had all belonged to companies or known names. None were likely to be cargo planes for stolen merchandise.

The criminal contacts had reported in with nothing more to add. No one was trying to discount a quantity of diamonds, nor was anyone selling bearer bonds. There were a few small drug buys being made, but all by reliable regulars. They were plainly annoyed that someone might be freelancing in their country.

"So, what have we got?" Al had asked when all the information was on the table.

"What we got is nothing," Igoe had answered. Then he restated his theory that Cindy had tied in with the wrong guy. "She's dead, and some amateur just landed in New York with the money. New York, or Chicago, or L.A. or London. It could be anywhere. Someone just stumbled into this, deep-sixed Cindy and left with the goods."

"How did he get out?" Al had challenged.

"Probably on one of the innocent boats you buzzed in your helicopter. Maybe out through the airport with the stuff in his luggage. Who knows? Maybe it's a native. Someone who lives here and has the stuff in his closet waiting for a rainy day."

Al had paced back and forth for a few minutes while he drained the beer. There were no more leads that he could think of. If Cindy was gone, he had lost all links to the money. And if some average citizen had taken it from her, then there was no way he was ever going to find it.

"I guess there's not much more for you to do here," he had told Igoe. Johnnie had agreed, and decided that he and his helpers would head back to Florida the next day.

"This going to be tough on you?" Johnnie had asked as he was leaving the room.

Al had given a lot of thought to what Walter Linz's reaction was going to be. "Nah. Walter knows I'm loyal. He's got a good system, and he's not going to go crazy over one busted deal. But I wouldn't want to be Cindy if he ever finds her and figures that she screwed him over. And I wouldn't want to be anyone she was working with."

The action started before sunrise, when he called Linz to report the failure of his efforts.

"Maybe we've been following the wrong courier," Linz offered.

Al was confused. There was only one courier to follow. He had carried the other one out of the shed and sunk him off the end of a pier.

"I've talked with the other side in this deal. And they've been very reasonable. They used a new man, and they pretty much accept your view that he may have talked too much. I've been wondering if perhaps he talked to someone else. Someone besides your taxi driver."

Yeah! Why not? Al had been concentrating on people that Cindy might have known. And people who knew the cab driver. Maybe it was someone who knew the dead courier.

"What's his name?" he asked.

"Peter Heinz. Like the ketchup. He left Zurich on Thursday, connected in New York, and then flew out to Tortola on Friday."

"By himself?"

"Yes," Walter answered. "There was no backup. They're very embarrassed about that."

"They gave a new guy uncut diamonds and sent him off on his own?"

"Apparently his sister works for them also. They had no doubt that he would be coming back."

"Where was he staying?"

"The Harborside."

"Shit," Al cursed. "That's on the same road where we're staying."

"You don't think he could have gotten together with Cindy?"

Al answered immediately. "No way. I was watching her from my room. She spent the whole day on her patio until she got the call. She called me fifteen minutes later."

"Perhaps that night?" Walter asked.

Al spun around in the phone booth. "Yeah. I suppose they could have gotten together at night. But it doesn't figure. I mean, if they were working together they'd have disappeared together. And they wouldn't have needed to involve the taxi driver."

He had waited, holding the silent line, while Walter Linz thought it through.

"Well, it's probably another long shot, but maybe you ought to check up on Mr. Heinz. Find out what he did while he was waiting for the meeting."

Al agreed. Then he put another coin in the phone and woke up Johnnie Igoe.

They began at the Harborside. Heinz, they learned, had been scheduled to check out on Tuesday. But he was still registered. His things were still in the room. They paid the bell captain to use his pass key and searched Heinz's belongings. There was nothing suspicious. But Al did notice that the telephone directory was turned open to a listing of bars and nightclubs. One of Johnnie's men tore out the page and left to check them out.

Al handed another bill to the bell captain. "I'd

like to take a look in his car." He trailed the captain outside the open parking area where the guests' cars were kept, and talked to the parking attendant who kept the keys. The man shook his head as he studied his board. "No car," he said.

"He took it with him, and never brought it back," Al speculated out loud.

"No, mon. He had no car. Must have come in a taxi."

"So, how did he get to Parson's Boatyard?" Al asked Igoe as they were walking away.

"Another taxi," Johnnie answered. He left to visit the taxi drivers he had already talked with. He had been asking them about their friend. This time he was going to ask them about a fare they might have picked up at the Harborside. It should be easy for someone to remember driving a fare to a deserted boatyard and not bringing him back.

It was too early to check back at Drake Channel Charters. Weston decided to walk back up the road to his hotel, change his clothes and get some breakfast.

He had finished shaving, taken his shower, and was toweling himself off when he saw his own phone directory lying on the night table. He broke it open to bars and began running through the names. Did any of them sound familiar? Did anything ring a bell?

It was then that he saw "Boats," and halfway up the next column, "Boats for Hire."

A boat! Why not? Peter Heinz had picked Parson's Boatyard for the exchange. He had picked a place right on the water. With piers. He could get there by boat. It was one damn smart way

342

to make sure he wasn't being followed. And it would give him a separate escape route after he made the deal.

He dressed quickly and dashed down the path toward the pool, where the hotel grounds touched the sea. Far across the water on the eastern shore, well outside the sea wall, he could see the shapes of the industrial and commercial buildings that were near the boatyard. It was a straight line. Rent a boat in the inner harbor, a couple of hundred feet from his hotel, and run straight across the inlet to Parson's Boatyard. He could see anyone who was following him going and coming back. And once he was back in the inner harbor it would be easy to get lost in the labyrinth of docks that were masked by the rows of tied-up yachts.

He walked quickly to the waterfront, the page of boat rental listings crumpled in his hand.

The places were just opening for the day. At his first stop, he had to dance around a jet of water where a workman was hosing down the pier. In the second office that he entered, Al got his answer. The manager remembered very clearly that he had rented a boat to a man who fit Peter Heinz's description. Remembered clearly, because Heinz had never brought the boat back.

"He took it out Saturday afternoon," Weston heard. "Maybe eleven in the morning. Sometime before lunch. And he brought it back a couple of hours later. Tells me he's going to want it on Sunday. All day. And he pays me in advance. That's the last I saw him. He took it out again sometime Sunday morning and never came back."

"What kind of boat?" Al asked. He was already unfolding his roll of bills.

"Little outboard runabout. Fast. Okay for hanging around close to the beach, but nothing you'd ever want to take to sea."

Al handed him twenty dollars. "You have a picture of it?"

"No. We don't keep pictures." He looked at the money. "But I can show it to you."

Al was stunned. "I thought you never got it back."

"He didn't bring it back," the manager corrected. "But it turned up down the harbor a ways. He just pulled it in between two yachts, tied it up and left it. Someone reported it, and the police brought it back to me."

"Where? Where was it found?"

"Down a ways."

Al counted out two more twenties. "Take me there, will you?"

"Sure. I can run you over in one of the boats."

As they walked down the ramp and picked out a small whaler with an outboard engine, Al put the pieces together.

Peter Heinz didn't bring the boat back, because Peter Heinz was lying dead in the center of the shed with a couple of holes through his chest. But someone else had taken it from the boatyard, back across the harbor. Someone who was carrying a camera case full of money. It had to be Cindy. Cindy and whoever was with her. If someone was with her. Maybe Cindy never completed the crossing. But the money probably did. And it was landed somewhere up the harbor, at a point where he was now heading.

Once in the boat, they passed the ends of the piers that reached like fingers from the shore out into the water. Al tried to look over the masts of the tied-up yachts. There were buildings at the tops of the gangways that led down to the piers, some with the names of the charter companies painted on them. Up ahead, he spotted "Drake Channel Charters" on the shed where he had made inquiries about *Cane Maiden.* He watched impatiently as the little runabout flashed past two more rows of docked boats, and then he heard the engine slow. The manager turned her into a channel with the Drake dock just to his right. Then he killed the engine. "Right in there. Behind that sloop," he said. "That's where he left it."

"Drop me off here. Anywhere," Weston said.

He walked out to the end of the dock where the launch was tied up. The launch pilot, a young kid in his late teens, was standing on the bow, mopping down the foredeck.

"You keep this thing running all night?" Al asked.

"Yes, sir. As long as we have a boat in the harbor."

"How about Sunday night? Was it running last Sunday night?"

"Sure. That's a big night in town. Most of the charters who are moored out want to come ashore on Sunday night."

"Were you on duty?"

The pilot said that he was, but his customer-pleasing smile began to narrow. "Why? What's up?"

"I'm looking for someone, a young woman who would have needed a ride out to *Cane Maiden.*"

The pilot shrugged his shoulders and tried to get back to his mopping. "There's always lots of people coming and going. I wouldn't remember any one in particular."

Al stepped closer and took out his bankroll. "Try," he said. "A real good-looking girl. Early twenties. She'd have been carrying an aluminum case. One of those things you pack camera equipment in."

The kid saw the money, but tried to ignore it. "It gets pretty hectic. Especially on weekends."

Al persisted. "She would have been looking for Steve. Steve Berlind. He was captain on *Cane Maiden.*" Two twenties came free from Al's roll.

"Listen, Mister. Steve's a friend of mine."

"I'm not looking for Steve," Al answered. "I'm looking for the girl. And it's very important."

The pilot climbed down off the bow. "I don't want to get Steve in any trouble," he said confidentially. "The captains aren't supposed to bring their girlfriends out to the boats. I mean, sometimes they do it. But the company doesn't like it."

Al wrapped a friendly arm around the kid's shoulders. "Look, this has nothing to do with your friend. The girl's family is trying to find her, that's all. I just need to know if she went out to *Cane Maiden* on Sunday night. And if she was alone. I don't have to mention Steve at all."

He hesitated.

Al put the money into his hand. "Please. It's important to the family."

"Yeah. About seven o'clock. I brought two couples in from *Cane Maiden,* and then she came up from one of the other boats. A real foxy-looking lady. She asked me if Steve was around and where she could find him. I told her he was moored out on *Cane Maiden* and she asked me to take her out. She said it was real important."

"She was alone?" Al asked.

"Yeah. And she had a case. Aluminum. Like you said."

"Did you bring her back?"

"No. She was still out there when I went off duty." He closed his fingers around the money and stuffed it into his pocket. "But all the guys do it. It's no big deal. I wouldn't want Steve to get into any trouble."

"I'll never mention his name," Al said. He started up the dock toward the shed.

She was alone. And she had the case. Al tried to put the pieces together. Peter Heinz had taken the small runabout across the harbor to his rendezvous at Parson's Boatyard. And then Cindy had used the boat to escape with the money. She had been alone, which meant that she was the only person who could have shot the taxi driver and the courier. But Al couldn't believe that Cindy could have used a gun even if she had one with her. So, the taxi driver must have tried to make a score and gotten into a shootout with Heinz. When they killed one another, Cindy found herself alone with the money.

And then, Al figured, she had gotten creative. Instead of bringing everything back to him, she had decided to keep it for herself. She must have known *Cane Maiden* was in port. Maybe she had even talked with her boyfriend about getting together while she was on Tortola. So she had gone to him, with the money.

But what about the passengers? What about the guy who had run into her in the airport and had shown up aboard the yacht? How did he figure in? Did he know Cindy? Or was he just an unconcerned bystander? Al knew he didn't have all the answers. But he had the most important one. Cindy was still alive, and she was probably still aboard *Cane Maiden*.

He ran up the gangway and charged through the open door of Drake Channel Charters. His clerk greeted him with a sad, despairing shake of his head. There was still no report from *Cane Maiden*.

"The company's beginning to worry that she might have been lost in the storm. They're going to put out a request to report sighting, so any boat that sees her will call in and let us know."

Al weighed the information. If she was in one of the nearby ports, then they ought to hear pretty quickly. But more than likely, *Cane Maiden* was already well outside the normal cruising grounds, making her escape. Out in open water where she wasn't likely to be recognized. "What happens if you don't hear anything?" he demanded.

"Then we start search and rescue."

"Meaning?"

"Meaning we call in the navy, and they start searching."

Al looked suddenly glum.

"But believe me," the clerk said. "It won't come

to that. Lots of boats go quiet for a couple of days, but they always turn up. They're probably sitting on top of some reef, and snorkeling over the side."

Al nodded, pretending to agree. "Hope you're right," he said. But he knew the kid wasn't even close. *Cane Maiden* wasn't "lots of boats." She was the only one that was carrying a couple of million in stolen money. So she wouldn't be lingering over a reef. No one would be snorkeling over the side.

41

They were all on deck as the sun came up, anxious for a new dawn that would help put the horrors of the past two days behind them. Marilyn brought up a pot of coffee and tall glasses of fruit juice. "I think I can make some eggs," she offered. "But I wouldn't risk the bacon. The ice was knocked out of the ice chest, and nothing has been chilled. Last thing we need now is a round of food poisoning."

Jeanne and Bill struggled the mattresses and the seat cushions up on deck where they could dry in the sun. Howard laid out the water-soaked charts, and began making calculations to try to fix their position. Cindy went below to offer Marilyn help with the cooking.

They tried simple conversation, and found they could create the sound of normalcy as long as they stuck to the details of their work. They could talk about the best places to stretch out the damp bedding, which plates they should wash for serving the breakfast, and how they might manage showers with the door broken off the head. They weren't yet ready to venture into the important issues that had to be decided, like what they would do with Cindy and the money, and what they would say to the authorities. None of those things could be discussed without calling up memories of Steve pointing the gun at them, of the terrible storm, and of the battle in the cockpit between Howard and the young captain. Most dreaded was the image of Steve disappearing under *Cane Maiden*'s bowsprit, and the futile search for his body. Those were the thoughts that filled their minds. They weren't yet ready to put them into words.

Bill joined Howard at the helm, and took the wheel while Howard worked on the charts that were spread out on the bench. "Any idea where we are?" he asked.

Howard drew a line across his parallel rulers, and then picked off a distance with the dividers. He then marked the spot with his pencil. "Somewhere around here, I think."

Bill glanced at the chart and then at the scales. The point was about a hundred miles southeast of St. Croix, perhaps seventy-five miles southwest of St. Kitts. "That far out?"

"I figure it this way," Howard answered. "We saw St. Croix off our port quarter around eleven A.M. on Monday. So we were sailing southwest. I'm guessing something like two one five." He indicated the line he had drawn out of Road Town along that heading.

"We held that course for a couple of hours before we saw the helicopter, and then probably another hour or so after the helicopter left. That would put us out here." He indicated the end of the pencil line, at a point nearly a hundred miles southwest of St. Croix.

"Then we turned to the east. But he was sailing

351

off the wind, so I figure we were heading more like one one zero." He indicated the second sector of the pencil line that crossed back under St. Croix to the southeast. "We were making damn good time, so I put us right about here when the storm hit." The point he touched was over a hundred miles south of St. Croix, northwest of tiny Aves Island.

"Then, I'm figuring we didn't make much progress during the storm — that basically all we were able to do was hold our own against the sea. We started out pointing to the southeast, but by the time it died down, I think we were heading more like northeast. But I don't think it matters because we weren't making a lot of headway."

Bill nodded. So far he had been able to keep up with Howard's logic.

"Then, yesterday, from the time we came out of the storm until . . . the accident, Steve was heading us eastward. I figure maybe ten hours, at pretty good speed. That would have put us right here" — he indicated a point on the third sector of his course line — "when . . . we lost Steve."

The last point was about sixty miles west of Montserrat, perhaps seventy miles southwest of St. Kitts.

"And then we searched for a couple of hours. Since then, for the last sixteen hours, we've been running on three four zero. But we've been making lousy time. Maybe fifty miles in total. So, we should be about here." The final point was forty miles west of St. Kitts, seventy-five miles east southeast of St. Croix. "This is all pretty rough, but I think it's in the ballpark."

352

"Sounds logical to me," Bill agreed.

"So," Howard concluded, "I think our best bet is to turn a little further to the west. Steer something like three two five. That would point us close to Road Town. We'd probably see St. Croix off to our west sometime in the early evening. We'd certainly see the lights after dark."

Bill tried to complete Howard's course line. "And, we'd be back in Road Harbor . . ."

"Early tomorrow morning," Howard told him.

They both studied the chart.

"Looks good," Bill repeated.

Howard was pleased with his work. "And it's safe. Suppose I'm off by fifty miles. Suppose we're actually here . . . or here . . . or here." He drew light circles to indicate each of the positions. "Steering three two five still gets us to land. St. Croix, if we're here. Or Virgin Gorda if we're all the way over here."

"No matter," Bill was able to agree. "You'll get a fix someplace, and we'll still make it into Road Harbor early tomorrow."

Howard rolled the chart. "Which means we've got decisions to make. We have to get everyone together and get our stories straight. And if we decide that it's best to put the girl ashore someplace, we have to decide where."

The opportunity didn't come right away. Marilyn came topside wrapped in a towel and carrying a pot of fresh water. "I'm bathing up on the bow," she told them. "I want plenty of warning before anyone comes up there to change a sail." She also announced that the cabin would be out of bounds. Jeanne was going to take her shower below, and with the broken door, she would need the pilot-house to herself.

The men stayed in the cockpit, Bill at the wheel and Howard on one of the benches. "This is the way it was supposed to be," Bill said, taking in the calm seas and the clear sky. "A week of nothing more than bumming around the islands. Easy winds. Swimming. Sightseeing." He shook his head. "It wasn't supposed to be the vacation from hell."

Jeanne came up on deck in fresh jeans and a new blouse. She wore Bill's baseball cap to keep the sun off her face. Marilyn finished splashing under her towel and then disappeared through the broken greenhouse hatch. When she came up into the cockpit, she was wearing a casual skirt and a tank top. Cindy climbed out on the bow and took up her solemn watch into the distance. Howard went below, put on fresh clothes, and then Bill followed once his friend had come back up to take the wheel. The meeting was already assembled when Bill came back up on deck.

"I asked the girls about agreeing that Steve was lost in the storm," Howard announced, glancing from Marilyn to Jeanne for confirmation. "They think it's the best way, and Marilyn has agreed to talk with Cindy. It will save all of us a lot of problems."

Bill wasn't sure that it was the right decision. What Howard had done was certainly defensible. Steve had been holding them all prisoner, threatening to kill them. Howard had struggled with him and thrown him over. Then he had turned back to rescue him. If they told the truth, there was no reason for them to expect any trouble.

But if they lied, and if a zealous official saw through their story, he could certainly persuade the truth out of one of them. And then their altered version of the truth would put them in even greater difficulty.

He had closed his mind to the possibility that what Howard had done was a calculated killing. His bottom line was that his friend had blundered badly, first in throwing Steve over and then in botching the rescue. It was, in the final analysis, a tragic accident, and it didn't seem to make a great deal of difference what kind of accident they reported. But still, he felt uneasy about the lie.

"Don't you think the money will make the police suspicious?" he asked the others.

"That's the next thing we have to talk about," Howard said, continuing his role as the chairman for their meeting. "The money."

He held up one of the certificates that he had taken from the film packets. "This is a bearer bond. It's a financial instrument that's just as good as cash. Bring it to a bank or a brokerage house, and they pay the bearer on demand. No questions asked. No way to trace how the bearer got the bond. Cindy was carrying a suitcase full of these things."

He passed it to Marilyn who glanced at it and then handed it to Jeanne. She studied it carefully.

"There's two million dollars worth of these things," Howard told Bill. "Two million dollars!"

"My God," Marilyn managed. She snatched the paper back from Jeanne and examined it more closely.

Howard reached into his pocket and took out a small cloth pouch. "This is what the bonds were going to buy." He felt all their eyes on him as he untied the drawstring, and he milked the moment, smiling at each one of them before he poured some of the contents out into his hand. Then he extended his palm out in front of them.

They all looked at the dull, silky shine on the surface of the small stones.

"Diamonds," Howard told them. "They're not finished. Still uncut and unpolished. But Steve talked about diamonds. And look at the size of some of them."

Marilyn carefully took one between her fingers and examined it. She held it in the sunlight and turned it slowly. "It doesn't seem as bright as a diamond," she decided.

"What are they worth?" Jeanne asked.

"I guess another two million," Howard said. "I don't know much about diamonds, but someone was willing to pay two million for them just as they are. I figure they have to be worth a great deal more once they're cut."

He looked at Bill. "What we've got here are both sides of the deal. The diamonds. And the money that was going to be paid for the diamonds."

"Four million dollars?" Jeanne gasped.

Marilyn meticulously placed the one she had examined back into Howard's hand. "You'd better put those away," she said. "Very carefully."

He poured the stones back into the pouch and tied the string. "There are four pouches of stones, and twenty packets of the bonds. The bonds are

356

worth more the longer you hold them. And the diamonds . . ." He threw up his hands helplessly. "Who knows? But I'd guess that if you used them slowly . . . had each one cut as you sold it . . . they'd be worth a hell of a lot more than two million."

Bill was confused.

"Figure it out," Howard told him. "Why would anyone spend two million dollars on these things if he didn't know that he could sell them for a hell of a lot more? Maybe, over time, he figured to double his money. Or even triple it. He wasn't going to go to all this trouble just to break even."

"How much do you figure, Howard?" Jeanne asked. "What's your best guess?"

"Five million, anyway," he answered. "Probably closer to six. That's if you spend it slowly. And carefully."

Bill stared at Howard. "Five million dollars?"

Howard nodded. Then he smiled. "At least. Probably more." His eyes stayed with Bill until he knew that the amount had sunk in. Then, still smiling, he swept his gaze slowly across the wide-eyed expressions of the wifes.

"And all of it is untraceable. It's as good as finding a pot of gold in your backyard."

They were stunned into silence. Bill looked forward and noticed Cindy sitting quietly on the bow. Then he glanced back at his wife and his friends.

"You're not thinking about not returning it?" he said to Howard.

"Return it to who?" Howard answered, his smile broadening.

"To . . . whoever owns it." Bill knew his words

357

sounded silly the moment he had spoken. They had no idea who owned the bonds and the stones.

"We can't take them back to Cindy's friends," Howard continued. "Jesus, we know we don't want to identify ourselves to them. You remember what Steve said: 'These guys are killers.' You saw how frightened Cindy was of them."

Marilyn and Jeanne had been facing Howard as he spoke. Now they turned to Bill.

"To the authorities, then," Bill said. "The police, I suppose."

Howard stared at him, waiting for Bill to recognize the folly of his own suggestion. Then he filled in the confused blanks in Bill's thinking.

"We're in the Caribbean, Bill. These guys aren't the FBI. You give them five million dollars, and you think they're going to announce it in the papers under 'Lost and Found?' They'll say 'thank you very much,' and maybe give us the good citizenship award. Then they'll cut this up among themselves. What you'll have is a couple of the world's richest civil servants."

Another silence covered the cockpit. Then Jeanne told Bill, "It could also be dangerous. The police might not want us hanging around to see if there's going to be a reward. It would make things easier for them if we just disappeared."

"Wait a minute," Bill protested. "Let's just hold on for a minute. We can't just assume that the police are going to be a bunch of thieves." He looked at his wife. "Murdering thieves, at that. There has to be someone who would take the bonds, and the diamonds . . . and do what has to be done."

"Who?" Jeanne challenged him. "How are you going to find out?" She turned to the others and laughed derisively. "This is just like Bill. Walking around with his lantern, looking for an honest man." She snapped back toward her husband, "The first person you asked could be exactly the person who would kill us all. And why do a few officials have any more right to the money than we do?"

Cindy stood up on the bow, turned slowly and started aft. Then she looked up and saw the two couples clustered in the cockpit. She hesitated for an instant, trying to decide whether she would be welcome. One by one they saw her and acknowledged her with quick smiles or simple dips of their chins. But no one waved for her to join them. She stopped, and then went below through the greenhouse hatch. They waited silently until she had disappeared.

Howard leaned forward into his circle of friends, and spoke in a softer voice. "Did you ever think about committing the perfect crime? You know! You pull off something so clever that nobody even knows it happens. And you walk away with a fortune that no one will ever know about."

Bill knew exactly what Howard meant. He had enjoyed fantasizing about a foolproof system at roulette. Of being able to envision, in advance, the exact slot on the wheel where the ball would drop. Then he could go to the casinos from time to time, winning big one day and then letting himself lose the next. All he would have to do would be to lose frequently enough so that no one would suspect he had a system. But he would win just often enough to gradually accumulate a fortune.

Jeanne could identify with the thought. Working in interior design for corporate customers, she frequently had free run of executive offices. On one occasion, she had been asked to select the appropriate painting to hang over a personal wall safe. In her imagination, the safe was filled with embezzled funds; money the executive could never even admit existed. And then she would find the combination, taped to the bottom of a drawer in a desk she was replacing.

"Well, this is it," Howard continued. "The perfect crime. Only somebody else has committed it for us. Nobody knows that Cindy came aboard *Cane Maiden.* So nobody knows that we have the money. And whoever set this up made damn sure that none of the money could ever be traced. We bring this stuff home with us and just put it in our safety deposit boxes. Then use it for whatever we want. Whenever we want. It's a free ride that could last each of us for years. And it just fell into our laps."

They were all intrigued by the possibilities. Jeanne was evaluating the idea seriously. Bill and Marilyn were toying with it almost as if it were a delicious joke. Marilyn began to giggle. "It *is* just like finding a buried treasure in your backyard, isn't it?"

"Exactly," Howard told her. He looked at Jeanne.

She shook her head slowly. "No, it's not like we just found it. It didn't just fall into our laps. We almost got killed because of this money. Howard got smashed over the head with a pistol. Bill

360

came within an inch of getting himself shot. And then we were dragged through that storm. I don't know about the rest of you, but when the boat was being tossed around . . . when it turned over on its side, I was sure that I was about to be drowned. Those few hours were absolute terror. I'll never be the same." She turned directly to Marilyn. "How are you ever going to forget that girl leaning back on the ladder and pointing a gun at us? Even if she wasn't planning on killing us, it could have gone off accidentally any one of the times that she was thrown off the step and banged by the ladder."

Marilyn nodded slowly. "I thought for sure that I was going to die."

"The money didn't just fall in our laps," Jeanne concluded. "We earned it. We have a right to it. More of a right than some official back on Tortola."

Bill's silence made him the center of attention. They all waited for his decision.

"I think this could be very dangerous," he finally said. "Somebody will be looking for that money."

"You're right," Howard agreed. "Which is exactly why we can't admit we have it. Remember what Steve said about the guy in the helicopter? I don't know about you, but I don't want them to find me. And I sure as hell don't want to go looking for them and make it that much easier for them to find me."

Jeanne joined in with Howard. "They have no reason to suspect us. We're just one of a thousand groups taking a vacation on a charter boat. They don't know that this is the boat that Cindy came running to. They don't know we have the money. For God's sake, Bill, they don't even know that we exist."

"And they won't," Howard added. "Unless we start talking about it when we get back to Tortola. Don't you see? The most dangerous thing we could do would be to go back to port and announce that we've found a fortune in bearer bonds and diamonds."

The sails began to flap. Bill had been so absorbed in the conversation that he had lost his heading and let *Cane Maiden* steer herself into the wind. He turned down. The sails stiffened and the compass rose swung back toward his course.

"What do we say when we get back to port?" Bill asked. "That none of this ever happened?"

Howard was ready with the answer. "We tell them that we were doing some open water cruising and that we got caught in the storm. We were all below deck. The boat was getting knocked about but it seemed like we were going to be okay. And then, all of a sudden, we felt it broach. It fell off sideways, and we knew something was wrong. Before we could go up on deck to ask the captain, we were knocked down. Rolled right over on our side. When we finally made it up to the cockpit, the captain was gone. Lost over the side. We don't know how. We don't know where. We can't even be sure exactly when."

"That's what we'd have to say if we want to keep Howard from having to go through a police inquiry," Marilyn reminded Bill.

Jeanne added enthusiastically, "Most of it is true. It's really what we were going through."

"So then you and I were able to get the boat turned back into the wind," Howard continued. "Together, we reefed in most of the sail. We were able to ride out the storm. And then we sailed her back in."

Bill was still calculating.

"Look at the boat," Howard said to him. "The hatch is smashed. The dinghy cover is torn to shreds. The doors below are off their hinges and half the cabinets are smashed. You think that anyone will have a hard time believing that we've been through one hell of a storm?"

He was right. Howard's story was close enough to the truth that no one would have reason to be suspicious. Even more convincing was that fact that there was nothing to be suspicious about unless you knew that there were several million dollars aboard. And no one, other than themselves, knew that.

"Then I can show them the charts. I can show how I figured out where we probably were, and how I was able to plot a course back to Tortola, or wherever we land. It all works, because it's all true."

Bill's expression was still critical. "And you think they'll just let us take the money and leave? No questions asked?"

Howard laughed. "I think they'll give us a police escort right to the plane. The charter company isn't going to want us telling our story. Hell, it was their captain who fucked up and took us right into a tropical storm. And then left us out there to fend for ourselves. They'll be scared stiff that we're going to sue them for all they're worth. And the authorities aren't going to want us hanging around. The whole economy of this place is built on tourists. You think they're going to want a public hearing about how their visitors were damn near killed?"

Cindy came back up through the greenhouse. She had changed into Steve's shorts and company monogrammed golf shirt. The belt was pulled tight, holding the oversized clothes bunched around her waist. She glanced aft, waiting for an invitation. When none came, she slipped forward and settled back down on the bow.

"What about her?" Bill asked.

"What *about* her?" Jeanne snapped back. "She wasn't all that worried about what was going to happen to us."

"No," Howard contradicted. "We'll give her a share. I figure there are five of us. Everyone gets an equal share."

Jeanne was about to argue, but Howard cut her off. "We have to," he said. "She's going to be on the run. What we have to do is make sure that she's able to run very far, where no one will be able to find her. It's buying our own safety."

Bill's eyes narrowed toward Howard. "You've really thought this through, haven't you?"

Howard nodded. "Last night. When things calmed down and I realized how much money we had. I knew we would be in danger. I began trying to figure out how we could protect ourselves."

Bill studied the faces that circled him. "You go along with this?" he asked Marilyn.

"I don't want Howard to have to go through an investigation. And I don't want to cause us any problems with Cindy's friends. I don't want them knowing that we saw the money."

He gestured toward the bow where Cindy was sitting. "What makes you think she'd go along with it?"

"I think she's in the same boat we are," Howard answered. "I don't think she has any choice."

Marilyn volunteered to talk with Cindy. "I think she trusts me. I'll explain it just the way Howard did." She looked around at the others. "At least we ought to ask her."

Bill agreed. "Okay. Talk to her. But let's keep thinking about this. I don't like the idea of lying to the authorities, no matter what they might do. I'm not sure you can just put a million dollars in a safe deposit box without telling someone about it. Let's just take some time and try to think this through."

"What's to think about?" Jeanne demanded of her husband. "It's the only way. Why can't you just grab it when it's right there in front of you?"

Howard put a gently restraining hand on Jeanne's shoulder. "No, Bill's right. We want to be sure." Then he said to Bill, "But we have to decide pretty quickly. We'll have to put Cindy ashore someplace before we show up in Road Town. We ought to be figuring where the best place is to let her go. Once I get a fix on land, we ought to know where we're going to take her."

42

Drake Channel Charters had waited as long as it could. There had been no response to its general request that sightings of *Cane Maiden* be reported. The last communication with the yacht had been on Sunday evening, when it checked into Road Harbor and tied up at one of the company's moorings. Sometime later in the night, or early the next morning, she had set sail. And then it was as if she had disappeared off the edge of the Earth.

The tropical storm on Monday night had been sudden and furious. Lurking in the company managers' minds was the possibility that *Cane Maiden* had been lost, capsized so unexpectedly that her captain had no time to put out an SOS.

But her sinking was not the most likely of explanations. For one thing, there had not been a single report of any boat being lost, or even of a boat being damaged enough to require assistance. That fact alone made the storm an improbable answer, because *Cane Maiden* was far more seaworthy than any of the more commodious cruisers, and her captain was a good deal more experienced than the amateurs who took to sea in bare boats. Another factor was that all the boats were equipped with location beacons — small, low wattage radio transmitters that were designed to break free from the decks of sinking boats. The beacons broadcast directly to communications satellites that fixed their positions to within ten yards and notified the appropriate authorities. If *Cane Maiden* had gone down, her location beacon should have been heard, and her last position fixed with uncanny accuracy.

A more likely explanation was that she had sailed well outside the cruising grounds, and that possibility raised new dangers. The only reason for her taking to the open seas was that someone aboard was making for a distant, unknown port. Perhaps the passengers had used the pretext of cruising as a cover for a secret agenda. Or, outsiders might have taken over the boat for their own purposes — for running drugs or smuggling contraband.

All that the charter company knew for sure was that *Cane Maiden* was missing, and that if she were to be found afloat, it would be somewhere within her 150 mile-per-day cruising radius.

They conveyed this information to the police, who relayed it to the U.S. Coast Guard in San Juan. The coast guard rolled out a giant Sea King search-and-rescue helicopter for a look over the southern approaches to Tortola, and down the Leeward chain. At the same time, it sent messages to its British counterpart in the Bahamas, which regularly patrolled the Turks and Caicos islands to the northwest. There was no great urgency. The boat wasn't known to be in danger, and three days without reporting didn't constitute an emergency.

Al Weston's telephone rang a few minutes after noon. "We've started an air rescue search for *Cane Maiden*," his clerk at Drake Channel Charters told him. "I thought you'd want to know."

"What happens next?" Al asked.

"If they see her, and she doesn't seem to be in any trouble, they'll just call us and give us her position."

"Will you know about it?"

"Probably not," Ty Sherwood said. "But I know the people who would be the first to hear. I could nose around. Keep asking."

Al smiled. Everyone would sell out for the right price. "Why don't you do that. And let me know the minute you hear something. I'll double what I already gave you."

43

Howard was standing at the wheel, steering easily in the calm, slow weather. Marilyn had gone forward to sit beside Cindy on the bow, take her through their thinking and ask her to join their conspiracy. Bill had picked a place on the leeward deck, his feet against one of the lifeline stancheons, his back resting against the side of the pilothouse. He was supposed to be the lookout, keeping a sharp eye for the first trace of land. But the binoculars were resting beside him, the neck strap coiled around the focus ring. He was looking vacantly out at the sea, buried in his own private thoughts.

It was a simple decision. Take the money, which seemed to belong to no one. Or turn it over to the authorities and get on with his life. But he wasn't really thinking about bearer bonds and diamonds. And the decision was anything but simple.

He and Jeanne were unraveling. Not just during the last few days aboard *Cane Maiden*, but probably during the last few years. He was failing her, or at least failing her ambitions. And now he was beginning to realize that she was failing him.

Both of them had been deadly honest with each

other. When they had met, he had told her that he was a teacher, and that was exactly what he hoped to be. And she had found that more than enough. She had done her exciting time in the company of the upwardly mobile, dating many men whose expectations were as boundless as their ambitions. She had felt herself being evaluated as a suitable partner in the frenzied pursuit of success by young attorneys racing for partnerships in two-named firms. She had been put on trial as the intriguing escort of account executives who were only one office away from owning a major account. She had been a guest at corporate dinners with escorts who whispered that they had been moved inside to the fast track. Perhaps the fast-trackers had rejected her, but it was certainly just as true that she had rejected them. As she moved closer, she found them to be frightened lackies, trying to dress mediocre talent in approved organizational uniforms. Eventually she backed away. Instead, she had fallen deeply in love with a teacher who accepted himself as he was and dove wholeheartedly into work he thought important, without particularly caring what value others put on his choice.

In turn, Jeanne had told him exactly what she was: an aspiring interior designer with realistic hopes for her prospects; someone more interested in people than in their titles. Honest in her opinions, and hardheaded in defending her tastes against current fads. Not the socially connected conformist who would earn big fees. Not a mover in the trendy circles. Just a good, reasoning, competent designer.

They had been ready for each other.

But time had worked its changes. Bill had begun to seem to Jeanne to be unambitious, a man content in the service of failed causes. If, that is, the school really *was* a cause. Over the past year, Jeanne had begun to think of it more as his hiding place; the safe harbor where he would never have to test himself. She had accused him of running away from challenges, and at times he had wondered if she might be right. His work seemed important to him. But was that just an excuse? Was the school really his refuge?

Jeanne had seemed unsatisfied, in need of a bigger, more visible arena in which to perform. She seemed to regard the life they were living together as nothing more than a rehearsal. She was waiting for opening night when she would have her chance to star. He lingered while she goaded, and the magic had begun to tarnish with bitterness.

"We could live like this all the time," she had told him only a few days earlier, meaning that the life they were living was inadequate. In her moment of fear, she had turned to Howard, which said that she couldn't count on him any more.

And then came the money, which was suddenly important not as a cash amount but more as a test of where she fit into his life. It could change everything, and change was what she was yearning for. "Why can't you take it, when it's right there in front of you?" she had challenged. A fair question. But he didn't have an answer. He knew it was important to her, so what was holding him back? Was this the test of his strength that Jeanne thought he had been avoiding? Should he run roughshod over what he thought was right just to demonstrate that he was strong and daring?

Certainly, there was nothing wrong with buying her the freedom she needed to grow. Jeanne deserved the chance to set her own direction, and the money would give her that chance. And what was wrong with using part of the fortune to keep the school running, even if only for another year or two? He and Jeanne could make it count for more than the thieves who had assembled the murderous deal. All that was holding him back was a gnawing sense of wrong in building their futures on a lie. And a foreboding of danger in trying to protect their dark secret. Did that really count against the opportunities that the money would bring? Didn't other people build their relationships on shared lies?

Their lives were at a crossing. They could go ahead together, or they could part in separate directions. That choice, he felt, would depend on the choice he made about the bonds and the diamonds.

Jeanne came up from the cockpit carrying two glasses of rum-spiked punch and settled on the edge of the pilothouse, just above his head. She passed down one of the drinks, and he drained half of it before he realized what it was.

"That's potent stuff," he laughed.

"We need it," Jeanne said. Then she asked, "Nothing yet?" referring to the empty horizon that curved around them.

"No, but Howard really wasn't expecting to sight anything until later in the evening. We still have a ways to go. And we're not making much speed."

She hesitated, but then asked the question that had brought her out on deck. "What have you decided?"

"I'm still trying to put it all together." He took another sip of the drink.

"That money could make a difference," she prompted. "To both of us. I could get out of selling furniture. Open my own place. Go after my own clients. And you could stay on at the school. That's what you want to do, isn't it?"

Bill nodded. "I know it could make a difference."

"So, what's holding you back?"

"I don't like lying. Once it starts, it gets easier. Before it ends, you can't tell the lies from the truth."

"But Howard seems to think . . ."

"Fuck what Howard thinks. Howard doesn't care what's true. But we do care, don't we? Do you care, Jeanne?"

"I care what happens to us. This could be the chance we need. The chance I'd given up hoping for."

"An opportunity I haven't provided for you."

She didn't bring up past conversations. She said, "You can provide it now. For both of us."

It was a test. A test of how far he would go to keep her. He thought he still loved her, not because it was a question he ever asked himself but simply because he had never felt the need to ask the question. But he was no longer sure that she loved him. It was a lie that didn't have to hurt anyone. It didn't seem too much to do for the chance of winning back her love. "Okay," he said softly. "Okay."

"Should I tell Howard?" Jeanne offered.

44

Howard smiled at the decision. "It's the only thing we can do. The only thing that makes any sense. I can't see handing it over to the police. And I sure as hell would be afraid to go looking for Cindy's friends."

Marilyn came aft and joined them in the cockpit. Howard looked at her, waiting to hear the young woman's decision. But Marilyn shrugged in despair. "She doesn't care what we do. She doesn't even want to talk about it. All she keeps saying is that everything is her fault. If it wasn't for her, Steve wouldn't be dead. We wouldn't all be in danger."

Howard turned to Bill, his expression puzzled.

"Things haven't worked out for her, Howard. She was spilling her guts to me last night, and she's made kind of a mess of her life over the past couple of years. This is just her latest failure, only this time people have been killed. I don't think she sees much of a life ahead of her. I think she's telling the truth when she says she doesn't care what we do."

"Okay, then we'll decide for her. When we see land and get a fix on our position, we'll pick a place to put her ashore. Maybe somewhere on St.

374

Croix. Or, if we're further east than I've been figuring, maybe St. Martin. What we need is a busy tourist island with an airport. Someplace where she'd have a good chance of making her escape without attracting attention."

Marilyn didn't look enthusiastic. "I don't think she's interested in escaping. She didn't even want a share of the money."

"Well then we've got to talk with her," Howard said. "We can't have her just walk into a police station and give herself up. She'd implicate the rest of us."

"Maybe this isn't going to work," Marilyn warned. But Howard would have none of it.

"It will work," he insisted. "Unless Cindy screws it up. I've given this a lot of thought. She has to work with us."

Marilyn went forward to get Cindy. Bill dropped quietly onto one of the cockpit benches. He had suddenly become aware that Howard had, indeed, given a great deal of thought to his plan.

When did he *start* thinking about it? Bill wondered. It had only been that morning when Howard had first seemed to notice that the bonds and diamonds were untraceable. That was when he had first speculated that the money could be theirs. But had his sudden discovery been genuine? Or had his whole plan been carefully orchestrated? Had he just begun thinking about it during the night? Or had it been taking shape in his mind hours before, when Steve first mentioned *hundreds* of thousands? That would have been before Steve had died. And, if that were the case, could Steve's death have been part of the plan?

He jumped up from his seat and went back up to the solitude of the leeward deck. That's impossible, he told himself. Because if Howard had decided that the payment Steve offered them wasn't enough — that he could have a much bigger share — then his friend would have had good reason not to turn *Cane Maiden*'s bow away from the struggling figure in the water. Steve's death would have been part of a plan to make off with all the money. And Bill couldn't be sure that the entire plan had yet been played out.

Cindy trailed Marilyn aft along the windward deck and followed her into the cockpit where Howard and Jeanne were waiting.

"We're going to put you ashore," Howard started. "Someplace where the people who are looking for you won't be waiting. I've been thinking that we could give you Marilyn's passport. You could get by on her description and you can't tell anything from her photo. And we can easily explain that we lost the passport along with other things during the storm. It won't be a problem for us, and it will make things easier for you."

Cindy's expression remained blank and passive. It was as if she couldn't hear what he was saying.

"But you'll need money. You won't be able to go back to Tortola, or to Florida. You won't be able to contact your old friends. You'll have to disappear. At least for a year. Maybe longer. So you'll need to take a share of the money."

She still didn't register a reaction.

"Do you understand? This will keep you safe. It's your best chance of staying alive."

"I don't care what you do," Cindy finally answered. "It's my fault that Steve is dead. I never should have run away with the money."

"It's not your fault," Marilyn told her. "It was an accident."

"Yeah," she said. "But if it wasn't for me, there wouldn't have been an accident. He'd still be alive."

"And you'd be as good as dead," Jeanne snapped at her. "For God's sake, use your head. Do you really think he was going to take you with him?"

Cindy was shocked.

"You went to him because you thought he could help you. But he didn't help you. What Steve did was help himself. That's why he's dead. And that's why you'd be as good as dead if he were still running the show. You'd be the only link to the money. You'd always be a danger to him."

Howard nodded vigorously. "You don't really think you were part of his plan? Hell, your friends won't ever stop looking for you. And when they find you, then they find him. Believe me, Steve was planning on killing you along with the four of us."

Bill found himself fascinated as he heard Jeanne cut in. "So you shouldn't be worrying about what happened to Steve. The only thing you should be thinking about is what could happen to you."

"I already know what will to happen to me," Cindy answered, sounding aware for the first time. "I'm going to get killed. If I'm lucky. These guys can do a lot worse than just kill you."

Bill stepped back down into the cockpit, and focused on the young woman.

"If they find me on the run, they'll kill me,"

Cindy continued. "And if I go back to them with my share of the money they'll kill me. Either way, they'll know that I was stealing from them."

"We're giving you a chance to escape," Marilyn said.

Cindy smiled sadly at the thought and shook her head. "No way I can spend the rest of my life running. They'll keep looking until they know I'm dead."

It was Bill who broke the silence. "I think we've missed something, Howard." He looked from Howard to Jeanne. "We can't take the money. It just won't work."

Jeanne looked stunned. "Why?" she demanded.

"You just explained why to Cindy. You said she always would have been a danger to Steve. It's just as true for us. She'd always be a danger to us."

"But we're helping her escape," Howard insisted.

"We're trying to," Bill said, "but it won't work."

Jeanne asked angrily, "Why won't it work?"

He answered to all of them. "Don't you see? As long as the money is missing, they'll keep looking for Cindy. And when they find her, and she doesn't have the money, they'll want to know where it is." He sat down next to Jeanne and spoke directly to her. "If we take the money, we'll begin each morning wondering whether today is going to be the day that they catch up with Cindy. We'll spend each day wondering if this is the day when they're going to find us."

They listened morosely. Marilyn understood,

378

and added, "Not much of a life, is it?"

"How do you know they'll find her?" Jeanne challenged.

"How do you know they won't?" Bill answered.

Howard stood dumbly behind the wheel. Then he decided, "I guess that's a chance we'll just have to take." He looked at Jeanne. "We *know* about the bonds and the diamonds. Even if we don't have them, we'd be a danger to these people. So we'd still be in danger." Then he turned to Marilyn. "It's the same risk either way. You see that, don't you?"

"No, I don't see it," Marilyn answered. "I think Bill is right. It just won't work."

They stayed in thoughtful silence. Bill reached for Jeanne's hand, but she pulled it away. He was the messenger who had just brought bad news, and she hated him along with the message.

Howard tried to reassemble his plan. "We put her ashore. On one of the really crowded, commercial islands. Where people are coming and going all the time. We give her a passport that nobody has any reason to question. An American passport, so she can fly to any place in the United States. And she has . . . what? Four hundred thousand dollars, if we just divide the bearer bonds. Hell, half a million if she takes extra bonds because she's leaving the diamonds behind. That means she can go anywhere. Be anybody. She can even have her face changed. What are the chances of anyone ever finding her?"

"None," Jeanne answered. "None at all."

"Howard," Marilyn interrupted. "Is that a

chance you really want to take? A chance with our lives? Maybe even with the lives of our children?"

"They'll never find her," Howard nearly shouted. "I've thought this through. There isn't a chance in a million that they'll ever find her."

Cindy stood up slowly and started up onto the deck.

"Where are you going?" Jeanne demanded. "You're part of this."

Cindy smiled. "You all seem to be doing fine deciding how my life's going to come out. You don't need me."

She walked forward.

Howard turned on his wife. "Dammit, there's nothing we can do about the danger. They could come looking for us whether we have the money or not."

"Maybe not," Bill cut in. "Cindy just told us that she's as good as dead whether she has none of the money or just a share of it. But suppose she has all of the money."

Howard's jaw dropped. Jeanne seemed about to scream in rage.

"All the bonds," Bill said. "And all the diamonds."

"She leaves with everything?" Howard was aghast.

"Not leaves," Bill explained. "We put her ashore. In Tortola. But at a different port before we go back to Road Town. And she takes the case with all the bonds and the pouches with all the diamonds. She goes straight to her friends and she says, 'Here. Here's everything.' And then she tells them the story, exactly as it happened. She ran to Steve for protection because he was the only one she knew. But Steve wasn't interested in helping her. Instead, he kidnapped her and us, and tried to run with the money. We didn't know anything about the money. And then, when Steve was lost over the side we brought the boat, with Cindy aboard, back to Road Town."

"They'd never believe her," Howard snapped.

"Why wouldn't they? They have all their money. They have no reason to doubt Cindy because she saved their merchandise. They have no reason to think about us because Cindy didn't tell us anything."

"What if they don't believe her?" Howard challenged. "If they think we know about the money, we're as good as dead. Our best chance is for Cindy to get out of here, find an out-of-the-way place and get herself lost."

Bill nodded. "There's danger no matter how we play it. But I think Cindy is in far less danger if she goes to them with all the money, rather than risking them finding her with only part of it. And I think we're in less danger if Cindy's friends just take their money and run."

They looked from one to another, trying to evaluate the alternative that faced them. Howard's perfect plan, the one that Bill had agreed to only minutes before, didn't seem so perfect. Then Jeanne said, "Why are you so concerned about Cindy's safety? Doesn't it matter to you that only yesterday morning she was pointing a gun at me? Threatening to kill me? Why aren't you thinking about my safety?"

"I am," Bill argued. "Our chances are better if no one is looking for us."

Howard slammed his fist against the wheel. "Dammit! The fact is that we'd all be perfectly safe if that little slut had gone over the side with her boyfriend."

"Howard!" Marilyn couldn't believe what her husband had just said.

"I don't think you mean that," Bill told his friend.

"Well think about it," Howard snarled. "We're all in danger of our lives because a pair of thieves kidnapped us and used us to cover their escape. We didn't steal anyone's money. We didn't do anything wrong. But now we're putting ourselves in danger just to protect . . . her!" He jabbed his finger toward Cindy who was kneeling against the lifeline on the port bow.

"That's right," Jeanne agreed. "We're putting ourselves at terrible risk for the sake of someone who would gladly have killed us all."

"She wouldn't have killed us!" Bill yelled. His voice was loud enough to turn Cindy's face back toward them.

And then Jeanne screamed, "God damn you! She was pointing a gun right into my face!"

Marilyn tried to intervene. "Let's get a hold of ourselves. We're never going to work this out if we start fighting."

Bill controlled his response. "You're right. The goddamn money will make us all crazy. Just like it did to Steve."

"It's not just the money," Howard insisted. "We're talking about our lives."

Jeanne was still furious. "And I'm not about to spend the rest of my life in hiding just to protect someone who was going to kill me."

Then Howard said, "We ought to put her over the side in the dinghy and let her fend for herself. That's the best we could have expected from her."

"She'd die out here," Bill said to Howard.

"At least we'd be safe!" Jeanne yelled at her husband.

Bill looked at Jeanne and understood that he didn't know her anymore. And if he didn't know her, could he really be in love with her? Was there anything left to be saved?

Even at the forward end of the boat, Cindy could catch words from their argument. She understood what it was that they were deciding. They were like lawyers presenting their cases and demanding a verdict. She turned her face back to the open sea. She really didn't care what decision they reached.

45

The Sea King helicopter had lifted off from San Juan, flown easterly across the American Virgins and the Drake Channel, and then crossed the Anagada Passage that separated the Virgin Islands from the Antilles. It had window-shopped the approaches to St. Martin, overflown Saba and then headed south southeast. Flying at 2,000 feet, and making 120 knots, it stayed well west of the tiny islands that bent in an arc from the Virgins to the South American coast, sealing off the Caribbean from the Atlantic. The islands formed the eastern edge of the image on the surface search radar. The western edge touched St. Croix for a moment, when the helicopter held the island directly to the west. But now the screen's western side showed only open sea.

In the forward cockpit, the pilot and copilot were well settled into the routine of managing the flight instruments. Directly behind them, in a darkened compartment, the radar operator kept a plot of their position while directing the pilot toward any promising targets that appeared on his screen. In the Sea King's cargo bay, two observers were positioned at the open doors, scanning through powerful binoculars. They weren't looking for boats.

The radar would find any boats in the area long before they could make visual contact. Instead, they were searching for the nearly invisible traces of lost ships. An overturned raft. A floating piece of deck planking. A slick of diesel fuel. Small, nearly sunken clues too insignificant to reflect a radar signal.

Like Al Weston, the pilot wasn't looking into harbors, or overflying the thousands of tiny images that were close in to the islands. Inside the cruising lanes, there were too many boats to examine. And if *Cane Maiden* was among them, she would soon be identified by a passing charter boat, or logged into a familiar port. Instead, he was interested in solitary reflections from boats wandering far offshore. That's where he would find *Cane Maiden*, if he were going to find her at all.

Their plan was to sweep down the Leewards as far as Dominica, run west 120 miles to Aves Island, and then turn directly north for their return to Tortola. If *Cane Maiden* were moving offshore down the Antilles, they'd find her.

They held Nevis Island ahead when the radar operator began to pick up a reflection thirty miles to the west. "It's a hard target," he reported to the pilot, indicating that it was a fixed object, rising out of the normal return from the water's surface. "Small, but distinct. Looks like a small boat."

"You have a course on her?" the pilot asked.

The radarman turned a speedball to put the crosshairs on the target. Then he touched a button. "It will take a minute," he answered.

He waited a minute, moved the crosshairs a fraction to the pip's relative position, and hit the button again. A computer accounted for the helicopter's movement, calculated the effect of the change in relative bearing and range, and displayed the answer. "I get speed three knots. Course three two five. Looks like a sailboat making for St. Croix."

"Three knots?" the pilot questioned. "Either a sailboat, or maybe a fisherman trawling." He looked at his copilot. "What do you think? Should we take a run over?"

The copilot shrugged. "It will cost us twenty minutes over and twenty minutes back. Plus a lot of fuel. We'll be much closer to her on the way back."

"Right," the pilot agreed. "And at three knots, she won't be going anywhere. We've got plenty of time." He keyed his radio. "Just mark her. We'll have a closer look on the way back in."

The radar operator gave the target a number and, with the touch of a key, entered her into the system memory. The computer would continue to plot the target at its dead reckoning course, and identify her as soon as she appeared during the Sea King's run back to the north.

46

They moved silently about the boat as if they were each on a separate voyage. Bill had the wheel. Howard moved about the deck, checking rigging and tidying up lines. Jeanne was folding laundry off the lifeline and bringing dry things below. Marilyn was below trying to find the ingredients of a simple meal. Cindy had disappeared down into Steve's compartment in the bow, adding walls to her isolation from the others.

It was the money that had driven each of them into isolation. It was close enough to touch, and theirs to keep, a fortune that seemed to be a heaven-sent answer to the problems they had brought aboard *Cane Maiden*. To Howard, it was respectability. He could close his firm down to a skeleton staff and let the banks fight over his business assets. But he could maintain his lifestyle and afford all the trappings of his success. People might be tempted to pity his downfall, but they would be dismayed when he cranked up his display of affluence. Living well would be his temporary revenge, and he would be ready to launch an even more prestigious firm if the economy ever came back to life.

For Marilyn, the money could save the sanity

387

of her home. She was ready to pull in the purse strings, batten down the hatches and ride out the storm. But she knew her husband well enough to realize that he would never survive. Putting his house on the block would seem as great a disgrace as being hauled to the gallows in an open cart. Pulling his children out of private schools would seem as base as molesting them in public. He would keep up appearances until there was nothing left. And then, he would as soon drive his Mercedes at top speed into a tree as to admit his financial failure.

Jeanne saw the money as escape. Escape from a bare-bones loft that she considered hardly suitable for storing merchandise, much less for sheltering a family. Escape from the dictates of small businessmen who crumpled the edges of their estimates, and from the furniture companies who saw her talents as nothing more than a way to sell their trashy desks and side chairs. The money was an opportunity. A chance to let her imagination soar, to innovate. To create new decor, and turn her back on the midgets who could see only expense. She could open her own house, move out into new circles, find appreciation and respect for her art. She could rid herself of the damn debt-ridden school that had stolen her husband and forced him into the service of the city's neediest cases.

Even Bill could toy with its advantages. Just his share of the fortune would hold back the wrecking balls that were already poised over the seedy, paint-peeled schoolhouse that the creditors wanted to turn into a parking lot. And Jeanne's share would open new worlds to her, perhaps making her less critical of the limitations he had too willingly accepted. But while he could see the possibilities, he was more concerned with what the money was doing to them all. It had driven Steve to near-madness, and was now turning them all into enemies. It had created the silence that was separating them, and was threatening to launch each of them at one another's throats.

It was the money that dominated their thoughts. It had turned them all into liars, who pretended to be thinking only of their safety. "Screw the money," Howard had screamed. "We're talking about our lives. That damn girl is a threat to our lives."

"Why are we concerned about her?" Jeanne had demanded. "She was going to kill us. Why should we let her threaten us for the rest of our lives?"

They had argued on, long after Cindy had gone below. Marilyn had seemed unconcerned about her own safety. But she had raised the specter of vengeful mercenaries taking their anger out on her children. "If they find Cindy, then they're certainly going to find us. Our names and addresses are on the charter agreement. And they'll understand that the way to get our cooperation is to threaten our children."

Howard had agreed. "I don't give a damn about myself. But I'm sure as hell not going to put my children in danger for the sake of some bimbo who's probably screwed half the bartenders in Florida."

Jeanne had come back into the discussion. "It's not as if we were going to do anything to her.

Howard is just talking about setting her off in the dinghy, so that we can at least buy ourselves some time."

Bill's face had contorted in anger. "That's bullshit!" he yelled at Jeanne. "Throwing her over in the dinghy doesn't buy us time. It buys us an easier way to commit murder. Because that's what we're talking about, isn't it? Finding an easy way to get rid of her."

They had all been arguing against Bill who kept reminding them that their best chance of being left alone was if Cindy's friends weren't searching for their money. "But we're not really talking about our safety, are we?" he had challenged. "The real issue is whether we let her walk off with five million dollars that could be ours."

"That's not what I'm thinking of," Marilyn had shouted into Bill's face. And then she had stormed out of the cockpit and gone below.

Jeanne had fixed him in a cold, angry stare. "Is that all you think of me? God, but I despise you." She had gone up to the deck to sulk.

Howard had turned the wheel over to Bill. "I think that you ought to at least consider that you might be wrong. Maybe you need a little less sympathy and a bit more courage. Enough courage to do what has to be done."

"The fucking money," Bill had cursed to himself. "It's driving us all mad."

Or was Howard right? Was he wallowing in pity for a trashy girl just to cover his own lack of courage? Was Jeanne right, that the school was nothing more than his hiding place? Was he afraid to leave the safe harbors and put himself at risk?

390

How had they ever gotten to the point where they could talk seriously about jeopardizing the life of another person? Was it really the series of random events that it seemed?

They had discovered the money, which suddenly put them in danger. Then Steve had died, which left Cindy as the only link to the danger. Then they had understood that the money was untraceable, which made it theirs for the taking. They had planned a way to set Cindy free, and keep the money. And then, when they realized that the girl would always be a danger to them, they had begun discussing ways of eliminating her.

Or had it all been planned? Had Howard brought them slowly, one step at a time, to their damning conclusion? He had shown them the money. Let them handle the bonds and hold the diamonds up to the sun. Given them a chance to understand that they could be fabulously wealthy. Let the thought sink in. Then he had raised the problem that Cindy posed, but immediately offered a solution. "We have to give her a share so that she can run off and lose herself," he had suggested. Had he meant it, or was he just showing them that the young woman was the only thing that stood between them and the fortune? And then, perhaps he had simply waited for them to discover the flaw in his suggestion. Jeanne had stumbled on it when she realized that Steve would never have been free of the danger that Cindy represented. And Bill himself had clarified it. If Steve could never be free, then neither could they.

Had Howard planned to lead them to this point,

where they already felt that the money was theirs? Where they wouldn't be able to stomach the idea of letting a worthless tramp snatch it out of their hands and leave with it forever? Howard had said that they would have been better off if Cindy had gone over the side with Steve. Was that an unthinking comment, born in his frustration? Or was that the conclusion he knew they would have to reach sooner or later?

And if he had orchestrated their thinking, when did it all start? When Steve had offered them "hundreds of thousands of dollars," and Howard realized that the total fortune must be in the millions? Or after Steve had vanished, when Howard actually counted the bonds and the diamonds? Had Steve been the victim of a helmsman's miscalculation? Or had he been murdered?

"You hear that?" It was Howard stepping back down into the cockpit. He was shading his eyes and squinting into the southern sky.

Bill listened. He was used to the casual flap of the sails in the nearly dead wind. But there was another sound. A deep, throaty groan that seemed to be coming from beyond the southern horizon. "Yeah. I hear it. What is it?"

Howard kept searching. Then he stretched a finger out over the stern. "There. I think it's a plane."

Bill followed Howard's sight line. "No. It's a helicopter."

"Oh, Jesus!" Howard was instantly terrified. "They're back. Goddammit, they're back."

He raced forward to the bow hatch that opened into Steve's compartment. "Stay below," he shouted down. "It's your friend, in the helicopter." He slid the hatch closed, locking Cindy into the small cabin below. Then he raced back to the pilothouse hatch. "Marilyn, get up here. I need you on deck. Cindy's friends are coming back for another look."

Jeanne raced into the cockpit. "Why are they coming back?" she demanded of Bill.

"I don't know. Still searching, I guess."

Marilyn came up, and Howard directed her and Jeanne to the foredeck. "Same thing as before," he told them. "Just smile and wave. We're vacationers enjoying a cruise. You have to make them think that everything is normal."

He swung around to Bill. "What are we going to do about Steve? They'll see that he's missing. They'll want to talk to him."

He dashed back down the hatch. Bill looked back at the dot that was growing in the sky. The rumble of the engine was growing louder.

When Howard reappeared he had the microphone in one hand, trailing its coiled cord. He could show them the disconnected cord and gesture that the radio wasn't working. In the other hand he held the automatic pistol that he had retrieved from the locker in his cabin.

Bill gaped at the gun. "Jesus, Howard, that's the last thing we're going to need."

"Just in case," Howard answered. He slipped the gun under one of the bench cushions. "Just in case they try to board us."

"You're going to shoot them?"

"Jesus, Bill, you heard Steve. These guys are killers."

They both looked aft. They could see the heavy shape of the helicopter body, and catch the sunlight sparkling off the rotor.

47

"We hold it dead ahead," the radar operator said to the pilot.

"Right. I can see her. Looks like a sailing vessel. Maybe a ketch. She's carrying a lot of sail."

"Still making only a couple of knots," radar reported.

The captain nodded. He told his copilot, "Let's take her down and have a look."

They followed a glide path that would bring them down from 2,000 feet right onto the boat's stern. They were still two miles away, a good full minute of flying time. The copilot raised his binoculars to the windscreen. "Could be her. It could be a yawl."

They could see that there was no bow wave. The wake she trailed was hardly a ripple. There was barely enough air to keep her moving.

"Am I going swimming?" one of the observers asked over the radio. The Sea King could land on the water, and keep enough lift in its rotor to hold it upright. But standard procedure was to hover a few feet above the surface and send a swimmer to investigate wrecks or assist disabled boats.

"Not likely," the pilot answered. "She seems

to be doing just fine."

"That's her," the copilot announced. He was still studying the boat through his binoculars. "*Cane Maiden*." He could read the name that was printed across the transom.

They slowed and aimed off toward the leeward quarter.

"That's a different helicopter," Bill shouted to Howard. "It's got military markings. Looks like a search-and-rescue helicopter."

Howard hesitated in a moment of confusion. Then he screamed up to the women on the bow, "It's military. Maybe police. Don't do too much smiling. Remember, we've been through hell. We've lost our captain over the side."

Bill realized that Howard was giving stage directions. He was already setting the scene for the story he would tell in port.

"We want them to know we're okay," Howard instructed his friend. "We don't want them putting anybody on board. We're not ready."

The Sea King slipped up on the port quarter. The whine of its turbine engines was deafening, and it flattened the sea beneath it into misty rings. The side door was wide open. A crewman was waving at them. Howard waved back in acknowledgment. Jeanne and Marilyn raised their hands.

"Ahoy, on *Cane Maiden*!" the copilot's voice boomed from an amplifier.

Howard kept waving.

"Is everyone all right?"

He stretched out his arms in a gesture of helplessness. We're surviving, he was trying to tell them without any show of enthusiasm.

"Do you need assistance?"

He shook his head vigorously.

"Tortola police are looking for you. They've been trying to raise you."

He nodded that he understood. Then he held up his microphone with its dangling cord and made a cutting gesture with his free hand.

"You've lost your radio," the amplified voice suggested.

Howard's head bobbed up and down.

"Were you caught in the storm?"

He kept nodding.

"But you're seaworthy?"

Again, he responded with an affirmative nod.

The voice told him, "We'll report your position. Are you making for Road Harbor?"

Howard pointed to the compass binnacle. Then he nodded again.

He waited painfully while the crew of the helicopter digested the information.

Then came another question. "Do you have enough fuel aboard?"

Howard thought. If he had fuel, why was he drifting in the light air? He could be making six knots running on his auxiliary engine. He held his hand in the air with his fingers an inch apart. A little bit, he was signaling.

Again, the amplifier went silent. There was just the cry of the engine. Then the speaker crackled. "Okay. Smooth sailing!"

The Sea King lifted slowly and moved down the port side, only forty feet away from the women on the foredeck. The observer waved to them. Then the engine pitch changed and the pounding of the rotors grew frantic. It lifted off quickly and flew away to the north.

The pilot keyed his radio and raised his base in San Juan. "We've located *Cane Maiden*," he reported. "Under sail and headed back to Tortola. She had a testy time with the storm. Radios are out. Some damage on deck. They've got mattresses and seat cushions set out to dry. But she reports she's seaworthy. And she has reserve fuel in case she needs it."

"I copy," a voice acknowledged from the radio. "What's her position?"

"Radar," the pilot asked, "what's *Cane Maiden*'s position?"

The radarman cut in. "One thirty-four, East Point, thirty-one." She was thirty-one miles southeast of St. Croix's eastern tip. At her present slow speed, she would pass the island early in the morning hours, and make Road Harbor in the afternoon. But the winds would probably pick up after the effects of the storm had passed, and she could go to her engine once she was in close. Her position figured her to be back at her mooring sometime Thursday morning. If she held her present heading.

48

"You've already decided that Cindy's not coming back in with us," Bill said quietly to Howard as they watched the Sea King grow smaller in the sky.

Howard seemed stunned.

"The whole charade. The bit about only having a little fuel left. You want to make sure no one expects us in port tonight. You're leaving yourself time to get rid of her."

"No, that's not it," Howard protested. "I just wanted to cover for Steve. And I wanted to give us time to come to a decision."

"You've already made your decision," Bill told him.

Howard held a blank, innocent expression for a few seconds. Then he looked away. "I suppose you're right. I have already made my decision. But it's not up to me. We all have to decide."

"I've decided," Bill told him firmly. "We're taking her back to Tortola and putting her ashore with all the money. And then we're washing our hands of this whole mess."

"I understand your point," Howard answered. "But I don't think that any of us agrees with you. We don't want to spend the rest of our lives on the run."

"You're just going to put her over the side? Leave her to drown?"

Howard took a deep breath. Then he nodded slowly. "I don't think she's worth the four of us. I think it's either her or us."

"It's the fucking money." Bill spat out the words.

"That's part of it," Howard admitted. "If we turn in the money, we're in danger. And if they find Cindy, I think we're all as good as dead."

"You don't know that!" Bill shouted.

Howard pursed his lips and wagged his head. "No, I'm not positive. Nothing about this is positive. But that's my gut feeling. We all have to weigh the evidence. We all have to decide."

Marilyn and Jeanne brought up a simple meal of omelets with cut-up vegetables. Marilyn took a plate forward to Steve's cabin, but Cindy wasn't hungry. She came up on deck and sat alone on the bow, watching the western sky color itself in preparation for another sunset.

Howard tasted the omelet and then took a sip of the warm fruit punch. "I'm going below to fix us some real drinks," he told the others. "When I get back, we've got to talk. We've got to decide." They picked at their food in silence while they awaited his return, and then sipped the warm gin and tonics that he brought up with him.

"Well," Howard finally said to break the silence, "who wants to go first?"

He saw blank faces in response.

"I think we all ought to say exactly how we feel. We ought to face our problem honestly, and say what we want to do about it."

The two women nodded that they understood, but neither of them spoke. He looked at Bill. "Why don't you start?"

Bill set his plate and drink on the bench. "Okay, I'll start." There was an angry edge to his voice. "I'll start by saying that there's nothing to discuss. We can't put her over the side because we all know damn well that she'd never make it to shore. We haven't seen another boat in two days, so the chances of someone picking her up are slim to nonexistent. It would be just another way of killing her, and I don't think any of us is ready to kill someone. So, we're stuck with her."

He looked at the others. Only Marilyn was returning his glance, and her expression didn't reveal anything of her thoughts. Jeanne was looking out over the side. Howard was absorbed in the heading that was moving gently on the compass rose.

"The safest way to get rid of her is to put her ashore, with the bonds and diamonds, and then forget about her. Once her people have their money, I don't see why they would give a damn about us. Then I'll go along with Howard in telling the authorities that Steve went over in the storm. We get on an airplane, go home and put this whole trip behind us."

There was silence when he finished speaking. No one challenged him.

"Marilyn?" Howard gave his wife the floor.

Her face sunk into her hands for a moment. She raised her eyes and spoke over her fingertips. "I guess the only thing I'm thinking about is my children. I'll do anything to keep them out of danger. If there's even a chance that Cindy could lead those killers to our home . . ." She sat up straight and looked at her husband. "That's what I'm trying to decide. How much do we risk if we let her go with the money? Because I don't want to take any risk."

It was Jeanne's turn. She looked directly at Bill. "The only thing we should be thinking about is ourselves. Our own safety. As far as I'm concerned, that girl came at me with a loaded pistol in her hand. If I had grabbed for the gun . . . if we had struggled . . . it would have been her or me. And if she had been the one killed, I would have breathed a long sigh of relief."

Bill couldn't contradict her. So far, Jeanne was absolutely correct.

"I see this as exactly the same thing. It's her or us." She turned to Marilyn. "You wondered how much danger you and your children would be in. My answer is that *any* danger is too much. Why should you have to worry about the lives of your children just to protect someone who kidnapped us and was certainly thinking about killing us?"

Marilyn's expression relaxed. There was a hint of a relieved smile. Jeanne understood her fears.

"This girl is nothing more than a street hoodlum," Jeanne went on. "She pointed the gun at us, and what we're doing right now is struggling for the gun. If it kills her, that's her fault. She's the one who brought it aboard. She was the one who was ready to use it."

Bill carried her analogy. "So, we struggled. And now we have the gun. Does that give us the right to use it on her?"

"Right?" Jeanne fired back, as if the word were ridiculous. "Dammit, we're talking about the rest of our lives. Don't we have the *right* to protect ourselves?"

She turned away angrily.

Howard spoke very softly. "I agree with Jeanne. Frankly, I had some doubts, but I think she answered them for me. Bottom line is that it's either her or us. And I think, in this situation, we have to think about what's best for us." He looked at Bill. "I don't think we can afford to take her back."

"What about the money?" Bill demanded of Howard.

Howard shrugged. "There's nothing we can do about the money. We can't give it back. We can't announce that we have it without putting ourselves right back into danger. The only thing we can do is take it with us."

Bill jumped to his feet and walked away from his friends to the edge of the cockpit. He spent a few seconds looking at the reddening clouds. Then he wheeled back toward them. "So that's it? We're just going to kill her and take the money?"

"We haven't decided that yet," Howard answered. "We've just been discussing our problem."

"How do we decide?" Bill asked.

Howard glanced at the women. Neither seemed to have an answer.

"I suppose we have to vote."

Bill took the wheel while Howard went below. He could see Cindy sitting forward on the bow, looking idly down into the soft white wash that was stained with the red of the western sky. Her hair was tied behind her in a long ponytail. The short sleeves of Steve's shirt drooped down to her elbows. He could guess what she was thinking. She had heard enough of their conversation to know that her life was being decided. She was probably thinking that her life wasn't worth very much at all, and wondering if they had come to the same decision. In the ill-fitting clothes, with the lonely expression, she looked just like many of the lost kids that he worked with. "Get up. Get mad. Fight back," was what he tried to tell his students. Some of them listened. Others just shrank and waited for the world to deal with them. He didn't see any fight left in Cindy. "I really screwed up," she had told him, as if that were reason enough to let herself be destroyed. She was lost, unless somebody fought for her.

When Howard came back up, he was carrying an empty coffee mug. He set it on the front of the bench. "That's the ballot box," he told the others. Then he held up a handful of wooden kitchen matches. "These are the ballots." He gave each of them one of the matches.

"You don't have to tell anyone how you voted. If you want to turn her free with the money, put the match in the cup. If you want to leave her out here, break the match in half, and put half in the cup. Take your time. Think about it. I'll check the cup after sunset. And I'll tell you what we've decided."

Bill felt his throat go dry. He expected to explode in anger, but there was no anger in him. All he felt was a terrible sadness.

"We can't do this," he managed to say to the others. His voice broke. "We can't do this."

Howard sounded sympathetic. "We have to. We have to decide."

Bill looked down at the matchstick in his hand. "We have no right to decide whether someone lives or dies. It's not up to us."

Jeanne answered him. "We have every right to protect ourselves."

Bill took his match and broke it in half. Then he turned and fired both pieces over the side.

49

"They've found her!" Al Weston announced as he set the telephone back into its cradle.

"Cindy?" Johnnie Igoe asked in disbelief.

"No. *Cane Maiden*. Air Rescue spotted her thirty-five miles south of St. Croix."

"She's still at sea?"

Al nodded, his first smile in days playing across his lips. He glanced down at the location he had copied while his hired clerk at Drake Channel Charters was telling him the news. "She's headed north. They figure she'll either put in on St. Croix sometime during the night, or make it back to Tortola around noon tomorrow. It depends on the wind."

"Why is she coming back?" Igoe asked, aiming the question as much at himself as to Al. "If they have the money, they already made their getaway. So why the fuck are they coming back?" Then he answered his own question. "Unless they already put the money ashore someplace."

"Could be," Al allowed. "But if they did, then the people on board know where they put the money ashore. And that gives us a live lead."

Igoe's frown disappeared. He had given up on ever finding either Cindy or the money. Now they

406

had a chance. A damn good chance. How many flights were there out of the smaller Leeward Islands? One, maybe two a day at best. All they needed to find out was which island the money had landed on. Then they could take up the chase. And they would have that information within minutes of meeting *Cane Maiden*'s passengers. It generally didn't take longer than that for people to tell Al whatever he wanted to hear.

"You know," Al speculated, "there's even a chance that she never made a port. The kid told me that she had been beaten up in the storm. She lost her radios and took on some water."

Johnnie didn't understand the significance. He waited for Al to finish.

"If they were running out into the open sea, the storm could have changed their minds. Suppose they lost their navigation gear. And maybe they burned up a lot of fuel. Could be they decided they were in no shape to make an ocean crossing. Maybe they figured they had a better chance on land."

"Yeah, but why come back here? There's lots of land they could head for."

Weston nodded thoughtfully. "You're probably right. If I was in their shoes, this is the last place I'd head for. So, maybe they aren't trying to make Road Harbor. Maybe they figure St. Croix is a safe place to put in."

He jumped up from his chair and snatched his jacket from the sofa. "Let's go," he told Johnnie.

Johnnie was already on his feet before he asked, "Go where?"

"St. Croix," Al answered.

They raced to the airport, formulating their plan as they drove. The helicopter could get them down to St. Croix before nightfall. But it would be too late to search the waters south of the island. So, they would have to wait on shore for *Cane Maiden* to arrive.

"They wouldn't come right into Christiansted," Igoe suggested. "I mean, St. Croix is a big island. There's got to be miles of beach where they could land."

Al agreed. St. Croix was the biggest of the Virgins. And there was just Johnnie and himself to cover the beaches. So there wasn't much of a chance of intercepting *Cane Maiden*'s landing. But there was only one airport which would be very easy to cover during the night. And they could take off at first light to patrol the southeastern shore.

Their problem got easier when they talked with Paul Canavan, their helicopter pilot. The island's southeastern coast didn't provide many good landing points for a boat of *Cane Maiden*'s size. "There are shoals all along the beach," he explained, unrolling the chart. "Nobody in his right mind would try to go in there at night."

"So, where does she land?" Weston asked.

"Grass Point," Paul said, indicating a spit of land that stuck out past the shoals at the eastern end of the south shore. "Or maybe here." He pointed to an anchorage off Milford Point, three miles to the west. "Other than that, he's got to round East Point and put in someplace on the north shore. But if he's smart, he'll stay off until daylight."

Al figured that Johnnie could cover the airport,

and that he could easily keep track of the two most promising landing points. But from what he was seeing on the chart, *Cane Maiden* would most likely stay at sea until daybreak.

"Suppose we wanted to board her at sea. Could we do that?" he asked Paul.

"Depends on whether she wants to be boarded." It was tough enough to hold a hovering helicopter steady over a moving boat; impossible to lower someone down in a harness through the rigging. But he could set down in the water next to *Cane Maiden*, and she could send over her dinghy to pick him up.

Al knew *Cane Maiden* wouldn't be sending over a dinghy. "Can we bring our own boat?"

"We can bring an inflatable. But we'll need a bigger chopper. It's going to cost you a lot more."

They took off in a five-seat Jet Ranger, equipped with air bag floats for landing on the water. An inflatable boat, with a small outboard motor, was strapped to the side. Al sat next to the pilot, with Johnnie in the seat behind him, his feet resting on an automatic rifle.

Al had figured that the rifle gave him all the firepower he would need to convince *Cane Maiden* to turn into the wind and drop her sails. Then, with Johnnie providing cover from the helicopter, he could put the inflatable over and make it to the yacht. The gun in the holster under his jacket would be all he would need once he got aboard.

"Hey, I ain't flying into any gunfight," the pilot had protested. "It only takes one hit in the right place to bring this thing down in flames."

"Won't be any gunfight," Al reassured him.

"The way I figure it, there are some scared passengers on board with Cindy and her boyfriend. Nobody's going to be firing back. They'll do what they're told."

"What are we gonna do with them?" Johnnie wondered out loud.

"Take Cindy and take our money. Then we'll sink the son-of-a-bitch."

"What about the passengers?"

"Let them swim home."

As soon as they reached their cruising altitude they could see the low outline of St. Croix, a dark stain in the blood-red sea. To the west, the sun had just vanished behind the horizon, leaving the sky in flames. The color began to drain as they flew, and the lights were already on in Christiansted when they passed over the city. Ahead, they could make out the landing lights at the airport to the south.

They moved quickly once they were on the ground. Johnnie went to the terminal to check the schedule of the morning's departing flights. Al went to the general aviation desk to get a fix on any private planes that might be scheduled to leave. Then he rented a car and drove out along the southern coastal road.

It was hardly a road, really just a path of broken paving that wandered along the edge of the sea. At times, it cut through the heavy foliage across the tops of volcanic cliffs. Then it would drop down beneath the rock formations and run along the shore, with a wall overgrown with vegetation to the left and rocky beaches to the right. Al had to drive slowly as he negotiated treacherous turns, following the beams of his headlamps which were a poor match for the inky darkness. If they land out here, he thought, they won't get very far. Without a car, *Cane Maiden*'s passengers couldn't move more than a few hundred yards from where the boat put in.

But he was becoming more convinced that no experienced captain would even attempt a landing. Across the black water, he could see a white line of waves breaking over the offshore shoals. Even if they anchored outside, it would be dangerous to try to bring a dinghy over the rocks and onto the beach. If *Cane Maiden* were trying to make St. Croix, she would either lay off over night, or sail around East Point and try for one of the northern ports.

They would find her in the morning, probably as she turned around the Point. He hoped she would still be far enough out so that his automatic rifle wouldn't attract too much attention.

50

Bill looked down into the coffee mug that Jeanne had set before him on the saloon table. He tipped it over and let the matchsticks fall out. There were three of them. All of them were broken in half.

Jeanne slid into the bench across from him, studied the matchsticks for a moment, and then looked up into her husband's eyes. "We've decided," she told him. "Howard says that it has to be done now, before we get any closer to shore."

"That's because Howard wants to be damn certain that no one ever finds her," Bill answered. He looked angrily at the broken sticks. Then his hand flashed across the top of the table sending the mug and the matches flying.

"Dammit! You're lying to yourselves. If Cindy is found, then she can certainly tell who put her over the side. And why they did it. It wouldn't be just her friends that would come looking for us. The police would be after us too. When you put her in that dinghy, you're not hoping that someone will find her. You're counting on her dying out there. And that's murder, plain and simple."

"It's a better chance than she would have given us."

412

"It's no chance at all, and you all know it!"

She pulled back as if he had slapped her. His voice softened to a plea. "Jeanne, for God's sake, face the truth. You're counting on no one ever finding her, aren't you?"

"I'm not going to run for the rest of my life," Jeanne screamed into his face.

"You don't have to run. Just give her the money and let her go. Let her walk out of our lives and settle up with her friends."

She started to answer, but the words never came. Her mouth was open, and her eyes flashing, but she had no answer. She was lying to herself, and to the others who were lying to her. Bill was right, she had decided, even before she had broken her matchstick. The safest course was to give the girl the money and let her go. But she couldn't do that. Because it wasn't just the money that Cindy would take away with her. It was all Jeanne's hopes for the future.

"We've decided," she finally managed.

Bill studied her sadly. "The money means that much to you? You'd kill someone to have it?"

Jeanne looked away from the confrontation. "She would have killed us," she repeated. "If she had gone over the side during the storm, none of us would have cared. We'd have been damn grateful to be rid of her." She turned back to Bill. "Why is it different now? It's still her, or us. Why shouldn't it be us?"

He reached across the table and took her hand. "You know, we can still make a go of things. You and I can make a fresh start. I'll get out of the school. I'll give you your chance to do what you

413

want. I never meant to hold you back."

She studied him for a moment, and he thought he saw a softening in her eyes. But then she eased her hand out of his grasp. "It's too late for that," Jeanne said. "We have to act now."

She slid off the bench and started for the ladder. On her way, she stopped to pick up the coffee mug. Bill was left staring in confusion at the broken matchsticks that were scattered on the deck.

Their marriage, he reasoned, had just ended. She had walked away from him, from his values, from his potential. She knew what she wanted, and she knew that the money could buy it all. Nothing was going to stand in her way. Not him and the life he thought they had been trying to build together. Certainly not a young woman she had every reason to despise.

But, still, he couldn't believe it. He couldn't believe she was capable of killing. He understood the ambition that had been gnawing at her for the past few years, and knew her determination to break free. But he also knew Jeanne to be a moral, principled person. He couldn't believe that she was capable of crossing the clear line that ruled out killing another person. No matter what the reward.

What she had done, as she held the wooden matchstick in her hand, was blur the line so that it would be hard to see when she stepped over. "We're not killing her. We're just buying time to get away," she had told herself. Then, if she still couldn't bring herself to break the match, "She's a danger to us. We're just protecting ourselves." And finally, when her honesty wouldn't let her avoid the thought of killing, "She would have killed us." It was then that the frail wooden stick had snapped in her fingers. A quiet sound that she had tried not to hear.

Howard, Bill realized, had led her every step of the journey, even holding her hand when she stepped over the line. He had suggested, proposed, and rationalized, gradually revealing the decision that he had already made. It was the money that had infected Jeanne. But Howard had been the carrier of the infection.

A noise from the deck above stirred him out of his trance. There were footsteps walking overhead. And voices. Howard's, and then Cindy's. He jumped off the bench and rushed to the ladder.

They were gathered in the cockpit, Howard and Cindy face to face on the starboard side, Marilyn behind the wheel and Jeanne looking on from the port side. They all turned to him as he climbed up onto the deck. In the fading daylight, he could see the tension in their faces. Howard tightened his grip on Cindy's arm as Bill moved toward him.

"We have to do this, Bill," Howard said, warning his friend not to interfere.

Cindy's frightened eyes registered an instant of confusion. In Howard's tone, she recognized that Bill was an ally. But she made no move to pull away from her captor.

"What do we have to do, Howard?"

"I've told her. We have to leave her here. In the dinghy."

Bill glanced at the rubber boat that was waiting on the transom. The tie lines had been released and the small outboard motor had been removed.

He turned to Marilyn. "Is that what you have to do, Marilyn? Leave her out here to die in the sun?"

Marilyn didn't look back at him. "I'm afraid for my kids," was the only answer she could manage.

"Is that what we have to do, Jeanne? Put her on that raft and let her die slowly?"

"Someone will find her," Jeanne offered, but without any conviction.

Howard pulled Cindy back as Bill stepped down into the cockpit. "'We've been all through this," he said. "It's the only way."

Bill shook his head. "No. There's another way. Quicker. Cleaner."

Casually, he reached under the seat cushion and pulled out the gun that Howard had hidden. He slid his finger across the trigger. Howard spun away using Cindy as a shield. Marilyn jumped from behind the helm and fled to the port side next to Jeanne.

Bill smiled at their panicky retreat. He stepped past the wheel to the transom, raised the gun in one hand, and began firing. They all recoiled from the shattering sound as if the noise itself were deadly. Then, as the blasts died away, they heard the shrill hiss of air rushing out of the inflatable dinghy. They looked, saw the jagged tears that the bullets had ripped through the rubber, and watched the boat settle into a shapeless mass. Bill stood perfectly still, looking down with satisfaction on his work.

"Jesus," Jeanne breathed in terror, as if the boat had been her last hope of escape.

"You're crazy," Howard said, staring at Bill.

Bill was still looking over the stern when he said, "Now, let's talk about what you really have to do. Let's talk about which one of you is going to kill her?"

He turned to face them, Howard standing at his right, and Jeanne and Marilyn squeezed together at his left. Carefully, he turned the gun in his hand so that the handle and trigger grip were pointing to his companions. "Which one of you wants the honor?" Their eyes dropped from his face down to the pistol that he was offering.

"How about you, Marilyn?" He stepped toward her. "You're just trying to save your kids. It should be easy for you do it. Just take this, and point it at her carefully. If you hit her right in the face she probably won't even feel it. A lot quicker than leaving her out here to die."

He thrust the weapon at her. "Take it!"

Marilyn's hands fell to her sides and then moved slowly behind her back.

Bill grabbed her arm roughly, wrestled her hand in front of her and pressed the gun into her palm. "Take it, dammit. It's for your kids. You're killing her to save your kids."

"Stop it!" she screamed, tearing her hand free. She looked at the gun, and then at Bill. Her hands flew up to cover her face, and she knocked against Jeanne as she stumbled out of the cockpit and raced forward to the isolation of the bow. Bill and Jeanne were left inches apart, standing face to face.

"I guess you'll have to do it, then," he told his wife. He held out the gun. "It's rapid fire. Just squeeze the trigger. Hold it until you empty the

417

whole goddamn magazine into her."

"You bastard," she answered. But she didn't reach for the pistol.

"Not as easy as breaking a matchstick, is it?"

"You bastard." She backed away from him and dropped like a rag doll down onto the bench.

He turned to Howard, who was standing alone. "I guess the vote just changed, Howard. No one wants to kill her."

Howard broke eye contact with Bill. His glance found Cindy, but didn't linger there either. Then he noticed the wheel moving idly as *Cane Maiden* turned slowly into the wind. With his head bowed, he reached out and turned the boat back toward its course. "We weren't going to kill anyone," he mumbled as an excuse.

Bill crossed the cockpit and pushed the gun back under the bench cushion. "She's going to be below, in my cabin. And I'm going to be sitting right outside the door. If you change your mind, you'll know where to find us. But you'll have to kill both of us, Howard. Because I'm not going to let you get near her."

He steered Cindy out of the cockpit and up to the hatch. She climbed down, and Bill started down after her.

"I just wanted us to be safe," Howard called after him. "You have it all wrong. I wasn't trying to kill her."

Bill stopped, halfway into the hatch. "It wasn't an accident, was it, Howard?"

Howard blinked in confusion.

"Steve," Bill said in explanation. "Steve wasn't an accident, was it?"

418

51

Bill opened the door to his cabin and switched on the lamp. "You'll be safe in here," he told Cindy as he dragged the blanket off his bunk and took one of the pillows. "Just don't come out unless you know I'm here." Then he settled down on the deck with his back propped up against the door.

There were voices over his head. Howard and Jeanne were talking in the cockpit. He could hear Howard protesting that it was the only thing they could have done. Jeanne was agreeing that they were now all in terrible danger.

"What are we going to do?" he heard his wife beg.

And then Howard answered, "There's nothing we can do."

Marilyn's voice sounded from the hatch entrance. "We can do what we should have done in the first place. Get back to port, and tell the authorities exactly what happened."

Then he heard Marilyn's footsteps on the ladder.

She climbed down in front of him, looked at him for a second, and then turned away to the galley. Bill watched her as she filled the coffeepot, and lit the burner on the range.

"I guess I should thank you," Marilyn said out loud when she had set the pot over the flame.

Bill didn't answer.

She backed away from the stove so that she could look directly at him. "You kept me from doing something horrible." She shook her head slowly. "I never could have lived with it."

"None of us could," Bill said.

"Then what happened to us? What made us think . . ." She left the question hanging. So many mad ideas had gone through their minds. They had thought for certain that they were dead. And then, when they realized they were going to live, they had been thrust into a life different from anything any of them had ever experienced: the danger that hung over them, the money that suddenly seemed to be the answer to everything. And the isolation of the sea, that left them nowhere to turn for answers. Except to each other.

"We certainly saw ourselves at our worst," she continued. "Maybe that was it. We spent too much time alone with our fears and with our greed. It made us crazy."

She looked back at the coffeepot where the water was slowly darkening. "Thank God you kept your head."

"You couldn't have done it," Bill told her.

"No," she agreed. "But I was ready to watch it happen. And I would have watched her drift away from us, telling myself she'd be okay, and knowing that I'd never be able to stop thinking that I'd left her there to die. I was lying to myself. When you offered me the gun, I saw the truth."

She stretched up and took the cups down from

the cupboard. "See if she wants some coffee," she told Bill.

"Why don't you ask her?" he suggested.

Marilyn smiled. "Not much of a peace offering for someone you almost killed. A lousy cup of coffee. I think you better ask her."

She poured two cups, brought them aft and set them on the deck next to Bill. Then she took the pot and the other cups and started up the ladder. "I don't think I have any friends up there, either," she said.

As soon as Marilyn disappeared through the hatch, Bill tapped on the louvered door. It pushed open from the inside, and he saw Cindy sitting on the deck, her back leaning against the drawers under the bunk. He lifted one of the mugs and passed it in to her. Cindy stared at it for a moment, then reached out and took it with both hands.

"Thanks," she whispered.

"Marilyn made it. I'm just delivering it."

"For what you did up there," Cindy said, making her meaning clear. "For saving me, I guess." She looked childlike in the ridiculously oversized clothes she had taken from Steve's gear. Like one of his students dressed in an older brother's hand-me-downs.

"I didn't believe they could have hurt you. Intentionally, I mean. Not when they understood what they were doing."

"Everyone makes excuses when they screw you," she answered. "No one ever means to hurt you."

Bill felt the pressure of his own anger. "Well, why in hell didn't you fight them? What were you going to do? Just climb into the goddamn dinghy and make it easy for them?"

She shrugged. There wasn't much point in fighting back. What did it matter what happened to her?

"You're worth something, Cindy. You can't just let people . . . screw you. You have to believe in yourself." The words sounded ridiculous as soon as he said them. She wasn't one of his teenage charges. She was a woman who had seen a lot more of the world than he had. Seen everything, except perhaps herself.

She sipped the coffee, and with the cup still close to her face said, "You really bought yourself a lot of trouble, didn't you? It would have been a lot simpler to do it their way. My friends never would have known anything about you. You could have had a free ride with the money."

He nodded. "I suppose so. But it will all work out."

"Why'd you do it?"

He looked at her eyes. It was an honest question. She was truly puzzled, and really wondered why he had "bought himself a lot of trouble" when the answer was so simple. She was the problem. The smart play was to get rid of her.

"Because you're not for sale. Nobody is."

She sneered. "Not even for a couple of million bucks?"

He weighed the question. "I guess not."

Cindy shook her head, dismissing him as a madman. "People have bought me for a hell of a lot less."

"You've been with the wrong people."

422

"Ain't that the truth," she answered. She slid the empty coffee cup back through the door.

Bill reminded her, "You said you were hoping to get back home. Why don't you do that?"

"Christ!" She dismissed the notion. "I'm never going to get off Tortola."

"Why not?"

"The people I was working for are going to be looking for their money. I've seen what happens to people who mess with their money."

"Cindy, we're going to give you the damn money. Just take it back to your people and pay them off. Then get the hell out. Go back home."

Her eyes widened in disbelief. Then her mouth curled suspiciously. "You're going to give me the money?"

"Yes."

"All of it?"

"All of it. It's the only way for you. And it's the only way for us."

Her expression narrowed. "You're going to let me leave with a couple of million dollars? Just . . . let me go?"

He nodded, wondering why the idea was so difficult for her. There was no other way.

Cindy settled back against the bottom of the bunk. "He'll never let you do it. Your friend is never going to let me walk away with the money."

Bill eased the door closed, bunched the pillow and settled back against the bulkhead. Howard wasn't going to interfere with Cindy's leaving. They had had their confrontation and Howard had backed down. The conspiracy he had built so carefully among the women had unraveled. Howard had lost. But as he closed his eyes, he realized that Cindy was much more familiar with the dark sides of people than he was. Maybe she was right. Maybe Howard hadn't yet swallowed the idea of the money leaving with the young woman. Maybe he still thought there was a way of having it for himself.

"I meant it when I said 'thank you.' " It was Cindy's voice coming softly through the louvers from behind his head.

"It's okay," Bill answered.

"But just be careful, okay? Because you really have bought yourself a lot of trouble."

52

It was a light. It was faint, and seemed to flicker on the dark horizon dead ahead. But definitely a light. Howard stared hard at it. And then he noticed the vague halo that was barely visible behind it.

It had to be land. Probably the southern edge of St. Croix, exactly where he had expected to find it. He pulled the rolled chart up against the glow that came from the compass binnacle. If his figuring was correct then he was aiming somewhere into the island's south shore. And he was pretty close, probably something less than ten miles, if he was beginning to pick up the glow of ordinary roadway and household lights.

He glanced around him. Jeanne was stretched out on the port bench, rolled in a blanket and struggling for sleep. Marilyn had gone below through the greenhouse hatch, and was probably sleeping in the pilot berth. Bill was below, guarding the door to his cabin. Howard had the wheel. He was the only one on watch. *Cane Maiden* was his to command.

The breeze was freshening. He could feel the growing tension on the sheets and the heel of the boat, which had increased ever so slightly. The sound of the seas moving along the bilges had changed from the idle slapping when they were barely moving, to a steady hiss. The wheel in his hands was more nimble, responding more quickly.

The light ahead grew stronger. It was no longer a flicker, but a steady faint point. And in the halo behind it, he was beginning to make out individual points that sparkled. Within an hour he would be able to get his fix, and adjust his course. And then he would be sailing the final leg to Road Town.

But he couldn't go back. Not until everything was settled. Cindy was still on board, living proof that the money had been brought aboard. Bring her in to the mooring, and he would be identifying himself to her murderous associates. He would be surrendering his last chance at a fortune.

He also needed time to talk with Bill. They had agreed that Steve had been lost over the side in the storm. But Bill's last words to him had been that Steve was no accident. He was breaking the pact. That could mean an inquiry, with official suspicions as to how Steve had gone into the water, and with police questions as to how he had died.

It had all been so simple. Only a few hours ago, he had held all the answers. And now there were no answers. Only damning questions that led to deadly dangers.

It was all because of the girl. If they had only put her over the side. That was his mistake. He had waited for the others to realize what had to be done. He had wasted time trying to show them that there was no other way. He should have acted right at the beginning. The second she brought the camera case up on deck, the instant that it was in his hands, he should have grabbed her and flung her over with her boyfriend. And then never looked back. Just let the pair of them drown, exactly the way they were planning to leave him and his friends.

What could they have done? Bill would have tried to save them, but Bill didn't know how to turn the boat around. Marilyn would have wailed. But Marilyn always came around to his way of thinking. What could they have done? Turn him into the police? Why? For getting rid of the people who had kidnapped them and threatened to kill them? Demanded that he return the money? Where? They were no more anxious to find Cindy's friends than he was. Despise him? Maybe for a few moments. But it wouldn't have taken them long to realize that he was right. That there was no other way. That there was no point in doing anything other than taking the money and going home.

But he had hesitated. He had waited. And the waiting had brought confusion instead of clarity, with the confusion finally leading to chaos. Now there were no answers. Nothing at all that he could use to confront the people who were waiting on shore.

He couldn't bring the damn girl back. Let the others think what they may, there was no other way. They would have to see that. Sooner or later they would have to see it!

The lights were now clearly visible, a dozen shining points with others beginning to flicker into view. There was a new sound; the hum of the rigging beginning to strain against the air. *Cane*

Maiden was getting her wind. She was beginning to lean into the confrontation that he wasn't ready to face.

Slowly, carefully, he began to ease the wheel windward. The lights began to turn toward port. The edges of the sails started to flutter, and the sheets began to slacken. The bow eased across the wind, hesitated for an instant, and then swung across to the other side. Howard held the wheel over as he turned *Cane Maiden* away from the lights, and headed her back out to sea.

THURSDAY

53

It was still dark when Al Weston and Johnnie Igoe met Johnnie's two reinforcements at the airport. One of the new arrivals was assigned to cover the commercial and executive flights out of St. Croix. The other was sent to the island's north coast to watch the yacht harbor at Christiansted and monitor the traffic at the yacht club. It was a precaution against the possibility that *Cane Maiden* might make shore in the predawn hours.

But as they walked toward the helicopter landing pad, Al was certain that *Cane Maiden* was his. His tour of the southeastern coastline had convinced him that there was no way she could have made a nighttime landing in that area. And if the position report had been correct, she simply wouldn't have had the time to turn the island's east end and make it into one of the ports on the north shore. He expected to find her still at sea, probably just off East Point, possibly still making her way back to Road Town.

"You won't be able to see anything," Paul Canavan complained, showing his irritation at being roused out at night. "You won't have any visibility for another hour." He climbed reluctantly into the Jet Ranger's cockpit.

"I like sunrises," Al told him as he slipped into the copilot's seat.

As soon as they were above the tree line, they could see the first edge of light on the horizon, over the island's low-lying eastern end. But the sky was still a deep gray, and the sea still invisible. All that Al could make out was a thin line of white, where the waves were breaking over the reef.

"Run up towards Tortola," he ordered. "As soon as we can see something, I want to turn around and take a straight line to the south."

"Back to St. Croix?"

"Back past East Point and then straight out to sea. She's got to be someplace along the line."

Within a few minutes, they could see the lights on Tortola's mountaintops, and then the airport beacon on Beef Island. Al thought he was beginning to make out the shape of the landfall.

"She coulda turned east," Johnnie's voice speculated from the backseat.

Al shook his head. "She was heading north. Back towards port. If she wanted to go east, she would have made her turn yesterday."

"I can't figure why she'd be comin' back," Johnnie said. "Why not keep runnin'?"

"Why? Maybe they figure we don't know Cindy was ever aboard. No reason why they should think we're waiting for them. As far as they know, they're home free."

The sea appeared out of the darkness, a wrinkled fabric of hazy gray. Al pressed his face against the glass. The pilot rose up in his seat to get a better look through the glass window under the nose.

"Doesn't seem to be anything up ahead," he told Al. "Want me to turn around?"

"Not yet. I don't figure that she got this far, but I want to be damn sure."

The eastern horizon was now a bright silver, with traces of pink along the water's edge. The dark peaks of Tortola began to show their green color. Outlines of the small islands that bound the southern edge of the Drake Channel began to appear. Then the small cherry shape of the sun popped out of the sea.

Al looked ahead, and then down over the side. "Anything on your side?" he asked Johnnie.

"Nothin'," Igoe answered. "Everyone's still asleep."

Al took a last glance below. "Okay," he told Paul. "Let's head back. A straight line to the east end."

The helicopter banked into a gentle turn. When St. Croix swung back into view it was already bathed in sunlight.

"She has to be dead ahead of us," Al told Johnnie Igoe. "It won't be long now!"

54

Light leaked through the portholes and washed gently across Bill's face. He blinked, opened his eyes curiously and watched the rise and fall of the shadows as *Cane Maiden* rocked gently. Then he sat up with a start, suddenly remembering why he was propped painfully against the cabin door.

"Cindy?" He tapped lightly.

"Yeah," her answer came immediately. She hadn't been sleeping.

"You okay?"

"Yeah. I guess so."

"We should be near land. I'm going up top to talk to Howard."

"I don't see anything," she answered. "I've been watching through the porthole, but there isn't any land."

He stood wearily, went to the porthole above the chart table and looked out at a sun that was just breaking the horizon. His eyes suddenly widened. He was looking out the port side into the sunrise. The boat was pointing to the south. Howard had turned around and was heading away from land.

He bolted up the ladder, stuck his head through the hatch and found open sea in every direction.

434

"Where in hell are we?" he yelled.

"Back out a ways. I turned us around," Howard answered defiantly.

Bill bolted out of the hatch and started down into the cockpit. "Why? We settled all this yesterday. Dammit, Howard! We're supposed to be in sight of Tortola."

"Nothing is settled while she's still on board."

Jeanne stirred at the sound of the voices, and sat up on the bench where she had been sleeping.

"We're bringing her back," Bill said. "We all agreed."

Howard shook his head. "It's not the same for the rest of you. I'm the one who killed her boyfriend."

"We all agreed," Bill repeated carefully into Howard's face. "Nobody wanted to hurt her. Nobody wanted to pull the trigger."

"Everybody wanted to," Howard sneered. "But nobody had the guts. Well I don't have any choice. That little bitch could get me sent to prison. I'm going to pull the trigger."

Only the ship's wheel separated them. Howard was behind it, holding the boat's course against the angle of the sea. He had made up his mind and was ignoring Bill's protests, looking out over the bow at the empty sea that would hide his crime and solve all his problems. Bill stood on the other side, pressed up against the compass binnacle, his muscles taut with anger. He reached out and grabbed the wheel, his hand locking on it like a vise.

"Turn this thing around," he ordered.

"Not until I get rid of her."

"We're not getting rid of her."

Howard's eyes suddenly found Bill's. "*I'm* getting rid of her. No one has to be involved."

He looked from Bill to Jeanne. "Just go below and get out of the way. You know you want me to do this. I'm going to make you rich."

Jeanne stared back at him, her eyes slowly widening in understanding. "Oh my God," she whispered, recognizing what she was seeing. Howard had torn away the last veil of ambiguity. He had laid out clearly the course he was steering and the journey on which she had allowed herself to become a willing passenger. His plan had never been about their safety. It was about money and murder. She had found ways to avoid the truth, coloring the facts with thoughts of what Cindy and Steve might have done to her, and rationalizing the dangers of being connected to the bonds and the diamonds. She had even convinced herself that leaving the girl adrift in open water was somehow different from pulling the trigger. But Howard's eyes, as empty as those of a shark, left no place to hide. It was about money and murder and nothing more.

"Oh my God."

"It has to be done," Howard answered, almost kindly.

They stared silently at one another.

"Dammit," Bill interrupted. "Turn this thing around, or I'll do it."

Howard heard him. The empty eyes swung slowly back to Bill, but the only response was a thin smile. His hands dropped away from the wheel. He walked to one of the side benches and sat slowly, vaguely amused at the power he held by being the only experienced sailor on board.

Bill snapped his attention back to the wheel which was beginning to turn as the bow pointed up into the wind. He jumped around the binnacle and steadied the boat.

"Maybe you can get us back," Howard smirked. "Go ahead! Bring her around. Bring me back and turn me over to the police." He nodded toward Jeanne. "Bring her back to those killers who are looking for us."

Bill looked down at the compass and then up at the sails. He had watched Howard and Steve maneuver *Cane Maiden.* He understood the tight sequence of events that could bring her around and point her toward Tortola. But the information was still locked in his head. Now he needed it in his hands.

"If you don't get us all killed out here," Howard went on, "you sure as hell will get us all killed when we get back."

Bill checked the sheets that led aft from the giant genoa jib.

"Jeanne, help me," he asked.

She looked up at him uncertainly, without moving from the bench.

"Please, I need you."

She rose cautiously.

He pointed toward the winch on the starboard side. "Throw that line off when I tell you."

She understood what he wanted her to do, but still she hesitated, needing absolution from her crimes before she could turn away from them and put them behind her. "Bill . . . I'm sorry . . . I . . ."

He cut her off. "Pull it out of the lock so that it will run free," he said, nodding toward the line.

She suddenly jumped across the cockpit to where Howard was sitting, and grabbed the line that was drawn as hard as steel by the pull of the sail. "This one?" she asked.

"Right," he confirmed as he turned the port sheet around its winchhead.

"It has to be done," Howard shouted at Bill, suddenly afraid that they might not need him. "Just let me take care of it. For all of us."

Bill spun the wheel across the wind. He watched the genoa soften and then suddenly begin flapping, shaking the line that Jeanne was touching. "Now!" he yelled at Jeanne. "Throw it off."

She uncoiled the line from the winch and let it run free, pulled by the sail that was blowing across the bow. Bill pulled the other sheet tight and began cranking it in as the boat continued through her turn. The main boom swung across over his head, and he heard the mizzen sail snap into place behind him. He watched the compass rose spin, and then turned the wheel back to stop the bow at dead north.

"He'll get us all killed," Howard whispered to Jeanne.

She kept her attention on the line that she was now coiling. Bill steadied the boat, and then began trimming the sails, just as he had done for Howard and Steve. He could feel *Cane Maiden* begin to move under his feet.

"He's going to let her take all the money," How-

438

ard reminded Jeanne. "She's going to bring five million dollars back to her friends."

Jeanne nodded toward Bill. "He's right, Howard. He's been right all along. He kept us from doing something terrible."

Howard understood that he was now all alone. His carefully constructed alliance had crumbled. Bill would certainly be able to bring the boat back to land, even if he had to run her up on a beach. Cindy would leave with the money he needed to save his self-respect. And then, when the police began asking questions about Steve's death, even his freedom would be in jeopardy. He watched helplessly as Jeanne moved away from him, back across the cockpit to the bench near her husband.

But Howard was sure that she would need him, even if she didn't realize it. He had seen the look in her eyes when they had counted the money. Jeanne wanted it just as badly as he did. And he understood Marilyn's fears for the safety of their children. Nothing was more important to her. Cindy was a problem to the two women just as much as she was to him. Neither of them had been able to take the pistol when Bill had tried to force it into their hands. Both would recoil in horror when he dragged the young woman out of the cabin and brought her up into the cockpit. But once it was done . . . once she was gone and out of their lives . . . once they realized that they were free, and wealthy beyond their wildest dreams, then they would thank him. Then they would realize that he alone had had the courage to do what had to be done.

His hand slipped under the bench cushion, and

searched for the gun that Bill had hidden the night before. His fingers touched the cold metal stock.

Bill was the problem. He had to do something about Bill.

55

"Where the fuck is she?" Al Weston cursed. East Point was coming up on the right side of the helicopter, and there was still no trace of *Cane Maiden*.

There were no boats at all. The only one they had seen was a small water taxi, speeding north from St. Croix. The sailors hadn't taken to sea yet.

"Maybe she's already in," Paul tried, pointing to the row of masts that were visible just off the St. Croix Yacht Club.

Al shook his head. To be in port, *Cane Maiden* would have had to find the narrow break in the reef while it was still dark. That wasn't likely. And even if she had, he had the yacht club covered. Johnnie Igoe's man would have phoned the airport, and the helicopter would have been alerted over the radio.

"Just keep going," Al told the pilot. He leaned forward so that he could get a better view through the glass nose.

"How far do you want to go?"

"As far as it takes," Al snapped.

He was beginning to worry. Yesterday evening, *Cane Maiden* was only forty miles out at sea, heading back into Tortola. Even in the light air, she should have been able to make three or four knots. If she held course, she had to have reached East Point by now. He should already have found her.

Johnnie pulled back from the side window. "She must have turned, Al. We're probably looking in the wrong place."

Al's temper flashed. "So, where do you want to look? If you've got a better idea, Johnnie, I sure in hell want to hear about it."

Igoe shrugged. "I don't know. We've got St. Croix covered. Maybe we ought'a be lookin' further east. Over towards St. Martin. Or maybe we ought to get back to Tortola. That's where she's supposed to be heading."

"We just checked towards Tortola, as far as she could have gotten," Al answered.

"Well then let's check over to the east," Johnnie repeated.

Al's expression was set like stone. But he knew there was a chance that Johnnie was right. It was becoming obvious that the yacht hadn't kept to the course she had been sailing the night before. Maybe she was trying for St. Martin. Or maybe she had turned to the West and was making for Puerto Rico. The certainty he had felt when he boarded the helicopter before sunlight was quickly disappearing.

There was still another possibility. The Coast Guard had reported that *Cane Maiden* had suffered storm damage. Maybe something had given way. Maybe she had lost a part of her rigging, and was lying dead in the water. Or moving slowly under her auxiliary engine.

The fact was that she could have moved in any

442

direction after she was sighted. Or not moved at all. His careful calculations weren't really calculations, but just guesses. All he could do was make another guess.

"Let's stay on this course for another forty miles. That should bring us right to where she was sighted. Then we'll turn east and run towards St. Martin."

Paul Canavan nodded. Johnnie Igoe smiled and turned back to his vigil at the side window.

56

Bill was steering north, able to hold the boat close to its heading. Jeanne was slumped on the bench to his left, lost in her own thoughts. Howard was at his right, staring at him, watching his every move.

"How far out did you take us?" Bill asked Howard, almost as a peace offering. Howard turned away from him.

"Well, then take over the wheel while I go below and get the charts."

Howard shook his head. "You're going to get us all killed," he mumbled, even though he knew that Bill was beyond any argument.

"Jeanne, give me a hand here. Please."

She looked up at the wheel and the compass that Bill was focused on. They were strange to her, even frightening when she thought of using them to control the boat.

"I can't. I don't know anything about it."

"Just for a minute. All you have to do is hold it steady."

She got up slowly, slipped behind the wheel and stood next to him. She watched for several seconds as he made small turns to keep the heading marker over the ornate "N" on the compass rose. Then

444

she raised her hands carefully and tried to imitate Bill's actions. Almost immediately, the heading began to drift toward the east.

"I can't," she said to her husband, letting go of the wheel.

"You can. Just keep turning us back toward the heading." He eased the wheel left.

She put her hands back on the wheel. Bill watched as the boat swung past its mark, and saw Jeanne turn the wheel to stop the swing.

"That's it. Just keep steering it back to North."

He stepped away from her, leaving her alone at the helm, and saw that she could handle it. "You're doing great. I'll be back up in a minute." He stepped out of the cockpit and up onto the pilothouse. Then he swung his feet into the hatch and started down the ladder.

Howard sprang from his seat and started up after him. Jeanne looked up at the sudden motion and caught a glimpse of the pistol that was clutched in his hand.

"Bill!" she screamed. "He has the gun!"

Bill was totally vulnerable, his arms and shoulders already below deck, his head still above the hatch opening. He turned just in time to see the shiny metal arching down toward him. He tried to duck away, but there was no room for escape. The gun glanced off the crown of his head, and he dropped like a dead weight down through the opening.

"Bill!" Jeanne screamed again. She started around the helm.

"Stay there!" Howard ordered, stopping her in her tracks. "He'll be all right."

She hesitated in confusion, terrified by Howard's vicious attack. Bill was hurt, but the man standing between her and her husband was dangerous. He was completely out of control.

"Hold the course," Howard ordered. "Just the way Bill showed you." He climbed down the hatch.

Bill was in a heap at the foot of the ladder, a small ooze of blood matting his hair. Marilyn, who had jumped down from the pilot bunk when she heard Jeanne's scream, was rushing to his aid. She saw the gun that her husband was holding.

"What's happening? What are you doing?" she demanded.

"What we should have done yesterday," he answered calmly. He stepped over Bill's crumpled shape, pushed past his wife and turned aft toward the cabins. With one strong kick he broke the frail door to Bill's cabin off its hinges. As it toppled to the deck, Cindy retreated.

Howard stepped through the doorway, grabbed the collar of her shirt, and started to drag her out.

"Let go of me, you bastard!" Cindy lashed out and raked her nails across Howard's cheek. But he didn't show any pain. Instead, he punched the barrel of the pistol into her belly. He shifted his grip to her hair and smashed her head against the bulkhead. Then he fired her through the door, into the galley.

Marilyn had been bent over Bill when the cabin door smashed. Now, she didn't know which way to turn. Bill was hurt — alive, but unconscious. He needed help. And now there was Cindy, dazed and frightened, scarcely able to keep her footing as she hurtled into the galley. "Howard!" Marilyn screamed. "Stop!"

But he didn't seem to hear her. He locked his grip on the young woman's arm and twisted it up behind her back. Then he rushed her toward the ladder, lifting her painfully over Bill. Cindy twisted and tried to kick at him. But she had to climb in response to the searing pain in her arm as Howard pushed up on it from behind.

"No," Marilyn yelled. "We have to help Bill." She grabbed the back of Howard's shirt and tried to drag him back down. "Let her go! We have to help Bill."

Howard turned halfway and smashed at her hand, breaking her grasp. "I'm doing what I have to do," he shouted at Marilyn. "Don't try to stop me!" But as soon as he turned back to the ladder, she was holding him again, this time by the back of his belt.

"Don't be crazy, Howard! Let her go!"

He turned on his wife again, and swung wildly at her grip. The moment he was distracted, Cindy pulled her hand free and fired an elbow into Howard's gut. She scampered up the ladder toward the light that filled the open hatch. Howard winced, but he was able to hold his balance and started up the ladder after her. This time Marilyn locked her arms around his leg.

He kicked at her, but she wouldn't let go. Above his head Cindy was escaping through the opening. He looked up and then back down. Then he slapped the pistol across his wife's face. Marilyn lost the grip on his leg and fell back in pain. Howard turned immediately and raced up the steps.

Cindy jumped out through the opening, and slammed the hatch cover closed. Howard saw it coming down and put up his hand to stop its fall. For an instant the cover wavered, with Cindy pushing down, trying to hold it steady so she could set the lock, and Howard pushing up from below. But balanced on the ladder steps, Howard couldn't generate enough force to overcome Cindy's weight. He felt the hatch squeeze shut above his head, and heard the locking dog snap into place.

"Dammit!" he cursed. He dashed back down the ladder, stepping over Bill's motionless body and brushing by Marilyn, whose hands were up to her battered face. Wordlessly, he rushed into the saloon, and climbed up into the skylight.

Through the broken glass, he could see Cindy scampering forward on the leeward deck, racing to lock the skylight hatch. He raised the pistol awkwardly, bending his wrist to fit the angle of the opening. Then he pulled the trigger.

The blast inside the boat was deafening, followed immediately by Marilyn's piercing scream. The shots aimed wildly, punching a neat row of holes through the jib, far away from where Cindy had ducked down as soon as she saw the gun. But they had their effect. Cindy retreated back toward the cockpit, and Howard was able to push the hatch open. He pulled himself up onto *Cane Maiden*'s foredeck.

Jeanne had abandoned the wheel, throwing herself down on the deck as soon as she heard the gunfire. Cindy was disappearing over the cockpit edge. Howard stopped, and grabbed the lifeline to steady himself. There was no hurry. Cindy was

448

trapped in the cockpit, exactly where he wanted her. Bill and Marilyn were locked below. Jeanne, he felt certain, wouldn't stand in his way.

He took a deep breath. Carefully, he snapped the magazine from the pistol, pushed down on the ammunition to be certain that he still had several rounds left. Then he pushed it back into the bottom of the housing.

"Okay, let's get this over with," Howard whispered to himself. He started aft, with one hand on the lifeline, ignoring the flap of the genoa jib that was turning slowly into the wind. "Let's get this over with."

57

"What's that?"

Al Weston was pointing across the nose toward the pilot's side, indicating a shape that was suddenly visible through the morning haze. He couldn't make out any details, only a blemish that interrupted the emptiness of the sea.

"Must be a boat," the pilot answered. "There's no land out here."

Johnnie strained forward between Al and the pilot. "Yeah, I see it. But I can't tell what it is."

Al raised his binoculars and tried to steady them against the vibration of the helicopter. The blurry image dashed back and forth. He couldn't hold it still. But he could make out a white shape that seemed to climb out of the water.

"It's a sailboat," he decided.

Without waiting for instructions, Paul pushed the stick over, moving the target to dead ahead. "Looks like we're getting lucky," he told Weston.

They flew in silence for another minute, the soft shape ahead beginning to harden. Weston kept the glasses to his face, trying to keep them still while he struggled with the focusing wheel. He saw the shape of a sail appear and then, just as quickly, soften to a blur.

"It's a sailboat. No doubt about it."

"*Cane Maiden*?" Igoe asked from the back seat.

"Can't tell . . . yet," Al admitted. "I only saw one sail. But what the hell is she doing out so far? She must have spent the whole night dead in the water."

The helicopter began descending in a gradual glide path, dropping directly toward the boat. Al looked over the top of the binoculars. "I think I see another sail!" There was an edge in his voice. He felt certain that he was looking down on *Cane Maiden* even though he couldn't yet see anything of her distinctive lines. He tried to imagine what was happening aboard.

Were Cindy and Steve still with the boat? Was the money still on board? He could fill in a hundred scenarios to account for the fact that she was still afloat, moving under her own power back toward her home port. The most likely was that his courier and her boyfriend had gone ashore somewhere, taking most of the money with them. They had probably paid the two vacationing couples handsomely to make up some story that accounted for Steve's disappearance. The storm that had battered them made a damn near perfect cover.

But it didn't matter. Once he had them in his sights, it would take only a few seconds to get the truth out of them. And once he knew where Cindy and Steve had gone ashore, he could get back onto their trail.

Through the glasses, he got a clear glimpse of the second sail. It was a yawl, just like *Cane Maiden*, and not a very common rigging among the charter boats. And he could make out her direction. She was heading straight toward him, running just slightly to the east of the line he had laid out that would take her straight into Road Town.

"That has to be her," he announced.

There was a metallic click from the backseat as Johnnie Igoe pulled the bolt of his automatic rifle.

58

Jeanne stood cautiously, rising slowly above the edge of the cockpit, face to face with Howard.

"Where's Bill? Where is he?"

"He'll be okay," Howard snapped, his eyes panning as he searched for Cindy. "Get back to the wheel. Get us back on course."

"I want to see Bill!" Jeanne challenged defiantly.

Howard's eyes locked onto her. She was frightened by their wildness. Slowly she backed away toward the wheel.

"We should talk, Howard," Jeanne tried. "We should get everybody up here and decide what we're going to do."

He stepped to the edge of the cockpit, and saw Cindy cowering on the deck against the starboard bench. "I'm going to do what we have to do. There's nothing more to talk about." He kept the gun trained on the young woman as he climbed down.

"Howard!" It was Marilyn's voice screaming from the foredeck. He turned his glance carefully and saw her climbing up through the greenhouse hatch.

"Get below!" he ordered, snapping his attention back to Cindy.

But her voice persisted. "No! I'm not going to let you do this." He stole another glance forward. Marilyn was coming toward him, one hand on the lifeline, the other still pressed to her wounded cheek. "Put the gun down, Howard. Damn you! Unless you're ready to kill me, too, put the gun down."

"Get back," he ordered his wife. But he knew that she would keep coming toward him. He wheeled quickly toward Cindy who was easing slowly up to her feet. He had to do it now. Ignoring Marilyn, he aimed the automatic pistol directly into Cindy's face. With steady pressure, he began squeezing the trigger.

Jeanne's hands snapped like a lock around Howard's arm and pulled the gun off its aim. The quick burst of shots fired harmlessly over the fantail. Howard pulled his hand free and pushed Jeanne aside. But as he turned back toward his victim, she was already on him. Cindy had sprung like a runner out of her crouched position, aiming all her momentum into Howard's chest. He fell back onto the bench with Cindy on top of him, his vision lost in the wild thrashing of her hands. He kicked at her with his knee, got the flat of his hand across her face and pushed her back. He started to turn the muzzle of the gun into her body, but Jeanne had a new grip on his wrist and was leaning all her weight against his arm. Howard kicked free of Cindy and then tried to wrestle out of Jeanne's grasp. "I'll kill you, you bitch," he snarled into her face. "I'll kill you, too."

And then there was another arm around his neck. Marilyn had jumped down from the deck, and wrapped his head in a stranglehold. His hand with the gun was pinned under Jeanne, and Marilyn was holding him back. Cindy had recovered and was hurtling back toward him.

He caught Cindy with his free arm, deflecting her charge and pushing her on top of Jeanne. Then, as she started to turn back to him, he fired a short, tight punch into her cheek. Cindy slid to her knees at his feet. He reached over his head and grabbed Marilyn's hair, pulling her off balance until she rolled over his shoulder. Then he aimed a punch squarely across Jeanne's jaw, and dragged the gun hand free.

Cindy was starting to get up, swinging wildly at her assassin. He whipped the pistol at her, smashing it across her arm and shoulder. When she fell back, Howard snatched her other arm, and twisted it up behind her. She hung like a rag doll as he forced her toward the lifeline and pushed her head out over the side. Cindy was staring down at the white water that was rushing past. She could feel the cold metal of the gun barrel pressing into the back of her neck.

"Don't do it, Howard!"

It was Bill's voice. Howard looked up and saw Bill standing on top of the pilothouse, next to the open greenhouse. Then he saw the aluminum camera case that Bill had carried up with him.

"It's all over, Howard. There's no reason to kill her. The money's gone!"

Howard blinked in confusion. The money was right there. Bill had it in his hand. And then he understood. He watched Bill swing the aluminum case around behind his back. He saw it hesitate for an instant before it began to swing forward. He knew that Bill was about to throw the fortune over the side.

"Noooo!" he screamed into the wind.

The case gathered momentum.

Howard snapped the pistol away from Cindy, and fired at Bill.

The case slipped out of Bill's grasp, but continued its flight, turning end over end as it hurtled out over the water. Bill clutched at his shoulder, staggered back, and toppled down to the deck from the pilothouse roof. The lifeline caught him across the back of his legs, and flipped him over the side.

Jeanne screamed. She lunged out of the cockpit and slid on her belly across the deck, reaching the lifeline just as Bill's thrashing form slid along the side of the boat. She reached under the lifeline and caught his hand.

For a split second, she thought she had saved him. But the momentum of the big boat was much too strong for her. Bill's weight snapped her aft, while *Cane Maiden* kept charging ahead. She was jerked out under the rail as if she had caught onto a moving truck. Her head and then her shoulders were pulled out over the side.

The only way to keep from being dragged overboard was to let go of her husband. But she dug her nails fiercely into his wrist so that he couldn't get away. She held on with all her strength as she felt herself being dragged across the deck and out into the sea.

Howard heard Jeanne's scream, and then Marilyn's cry as Jeanne disappeared. Then he saw the wheel, spinning idly as the yacht turned its own course into the wind. He abandoned Cindy for a moment as he rushed toward the helm. But he was stopped by a new sound, the metallic whine of a distant turbine. He looked up off the port bow and saw the helicopter, still a good way off, but aimed directly toward him.

59

"It's the money!" Al Weston yelled. "They threw the case over the side!"

They were close enough so that he could see *Cane Maiden* clearly. He had watched the commotion in the cockpit without being able to decide exactly what was going on. "They seem to be fighting," he had mumbled to the others when a glimpse through the glasses had shown Howard struggling with the three women. Then he had watched Howard drag one of the girls across the cockpit. "Looks like a fucking barroom brawl!"

Then a figure had come out on the foredeck; a man with something in his hand. Al had steadied and focused the glasses. He had watched Bill pause for a moment and then had recognized the camera case as he swung it back. In horror, he had seen Bill throw the case and watched it topple through the air.

He wheeled toward the pilot. "It's in the water. The money is in the water. Get down there! Get down there now!"

Al tried to keep the aluminum case in sight. He watched one of the people splash into the water, and then saw one of the women glide over the side. "They're going in after it," he screamed over the noise of the engine. "Get down there!"

"It's wide open," Canavan yelled back. "We're going as fast as we can."

Cane Maiden was sailing directly under the helicopter's glass nose. Strung out in her wake, Weston could see the aluminum case, and the two figures thrashing about. He jabbed his finger at the case. "Get the money! Set this damn thing down right on top of the money!"

It wouldn't be that easy. Paul couldn't crash the chopper directly into the sea. He had to level it, stop it and then set it down carefully — a routine maneuver, but one that would take time. Precious seconds that would seem an eternity to Al Weston.

They raced by *Cane Maiden* at masthead height. Al could see the faces on deck. He recognized the man he had seen at the airport behind the boat's wheel, but he paid him little attention. He saw that the two people in the water, a man and a woman, seemed to be clinging to one another. But he was focused on the aluminum case that was bobbing up and down with the wave peaks, its shiny side barely breaking the surface of the water.

"It's gonna sink!" he screamed. He released the chest buckle of his safety belt, and tried to shoulder the door open against the blast of the outside air.

The helicopter eased over the two heads in the water, setting the surface whirling around them. Then it stopped in midair, hanging less than ten feet above the case. Gently, it began to settle on top of its target. Al pushed the door open, stepped down onto the folded rubber boat, and then reached his foot toward the inflated pontoon.

459

60

Howard clung to the wheel, frightened and confused. He knew he should take *Cane Maiden* into the wind to kill its speed, and then fall off into a tight turn that would bring him back to the two shipmates who had gone overboard.

But he was focused on the helicopter. As he watched it approach, he wasn't sure whether it was the police coming to his rescue, or Cindy's killers coming to destroy him. As it whizzed over the mast, he realized that it didn't matter. It was his gunfire that had spilled his friend over the side. If the helicopter rescued Bill it would be rescuing his accuser. He held his course and tried to make his escape.

And then there was Cindy. She was right next to him, pulling herself up on the lifeline that he had been trying to force her through. Seconds before he had held the executioner's pistol to the back of her head. But she was still alive, ready to confront him. There could be no escape as long as she remained on board. He started to step toward her, intent on finishing the job. But now there were new witnesses. The people in the helicopter were only a few feet away. They would see him fire, and see him push the evidence over the side.

And there was his wife, her face still bloody from

his pistol-whipping. He had counted on the fact that she could never turn against him. But he had turned viciously against her and made her an enemy. Now she was as dangerous to his desperate hopes as all the others.

He was surrounded by danger. There was no safe course he could follow. He threw the wheel over and headed back to his only friend, who was thrashing in the water.

Jeanne had clung to Bill, trying to keep him from sinking. But now he was holding her to keep her from going under. He had nearly lost consciousness in the seconds after Howard's wild shot had sliced through the flesh of his shoulder. He had felt Jeanne clutch his hand, and realized that she was in the water with him. And then he knew that she was tiring, quickly exhausted by her struggle to save him. He had wrapped his wounded arm around her, kicking furiously back toward the retreating boat, without thinking that the man who had just tried to kill him was waiting on board. Then came the shattering roar of engine. He had seen the helicopter moving over him, and felt the blast from its rotor. He had reached up toward it, expecting a rescuing hand to reach down to him. But the copter had drifted past.

Now it was settling down on the water only twenty yards behind him, much closer than the yawl that was still under sail. "We're all right," he kept repeating to Jeanne. "We're okay." He rolled her on her back and kicked toward the helicopter. But then he saw the man climbing out of the cabin onto the pontoon. He saw the pistol that the man was carrying. In that instant, he understood who he was.

61

The money was only a few feet away. Weston was staring straight down at the case that was floating just below the surface, its corners breaking the water as it bobbed. But he couldn't reach it. He was standing on the pontoon, holding a death grip on the bottom edge of the open cabin door. He couldn't let go to climb down lower because the downdraft threatened to blow him off his footing.

He pushed the pistol back into the helicopter and let it clatter onto the floor. "Land this fucker! Put it down!" he screamed, trying to be heard over the howl of the turbine. Then he reached with his free hand for the thin metal strut that supported the pontoon, and began to work his way carefully down to a kneeling position. The pontoon was settling lower, the wave tips lapping at its rubber bottom. He was only inches away from the camera case. But it was sinking under him. He could still see it, but it had settled further below the surface. Its edges were no longer bobbing up.

The pontoon touched down. Weston dropped to his belly. One arm was wrapped around the strut, the other reaching down into the sea. His fingers grazed across the metal surface. His hand clutched at the handle. For an instant, he thought he had it. But then it slipped from his grasp. He twisted until half his body was hanging into the water. But he couldn't feel it. Then he realized he could no longer see it. The case had vented the air it contained and was sinking rapidly.

The money was gone.

Al screamed in rage, and climbed back up the strut. Johnnie Igoe reached out of the cockpit and caught the back of his jacket to keep him from falling.

"It's gone! I had it in my fingers! I couldn't hold it," Al kept yelling as Johnnie wrestled him back into the helicopter. "The motherfuckers threw it overboard."

Johnnie nodded that he understood. He dragged Al back into the copilot's seat.

"The bastards!" Al wailed. "The lousy bastards!" He saw Bill and Jeanne, struggling in the water, halfway between the helicopter and the yacht. "You're dead, you fuckers!" he snarled as he snatched up his pistol from the cabin floor.

62

Bill was leading Jeanne back toward *Cane Maiden*, holding her in his wounded arm and swimming with the other. He had turned away from the helicopter when he saw Al Weston climb onto the pontoon, carrying a pistol. At first, it had seemed hopeless, with *Cane Maiden* sailing away, leaving him and Jeanne to their fate in the sea. But then Howard had turned into the wind, brought the boat about and begun moving back toward them.

"We can make it," he kept encouraging Jeanne. "We'll be okay." Jeanne was kicking, trying to swim along with him.

He had seen Al climb out onto the pontoon, and understood that Al's interest was in the money and not in them. For an instant he had hoped that Al would rescue the camera case and fly away. Now he heard the change in the engine's pitch, and felt the beating of the rotor as the copter lifted off the surface. He looked back just as Al leaned out above the open door, and saw the pistol panning toward him.

"Go under!" he shouted at his wife. He took a deep breath, put his hands on Jeanne's head and drove her under the surface. Then he dove down after her. When he heard the gunshots, they were faint rumbles, nearly lost in the sound of the engine.

Al was firing even before he aimed, screaming threats in his wild rage. He steadied the gun at the point where the two people had vanished beneath the surface and squeezed the trigger again and again. He kept firing as the helicopter lifted, watching the water explode over the heads of his victims, and trying to keep his aim as the chopper rotated. He was still screaming when the gun went silent.

"Gimme that thing," he ordered, and Johnnie passed the automatic rifle into the front seat.

As it rose slowly, the helicopter drifted with the wind, sliding up along the starboard side of *Cane Maiden* which was turning back toward Bill and Jeanne. The boat's genoa was blowing freely, forming a curtain across the cockpit. Al pulled the bolt on his rifle just as the sail was pulled taut. He saw Cindy, still clinging to the starboard lifeline.

She was alive! She was nobody's victim, which told him that she was part of the scheme to take the bonds and the diamonds. Standing there, aboard the boat he had been tracking, she was proof of Al's worst fears. He had been outsmarted by a dumb cocktail waitress who had taken his money, and then thrown it away when she knew he had found her. He swung the muzzle of the rifle away from the targets in the water toward the open cockpit. Then he set the stock against his shoulder.

Cindy saw Al and saw the gun. She grabbed Marilyn and threw her down on the deck and then sprawled on top of her. Howard dove from behind the wheel and slid up against the port side bench. They were all flat on their faces when the gunfire exploded across the cockpit.

The rounds hit like the blows of an ax. Great chunks of wood tore free from the pilothouse roof. The wooden strakes that formed the bench just above Howard's head shattered into splinters. The compass binnacle rang out musically as it was punctured with a row of holes, and then the glass that surrounded the compass shattered. Finally, an arc of the steering wheel was sawed off, and several of the elaborate spoke handles were blown over the side. Howard and the two women cowered from the mayhem all around them, certain that they would feel the bullets blasting through their bodies. But just as suddenly as it had begun, the shooting stopped. The sudden calm beneath the steady drone of the helicopter was nearly as terrifying as the gunfire had been.

Al Weston ripped the empty magazine out of the rifle, dropped it at his feet and held his open hand toward Johnnie Igoe. Johnnie slapped a new magazine into his palm, and Al snapped it into place.

"I'll get the bastards out into the open," he promised, as he again pressed the wire stock against his shoulder and sighted down the short barrel. This time he wasn't going to waste ammunition cutting up the woodwork over their heads. He was going to sink the boat under them.

Howard had gotten a grip on the pistol that he had stuffed into his belt and was just beginning to lift his face from the deck when the chatter

466

of gunfire sounded again. He pressed down flat, sure that this time the bullets would find him. But then he heard the rounds hit like hammer blows into *Cane Maiden*'s side.

They were firing at the waterline, punching neat holes into *Cane Maiden*'s flank. The holes linked together under the steady stream of steel-jacketed rounds, and then chunks of the wooden strakes shattered and fell away. Seawater began spilling into the hull.

There was another pause, with the engine noise and the beating of the rotors seeming to soothe the air that had been screaming with gunfire. Howard understood that his attacker was reloading, and thought about springing up and firing back at the helicopter. But he was suddenly aware of the smell of diesel oil. And then he saw the trace of black smoke that was curling over the cockpit.

Weston smiled when he saw the smoke. "We'll burn 'em out," he said to Johnnie, as he snapped another magazine into place. He ordered the pilot, "Keep me right here. Right on this side."

Cane Maiden had continued turning toward him under the momentum that Howard had created when he brought the yacht about. She had lost speed, nearly jibing as her stern reached the wind, making her a still target for the hovering helicopter. But then the wind had driven against her mizzen sail, pushing the stern downwind and checking her turn. *Cane Maiden* was beginning to move again, and Al wanted the pilot to keep him lined up with the gaping hole he had blasted in the boat's side. He aimed and fired.

Chunks of wood flew off the yacht's hull, carving

an even wider hole into the waterline. Bullets sparked off the engine and the fuel tank, and spilled diesel oil fed the smokey fire. While he was still emptying the magazine, Al could see a red glow dancing inside the shattered hull. *Cane Maiden* was afire, and taking on water.

"Let's go up over her," Al ordered. No matter where they were hiding, he thought, the fire would drive them up onto the deck. He wanted to be right above them, with the rifle pointed down into their faces.

"We have to be careful of the rigging," Paul Canavan said, shaking his head.

"Get on top of her," Al snapped.

The order rang like a threat. The pilot lifted higher, and turned the helicopter toward the boat.

Al leaned out, squinting against the cloud of smoke that was thickening around him, trying to see through the sails into the forward end of the cockpit. He caught a glimpse of the bodies pressed flat against the cockpit deck, and raised the rifle against his cheek.

63

Bill had held Jeanne down beneath the surface even when he felt her fighting to get back up to the air. The pale blue water, with its shimmering columns of light, was their only shield against the killer who was waiting above, and the soft stillness was their haven from the violent gunshots that would probably be the last sound that either of them heard. He had stayed below until his lungs were screaming in pain, and then had kicked to the surface dragging Jeanne along with him.

They had come up into hell, blinded by the white sunlight and deafened by the roar of the helicopter. Bill had drawn a deep breath, intending to take Jeanne back down to safety. But she was choking on the water she had swallowed, struggling to catch her breath. He had to hold her up.

He was surprised to see *Cane Maiden* turned and heading back toward him. But he was horrified as he saw the helicopter drifting up against her side. Then there was the explosion of gunfire, and he watched helplessly while the bullets tore the boat's decks to pieces.

Cane Maiden kept turning until her bow had crossed between him and the helicopter. He flinched from a second burst of shooting, unable to see the destruction on the boat's other side. Then, the boat had caught the air and moved toward him, almost as if it were trying to escape from its tormenter. But the helicopter had moved along with her and there had been new bursts of rifle fire. Then he had seen the smoke and realized that *Cane Maiden* was burning.

"We've got to help them," Bill shouted at Jeanne. She nodded, still trying to catch her breath. He hooked his arm under hers, startled by the stab of pain from the wound he had completely forgotten. Then he kicked toward the hull that was slowly turning back toward him.

The pitch of the whining engine changed, and in a second the helicopter appeared over the blanket of the mainsail. Bill watched it climb up over the stern, and then slide forward to position itself directly over the cabin. He could see the pilot through the side window, and through the glass panel under the nose he could see one side of the man who was leaning out the opposite window. Even though he couldn't see the rifle, he knew that the man was taking aim at the victims he had trapped on the burning boat. He knew that there was nothing he could do to save his friends.

Howard had rolled onto his back when he heard the helicopter start its maneuver. He was no longer thinking of Cindy or the danger she posed. As the mantis shape popped up above the mizzen sail and began easing forward over his head, Howard was fighting for his life. He raised the pistol in both hands, aimed it up at the craft's belly, and pulled the trigger at point-blank range.

Holes tore into the helicopter's thin skin, and the glass nose panel shattered. Instantly, the chopper went into a sharp bank and rolled away off the port quarter.

"Go back, goddammit!" Al Weston screamed as he turned on the pilot. "I'm gonna finish those fuckers off!"

The pilot shook his head furiously. "No way!" he yelled back.

"All he's got is a lousy pistol," Al said, grabbing the pilot's arm. "Get me back there."

"One hit could bring us down," the pilot answered, tearing his arm out of Al's grip. "You need a couple of hundred hits to sink that thing. But one bullet in the right place and we go down in flames. No way I'm going back."

With his free hand, Al reached for the pilot's throat. Johnnie Igoe caught his wrist before Al could get a chokehold.

"He's right, Al. We already got holes through the floor. Let's get out of here."

"I'm not leaving them alive!"

"They're as good as dead. The fucking boat is sinking."

"Turn around," Al hissed at the pilot. "I'm not leaving them alive."

"It's too risky," Paul pleaded. But he realized that Al was beyond reason. "Okay. But we can't hover. A couple of quick passes, and then we get out of here."

Al turned and looked back over his shoulder. He could see the boat foundering at the base of a thickening column of smoke. There were people struggling at the edge of the cockpit. "A couple

471

of quick passes," he agreed. "That's all I'm gonna need." He took a fresh magazine from Johnnie and loaded it into the rifle.

64

Howard had kept firing until his pistol emptied. Then, in the sudden quiet, he realized that the helicopter engine was no longer a painful whine. The sound was dying. He scampered to his knees, and then pulled himself up onto the shredded boards of the port side bench. He saw his attacker, low to the water, and heading away.

Bill's voice called from over the side and, for a split second, Howard hesitated. Bill was a danger to him, he remembered. At a confused moment that now seemed only a dream, he and Bill had been mortal enemies. He had fired at Bill. He had tried to kill him. No! Not kill him. Just stop him. Stop him from what? Why had he fired?

Cindy rushed past him, and freed the swimming ladder so she could swing it over the side. He reached to help her, but his hand stopped in mid-air. Why was he helping her? Wasn't she the one who had brought the gunmen? Of course! She was the one who was going to take his money.

And then Marilyn's voice screamed behind him. He turned, and saw the tips of orange flames dancing above the lifeline. There was a fire! The boat was sinking. He had to fight the fire. He was frozen in confusion, trying to reassemble the reasons for

473

what had happened, and trying to decide what he should do.

The abrupt change of the helicopter's engine noise hit him like a slap in the face. His head snapped around and he saw that it was turning back toward them. The clear threat cut through his stupor. He remembered vividly that his gunfire had driven the attacker off. He remembered that his gun was now empty. Howard bolted out of the cockpit and raced forward along the starboard side. He pulled open the hatch to the bow compartment where Steve had bunked, dropped down the ladder and scooped up the ammunition clips.

Bill pushed Jeanne up the swimming ladder to the point where Cindy and Marilyn could lift her aboard. Then he followed her over the deck and rolled into the cockpit.

"Get down!" he yelled, when he saw the helicopter heading back toward them. He grabbed the women who had just rescued him and dragged them down to the cockpit deck. The helicopter roared and raced across the stern. Gunshots exploded into the bulkhead, inches above their flattened bodies. The mizzen sail rigging tore to shreds, the stays went slack and the mast toppled forward, bouncing off the mainsail and crashing down across the pilothouse. They cowered under the crushed Bimini awning until they heard the engine noise growing faint.

Bill sprung up and pushed his way through the tangle of canvas and rigging. Through the billowing smoke he could see the helicopter banking into a turn far off the starboard side. She was coming back for another pass. Then he saw Howard climb

474

up onto the foredeck, drop to one knee and steady the automatic pistol over the lifeline. He glanced out at the helicopter and saw the rifle hanging out of the window. Then he looked back at Howard who was out in the open, framed by the white sail that was hanging behind him.

"Get down, Howard!" Bill screamed. "Get below!" He was gesturing to Howard with both arms, and yelling with all the breath he had left. But Howard wasn't noticing. He was totally focused on the helicopter which had swung out of its turn and was accelerating back toward its doomed victims.

Bill jumped out of the cockpit, stepped over the tongue of flame that was wrapping around the curve of the hull, and raced forward.

"Howard! Get down!" His voice was lost in the blast of the pistol as Howard began firing at the chopper. He charged toward his friend, already crouching into the tackle that would knock him down and roll him to the safety of the open hatch. But then the deck under Howard's feet exploded. The automatic rifle rounds tore through his legs, and blasted into his back as he spun along the lifeline. He seemed to sit for an instant on the top of the lifeline, and then he rolled out over the side.

Bill dove onto his face as the gunfire hit ahead of him. His hands locked over his head, saving him the sight of his friend's agony. He looked up when the shots strayed past him and blasted back toward the cockpit. Howard wasn't there.

He was on his feet the second that the helicopter whizzed across the stern. He looked over the side.

The boat was nearly dead in the water, so Howard should be right beneath him. But there was no trace. Then Bill saw a crimson smear on the white side of the boat. He backed away and saw the bloodstains spotted across the deck, each counting one of the rounds that had struck his friend. There was no doubt that Howard was dead.

He picked up the gun that had fallen into the scupper, and wiped the blood against his wet pants. Then he turned away, ducked under the idle genoa jib and followed the helicopter as it flew off to port. It once again banked into a turn. It was coming back for still another murderous pass.

"Howard!" It was Marilyn's voice calling from the cockpit.

"Get down!" Bill ordered. "Get below! They're coming back!"

"Where's Howard?" she demanded.

"Get down, dammit!"

Marilyn heard the engine, turned and saw the helicopter coming back toward her. She dropped down out of sight.

The chopper was coming straight at him, aimed toward *Cane Maiden*'s bow in order to give the gunner a firing angle out of the window. Bill saw the muzzle flash and instantly the port side deck began to splinter. The greenhouse shattered and dropped debris down into the cabin, and then the pilothouse portholes blew away.

He held his fire, knowing that at the last second, the helicopter would bank and turn across the stern. At that moment, the copilot's window would be turned away from him, and the gunman would be unable to fire the rifle.

The stream of explosions ran down the top of the pilothouse and chewed into the mizzen sail that had fallen across the cockpit. The decking on the transom blew away in huge splinters. And when the chopper was right on top of them, the gunfire tore into the deck of the cockpit. Bill heard the women's screams.

The rifle fire stopped. The helicopter banked. Bill jumped up and opened fire.

He watched his shots rip through the helicopter's side, and saw the passenger window explode into a spider web. He swung the pistol to keep it trained on the helicopter engine, and kept the trigger squeezed.

"I'm hit, Al. I'm hit," Johnnie Igoe groaned. Pieces of the broken window were scattered across his lap. He was clutching his leg. A red stain was spreading out from under his fingers, soaking through his trousers.

The pilot was battling the controls, trying to keep the helicopter upright. Bullets had smashed against the pitch control rods under the rotor, and the plane was banking steeply into a tight turn.

Al had been thrown against the door, banging his face against the edge of the open window frame. The rifle had dropped from his fingers, bounced off the folded rubber boat and then dropped into the sea.

"Come back! Come back!" the pilot begged the control column that he was forcing against the turn. Slowly, the helicopter rocked back toward level. He eased back on the stick that was next to his seat, and they began to climb away from the water surface. "Jesus, that was close!" he whispered. Then he yelled at Al, "We're heading back! Right now!"

Al nodded in agreement. "Yeah! They're finished." Flames were billowing out of *Cane Maiden*'s hull. The rigging was in shambles, and the yacht was beginning to list. "Let's get out of here."

He twisted around so he could see Johnnie. "You gonna be all right?"

"Yeah! It's just a cut. But it hurts like a bitch." He had pulled off his belt and was tying it tight around his leg to slow the bleeding.

Al nudged the pilot. "Raise your man at the airport. Tell him to have my guys charter a plane. We'll want to take off as soon as we get in."

"Take off for where?" the pilot asked as he picked up the radio microphone.

"Florida," Al said. "Back to the States."

65

Bill screamed toward the cockpit. "Are you all right?"

Three uncertain voices answered. Nobody had been hit.

"Stay down!" he told them. "They might be coming back!"

He couldn't be sure what the helicopter was going to do, but he couldn't wait to find out. There were new dangers, just as deadly. The oily fire that had already burned through the starboard side was about to break into the cockpit. And *Cane Maiden* was sinking. As she settled lower into the water, more of the holes that had been shot through her side were pulled beneath the surface. The rate at which she was taking on water was increasing.

He dropped down through the greenhouse opening. The stern was down, under weight of the water that had poured into the bilge. As he moved aft, he could smell the smoke that was still contained under the engine room hatch. Bill took the fire extinguisher and pulled the safety pin out of its handle. Then he opened the hatchway, and aimed the blast of foam ahead of him.

The frames and planking on the starboard side

were burning, venting out through the hull. Inside, the smoke was choking. Seawater had closed over the tops of the engine and fuel tanks, but the batteries were still above the tide. Fire was dancing in patches across the floating oil. Bill ducked his head and plunged into waist-deep water, spraying the foam around him. The floating fires died, and the smoke began to clear. Then he concentrated the extinguisher on the burning wood. As the fire died and the smoke vented, he could see the opening in the hull, chopped clean at the bottom by the rifle rounds and burned irregularly up toward the deck. It was a gaping hole, but it reached down only two feet below the level of the sea. If he could raise the starboard side by just a few feet, he could stop the flow of water into the bilge.

He dragged the extinguisher out of the engine space, and then up the ladder. The hatch cover was still locked, so he had to use the extinguisher to smash it open. When he climbed out of the hatch, he was stunned by the destruction that surrounded him. The fallen mizzenmast was angled across the cockpit, its rigging a tangled rat's nest, the sail smeared with the oily smoke. The Bimini awning was smashed and spread across the deck like a torn shroud. The women who were struggling out from beneath it were close to shock, oblivious to the fire that was burning next to them. Their expressions were more numbed than frightened.

Marilyn's face was swollen and stained with soot. Cindy's shirt had torn to shreds as she dragged free from the fallen rigging, and there was a gash across her shoulder. Her blond hair was a murky gray. Jeanne was still soaked from her plunge into the sea, her hands and face black with oil. They all needed attention, but there wasn't time.

Bill pushed past them and blasted the extinguisher toward the flames. First he killed the fire that had caught the edge of the Bimini canvas. Then he doused the deck and the bulkhead inside the cockpit.

"Get that mast untangled," he told the women. Marilyn, who had slumped against the shattered port side bench, raised her reddened eyes and understood the problem. The fallen mizzenmast was across the helm, its tangled rigging wrapped around the wheel. She began pulling the lines free. Cindy saw that the extinguisher had the fire under control and moved to help Marilyn. Jeanne saw that they would need to cut the rigging wires in order to free the mast. She began searching the cockpit lockers, looking for the tool kit. Through their exhaustion, they began fighting for their lives.

Bill jumped up onto the smoldering deck, and sprayed the flames that were licking at the side of the hull. The fire flickered and then died. Next, he climbed on top of the pilothouse and lifted the top of the fallen mast over the lifeline. Seconds later, he and the women were able to lever the mast over the side. He used the wire cutters that Jeanne had brought from the tool kit to cut the last wire, and the mast sank beside them, pulling the small spanker sail down with it.

Cane Maiden had slowly turned herself into the wind, luffing the sails that were still flying. He checked the sheets that were attached to the sails, and made sure that they were still running free.

"Okay," he told his crew with more confidence than he felt, "Let's see if we can sail this thing."

Jeanne seemed shocked at the thought. "We're sinking," she said, putting words to what was obvious to all of them.

But Bill remembered the uncomfortable heel of the boat when it was sailing across the wind. If he could head her north, the wind would be coming over the starboard side. And if he could haul the sails in tight — the way Howard and Steve had taught him — the boat would lean to port. It wouldn't take much of a heel to lift the shattered starboard side out of the water.

He hauled in on the working jib which was flapping uselessly. But even when it was all the way in, it didn't catch enough wind to deliver any power. The boat was dead into the wind. He turned the broken wheel as far as he could to port. "Hold it here," he told Cindy, who stepped up next to him. Then he left the cockpit and raced forward.

Bill took the boom of the working jib and dragged it into the wind, exactly as Howard had ordered when they were first getting under way. By backing the sail to the starboard side, he hoped to start the bow swinging to port.

The sail filled, but *Cane Maiden* didn't respond. With her bilges filled, she was settled below her sailing lines. She was as immobile as an anchor. Marilyn saw what he was trying to do, and raced forward to help. Jeanne followed, and the three of them were able to drag the sail further across the wind. The yacht's bow began to edge around.

482

As she turned, the wind moved down the starboard side. The huge genoa began to fill.

"We've got it!" Bill nearly laughed. He ran aft, and joined Cindy who was still holding the wheel hard over. Bill cranked in on the genoa and the boat began to move, turning first to the east, and then continuing on toward north. The mainsail caught some air, and he cranked it in until it stiffened.

Cane Maiden began to heel, heavily because of the weight of water she was carrying far below the water line. The starboard side inched upward.

He took the wheel and spun it back toward the centerline. "Hold that!" he ordered Cindy. She nodded. But the compass had been shot away. She had nothing to guide her steering.

Bill went to the starboard rail and looked down over the side. The big holes, where Al had shot away huge chunks of planking and where the fire had burned, were out of the water. The flood into the boat had slowed.

Now, it was all up to the batteries. He found the console switch that Steve had used to pump the bilges after the storm, and toggled it back and forth. Nothing seemed to happen. But then he was aware of a different sound. Water was splashing next to the boat. He looked over the side and saw a steady jet of water firing out from the stern and into *Cane Maiden*'s wake. The pumps were working. Water was being lifted out of the bilge and hurled over the side.

Cane Maiden began to gather speed, sailing to the north, with a southeasterly wind blowing across her decks. That was the only heading she could steer. She had to keep the wind to starboard in order to maintain the heel that held the damaged hull out of the water. But for her crew, it was the only heading they needed. Bill wouldn't be able to pick a precise course off the charts. He knew nothing about navigation. And even if he did, there was no compass or radio navigation system to use for guidance. But he knew that the Drake Channel, with its dozens of islands and cays, was spread across his northerly heading. If the wind stayed steady, and they could keep it on their starboard side, they were bound to reach land.

"We're going to make it," he told the others. The moment of crisis had past. But there was little joy in the weary faces that looked back at him. They were all wounded. Marilyn had seen her husband sink into black madness, and then vanish from her life. Jeanne's consoling words, and Bill's assurance that he had died trying to save them, were of little value. Jeanne had traded her marriage for a glittering glimpse of a more rewarding future. Now, even as she bandaged the torn flesh of her husband's shoulder, she knew that wounds had been opened that would never heal. And Cindy was still in mortal danger. Bill had thrown the money over the side in a desperate attempt to save her life. But without the money to return, her life would always be at terrible risk.

The problems that had driven them all to the edge of destruction were still traveling aboard *Cane Maiden*. The faster the boat sailed, the sooner they would have to be resolved.

66

Johnnie Igoe hobbled away from the helicopter, his arm draped across Al Weston's shoulder.

"I'll be all right," Johnnie kept insisting. "Just get me on a plane and get me the hell outta here!"

"The doctor is just going to look at you. Clean up the wound and put a decent bandage on it," Al told him. "You'll be on the plane in an hour."

Al had radioed ahead and arranged for a doctor to treat Johnnie privately. He didn't want to go near a hospital where the police were apt to ask questions. He helped his friend into the backseat of the rental car, and eased his leg through the doorway. "Have him give you some painkillers. Maybe a shot of morphine. You might enjoy getting high legally."

"Yeah!" Johnnie managed, forcing a thin smile. "Maybe I can get an extra hit for you."

Al shook his head as he eased the door closed. "I won't be going back right away. Think I'll hang around Tortola for a couple of days, just to keep in touch with my contact at the charter boat company."

Johnnie looked disappointed. "Give it up, Al. The money is gone. Cindy and her friends went down with the ship. There's nothing left."

485

"Yeah," Al agreed, "but I just want to be certain. Walter Linz likes to have everything buttoned up. He doesn't like loose ends."

As soon as the car pulled away, Al went to a telephone and called Ft. Lauderdale. Walter Linz picked up on the first ring, took the number of Al's pay phone, and then called back ten minutes later. There were traffic noises in the background, indicating that he was talking on the cellular phone in his limousine.

"I lost it, Walter," Al told him contritely. "When we were closing in, the bastards threw the case over the side. I had my hands on it, but it sunk right under me."

"And Cindy?" Walter asked.

"She was aboard. I guess that means she was in on it, because if someone had taken it from her they probably wouldn't have kept her around."

"I tend to agree with you," Walter Linz said. Then he asked, "Will we be able to talk with her?"

"I don't think so," Al answered. "The boat was on fire and seemed to be sinking. She was still aboard."

"You're telling me that she went down with the boat?"

"That's the way it looked. I'm planning to hang around for a couple of days just to be sure."

"Be very careful," Walter advised. It was more an order than an expression of personal concern. "We've been very fortunate that none of this has come to the attention of the officials. I hate to lose the money, but it's much more important that we don't stir up a lot of interest, and raise a lot

486

of questions. The people on the other side of this deal are a good bit bigger than we are. They expect me to protect them. They've made it clear that I shouldn't do a lot of complaining about an occasional loss."

"I understand," Al answered. "I'm not going to cause any problems. I just want to be sure."

He slammed his fist against the wall of the phone booth as soon as he hung up, breaking the skin on his knuckles. "Fuck the people on the other side," he cursed. He knew that Walter dealt in circles where a million was the lowest value chip. When they said "one," they didn't mean a dollar or even a thousand dollars. "One" meant a million. Anything less was pocket change, hardly worth the effort. Walter and his friends could write off the loss and get on with their next deal.

Not that they were indifferent. If the people on the other side had found their loudmouthed courier alive, they would certainly have made an unforgettable example out of him. And if Walter had caught Cindy in the act of betrayal, he wouldn't have hesitated to order her punishment. Management in any organization had to keep its workers in line. But they were businessmen, very forgiving of their own mistakes and anxious to put embarrassing oversights behind them. It was important to them that Al not do anything that would attract attention to their failure.

Al's priorities were different. He had been sent to safeguard the transaction. Cindy had been his responsibility, and she had turned on him and outsmarted him. A goddamn cocktail waitress and her waste of a boyfriend had figured they could take the bonds and the diamonds and get away with it. And they damn near had pulled it off.

He wasn't sure how the others were involved. He couldn't believe that the architect and the schoolteacher were in on the plot. But one of them had come out on deck with the camera case and thrown it over the side, so they had to know that they held a fortune right in their hands. And people who found a fortune didn't generally throw it away. Al figured that before they had tossed the case and the money over the side, they had paused to stuff some of it into their own pockets.

If they had all gone down with *Cane Maiden,* then what they had planned or what they had stolen didn't make a damn bit of difference. They had gotten out of line, and they had paid for it. Sure, he would have liked to have had a few minutes face to face with Cindy and her boyfriend. And if the passengers were in on it, he would have enjoyed pointing out their error. He was sure he had already settled the score with at least one of them. As he fired from the window of the helicopter, he had seen one of the men disappear into the sea. And he had left the boat a burning hulk. It didn't seem likely that there would be any survivors.

But he wanted to be sure. He wanted to see an official report that said *Cane Maiden* was lost, and maybe a coroner's report on the bodies that had been picked up off a beach. Al couldn't live with the thought that Cindy was ashore someplace laughing at him. He couldn't stomach the possibility that the vacationers would leave Tortola with their luggage stuffed with bearer bonds, or with packets of diamonds taped between their legs. He had to know that no one had made a fool of him. He had to be certain that the people who had crossed him had paid for their crime.

67

The wind held steady, and the crippled yacht kept moving. The batteries had died before all the water was pumped out of the bilge, and there was still a flow into the boat whenever the waves lapped up over the holes in her side. But Bill was able to keep it under control with the hand pump, while Cindy and Jeanne took turns steering the bow off the wind.

They tried to guess at the progress they were making. The eastern end of St. Croix appeared on the horizon in the early afternoon, and moved slowly down the port side. But they couldn't turn toward it without changing the lean of the boat and flooding new water into the bilge. They wouldn't be able to reach land before the yacht filled. Bill tried a calculation based on the time it took for a point of land to pass abeam. He guessed they were making about five knots, which would leave them seven more hours of sailing before they reached the islands to the north. They should see land clearly in the late afternoon, but it might well be dark before they reached it.

During her search of the lockers, Jeanne had found the signaling pistol with its flare cartridges. They could see other cruising yachts, two to the west that seemed to be traveling between St. John and St. Croix, and several far to the east that were probably running between the Virgins and the Leewards. A flare fired into the sky should bring one of the boats to their aid.

But that had to be their last resort if they hoped to put Cindy ashore and let her run for her safety. They hadn't decided exactly what their story would be, but if they called another boat to their rescue, then there would be no escape for Cindy. She would be met by police just as they would be. Her name, and their connection to her, would become public information. They had decided to hold their course until evening. Then, if they saw no hope of reaching land, they would fire the signal.

They were together in the cockpit. One at a time they had gone below, peeled off the torn and oil-stained clothes that had seen them through the ordeal, and found fresh things to wear. Jeanne had come up with shorts and a blouse that fit Cindy, and given her a pair of sneakers. She had found jeans and a shirt for herself. Marilyn changed into a pair of slacks and a windbreaker. Only Bill had stayed on deck, changing into a clean shirt that Jeanne had brought topside. She had redone the dressing on his shoulder, but tiny spots of red were beginning to show through.

They were exhausted. Sleep the night before had been fitful and none of them had been prepared for the physical ordeal of the morning — much less the terrible mental strain. But they couldn't allow themselves the rest they needed. Just sailing the boat, a simple task for Steve, took their full attention. Cindy and Marilyn shared the steering, using the flow of the waves as their wind indicator. By keeping a constant angle off the sea, they were able to keep the sails filled and the boat heeled. Bill worked the pump, which was the most physically demanding task that they faced. And when Marilyn wasn't spelling him, she was leaning all her weight against the winch handles as they tried to keep the sails taut.

They were also famished. They had bottled water to ease their thirst, but there hadn't been time to bring a meal up from the galley. All they had was some fruit that Jeanne had salvaged from the ice chest.

And then there was the heat. In clearing the cockpit, they had thrown the shreds of the Bimini overboard. They were now exposed to the torturous midday sun with no protection other than the suntan lotions that they had brought aboard.

"We have to make some decisions," Jeanne finally offered.

Bill nodded that he understood, but he was too tired to take up the conversation.

"I still have some clothes that Cindy can wear. And she can take my passport. It's an old picture that doesn't look like anybody. I think it would get her on a plane."

He glanced up from the pump handle toward his wife. Only hours ago she had broken a match, selling Cindy to the sea for a chance at the fortune that Howard was offering. Then, in a violent act of contrition, she had fought with Howard to save the girl's life, and hurled herself overboard to rescue the husband she said she despised. Now she was the only one among them who was thinking clearly about helping Cindy escape.

"Don't worry," Cindy answered Jeanne. "I can take my chances."

"No," Jeanne contradicted. "I need to help you. I owe you that. Howard and I . . ."

She looked at Cindy, imploring her for forgiveness. Then she turned back to the helm.

"We can't be certain of anything until we make a landing," Bill said. "We'll have to know where we are before we can plan an escape."

He had been thinking of the possibilities. It would be sheer luck if they found themselves aimed at a harbor or even at a coastal village. They might run aground on one of the small cays where there would be no route of escape, and where their only choice would be to wait to be rescued. Or they could sail right into the arms of the police who were probably expecting their arrival. But still, it was smart to start preparing, and Jeanne's suggestions might prove workable. If they landed on one of the bigger islands, Cindy would have lots of escape routes. But, sooner or later, she would have to pass through customs and passport control. That was the bottleneck where her danger would be the greatest. In Jeanne's clothes, perhaps with her hair hidden under a hat, she could look very different. The people who were looking for her probably wouldn't recognize her. And Jeanne's passport would give her a new identity for the few minutes she would need to get on board a plane.

Jeanne wouldn't need her passport. Unless they were intercepted, it was most likely that *Cane*

493

Maiden would slam into a rocky coastline and face destruction at the hands of the tides. They wouldn't be able to carry all their things ashore. It would be simple to let the authorities assume that the passport was lost.

But at this moment, there were more demanding problems. The seas were churning under a freshening breeze, sending stronger waves against the hull. More water was lapping in and Bill was falling behind with the hand pump. He had to rig some sort of cover to give them protection from the sun. Then he had to work out a schedule that would give each of them a few minutes rest, and a chance to go below and find something to eat. They still had hours of struggle left ahead of them. The mountains of Tortola still weren't in sight.

68

Al Weston went straight to Drake Channel Charters as soon as his helicopter touched down. Ty Sherwood jumped up from behind the counter the moment he came through the door.

"What have you heard?" Al demanded.

The young man threw up his hands. "Nothing. Not since yesterday when the Coast Guard spotted her. We expected her in this morning. This afternoon at the latest. We even had our chase boat out looking for her. But nobody's heard anything."

It was the answer that Al was hoping for. The puff of smoke hadn't attracted any attention. She had simply disappeared. But even with the boat gone, he couldn't be sure of the passengers. "Well if they're missing, why ain't someone out looking for them? Maybe you've got people out there floating around in life jackets."

The kid shrugged. "They weren't in any danger yesterday. The Coast Guard said they were doing okay."

"Then where the hell are they?"

"I don't know. Still heading home, I guess. They didn't duck into St. Croix, because if they did someone would have called us."

"I'll be back at my hotel," Al told him.

"Yeah," the clerk assured him. "I have the number. I'll give you a call as soon as I hear anything."

Al walked wearily through the sculptured garden and around the swimming pool, past Cindy's cottage. The door was open, and the maids were making up the room for other guests. Al figured they were probably holding Cindy's belongings as security against her unpaid bill. He wondered how long it would take them to figure out that she wasn't coming back.

As soon as he was in his own room he dialed the bar and ordered a bottle of Scotch and a setup. He tipped the boy lavishly, too anxious for a drink to wait through the hassle of making change. It had been an agonizing day on top of a frustrating week, and he felt no need to keep the sharp edge of his senses. It was over, he figured. All except the phone call telling him that someone had wandered across the debris from the sunken *Cane Maiden*. He wouldn't need to be sober to understand that.

Al poured a full glass over the ice cubes and drained half of it in one swallow. Somehow, he had to get rid of the image of the camera case floating just beneath the surface. He had to forget the feel of it slipping through his fingers.

69

They saw the hilltops through the evening haze and, as the shadows began to fall, the first lights on top of Tortola. Bill guessed that they were still ten miles out, and that they still had two hours of sailing ahead of them. But just the sight of their goal lifted their spirits and seemed to flood them with new energy. The women, who had fallen into a heavy silence, began talking again. Bill bent his back to the pump handle, determined not to be forced into firing the flare.

Next, they caught a glimpse of the islands on the southern border of the Drake Channel and managed to join in a cheer. If they were in any danger, they could run the boat aground on any of them. But it would be difficult to get Cindy off the small islands without her being identified. They still hoped to sail between them, and make it all the way back to Tortola.

"I think it's time to find her some clothes," Marilyn told Jeanne. "We ought to be ready." Jeanne went below and then came topside with an armful of things she had rescued from her duffel. Cindy picked the most likely fits and went below to try them on.

While she was gone, Marilyn and Jeanne began

talking about makeup. Cindy, they agreed, needed something to darken her complexion. But it couldn't be enough to attract attention. Their conversation was serious, but it struck Bill as incongruous against the dangers they had just come through. They were debating shades of eye shadow and lipstick, oblivious to the dangers they would face when *Cane Maiden* crashed ashore.

Land rose up on each side of them, a large island with occasional lights to the west, and a small dark island to the east. A glance at the charts suggested two likely combinations; they were either passing between Peter Island and Salt Island, or between Cooper Island and Ginger Island. It didn't matter which. Either way, the land dead ahead was Tortola. They could see the light atop the radio antenna at the high point of the land mass to their left, and the rotating aircraft beacon on Beef Island to their right. They had less than two hours of sailing ahead of them, and the sun was just touching down on top of a huge island far to the west. There was a good chance that there would still be light in the sky when they reached shore.

Cindy brought up a waterproof pouch, packed with the clothes she would wear. It seemed likely that she might have to wade ashore, and the clothes would have to be dry and pressed if they were going to make her invisible to emigration agents. The women took turns going below to gather their most valuable possessions and bring them topside. Like Cindy, they put their essentials into watertight containers that were emptied of matches, flares and navigation instruments. Their working assumption was that they wouldn't be able to bring

Cane Maiden to a dock. Most of their things would be lost.

The wind picked up as they cleared the southern islands and moved into the center of the Drake Channel. But its direction never budged. It kept blowing from the southeast, over their starboard side, holding the boat tipped to port. The damaged sections of the hull rode high out of the water.

With the noticeable increase in speed, they assumed that the last miles of their journey would certainly be shortened. But the night came more quickly than they had expected. As the sun fell behind St. John, the shadow of the island closed down over the Drake Channel. The mountains of Tortola faded, replaced by confusing clusters of lights. Their confidence ebbed as they felt themselves suddenly lost in the darkness.

Bill figured that they should reduce speed for their final run toward their unknown landing. He rolled in the giant genoa, watching carefully the effect on *Cane Maiden*'s list. Even when it was completely furled, the hole in her side was still a bit above the waves. In the distance they had left, they wouldn't take on much water.

He picked a target toward which they could steer; a bright cluster of lights dead ahead. "That's your mark," he told Marilyn, who was at the wheel. "Just hold it until we hit something."

It would also be their goal if they had to swim for it. They agreed that if the boat swamped before they reached shore, they would stay together and cling to the wreck. If the boat sank, they would leave everything behind and swim together toward the cluster of lights. "It's probably a couple of houses. Or maybe a crossroad," Bill speculated. "Someplace where we can get help if we need it."

Jeanne volunteered to handle the signaling pistol. They wouldn't use it if they made it to shore. They hoped not to attract attention until Cindy could slip away. But if the boat foundered off shore, they might need the distress signals.

"Anything else?" he asked, when he had exhausted his meager knowledge of boat emergencies.

"Just a prayer for a sandy beach," Jeanne said.

Bill took the powerful, multi-cell flashlight and started toward the bow.

"Hey!" It was Cindy's voice from the corner of the cockpit. Bill stopped and turned with the others.

"In case we get separated . . . thanks!"

She found them all looking back at her. But nobody answered.

"I caused you guys a lot of trouble." She focused on Marilyn. "Not just trouble. A lot of pain."

Still, no one said anything. Cindy turned her eyes away from them, and tried again. "For a while I thought the best thing I could do was just slip over the side. That would have been the best thing for all of you. I mean, I was the one who brought all the problems on board. I'm the one who should have died with them. But I don't feel like that any more. I'm glad I'm still alive. I guess it's wrong for me to feel that way after what I've put you through. I should be sorry. But I'm just grateful. I owe you guys my life. So I want to say 'thanks.' "

She was still looking away when she heard

Marilyn's soft voice. "You have nothing to be sorry for. You didn't bring our problems aboard. We brought them aboard ourselves."

70

The lights in the cluster they were steering toward began to separate. From his place on the bowsprit, Bill could make out individual buildings. And then he saw that some of the lights were moving. There were cars passing along a road close to the shore. They seemed to have stumbled across the perfect landing point, with roads that could carry Cindy away, and with homes where they could go for help. If only they could get there. If only there were no barrier reef or outcropping of rocks to block their way.

He saw waves. There was a thin line of white foam, illuminated by the lights on the land, directly ahead. He listened carefully, and thought he could hear the distant rumble of a light surf. He aimed the flashlight toward the sound, and saw a spray of white water explode from a rock just off the port bow. But when he swung the light directly ahead, the sea was still calm.

"Bill!" It was Marilyn's voice calling from the cockpit. She could see the waves breaking on the rock.

"Hold your heading," he screamed. If he tried to turn away from the danger, the sails would luff and the boat would stop. They'd be filling with water while the sea was pushing them onto the rocks. He had to gamble that he had a clear passage dead ahead.

"Hold your heading!" he repeated, aiming the light beam at the angry spray. *Cane Maiden* tracked a straight line. The jagged point slid by, ten yards off the port beam.

The surf ahead was getting louder. He could see the small waves that formed the white line, reflected in the shore lights that were now clearly visible. They couldn't be more than a thousand yards from land. But the line of waves was only half that distance ahead, and it was blocking their approach. Bill backed off the bowsprit and raced aft to the cockpit.

"There's a bar, or a reef dead ahead." He took the wheel from Marilyn. "Hang on!" he told the others. "We're going over it."

They could hear the surf, and then suddenly they could all see the row of waves. There were points of rock all along the surf line, with narrow patches of blue water between the rocks. As they raced up to the line, Bill saw a narrow break in the surf just off the port bow. He spun the wheel.

Cane Maiden turned toward the opening and raced ahead. White water splashed on either side, but the sea was flat under her bow. She was almost through, when she suddenly shuddered, and lurched violently to port. She heeled steeply, and then there was an explosion of crackling wood. The women were thrown across the cockpit. The wheel spun out of Bill's hands, and he rolled out across the deck and bounced against the rail. He caught the lifeline to keep from falling out into the sea.

But as abruptly as she had slammed to a stop, *Cane Maiden* drifted free. The wash from the waves nudged gently against her stern and she eased forward, the wind again tugging at her sails. Bill scampered back to the wheel, thinking that he could turn the bow and straighten her out. It was when the wheel turned freely that he realized the boat had lost her rudder. Seconds later, he heard the rush of the sea into the cabin below. He jumped up to the hatch and shined the flashlight down through the opening. There was a whirlpool of water working its way up the ladder. *Cane Maiden* had torn her bottom open on the rocks.

She was sinking, but still moving toward the shore. He freed the mainsail and let it swing out so that it could catch the air, and then he threw off the sheet to the jib. The boat was blowing freely before the onshore wind, moving ahead, but settling down into the water as she traveled.

The women had recovered, and understood that they would never make the beach. "What are we going to do?" Marilyn asked in a calm voice.

"Ride her as far as she'll take us," Bill answered.

It wouldn't be very far. She was filling quickly, indicating that the damage to her bottom was massive. But somehow, the sails were still pulling. And she was being pushed by the small rollers that washed over the reef.

And then she broached, turning her side to the sea. The sails flapped uselessly, and she dipped her port rails into the water.

They slipped down the steep slope of the cockpit, and then were thrown backward as the boat righted. But once again, she leaned precariously. There were more crashes from below, as giant timbers snapped under the enormous strain. *Cane Maiden* was screaming in her death agony. When she righted herself again, water washed over her decks. The cockpit began to fill.

"Should we swim for it?" Jeanne asked.

"Stay with the boat," Marilyn answered instantly. They held on as the water flooded in around them.

Cane Maiden slammed to a stop. Her wire shrouds howled under the strain, and then snapped with a musical twang. They ducked down as the mainmast snapped at its base, and fell over the side, dragging the sails behind it. There was an instant of terror as they waited for the boat to follow its mast and turn over.

But the boat was perfectly still, unaffected by the sea that was swirling around it. They looked up cautiously, and then at one another.

"What's happened?" Marilyn asked.

Bill looked out over the side, and saw that the mast wasn't sinking. It was propped on an angle, its top jabbed into the water and its base resting on the broken roof of the pilothouse. "I think we're aground," he answered cautiously. He aimed the flashlight out past the end of the mast and saw a sandy beach.

71

Al blinked at the telephone, and listened to its second ring. He poked around, wondered where he was, studied the strange furniture and then recognized the half-empty Scotch bottle on the table by his feet. The phone rang again.

He sat up abruptly. He was on the sofa, still fully dressed. The ice in his glass had melted, and there were wet circles on the coffee table. He stood carefully, and reached the telephone as it started still another ring.

"We found her!" the voice said.

"Found who?" he asked, still trying to remember why he was back in his hotel room.

"*Cane Maiden.* She came ashore a couple of hours ago. Ran aground out by Brandywine Bay."

He recognized the voice. The kid from Drake Channel Charters.

"She made it in?" Al asked without disguising his surprise.

"Just barely. Broke up on a reef and washed up on the beach. She lost her captain a couple of days ago. One of the passengers sailed her back."

He was wide awake now, and fully alert. "Who was aboard?" he demanded.

"The guy and the two wives. One of the husbands was lost along with the captain. I don't have all the details, but it sounds like they went through hell. I heard someone tried to sink them."

"Just the two wives?" Al asked. "No one else?"

"That's what I heard. I didn't ask a lot of questions. You told me to call you right away."

"Yeah, of course," Al answered. "And I appreciate it. I'll be by to see you tomorrow." He let the hint of another payment sink in and then he asked, "If you hear anything else, call me back. It's important."

It doesn't figure, he thought as he hung up the phone. Cindy had been aboard. He had seen her standing in the cockpit. So if the boat stayed afloat, and made it to shore, Cindy should still be on it. Even if he had hit her when he was firing into the cockpit, they still would have brought her back. Unless . . .

He went into the bathroom, turned on the cold water tap full blast and splashed handfuls of water into his face. Unless . . .

Unless they were happy to get rid of the only link to the money. Suppose the case they had thrown over the side had been empty. Suppose they had already put the money ashore, maybe with the captain who, they were claiming, was washed overboard. Or suppose the money was still on board. Then maybe they wouldn't want to have to explain Cindy. Maybe, if he had killed her, they would have decided to bury her at sea.

Or maybe he hadn't killed her. Maybe she had come back with them and had simply gone into hiding once they reached the beach.

The only explanation for Cindy not being on

board was that the passengers had something to hide. They either had the money, or they knew where it was.

Where would he find them? Probably at the hospital that looked out over Road Harbor. If they wrecked the boat, they might well need medical attention. Or maybe with the police. The police would certainly have to ask questions about a captain lost over the side and about the people they claimed tried to sink them. Al knew he wouldn't have any trouble finding the architect or the schoolteacher, whichever one of them had survived.

He peeled off his clothes and stepped into the shower. He would need to be wide awake for the hours ahead.

FRIDAY

72

Cindy watched the sun lift over the glowing hilltops and fill the basin of Road Harbor with soft
light. She looked out toward the open sea, and
saw the power boat, right on schedule, turning
the southwest point. It trailed a white wake as
it raced toward the inner harbor.

She stepped carefully from behind the equipment shed to get a better view. The cab driver,
who had picked her up the night before, had told
her that she couldn't miss the water taxi to St.
Thomas. "A big blue boat with two decks and
rows of white benches. It lands just outside the
seawall." But the boat that was approaching was
still too far away for her to make out the details.

She had been hiding behind the shed for most
of the night. As soon as they were safely ashore,
Bill had told her to get moving, refusing her offer
to help bring their belongings in from the wreck.
"Get up to the road. Find a ride and get out of
here. You don't want to be seen with us. You
don't want anyone to figure you were on the
boat."

"I can't just leave you," she had argued.

"You have to. We're safe. You have to get away
from here."

Cindy had carried the small bundle of Jeanne's clothes across the beach, taking a roundabout route to avoid the pool of light that spread out to the water's edge. She had hidden for a moment as people from the small, cinder block houses rushed down toward the wreck that had just washed ashore at their doorstep. Then she had made her way up to the road they had seen when they were approaching the shore. She had walked to a shed-like nightclub, where a reggae band was entertaining the natives, and a few tourists were soaking up the island culture. Two taxi vans were waiting by the roadside, hoping to take the tourists back to the wharfs.

She was already in one of the cabs when she had realized she had no idea where she was headed. "Best way to get to St. Thomas?" she had asked. She turned down the suggestion of one of the flights that would leave Beef Island. If Al were still looking for her, the airport would certainly be covered. Then the driver had suggested the water taxi. "Runs all day, starting at sunrise. There's a boat every couple of hours."

As soon as he had pulled away, leaving her standing on the roadside across from the dock, she had gone into the shadows behind the equipment shed and changed into Jeanne's clothes. The island's hospital was directly across the street. Lights burned in many of the windows, and there were people coming and going throughout the night. She had stayed awake, pulling herself up against the water side of the battered structure every time there was activity out on the road. Now, with the ferry in sight, she felt numb with fear. To board

512

the boat, she would have to walk out into the open, and come face to face with the crew and passengers. That would be the most vulnerable point in her escape from Tortola.

Cindy checked her outfit. She was wearing a long tan skirt and a flowered, long-sleeved blouse. There was no hint of her figure. The straw sailing hat, tied under her chin with a ribbon, completely hid her hair, and the wide brim kept her face in shadow. At a glance, nobody would recognize her. But there was no costume that would save her if she came face to face with Al or one of his men.

People began arriving, strolling past the shed and down to the dock. A taxi pulled up, and a family of visitors with two small children climbed out. Other cars stopped, dropping off more passengers for the ferry. Within a few minutes, there were twenty people forming a line at the edge of the pier.

The boat was racing closer. Cindy could see its open decks and the wide passenger benches. There were a few people aboard who were coming over from St. Thomas, and one of the crew was out on the bow, ready with a docking line. But she stayed close to the building. She didn't want to risk standing out in the open. She would wait until everyone was crowding aboard before rushing out into the open.

She glanced back toward the road. A steady stream of cars was arriving at the hospital, and several more cars had pulled up with passengers for the water taxi. She could see people running toward her along the road's edge, afraid that the boat would leave without them. Cindy breathed a bit more easily. There was suddenly a great deal of activity that she could blend in with. She wouldn't be standing alone, attracting attention.

Then she saw Al Weston.

He stepped out of a van that had pulled to the edge of the roadway, and spent a few seconds talking with his driver. Then he turned and looked around slowly, at first away from Cindy as he searched the hospital parking lot, and then toward her as he completed the full circle. She ducked around the corner of the shed, putting the building between Al and her, and pressed her back against the wall.

He had found her. Somehow, he had found her. Probably the cab driver who had brought her here. Of course! All he had to do was check with the island's drivers. A girl fitting Cindy's description would be easy to remember.

She couldn't see the road, but she had a clear view of the dock where the water taxi was throwing over its bow line. Al, she guessed, would walk into sight on his way down to the boat. She would slip around the next corner of the shed, keeping it between them until she was facing the road. Then she would make a run for it.

Slowly, Cindy was telling herself. Just walk away. Maybe toward the hospital. He would never recognize her from a distance, particularly if she were walking away from him. She was just another tourist. But if she ran, she would attract attention. Don't panic, she tried to persuade herself. Just walk away.

But Al didn't come into sight. It should only have taken him a few seconds to walk down from the road. She never would have missed his large frame, and the straw hat with the colorful band that he was wearing again. What was he waiting for? Had he seen that she wasn't among the passengers, and decided to watch the new arrivals coming along the road? Or had he seen her, and decided to wait until she committed herself one way or the other?

She froze for a moment, not knowing what she should do. Then, slowly, she edged back to the corner and peeked around. When she didn't see him, she stepped out a bit further. His cab was waiting, the sliding door wide open, and the driver lounging in the front seat. But there was no sign of Al. She was tempted to make her dash toward the boat which was beginning to board passengers. But that seemed too risky until she knew where he was. She might rush right into his arms.

She saw his hat above the traffic of people who were passing through the main door of the hospital. He had started into the hospital, but now was coming back out. He came down the steps and walked the path to the road. But instead of continuing on to his waiting taxi, he turned up the road and stopped by the ambulance driveway. Then he stood there, half turned away from her, his attention locked on the hospital door.

He wasn't looking for her, Cindy understood. He was waiting for someone. Someone who was visiting at the hospital. At least for the moment, he wasn't paying any attention to the water taxi, or to the passengers who were nearly all aboard. All she had to do was step out and stroll casually toward the pier. There was nothing about her that

515

would attract his attention. Even if he turned toward her for a moment, he wouldn't recognize her at this distance.

Then she saw Bill, with Marilyn on one side and Jeanne on the other. Bill's left arm was in a white sling. There was a white bandage showing beneath Marilyn's sunglasses. They had come through the front door of the hospital, and were talking with a policeman on the top step. They started down, the officer in his blue and khaki uniform only a few steps behind, and came toward the road, following the path that Al had just walked. Cindy could see them all together. Her shipmates walking toward her. Her executioner waiting a few feet away from them, watching them. It was at that instant that she understood who Al's victims would be.

The scream was on her lips. She should cry out to warn Bill and the two women that they had been found. But they were too far away. Al was much closer to her, and if she alerted him, all she would be doing was handing him another victim.

The water taxi blew its whistle. The last straggler, walking along the road, began to run so as not to miss the boat. It was Cindy's chance. With Al absorbed in her friends, all she had to do was join the last-second rush, and scamper aboard as the gangway was pulled back. She would be away from the island in less than a minute.

The police officer helped Bill and the two women into a taxi. Al hurried across the street and jumped through the open door of his own cab.

The water taxi whistle sounded behind her.

Cindy glanced toward the sound. The last passenger was running down the dock. The crewmen were waiting impatiently, holding the docking lines in their hands. It was now or never.

The police officer waved at the taxi as it edged into the ambulance driveway to begin its U-turn. Al's van pulled out onto the road, hesitated, and then began a turn toward the taxi.

The whistle on the boat gave a long, threatening blast. Cindy looked back just long enough to see the gangway being pulled away. Then she ran up to the road and raced through the door of a waiting taxi. Bill's cab and Al's van had already disappeared around the turn. "That way! Fast!" was the only instruction she was able to give to her driver.

73

As soon as they were out of sight of the hospital, Bill slipped his arm out of the cast and tested his shoulder. He was able to stretch the arm out ahead of him with no difficulty. There was pain only when he tried to reach above his head.

"You should rest it," Jeanne chastised.

"If feels fine," he answered. And then he glanced away, out through the window. An anxious silence filled the taxi.

The dangers that had threatened them were in the past. The crisis that had drawn them together had ended when they reached the beach. The young woman, who had been their common cause, was gone. Now they were sinking slowly back into their own thoughts, and beginning to face the truth of the past week.

The brief inquiry they had faced a few hours earlier had little to do with truth. It had been concerned with facts. Marilyn had answered all the police officer's questions with a firm voice, and told the entire painful story. The takeover by the captain and the young woman. The storm. The captain's death, which she believed accidental, during his struggle with her husband. And then the attack that had killed her husband

and set the yacht on fire. The only thing she had left out was what actually happened to Cindy. "She was with us when we hit the reef. And then she vanished. I can only hope that she's alive and well."

Every word was true. But the story avoided the real truth. It didn't get into the change that had been worked on them by the sight of the money. It never mentioned the three broken matchsticks. Nor was Marilyn clear on exactly what her husband was doing when the helicopter had appeared and shot him dead.

"And the money?" the police officer asked politely.

"I threw it overboard," Bill said. "I thought it was going to get us all killed," he added when the officer reacted with a look of astonishment. That was certainly true. But the truth that Bill was avoiding was that they were in great danger of destroying themselves over the money long before the helicopter had arrived.

Jeanne had told the same story, giving an account of the events that was devoid of their meaning. She accepted the officer's congratulations that they had all survived the ordeal, without sharing her feeling that nothing had survived. The relationships that had brought them together aboard *Cane Maiden* had been destroyed.

"I hope she made it," Jeanne said to break the silence. Bill and Marilyn nodded in agreement. They had all been thinking about Cindy. Their own survival seemed to depend on her making it off the island and back to her home. They had come so close to killing her, they needed to believe that they had helped save her.

The taxi turned through the gate of the hotel where the police had found them rooms. It was on the shore to the west of Road Town, a sprawling complex of bungalows built around a marina. There was one bedroom, which Bill had given to Marilyn and Jeanne. The pillow he had borrowed from them was still on the sofa where he had managed a few hours sleep before they had been taken to the hospital.

"You two should have the room," Marilyn offered as soon as they had stepped inside the bungalow.

"We won't be here long," Bill answered. "I think they're hoping to get us off the island today." The police officer had been more than satisfied with their answers and completely apologetic with regard to their difficulties. He had mentioned a routine report which would be prepared quickly for their signatures so as not to delay them.

Bill could understand why. Renegade charter captains, sudden storms and attacks from armed helicopters weren't good for the tourist business. One of the islands had nearly been closed down a decade ago when two vacationers were murdered on a golf course. The police, he figured, were anxious to wrap up any doubts about *Cane Maiden*'s fate as quickly as they could. They would want to offer the boat's crew every possible courtesy, give them a royal sendoff and hope that they didn't tell their story to one of the television networks as soon as they got home.

Marilyn went into the bedroom, leaving Jeanne and Bill alone together for the first time since they had boarded *Cane Maiden.* They both feared the moment as they settled into separate chairs, like strangers in a waiting room. Jeanne forced words of concern about his shoulder and he gave bravely reassuring answers. Then he asked about the bruises she had suffered during the storm and noticed a skinned elbow that she had gotten during the beaching. For a while, neither of them dared come near their true thoughts.

"Bill," she finally managed in a much softer tone. He heard the change in her voice and was instantly apprehensive. "Can you ever forgive me for what happened out there?"

"I've been trying to forget what happened out there," he answered. "You should try, too."

"I can't. I'll never forget snapping the matchstick. And wishing that she was . . . gone."

"Then don't ever forget saving her from Howard. Or diving into the water to save me. Be fair to yourself. When it really counted, you came through for all of us. Don't forget that."

She shook her head, denying herself the forgiving words. "But I wanted the money. I wanted it so badly I stopped thinking. . . ."

"Jeanne," he interrupted, "we all saw ourselves at our worst. *Cane Maiden* sailed us through hell, and we all recognized parts of ourselves that we didn't like. Now we have to try to live with ourselves the way we really are."

"You did nothing to be ashamed of," Jeanne said.

"That's what I'm ashamed of," he confessed. "That I did nothing. Nothing to help Howard when he wanted to take the gun away. If I had

521

acted earlier, maybe I would have saved us a lot of problems."

"Or made things even worse," Jeanne answered. "What you told me is much more true for you. When it really counted, you came through for all of us."

Now Bill couldn't accept forgiveness. "And I've done nothing to help you," he admitted. "I don't think I ever even listened to you. Until we were aboard *Cane Maiden.*"

"When I was saying things I wish you had never heard," she added.

He eased up out of the chair. "I'm going for a walk."

She wasn't sure it was an invitation. She let him go by himself.

He followed the concrete path through thick plantings of hibiscus and small palm trees, until the walkway turned into a planked boardwalk. To his left were a half dozen floating wooden fingers where white yachts were tied closely together. The riggings were silent. The air hadn't yet begun to move.

He needed the quiet. He needed a moment to pay his respects to the memory of a friend he had never really known. Had Howard ever been happy? Had he always been terrified of failure? Who was the real Howard? The one who had carefully organized the murder of Cindy? Or the one who had gone to battle with the killers in the helicopter?

Who was the real Jeanne? She had been his wife for the past seven years and he didn't know her. Was she the one who had dumped the broken matches in front of him and calmly pronounced

Cindy's death sentence? Or the woman who had dived overboard in order to save him? Did she despise him, as she had said, or did she love him, as she had shown? Did he love her? If he did, why had he never listened to her needs?

He reached the end of the walkway, where the last floating dock turned off to his left. There was no room left for him to wander aimlessly. He had to turn back.

Bill saw the big man walking toward him, a vacationer in a colorful straw hat. He started to smile in greeting, but realized that the smile wouldn't be returned. The man was narrow-eyed and thin-lipped. He wasn't wandering, but rather moving with tightly focused purpose.

Bill remembered the face, squinting over the top of a pistol as the barrel of the gun panned toward him, and the thin lips, tight with rage. Then he knew who the man was and why he had come. He wasn't at all surprised when his hand started under the edge of his jacket, or when the dull metal case of the pistol appeared. They both stopped walking, and stood ten feet apart, facing one another.

"You have something of mine," Al Weston said quietly.

Bill was looking past the pistol, straight into Al's eyes. "What have I got?"

"The stuff that was in the case you threw overboard."

"Anything that was in the case is still in the case," Bill answered.

"I don't believe you," Al said, showing a cynical smile.

"And I don't give a fuck what you believe," Bill answered with a smile of his own.

Winston sneered. "You're making a big mistake, pal. This can be real simple. You give me what's mine and I'm out of your life. You try to give me a hard time, and you're gonna get you and your friends hurt real bad."

"I have nothing of yours."

Al shook his head sadly. "Okay, we'll do it the hard way." He lowered the muzzle of the gun until it was pointing at Bill's left knee. "Like I said, you're making a big mistake."

"Stop!" A woman's voice screamed out over the water. Al Weston wheeled and saw Cindy running toward him. "Stop! He didn't do anything! I'm the one you're looking for!"

Bill lunged forward the instant Al's face turned toward Cindy. He caught Al's wrist before the gun aimed back toward him, and smashed it down across his knee. The pistol bounced across the wooden walkway.

The momentum of his rush had knocked Al off balance. Bill was able to twist his arm, get a leg behind him, and topple him. Al fell like a tree onto his back, with Bill slamming down on top of him. Then Bill got a forearm across his throat and pressed down. He had the big man pinned.

"Get the gun," he screamed at Cindy, who was running toward them. "Get the gun!"

But Weston wasn't helpless for long. He kicked up with his knee, lifting Bill's weight off him. Then he got a forearm under Bill's shoulder, and threw him to one side. He rolled up onto his haunches. Bill was already on one knee. As Al's face came up off the deck, he drove his fist squarely across his nose. Weston's face gushed blood.

Bill cocked his hand for another punch. But Al's fingers flashed out and locked around his neck. In an instant, Bill was no longer the aggressor. He had both hands around Weston's wrist, trying to break free from the stranglehold. Then Weston's punch came around Bill's hands and crashed against his jaw. He fell onto his back with Al rolling over on top of him.

Now it was Bill kicking with his knee, rolling Al off. And then Al was falling as he rolled past the edge of the walkway. Bill saw him splash into the water, and then felt himself being dragged over the edge. The next moment, he was in the water, face to face with Weston, each of them with their hands curled around the other's neck.

Bill used Al as a lever, pushing himself up out of the water. He shifted his hands to Al's head, and then pushed down with all his weight to drive Weston under. But Al was like a rock. Bill couldn't move him. And then Weston got a grip across Bill's shoulders and began pulling him down.

It was a brutal test of strength. Bill had the higher position, which should have been decisive. But Al Weston was much stronger. Slowly, Bill began to sink. He came eye to eye with the killer. Then Weston's face rose above his. He could see the grim smile on Weston's battered face. Then he could barely make out the outlines of a face through the water. And then Al was just a shadow. A dark blot against the blue light that was filtering down through the water.

Bill fought with his last breath. He released the

useless grip on Weston's shoulders and punched at his gut. But his punches and kicks were slowed by the water, and fell harmlessly. He reached up, and got his fingers around Al's neck. But it was like choking a tree trunk. He had no leverage. His strength was ebbing. His chest was screaming for air.

He heard a roar, muffled in the distance. At the same moment, Al shuddered; a quick tremble, almost as if he had caught a sudden chill. The powerful hands that were driving him under slowly relaxed. Bill broke Al's grip, and kicked back up toward the surface. He saw the shadow of the head above him. But the light that was filtering down around it was no longer blue. It had been stained a brilliant crimson.

When he broke through the surface, the eyes that faced him were wide with amazement. There was a bleeding hole in the center of the forehead. He watched the face sink away.

He grabbed the edge of the pier to keep from sinking himself, and coughed up the water he had swallowed. When he looked up, Cindy was staring down at the spot where Al Weston had disappeared. She held the pistol in both hands, its muzzle pointing at the center of the spreading rings.

Bill dragged himself out of the water and onto the dock. He was standing beside her before Cindy lifted her eyes away from the water and noticed him. Carefully, he took the gun out of her hands.

"He's gone," he said to Cindy.

She was paralyzed by the horror of what she had just done.

"You saved my life," he told her.

She looked at him, beginning to understand.

"Now you have to go. Just walk out of here and keep going. There's no one to stop you."

She hesitated.

He took her arm and led her back to the stone path. Then he pointed her toward the entrance to the hotel grounds. "Just go, and don't even look back. Go home, Cindy." She nodded, but she didn't move until he gave her a gentle nudge. Then she took a breath, and walked away confidently.

Bill watched her until she had gone through the gate. Then he walked back to the cottage where Jeanne and Marilyn were waiting.

"Call the police," he told them.

SATURDAY

74

The plane took off to the east, circled around the end of Beef Island, and flew back past the rocky face of Tortola. Brandywine Bay, where the wreck of *Cane Maiden* washed gently in the surf, passed under the right wing, and the deep basin of Road Harbor came into view. Bill turned and looked across the cabin, past Marilyn and out to the left side. He could see the tops of the islands to the south of Drake Channel, and further to the south, the hazy outline of St. Croix. Their voyage aboard *Cane Maiden* hadn't taken them very far. He could see most of the route they had sailed in a glance. It gave no hint of the distance that they had all traveled.

Jeanne sat next to him. She had reached out and taken his hand as the plane had begun rolling down the runway. She still held it tightly. Marilyn was in the single seat across the aisle, hunched toward the window. She was staring out at the edge of the horizon, trying to find the point where Howard had disappeared.

But it wouldn't be the place where she had lost him. Marilyn didn't know exactly where that had been. They had begun drifting apart somewhere in the past, at the point where Howard had decided that his success was more important to his life than she was. She had lost him at the turn where he had seen his business world crumbling and aimed all his efforts at holding it together. Marilyn knew that she wouldn't be able to see the place where her husband had died. The Howard she knew, the man she had hoped to save, had died the instant that he had seen the money and realized that it could be his. That place was much further to the south, well beyond the horizon she was searching.

Bill could only guess at what she was thinking. He had told her once again how Howard had died, standing alone on the bow in battle with the gunman who was about to kill them. She had thanked him. That was the story she was going to tell his children. That was the image she would hold on to and try to make herself believe. Perhaps it would become more vivid than the awful picture of her husband dragging the young woman into the cockpit.

It was harder for him to imagine what Jeanne was thinking. She had sold everything they shared for the fortune that was in the camera case. Yet she had risked everything to save him, and then to save the woman she had so openly despised. She had left him, and yet now she was holding on to him. She didn't seem to want to let go.

Had he ever known what she was thinking? Was her anger toward him as sudden as it had seemed? Or had it been heated slowly, over the years, by his own lack of understanding? By his indifference to her hopes and dreams? Had the money driven them apart? Or had it simply served to show them

532

how great a distance had grown up between them? He looked down at her hand, clutched tightly around his own. Could they try again? Or had they revealed too much of themselves to one another to ever fall in love?

No one was chasing them. The police had identified Al Weston's body when they lifted it out of the water. They had traced the helicopter that had flown from Tortola down to St. Croix, and located the pilot. He had described Al as the person who had hunted for *Cane Maiden*, and then attacked her at sea. As far as they were concerned, it was open and shut. Visitors to their island had been viciously assaulted. The killer had even tracked them down to their hotel where he had attacked Bill. And Bill had killed him in the struggle. They had taken statements and signatures, and then escorted the victims to the plane. The quicker they were gone, the better for everyone. There were no legal questions left to be answered.

But to Bill's mind, all the important questions were still unanswered. They had seen themselves at their worst, and then perhaps at their best. Could any of them survive the experience?

They set down on St. Thomas, and transferred immediately to the wide-bodied jet that would take them back to New York. Bill had offered to continue on with Marilyn until she was safely home, but she had refused the offer. She was all right, she had insisted. And this was as good a time as any to begin making her own way.

They were sitting together in three adjoining seats, when Marilyn handed Howard's camera case over to Bill.

"I don't think I want any of the pictures," she said. "Maybe there's something you want. Or maybe you can just get rid of everything."

He nodded. After a few seconds, he opened the case, planning to take out the film and hand back the camera. As Howard had said, it was the best that money could buy. Marilyn might not want it, but her children would certainly prize it.

He lifted the camera, and gave it to Jeanne to hold. Then he scooped up the cylinders that held the exposed rolls of film. The last thing he lifted from the case were two small cloth pouches.

"Oh my God!" he said softly. He didn't have to open them to know what they were. Howard had determined not to leave *Cane Maiden* empty-handed, no matter what. The diamonds had outlasted him as a mockery of his greed.

"I'm sorry," Bill said to Marilyn.

"Howard," she said sadly, as if that were the answer to all their questions. "He just wasn't ready for *Cane Maiden*."

Bill dropped the pouches into the bottom of the camera case and then set the camera and the lenses carefully on top of them. He put the case back into Marilyn's lap.

"Keep them," he told her. "It's going to be difficult. They may help."

"I can't," she said, pushing the case away.

"You can't give them back," he reminded her.

Marilyn studied the case for a few moments. Then she turned to Bill and Jeanne. "You should take them. There's that school you want to save. And Jeanne wants a chance to work on her own. The two of you could make this count for something."

Bill looked at Jeanne.

"I'll take my chances without them," she said. He smiled. "So will I."

Marilyn studied both of them, and then slipped the case to the floor at her feet. Maybe the diamonds would do something worthwhile for all of them if she used them well. They already seemed to have brought Bill and Jeanne a little closer together.